'Don't send me away,' she whispered, moving towards him and watching his eyes darkening with desire. She lifted a hand, and gently moved her fingertips from his jaw to the base of his throat. She saw that his hair was clinging damply to his forehead, where perspiration had formed.

'For the love of God, Catrina, get away from me, before I . . .'

'I love you, Dominic,' she said simply.

A groan escaped him. 'If I were—halfway drunk before,' he muttered, 'you are accomplishing—what an entire barrel of rum could not do . . .'

'Dominic,' she said seriously, 'I was not brought up in a delicate way, and so I cannot help it if my love is without shame . . .'

He uttered a low, unsteady laugh. 'Yes, the one thing you lack is shame, is it not . . .'

She hesitated for only a fraction of a second. Then, recklessly, she shrugged her arms out of the sleeves of the *peignoir* so that it fell to the floor . . .

Born of Afrikaans-speaking parents in Johannesburg, South Africa, Christina Laffeaty describes her education as 'erratic'. Between the ages of seven and fifteen she attended twelve different schools where her attendance depended on whether or not she was needed to help out with the ploughing or harvesting! She attributes the fact that she acquired any kind of education at all to her own obsessive reading.

She was nineteen before she learned English—from her husband, who brought her to live in England—and she started writing professionally shortly afterwards. Her work includes short stories for the BBC, the *Evening News* and various women's magazines; radio plays, serials and about sixty books, including eight novels written under the pen-name Netta Carstens. Mrs Laffeaty has a son and a daughter and lives in the West Country.

ILLICIT OBSESSION

BY

CHRISTINA LAFFEATY

WORLDWIDE BOOKS
LONDON SYDNEY TORONTO

First published in hardback in Great Britain in 1987 by Worldwide Books, 15-16 Brook's Mews, London W1A 1DR

ISBN 0 373 50947 2

10/0587-135572
Set in Monotype Times 10 on 10 pt.

Typeset in Great Britain by
Associated Publishing Services
Printed and bound in Great Britain by
William Clowes Limited,
Beccles and London

CHAPTER ONE

CATRINA OFTEN THOUGHT back to that last morning of the sea voyage, and marvelled at the fact that there was nothing whatever to warn her of the devastating trip-wires which Fate was already laying in her path. The only thing that was different was that the bulkheads of her cabin were not dipping and swaying in the crazy dance which they had been performing for so many days. Instead, she was aware of a gently rocking motion that was almost soothing.

Even more miraculously, the dreadful nausea which had claimed her, virtually from the moment *Oriole* had left England's shore, was totally missing this morning. Not even the pervasive ship-board smells, compounded of a mixture of rope and tar and cooking odours wafting from the galley, produced more than a grimace from her.

She pushed the covers away and swung her legs gingerly over the side of the bunk. Lord, she was as weak as a kitten! The miracle was less than complete, after all, for a wave of dizziness seized her, and she forced herself to fight grimly against it.

Violet had said they would be reaching the Bay of Gibraltar later in the morning, and Catrina knew that she needed to muster all her strength and resolution to deal with the task of dressing for the disembarkation. She reached for a looking-glass, and studied her reflection with dismay. Her heavy, copper-coloured hair only intensified the pallor of her skin, and her wide green eyes were shadowed. And she had been so determined to cut a dash when she arrived in Gibraltar; it was, after all, part of her major reason for embarking on this voyage, and she could have wept with frustration as she thought of the picture she would be presenting instead.

Just the mere thought of dressing her hair, and choosing from among her trunks an ensemble in which to go ashore, daunted her.

'Mr Stanmore was right.' she acknowledged aloud. 'I should have employed a lady's maid. Why didn't I listen to him?'

The question was a rhetorical one, as she well knew. She had rejected her lawyer's advice because her own years of servitude to Lady Prudence had left her with a repugnance at the thought of having another human being at her own beck and call. But who could have foreseen that she, always so healthy and strong, her powers of endurance honed by years of drudgery, would be laid low by sea-sickness? It was grossly unfair, when one considered that others like Violet took the turbulent motion of the ship in their stride.

Catrina thought back to their first meeting. They had been standing by the rail and watching the land slowly recede as the wind and the current took *Oriole* on her way to Gibraltar.

'Well, that's me last sight of England for a good while,' Violet had commented ruefully.

'Are you travelling to Gibraltar to marry one of the soldiers?' Catrina had asked, making conversation.

'Lord, no!' Violet had giggled. 'I'm an actress. I entertain the troops. And you, miss? *You* going to be hitched?'

'Hitched? Oh, I see . . . No, my parents and my married sister have been living in Gibraltar for years. My father is an army officer and so is . . .' Catrina had been forced to stop, her stomach heaving.

'My word, miss,' Violet had exclaimed, staring at her. 'You've gone quite green at the gills! Come, I'll help you to your cabin.'

And this wretched, poky cabin had remained Catrina's prison ever since. She was still asking herself what she would have done during the voyage without that ebullient, warm-hearted stranger who had guided her to it, when Violet herself came bouncing in, carrying a bowlful of gruel on a tray.

She was small and pert and pretty, with rosy cheeks and sparkling dark eyes and a mass of elaborate black curls. That was how she had looked when they first exchanged those casual remarks at the rail of the ship, and that was how she had continued looking all through the wretched voyage.

'So the patient's on the mend!' she exclaimed with approval, setting the tray down on a fixed ledge which was intended to do duty as a table, a wash-stand, a writing-desk or anything else for which it might be required in that cramped space.

'I've been sitting here, thinking how much I hate you, Violet,' Catrina joked. 'How could you have remained so unaffected by the tossing and heaving of the ship, when all I wanted to do was die?'

'Got me sea-legs long ago, love, haven't I? Been backwards and forwards between England and the Rock more times than I care to remember. Now, get this gruel down you. We don't want you going ashore looking as peaked as I-don't-know-what.'

Catrina rested the tray on her lap, and picked up a spoon to dip it into the gruel. She made a face at the food, but she began to eat mechanically, accustomed by now to being bullied into taking nourishment.

Violet sat down on the edge of the bunk, and went on, 'If I was you, ducks, I'd take a stroll on deck when you've finished that lot, and get some fresh air. The sea's as quiet as a mill-pond now, and if you keep to your cabin until we dock, you're like as not to faint clean away the moment you set foot on land. And that'll frighten your folks out of their skins!'

They don't know that I'm coming, Catrina thought. They never wanted me in Gibraltar in the first place, and it would be a matter of complete indifference to them whether I look ill or not. Aloud, she said, 'You're right. Will you go on deck with me?'

Violet hesitated for so long that Catrina went on contritely, 'I'm sorry. I have no right to make so many demands on you. You'll have your own packing to attend to.'

'It's ain't that, love. The fact is, you're a lady, and if the top-lofty coves aboard was to see you hob-nobbing with the likes of me . . .'

'Listen!' Catrina interrupted vehemently. 'You held my head when I was sick; you changed my nightgown and washed me; you brought me food and forced me to eat it.

You bullied me into leaning on you and walking around in my cabin, when all I wanted was to be left lying in my bunk. *I* was too far gone to care whether my muscles withered or not, but you forced me to exercise.'

'Yes, well, but that don't . . .'

'I suppose you're trying to say that the fact of your being an actress cancels all that out! Well, it doesn't. If it had not been for you, I would probably have died! So do you think I care a jot what anyone might think because I'm seen to be your friend?'

Violet flushed with obvious pleasure, but she said deprecatingly, 'I blew me own trumpet a bit loud and false when I told you I was an actress. I'm just an ordinary entertainer, dearie. You know—concerts for the troops, that kind of thing.'

'I never supposed you were in the same class as Mrs Siddons,' Catrina teased affectionately. 'I *can* picture you singing and dancing and reciting monologues to cheer up the soldiers in the garrison, on the other hand. It changes nothing. I am still proud to call you my friend!'

Violet said gruffly, 'Well, if that ain't as pretty a speech as ever I heard!'

'And meant from the heart! Now, *will* you help me to get dressed so that I may take the air on deck?'

'Of course I'll help you. You just wait a tick and I'll get some hot water for you to wash.'

After Violet had left the cabin, Catrina reached for her fitted writing-casket, smiling wryly as she remembered her intention of filling her diary with a day-by-day account of the voyage. Now she dipped her quill in the inkwell set into the box, and wrote:

> Soon we shall be disembarking, after a journey which I shudder to recall. I hope I will have the courage and the spirit to acquit myself as I had always meant to. Oh, Lady Prudence, how you must be turning in your grave if you are able to see how your former domestic drudge has had her life transformed! One should not speak or think ill of the dead, they say. Well, humbug is what *I* say. I have but one thing to thank you for, and that has come about without you ever meaning it to . . .

At that moment Violet returned with a jug of hot water and poured it into the recessed bowl set into one side of the ledge. Catrina took a pinch of sand from another small receptacle set into the writing-casket and scattered it over the page of her diary so that it would absorb the wet ink. Then, after carefully putting away her writing materials, she washed, grateful for Violet's help.

'I'll have to decide what to wear for the disembarkation,' Catrina remarked, glancing at her trunks piled up in one corner of the cabin.

'Spoilt for choice, you are,' Violet returned enviously. 'When I was rooting through your trunks for clean night-wear, I couldn't help seeing all them lovely gowns of yours.'

'They haven't been much use to me during the voyage. Would you like to help me go through the trunks and choose what to wear?'

She smiled at Violet's childlike enthusiasm as one gown after another was lifted from its envelope of protective tissue paper and inspected.

'Oh, this one is lovely!' the girl crooned, holding a creation of deep-rose silk against herself and stroking the material. 'Wear this one!'

'No, I think I've decided on the emerald-green muslin.' Impulsively, Catrina added, 'I want you to have the silk. The colour suits you far better than it does me.'

For a disconcerting moment she thought Violet was about to burst into tears. The girl was always somewhat gaudily dressed, in a way which no doubt fitted her occupation as an entertainer, but Catrina had noticed that the fabrics of which her gowns were made were generally cheap. She was clearly overcome at the notion of owning a silk dress, and Catrina, fearing that she meant to refuse the offer, added quickly,

'In exchange, I want you to help me appear as attractive as possible when I step ashore.' She grinned. 'I peeped at my face in the looking-glass, and I know what a tall order that is with such unpromising raw material. But even though nothing could make me less pasty-faced . . .'

'Lord love you, d'you think *my* complexion is a present from Old Ma Nature?' Violet giggled. 'Just wait a moment, love, while I fetch my box of tricks.'

Catrina had to concede, a while later, that there really was something almost magical about the way in which Violet succeeded in transforming her. Rouge was skilfully applied to her cheeks, and powder hid the dark shadows underneath her eyes. Violet pinned her hair up, and allowed fashionable ringlets to fall to her shoulders.

The fact that Catrina had lost weight during the voyage was easily camouflaged, at Violet's suggestion, by merely tying her stays less tightly than usual. Viewing her reflection by sections in the looking-glass, Catrina saw that the emerald-green muslin gown added to the illusion of voluptuous good health. Its low-cut bodice was trimmed with ruched flounces of the same material, and a satin sash in a deeper shade was tied tightly just below her bosom, leaving the ample skirt to skim her hips.

It was the very latest fashion from Paris, the modiste had assured Catrina. It was designed to be worn without hoops, and the layers of transparent muslin which formed the skirt were intended to give brief, tantalising glimpses of her thighs and legs as she moved.

When a matching straw bonnet trimmed with dark-green satin had been titlted upon the back of her head, Violet clapped her hands with pleasure at her own work. 'You look good enough to eat, love! It beats me why you ain't married, with your money and your beauty and all. I'll wager you've left many a broken heart behind you in England!'

Catrina smiled wryly, but made no comment. Violet, she thought, would probably not believe her if she told the truth—that she had never even met anyone who could conceivably have filled the role of a beau.

'I'm goin' to help you on deck now,' she heard Violet say, 'and leave you there while I do your packin'. And then I'm goin' to pin up the hem of that lovely gown you give me.'

Catrina was dismayed at the unsteadiness of her steps as she left the cabin for the first time since the beginning of the voyage. She was grateful for Violet's support, particularly when they reached the deck. Everything was swimming momentarily before her eyes as the blinding light of the sun's reflection on the water struck her. She was aware of being pulled towards the rail, and she clung to it grimly with both hands while taking deep breaths.

'Think you'll be safe by yourself now,' Violet asked, 'while I pop back below?'

'Thank you, yes. I feel much better.'

She would *will* herself to feel perfectly well. The young woman who stepped ashore at Gibraltar would be self-assured, strong and sophisticated, requiring pity from no one.

She thought of the presents she had bought for her family, and which were packed away in the trunks in her cabin. There were expensive luxuries liked sugared dried fruit, drinking chocolate, tea of the highest quality, and a case of fine brandy for her father.

For her mother she had bought a pocket-case of white satin worked with gold, and containing sewing-materials of gold and mother-of-pearl. And for her sister Millicent she had bought a length of blue watered silk.

Coals of fire, Catrina thought with satisfaction. For years her parents had refused her heartbroken requests to be allowed to join them and Millicent in Gibraltar; they had dismissed as selfish exaggerations her claim that she was living the wretched life of a skivvy to Lady Prudence. Well, now she was about to foist herself on her family, still unwanted but defiant, and bearing gifts . . .

It struck her suddenly that for all the difference in their stations, and even though their acquaintance was so brief, Violet was far more like a sister to her than Millicent had even been.

She could feel her facial muscles tensing involuntarily as she thought of her younger sister. With the uncanny instinct of children, Millicent had known from an early age that *she* was the beloved, favoured daughter, while Catrina was merely someone to whom duty visits had to be paid whenever their father received home leave from his regiment and they were able to return to England. Millicent had never failed to rub salt into the wounds by emphasising the fact in any way she could.

With bitterness, Catrina recalled the formal invitation which had arrived for her, requesting the pleasure of her company at the wedding of Millicent to an army captain named Dominic Ross. That invitation had been a pointed slap in the face, because her parents were perfectly aware that Catrina did not have the means to travel to Gibraltar, and that it would have been worse than useless to expect Lady Prudence to provide it.

Her thoughts were interrupted by the arrival of Violet, looking extremely fetching in the rose-coloured silk gown.

'My goodness!' Catrina exclaimed. 'You've certainly worked quickly at taking up that hem! The gown suits you to perfection!'

Violet beamed with pleasure. 'See, I even found a hair ribbon what matches!'

'Tell me about Gibraltar,' Catrina asked. 'What is it like to live there?'

'Well, the gentry—the officers and their wives, that is—they entertain, and they get invited to all the galas and balls the Governor gives. They live in grand Spanish houses from where you can see right across to Algeciras in Spain. Me and the girls, we have a house near the Casemates Barracks.'

'You and the girls?' Catrina echoed, a question in her voice.

'Yes, well, the other members of the concert party, see. We take turns every year or so for a visit home. I just been to see me old Ma and Pa.' She broke off. 'Funny that, ain't it? 'Cause you're about to visit *your* Ma and Pa. And I'd say you was about the same age as me. I'm twenty-three. And you?'

'Twenty-two.'

'There, now, hardly any difference.' Violet's voice was dry. 'Except that you're a lady, and I'm not. Miss Beaumont . . .'

'I've asked you not to call me that!'

'Well, I can't call you Catrina neither. It don't feel right. So you'll just have to put up with "dear" and "love" and "ducks".'

'What were you going to say a moment ago, Violet?'

'It don't matter. Your Ma and Pa'll soon set you right about life on the Rock.' She studied Catrina. 'I s'pose they left you in London so you could meet Their Majesties and do the season, and all that.'

'Hardly.' Catrina could not keep the bitterness from her

voice. 'They gave me away to my godmother when I was small. I grew up in a dreadful, gloomy house in Belgravia, where everything smelt of mildew and decay. My parents did not care that Lady Prudence treated me as little more than a slave.'

'Is that right?' Violet looked shocked. 'And there was me, thinkin' you've lived in the lap of luxury all your life, with all them lovely gowns and everything . . .'

Catrina gave a short laugh. 'Lady Prudence fooled everyone. She forced the two of us to live a miserly existence, scrimping and scraping and going without, and when she died it turned that she had not only been extremely wealthy, but she had left everything to me.'

'My goodness, it sounds like a fairy story! So now you've come to try and buy your Ma and Pa's love, poor ducks. I seen all the presents packed away in your trunks.'

Catrina felt her face suffusing with angry colour. 'I have not come to buy their love! I've always known that it belonged to my sister Millicent alone. They kept her and took her with them wherever my father's regiment was posted to, while they gave me away to Lady Prudence just as they would have given away an unwanted puppy.'

She stared fiercely at the ever-approaching land. 'I've come to show them that I don't need them now. I've come to show them how rich I am. I—I've come to crow, and embarrass them, and to make Millicent as jealous of me as I've always been of her!'

'There, there, dearie,' Violet said soothingly and sympathetically, almost as if she had not believed a word of Catrina's angry statement. 'Look, you can see the Rock now.'

Catrina found it impossible to suppress a feeling of awe. The Rock of Gibraltar was a glowering, mountainous promontory stretching itself out to sea. Of breath-taking sheerness and height, and tilted at an angle, it consisted of an immense shelf of rock, looming threateningly over the bays which surrounded it, defying anyone to storm the fortress which it represented.

Violet pointed out several vessels anchored in the bays. 'Spanish ships,' she explained. 'The Governor must be giving a reception for their naval officers. I remember, last year—no, '77 it was—we had the Spanish fleet in, and there was fireworks and all . . .'

Catrina was trying to divide her attention between what Violet was saying and concentration on watching the Rock looming closer. She could feel the ship speeding towards one of the bays, helped by a following breeze, but in the protected waters the vessel was steady and did not induce the slightest queasiness.

From the sea the town of Gibraltar itself, Catrina saw, was surrounded by high walls crowned with cannon, and broken by various batteries. The main part of the town was built upon a flat surface, but a section of it climbed up the lower slopes beside the water. The greater mass of rock seemed totally unscaleable, and viewed from the sea it had a craggy, barren appearance which suggested that it was of no practical use. The waterfront was crowded with conveyances and with people of every description, from scarlet-coated militiamen to swarthy, foreign-looking labourers and civilians.

'My goodness,' Catrina said faintly. 'Surely the arrival of a ship from England doesn't merit such a turn-out?'

'No. See, many of 'em has luggage. Other ships must be getting ready to sail soon. There's lots of folks go back and forth to their homelands—Portugal, Genoa, Morocco. Though why they're all crowding into this bay beats me.' Violet frowned slightly, and changed the subject. 'Will your Ma and Pa be there to meet you?'

'No. I did not write and tell them that I intended imposing my presence on them.'

'One of the girls will be waitin' for me with a cart,' Violet said. 'Soon as I've found her, I'll help you to hire a gharry.'

'A gharry? What is that?'

'A kind of small carriage, love. Step careful now.'

Catrina was glad of Violet's supporting arm as she stepped on dry land for the first time in more than two weeks. The heat would have been difficult to bear, were it not for the invigorating breeze.

While Violet stood on tiptoe and peered around for the colleague who had come to meet her, Catrina scanned the mass of people on the waterfront. Her gaze fell almost instantly upon a man would never have failed to stand out in any crowd. She studied him, half-hypnotised by a combination of his arresting physical presence and the babel of different tongues and the unfamiliar odours that assailed her senses.

Catrina did not know enough about military matters to be able to guess his rank, but she knew that he was an officer by the tight-fitting white buckskin pantaloons which displayed his long, hard-muscled legs and almost aggressively male thighs. His scarlet cut-away jacket emphasised his broad shoulders and narrow waist. Shc judged him to be about thirty years old. His face was clean-shaven, and brown from exposure to sunlight, and it wore the look of a man who was accustomed to giving orders and being instantly obeyed.

With an inexplicable pang, she realised now that he was escorting a pretty, dark-haired young woman, his arm protectively and possessively about her waist. Then Catrina's mesmerised gaze returned to his face, which she could see more clearly as he approached. His silver-grey eyes formed a startling contrast to the dark lashes and brows which framed them, and he was frowning slightly. His features were strong and clean-cut, and his wide mouth suggested both humour and sensuality.

'Violet,' Catrina asked, 'who is that man? The tall one coming this way, escorting a young woman?'

'He's one of the gentry. Look, you stay here while I go see if I can find me mate anywheres.'

Violet plunged through the crowd, and the tall man and his companion were now close by Catrina and within earshot.

'I shall miss you,' she heard him say. His voice was deep and faintly husky, and reminded her of brown velvet.

'To be sure, and I'll miss you too, me darlin'. But I've no doubt at all you'll soon find someone else to take me place!'

Catrina heard him laugh. 'Since you put it so bluntly—yes, I probably will.' At that moment he turned his head slightly, and Catrina found their glances locking. A faint smile played about his mouth, and his eyes studied her appreciatively. For some reason, she felt herself flushing.

His attention returned to the Irish girl by his side. 'I'd better take you to embark now. Your trunks have been carried aboard.'

Catrina watched them moving towards the waterfront, and out of earshot. The jostling of the crowd became so frantic with haste and impatience that she was carried along willy-nilly with the tide of people, and there was no sign of Violet anywhere.

Unexpectedly, she found herself face to face with the tall man. He was alone now, so his Irish companion must have gone aboard one of the vessels preparing to sail.

'Your friend . . .' he began to address Catrina.

At the moment the surging crowd behind her forced her to move forward, and as she did so she tripped and lost her balance, pitching forward.

He caught her in his arms, and did not let her go. Tactile experiences had not figured much in her life, and this was the first time she had ever felt a man's arms about her. She found herself in a strange state of unreality, aware of nothing but the warmth of his hands through the thin fabric of her gown, and of his breath stirring her hair.

She forced herself, at last, to draw away from him. 'Thank you for . . . for breaking my fall.'

He uttered a low, throaty laugh. She was as bewildered by his laughter as by the look of knowing amusement in his silver eyes. But at that moment Violet returned, looking flustered and anxious.

'Good day to you, Violet,' the man said. 'I am afraid the house near the Casemates Barrack has been closed, and the other girls have left for home. It's a pity that you did not delay your own departure, because you and your lovely companion would have received the news and been saved a fruitless journey.'

Catrina found herself flushing furiously as that same knowing, inwardly laughing glance of his rested upon her. He had removed his hat in a gesture of courtesy before addressing them, and she saw that he wore no wig. His hair was dark and the slight breeze was ruffling it.

'News? What news?' Violet demanded shrilly.

'Spain has declared war on Britain, and France has joined her. The Spaniards are laying claim to the Rock.'

Catrina had been listening to him in bemusement, hardly registering the sense of what he was saying. Totally unfamiliar feelings were coursing through her, stirred into life by his physical magnetism.

Then she became aware that Violet had flown into a panic. 'Oh, dear Lord! I ain't staying to be shot at! I'm going to see about a passage back!'

She plunged through the crowd again, but Catrina remained where she was. The knowledge that she had blundered straight into a war situation was almost lost in the impact the man was having on herself.

She heard him say with speculation in his voice, 'Since you do not appear to share your colleague's urgency to return home, would you consider accepting a—mutually congenial—position?'

'I beg your pardon?' Catrina blinked at him.

'The pickings really promise to be slim, you know, even for someone as beautiful as you. Your colleague realised that it will prove well-nigh impossible to make your living in the usual way.'

'*I* am not a concert entertainer . . .' Catrina began.

His mobile lips flickered at the corners, and his eyes danced. 'I never supposed you were,' he interrupted drily. 'Any more than Violet is one. But, as I said, the men are going to have to spend their money on food to supplement their rations, and there won't be anything to spare on the pleasures offered by a lady of the night. If you do intend staying, you'd best accept my proposition.'

She felt the colour drain from her face as the full implication of what he had been saying struck her. 'You—You insulting brute!' she stuttered. 'Violet isn't . . . And I'm not . . . I'll have you know—my father is a colonel.'

He threw back his head with a roar of laughter. 'You certainly have style, by God! Masquerading as a colonel's daughter, no less!'

'I *am* a colonel's daughter . . .'

'A colonel's daughter,' he mocked, one dark eyebrow raised in sardonic amusement, 'painted and powered, with all her charms on display, arriving in a garrison town chaperoned by a whore! And throwing herself at the first affluent-looking man she claps eyes upon!'

Catrina drew back one elegantly-booted leg to kick him as hard as she could on the shin. But he had anticipated her, and moved deftly away. He replaced his hat with a flourish, and made her a mocking bow.

'If you are staying, colonel's daughter, we shall meet again, for the Rock is a small place!'

As he pushed his way through the crowd, she stared after him, simmering with rage, but mixed up with it was something else. Something that she could not identify, because she had never experienced anything remotely like it before.

CHAPTER TWO

CATRINA GAVE HERSELF a mental shake. She would have to go after Violet who, whatever her true profession really was, had been a staunch friend during the past weeks and who would probably need help.

But before Catrina could plunge through the crowd, Violet herself returned, her face streaked with tears. 'They—they're asking three times the proper fare for a passage home!' she wailed. 'What'm I to do?'

'Violet, is it true that—you and the girls . . . You said you entertained the troops . . .'

Violet's shoulders slumped. 'Yes, well, concert entertainers is what we calls ourselves. Sounds more respectable, don't it? Besides, if you had known, you'd have turned your nose up at me, same as others do.'

'What you are,' Catrina said at last, 'does not in any way cancel out what you have done for me.' She fished inside her reticule and withdrew a draw-string bag, and counted out several sovereigns. 'Will this be sufficient to take you back to England?'

'Oh, love! Oh, ducks . . .' Tears were streaming down Violet's cheeks. 'I ain't goin' to forget you . . .'

'Or I you. Go now, quickly, before they put the fare up even more. It's obvious that there is fierce competition for passages home.'

Violet dropped the sovereigns inside her own reticule and then plunged through the crowd to secure her passage back to England.

Feeling bereft and confused and physically drained, Catrina went in search of her trunks among the unloaded luggage, and wondered what to do next.

'Gharry, mistress?'

She turned. A swarthy middle-aged man with broken teeth but a reassuringly honest face pointed towards a mule-driven vehicle standing a short distance away.

'Thank you,' she accepted with relief, and gave him the address where her parents lived with Millicent and the latter's husband.

The driver made short work of loading her trunks on the gharry, and helped her into the seat beside him. He was a garrulous man who spoke fractured English with such staccato rapidity that she had difficulty in understanding him at times. But she did learn that he was a Genoese who was debating whether to remain there with his family during the coming hostilities, or to return with them to their homeland.

'You fine, mistress,' he assured her. 'You safe. British army, they soon send home all wives, all families, in ships.'

She would, Catrina thought with satisfaction, take her mother and Millicent and her small niece home with her. They would see the changes she had wrought in Lady Prudence's previously grim, hideously neglected house in Belgravia. And more coals of fire would be heaped upon their heads in the shape of lavish hospitality.

But not yet. She would delay their departure until she had had a chance of meeting the silver-eyed officer again. Her father would recognise his description and she would ask to be introduced to him. Oh, how she would make him grovel!

She forgot about him for the moment in her surprise at seeing that the town bore a startling resemblance to a London suburb, with inns sporting such names as the Queen's Head and the Tower of London. They had entered the town through a single arch cut in the outer wall, and a drawbridge and moat added to the impression that the Rock was a distant extension of Britain. But there were conflicting features also, Catrina saw. The gharry passed a beautiful but austere-looking old building set in extensive grounds, and she asked the driver about it.

'Convent once, mistress,' he told her. 'Long ago, Spanish times. Now, barracks.'

Catrina realised that they were now travelling on higher ground, where the houses occupied by officers overlooked the Bay of Algeciras. The house in which her family lived was a long, low and unfamiliar structure. Of one storey only, its walls were a dazzling white, and there were ornamentally-shaped iron grilles over the windows. Leading to an arched front door was a courtyard of tessellated mosaic tiles.

The driver carried Catrina's trunks to the door. She paid him, and then found that her heart was racing and the palms of her hands were clammy as she tried to summon the courage to lift the iron knocker. It was as if she were a child again, expecting rejection. When she did knock, the door was opened by a maid-servant who, judging by her colouring and accent, was also Genoese.

Feeling more than ever like a child expecting a rebuff, Catrina stammered, 'Please—Please tell your mistress that Miss Beaumont has called to see her.'

The maid disappeared, and Catrina looked about her. Like the courtyard, the floor of the wide hall was tiled, but this time with beautiful ceramic squares, and Catrina could see several arched doorways leading off from the hall.

Forming an incongruous contrast with the Spanish or Moorish pattern of the tiled floor and the arches, the furniture was unmistakably British and had been shipped from England. With a painful pang, Catrina realised just what a stranger she was in her parents' home. The mahogany pedestal table standing against the wall, flanked on one side by a rosewood and marquetry chair, had a look of permanence about them, as if they had been acquired early in her parents' marriage and had accompanied them on many a foreign posting. And yet Catrina had never even laid eyes on them before now.

The maid returned, and beckoned Catrina to follow her. They passed through one of the arched doorways into what must now be a drawing-room, whatever its original use might have been. Again, the floor was tiled and scattered with rugs, and marble columns supported a magnificently carved ceiling. But the armchairs, the card and tea-tables, the carved sofas and the secretaire bookcase were all uncompromisingly British.

In one of the armchairs was seated a young woman, who stared at Catrina with a frown. Catrina stared back into the face of her younger sister.

Millicent was no longer the pretty, fair-haired girl Catrina remembered. Her mouth was pulled down in a look of discontent, and her once bright blue eyes seemed faded. Her hair looked lank and lustreless, as if she were forced to dress it herself and neither knew nor cared how to do so with any expertise. She was noticeably pregnant, and her black gown did nothing to improve her looks.

She made no effort to rise in a gesture of welcome. 'You have obviously been directed to the wrong house,' she said. 'I believe there is a Lieutenant Beaumont of the Royal Navy stationed in Gibraltar. His must be the house you are looking for.'

Catrina swallowed hard. If the thought had ever occurred to her, back in England, that Millicent might fail altogether to recognise her in her expensive finery, she would have experienced a sense of triumph. But there was no triumph at all; merely an obscure sadness.

No wonder Millicent had not recognised her. The last time her sister had seen her was six years ago. Millicent had been fourteen and Catrina, two years older, had been defeated and sullen, and dressed in one of the cheap, made-over drab gowns which Lady Prudence insisted was all she could afford.

Gently, Catrina said, 'Millicent, it's me—your sister.'

Millicent's eyes narrowed in a sharp look. 'Yes . . . Yes, now I can see . . . But what on earth . . .?'

'Lady Prudence died suddenly. To the surprise of everyone she was exceedingly rich. Even her lawyer, Mr Stanmore, was not aware that she owned numerous stocks and shares until he took away all her private papers after her death. And, in spite of the way she had always treated me, she left everything to me.'

Once again, Catrina found that there was no feeling of triumph to be gained from the flash of resentment and envy which crossed Millicent's face. Then the latter laughed shortly.

'You've come to the wrong place to spend your new-found wealth! What on earth brought you here?'

Catrina said quietly. 'I came to see you and Mother and Father, of course, as soon as I had the means to do so.'

A spasm crossed Millicent's face, and she stared at her hands in her lap. 'You're too late. Papa died of an apoplectic stroke just over two months ago, and dear Mama did not survive him for more than a few weeks.'

Catrina swallowed hard, and steadied herself against the back of a chair. 'Why—Why did you not write to tell me?'

'I have not been well.' Her voice took on an aggrieved, whining note. 'This wretched pregnancy . . . If *men* knew what one went through . . .'

'But . . .' Catrina insisted in a voice of dazed disbelief, 'not even to have written and told me . . .'

Millicent shot her a defiant glance. 'I would have done so, in time. There was no urgency, since you could not have attended either funeral.'

Catrina turned her head so that her sister would not see her expression. She felt quite certain that it had not even crossed Millicent's mind to inform her of their parents' death. That was how little she had figured in the charmed circle which had always shut her out.

She thought of that trunk of hers, stuffed with presents for her family. Coals of fire, she had christened them, meant to mortify and discomfort her family. She had been deceiving herself. Violet, shrewd judge of human behaviour that she was, had seen through to the truth.

She had hurried to Gibraltar in an attempt to buy what had never been freely given to her—the love of her family. But it was too late. Her parents were dead, and it would take more than a roll of blue watered silk to remove that expression of hostility from Millicent's eyes.

Catrina straightened her shoulders. 'If it is not convenient, and there is a respectable hostelry in town, I'll remove myself . . .'

'Oh, stay if you wish.' Millicent's voice took on an edge. 'But your finery is going to be wasted in this house. Apart from the fact that I am in mourning for dear Papa and Mama, my condition forces me to spend much time resting, and we do not entertain.'

After a pause, Catrina made up her mind. 'I must not delay my return to England for too long. I understood from the Genoese driver who brought me here that it is expected the Spanish will blockade the Bay.'

'Yes. At the moment they are content merely to show their presence. Dominic says they are clearly planning to play with us as a cat plays with a mouse before they begin hostilities.'

'Would you and your little girl like to leave with me?' Catrina suggested. 'I would gladly welcome you as my guests in London.' Once again, she found that there was no triumph in making the offer.

Millicent considered it for a moment and then shook her head. 'I feel wretched enough on land; the thought of a sea voyage in my condition is not to be borne. Besides, I dare not risk miscarrying if the ship should be tossed about by storms.'

She leant out of her chair to pull at a tasselled cord, and a moment later the maid-servant who had answered Catrina's knock entered the room. Millicent instructed the girl to show Catrina to one of the guest-rooms and to have her luggage brought inside.

'You will no doubt be glad of a rest, and some tea,' she added to her sister.

As soon as she entered the bedroom which had been placed at her disposal, Catrina's instinct told her that this had been Millicent's room before her marriage. It was wholly feminine and frivolous; the bedroom of a much-loved daughter of the house.

The four-poster bed was of carved giltwood, with many pediments and draped with pale-blue silk. The commode, armoire and dressing-table all had matching serpentine fronts and were embellished with ormolu and gilt. An oval mirror flanked by two branches of candles was set above the dressing-table, and Catrina could imagine a younger Millicent sitting there, excitedly watching her maid arrange her hair in a pretty coiffure. Pain and bitterness gripped her as she thought of the difference in their two life-styles.

She poured the tea which the maid had brought in, and ate bread-and-butter and small cakes without tasting any of it. She was, she thought bleakly, a stranger in the house of her parents. Millicent had never left it even when she married; she had merely left this girlish room and moved into a larger one.

After the maid had cleared away the tea-things, Catrina lay down on the bed. Dry, painful sobs shook her as she mourned the passing of the parents who had been little more than strangers to her. But after a while fatigue overtook her, and she felt herself drifting into sleep.

She dreamt of a man with silver-grey eyes and a mocking, sensual mouth. In her dream he was drawing her towards him, cupping her face between strong brown hands and murmuring bold, outrageous suggestions which filled her with both fury and a strange, pounding excitement.

She awakened abruptly, the dream still clinging to her mind. The man had seemed so real. She sat up, disorientated for a moment. Then she remembered. He *was* real. Everything else came rushing back. Violet; the death of her parents; the fact that she was a less than welcome guest in what was now Millicent's house, sleeping in Millicent's girlhood bedroom.

She realised that a maid had unpacked one of her trunks, and had brought in a jug of hot water which was standing inside the bowl on top of the commode.

The sun was low in the sky, and since Millicent had said nothing about dinner, Catrina decided she had better get ready in case the meal should be served early.

She washed, and as she removed the rouge from her face, the cold thought struck her that the only person who had ever shown her kindness and affection had been a harlot. Then, mentally berating herself for that brief flash of self-pity, Catrina put the thought behind her and sat down by the dressing-table to brush and arrange her hair.

The fact that she had slept, and that she had, for a blessedly continuous twenty-four hours, been free of nausea, had removed the dark shadows from beneath her eyes, and even her pallor was no longer quite so marked.

From among the gowns which the maid had unpacked for her, Catrina chose one of apricot gauze worn over a slim-fitting underdress of satin in the same shade. The colour reflected in her cheeks and gave them a glow, and this was enhanced by the necklet of Oriental topaz and gold which she fastened about her throat.

Through the open window came the sound of a bugle, followed by that of drums and other instruments swelling in a martial tune. Catrina hoped that the soldiers in the barracks would remember Violet and her colleagues with affection. Her thoughts were interrupted by a knock on the door.

It was another Genoese maid, delivering an invitation from the master to join him and the mistress in a glass of negus before dinner.

So Millicent's husband had returned home. Catrina had barely given him a thought. Now her curiosity was awakened as she made her way to the drawing-room. In the doorway, she came to a halt.

If Millicent had changed her gown, and done anything at all to her hair, the results were not obvious. She was seated in the same chair as before, and appeared to be alone in the room. Her husband, Catrina decided critically, could hardly be an inspiring creature if his home-coming did not give Millicent the slightest incentive to improve her appearance.

Catrina moved closer inside the room. 'Dominic,' she heard Millicent say. 'This is my sister Catrina, arrived today from England.'

For the first time, Catrina saw him. He had been standing in front of a bureau bookcase, and now he turned slowly.

'We have already met,' Catrina said.

Her voice was calm, but her heart was racing as she stared into the silvery-grey eyes of the man who had insulted her at the waterfront.

CHAPTER THREE

IT HAD BEEN one thing, hoping to meet him again so that she could force him to eat his insulting words. It was totally devastating to discover that he was her sister's husband!

He was regarding her with a totally inscrutable expression. Then he swept her a bow which she felt certain had more than a touch of irony about it.

'You've met before?' she heard Millicent demanding with amazement. 'When? Where?'

The husky voice which reminded Catrina of brown velvet answered without inflection. 'We encountered one another at the harbour. I mistook her for—someone she closely resembled at the time.'

Catrina gritted her teeth. The man had the effrontery to compound his earlier insult! What outraged her further was the fact that he was obviously confident she would not wish to hurt her sister by mentioning the mistress from whom he was parting, or the proposition he had made to herself.

She took the hand which he was extending to her and glared at him from under her lashes. He gave her a look of hard mockery in reply, and after a token handshake said, 'Please sit down, Miss Beaumont.'

One of the maids brought in a tray containing glasses encased in silver holders, and a heavy jug from which steam curled. When she had withdrawn, Dominic poured the mixture of hot, sweetened wine and water into glasses. He handed one to Millicent and then offered Catrina another. He addressed her, and this time Catrina noted that he made no attempt to disguise the irony in his voice.

'You have of course, hastened to come and pay your respects to the memory of your late parents and to visit their graves.'

Catrina was on the point of protesting angrily that she had had no knowledge of their deaths, but Millicent shot her a defiant glance and said, 'It would have been utterly hypocritical of her if she *had* arrived wearing deep mourning. After all, she had not set eyes on dear Papa and Mama above a dozen times during almost twenty years.'

It was obvious to Catrina that Millicent did not want her husband to know that she had neglected to write to her sister, informing her of their parents' death.

She found herself totally ignored by him now as he leant forward to address his wife. 'Since I am, for once, able to be home at an early hour, I should like our daughter to join us with her nanny.'

Millicent made a fretful gesture, and said, 'I have a headache, and the child's noisy chatter will only make it worse.'

Dominic's gaze rested on his wife. 'They are uncommonly frequent, these headaches of yours,' he remarked blandly. 'Since the child's presence has become one of the things likely to cause you distress, I shall go to the nursery to see her. If you will excuse me . . .'

'Please,' Catrina heard her own voice, 'I would like to meet my niece after all this time.'

She felt her colour rising slightly, for her statement was far less than the truth. She could vividly recall a passage from one of the few letters which Millicent had troubled to write to her since her marriage: *'Papa and Mama are quite besotted with their grand-daughter, and I have to guard against their spoiling Lucy completely.'*

Remembering her own bitterness at those words which had excluded her even more firmly from the charmed family circle, Catrina had no pressing desire to meet the latest member of that circle. But she could not bear the uncomfortable thought of being left alone with Millicent at the moment.

Her sister must be aware that Catrina had recognised the strain in her marriage, and pride would prompt her to try and explain it away. Knowing what she did, Catrina did not feel confident of being able to play a convincing part in such a game of make-believe.

However, Millicent changed her mind. 'Oh, very well,' she told Dominic resignedly. 'Ring for the child if you wish.'

Catrina was forced to bite off an involuntary sound when

the three-year-old Lucy skipped into the drawing-room, followed by her nanny, who also appeared to be Genoese.

Time telescoped, and it could have been Millicent who had entered, to jeer at her five-year-old sister, 'Papa and Mama love *me,* but not you!'

Lucy possessed the same bubbly fair curls which her mother had had as a child, the same bright blue eyes. And those eyes were now staring at Catrina as she demanded eagerly,

'Are you really my aunt? What is an aunt? Are you as rich as the Queen?'

Catrina parried the child's questions, and tried to hide her instinctive recoil behind a smile. She knew that it was grossly unfair to be prejudiced against Lucy merely because she looked and sounded so uncannily like the small girl Millicent had once been, but she could not help herself.

Dominic came unwittingly to her rescue, and picked the child up in his arms, holding her on his lap. The warmth in his eyes and his voice was a revelation as he responded to his daughter's chatter, and formed a painful contrast with the chilly neutrality which he employed towards his wife.

'If the lady is Mama's sister,' Lucy asked him, 'why do I not have a sister?'

'Perhaps,' Dominic said lightly, 'you may have one soon. But shall we hope for a brother for you instead?'

Millicent put in sharply, 'That is enough, Dominic. The child is becoming over-excited. Nanny, return her to the nursery, please.'

Catrina felt a stirring of pity for the little girl. There was something forlorn in the droop of Lucy's mouth as she was dismissed. Could history possibly be repeating itself, she wondered. Could it be that Millicent had as little feeling for her own first-born as their parents had obviously had for Catrina? Or was her sister perhaps jealous of Dominic's obvious affection for the child?

But then the little girl ran to her mother, who kissed her fondly enough before telling her to go with her nanny, and Catrina decided that it was merely pregnancy which was making Millicent so fretful and self-absorbed.

Dinner was announced soon afterwards, and they went into the dining-room. Catrina glanced about her with an interest not unmixed with pain. The dining-table was of mahogany, with a drop-leaf on either side, and supported by elegantly turned legs. The seats of the matching chairs were upholstered in finely-stitched tapestry work which she guessed had been executed by her mother. Against one wall stood a satinwood display cabinet with a serpentine front which housed a collection of porcelain. Another wall was dominated by an antique court cupboard in which Catrina guessed the table silver was kept. Again, the floor was ornately tiled, and to her mind it was spoilt by the scattered rugs which were quite beautiful in themselves, but which distracted the eyes from the mosaic pattern of the tiles. They sat down at the table, and two maids began to serve the first course.

'Catrina wishes to leave before the Spanish decide to blockade the Bay,' Millicent told her husband.

His brilliant, light-grey gaze flicked over Catrina. 'Understandable,' he murmured in a dry voice. 'She clearly did not anticipate that a war would interfere with her plans.'

Catrina flushed angrily. Whatever he had meant by that remark, she knew she had been right about him. He might pretend to be prejudiced against her for having journeyed to Gibraltar in the company of a whore, and because she was not wearing mourning for her parents. But the real reason why he disliked her was because she knew too much about him.

With the express motive of goading him, she said, 'Speaking of the coming war, it seems to me that right is on the side of Spain. How can Britain possibly justify holding on to what is an integral part of their country?'

He gave her a long, cold look. 'Spain has no legal or moral right to Gibraltar. It was yielded almost seventy years ago—in 1713, to be precise—to Britain by His Catholic Majesty, and the actual and irrefutable wording of the document was that it was to be held by us "for ever without any exception or impediment whatsoever." Now, merely because our military strength is over-stretched by the so-called war of independence which the Americans are fighting against us, Spain has decided to exploit the situation. And France, as always, is only too ready to join in any offensive against us.'

Millicent shuddered. 'All this talk of war . . . My head has begun to ache quite abominably. I am afraid you will have to excuse me. I shall have to retire to bed.'

She rose, and Dominic made a polite gesture of getting to his feet. At the door, Millicent turned and said, 'I shall require some assistance in undressing. The buttons on this gown are particularly awkward, and my condition has rendered me so clumsy.'

Catrina glanced at Dominic, but he was engaged in helping himself to vegetables. She stood up. 'I shall help you, Millicent. But why do you not have a personal maid?'

'She asked to be returned to Britain. She did not wish to be trapped here by the war. The Genoese girls are so clumsy, but I shall have to resign myself to put up with one of them, I suppose.'

As Catrina followed Millicent along the corridor, she wondered why her sister's marriage had deteriorated to such a stage that Dominic did not offer to perform such a simple service for his wife as helping her out of her gown. Quite inconsequentially, she began to imagine his fingers undoing the buttons of her own gown, and she flushed with guilt and anger at herself.

She experienced a curious reluctance to enter the marriage bedroom. When she did so, the light from the branch of candles which she was holding showed her an enormous four-poster bed with muslin drapings. On one side of it stood a commode, and on the other a rosewood and mahogany side-table with a deep drawer, on which she set the branch of candles.

Slowly, she took in the unmistakable signs that, in spite of the large bed, Millicent slept there alone. There was no sign of a man's hair-brushes on the dressing-table; no masculine boots shared the shoe-tidy which stood beside the wardrobe.

Then Catrina noticed a door, half-concealed by an ornamental screen, and realised that Dominic occupied an adjoining room. So appearances were not even being kept up for the benefit of the servants, for the positioning of the screen showed that the door had not been opened in a long while.

As she helped her sister out of the black gown and

loosened her stays, Catrina said, 'I am quite clever at arranging a coiffure, you know. I have always had to cope with my own toilette. If you like, I could attend to your hair while I am here.'

'You will not be here for very long,' Millicent interrupted bluntly. 'And my hair is the very last consideration on my mind at present.'

Feeling rebuffed, Catrina returned to the dining-room, where Dominic was now alone, the servants having withdrawn after serving the second course. He rose with automatic politeness and pulled out her chair. As he pushed it close to the table once she had sat down, his hand slipped and came to rest upon her shoulder. It was the most fleeting of physical contacts, swiftly broken by him, and yet she felt as if his fingers had left scorch marks on her skin.

Briskly, to hide from him the fact that her heart was beating stormily, Catrina helped herself to cold cuts of meat and to vegetables. What on earth, she asked herself in angry confusion, was the matter with her that the man should disturb her so? A man for whom she ought to feel nothing but contempt?

She looked up at him, and it was as if someone had thrown cold water in her face. If he disturbed her, she in turn evoked equally strong feelings in him, but of a completely different nature. And it could have nothing to do with to do with the fact that she knew of his infidelity to Millicent, for he was studying her with such undisguised scorn that she caught her breath.

'You know,' he said abruptly, 'I had far more respect for you this morning, when I believed you to be an honest whore come to earn her crust in the only way open to her.'

Catrina dropped her fork with a clatter. 'What . . . do you mean?'

'You enjoy flouting convention and drawing attention to yourself, don't you? Tell me—whom did you hope to embarrass and shame when you arrived, over-dressed and powdered and painted, and openly friendly with a harlot?'

For a moment she was quite unable to speak. What arrogant dual standards he applied, considering his own behaviour! How dared he claim the moral right to condemn her!

'To begin with,' Catrina exclaimed angrily when she found her voice, 'I was not aware of Violet's true profession. But even if I *had* been, I would still not have shunned her when we disembarked!'

'Since you were presenting yourself to all on the Rock as her sister-under-the-skin,' he put in with heavy irony, 'that does not surprise me in the least. Assuming the improbable to be true, of course, and that you really did not guess what she was. You have not answered my question. Whom did you wish to hurt by coming here in such scandalous circumstances? The memory of your recently-dead parents? Or Millicent?'

'When it comes to hurting Millicent,' Catrina interrupted furiously, 'I am sure, from what I have already seen and heard, that you have perfected that to a fine art!'

'Mind your own business!' he snarled. 'My relationship with Millicent is no concern of yours! Now answer my question! Who was your real target in coming here? Was it Lady Prudence's daughter? Were you carrying out some perverted dying request of the old woman's, and revelling in it?'

Catrina stared at him. 'Lady Prudence *had* no daughter!'

He laughed unpleasantly. 'You are not seriously trying to make me believe that you lived for almost twenty years as Lady Prudence's doted-upon and spoilt charge, without learning of the existence of her only child, Alice?'

'Doted-upon and spoilt!' Catrina echoed, ignoring for the moment everything else he had said. 'Nothing could have been further from the truth! Captain Ross, where did you get that notion?'

'Why, Miss Beaumont,' he returned with hard mockery. 'From your own behaviour, for one thing. From the fact that Lady Prudence left you her fortune. And from what your parents had told me.'

'Precisely *what* did they tell you? How did they account for the fact that they had abandoned me?'

'They did not abandon you, so don't indulge your taste for the melodramatic on me! You were a headstrong, difficult child from the beginning. The frequent moves which your father had to make whenever the regiment was posted elsewhere only worsened matters, and you became beyond their control. So your godmother agreed to keep you for a while, and when you became older, you refused to leave her and join your family.'

Catrina drew a long, ragged breath. How could they have distorted the truth like that? A moment's reflection told her that they could hardly have confessed to their son-in-law—or anyone else, for that matter—that they had rejected their elder daughter.

She pushed her chair back. 'From the way in which you spoke, Lady Prudence's daughter is here in Gibraltar?'

'As you are only too well aware. She is married to General Ridgeway, my commanding officer and also, incidentally, the commanding officer of your late father.'

'Take me to her,' Catrina demanded.

His jaw hardened. 'The devil I will! I'll not help you to make mischief there . . .'

'In that case, I shall hail a gharry and ask to be driven to the Ridgeway residence by myself!'

She had reached the door when he took hold of her shoulders and whirled her about to face him. Once again, in spite of her present agitation, in spite of the fact that his eyes blazed with anger and contempt, the mere physical touch of his hands brought feelings washing over her which she did not understand.

'I'll take you to her,' he rapped. 'But one word out of place—one gloating reference to the fact that you had ousted her from her mother's affections—and I shall personally wring that slender white neck of yours!'

He gave her a none-too-gentle push. 'Go and fetch a cloak. The night air is fresh.'

Trembling, she obeyed. When she rejoined him, she discovered that they were to walk to the Ridgeway residence. Dominic told her tersely,

'The Rock is only about three miles long and no more than three-quarters of a mile in breadth, so that we all live very much cheek by jowl. Only the Governor resides in splendid isolation, high above the town in what used to be a Franciscan convent.'

She made some non-committal response, her mind preoccupied now by the knowledge that she was soon to meet Lady Prudence's daughter. Why had the old woman never spoken of her, Catrina wondered in helpless bewilderment. She broke the silence. 'You believe that Lady Prudence doted on me, and that I refused to leave her. Has it not occurred to you that if that had truly been the case, I would have worn mourning for *her,* even if I do not do so for my parents?'

Dominic uttered a grim laugh. 'It is entirely in character that you don't! As I have said, you enjoy flouting the conventions. You relish the excitement of creating scandal. And you clearly have a taste for the theatrical, or you would not be indulging in this jeremiad of having been abandoned by your parents and brought up by a cruel godmother. The fact that Lady Prudence disinherited her own daughter in your favour provides a flaw in your tale of woe, so you are pretending that you knew nothing of her existence. Besides, Miss Beaumont, I don't believe your vanity would ever allow you to hide your charms behind mourning-crape!'

Catrina had been listening to his catalogue of insults with mounting anger. 'You insufferable hypocrite!' she hurled at him. 'You dare to malign me, when you know nothing about me at all! And yet within seconds of our first meeting, you offered me a proposition . . .'

'The offer has been withdrawn. Even if you were not Millicent's sister, I would not consider you as a possible mistress—now that I know a very good deal about you!'

At this final taunt her control snapped. 'You—warped—twisted . . .' she stuttered incoherently, and raised her arm to slap his face. But the moonlight had made her intentions clear to him, and at the last moment her hand was grasped in one of his.

The impetus which she had intended to put behind that frustrated blow caused her to fall against him. He was still holding her hand in a firm grip, but now he dropped his arm. They stood like that for what seemed to Catrina to be an immeasurable time; neither of them speaking or moving, her head against his chest and her hand clasped in his.

The husky note in his voice was more pronounced than usual when he said, 'We have almost reached the house of General Ridgeway. Please compose yourself, and let us get this visit over and done with.'

As he moved away from her, she had the oddest instinct

that he was experiencing considerable difficulty in composing himself. Why that should be so, she could not have said, for he had not appeared to lose his composure in any way. She was the one who had been goaded into attempted physical violence, while he had merely restrained her.

They did not speak again until they reached the house where the Ridgeways lived.

The grounds of the house were impressive, as befitted the status of a General. In the bright moonlight, Catrina could see various unfamiliar flowering shrubs surrounding the gracious old Spanish house. Again, the front door was arched in the Moorish style, and it was opened to them by a butler who could not have been anything other than British.

'Good evening, Hobson,' Dominic said. 'I know this is most unorthodox, calling unannounced. But are General and Mrs Ridgeway at home, and likely to receive us?'

'They are, Captain Ross. I'm sure they will, as always, be delighted to see you. I shall announce you and . . .?'

'Miss Catrina Beaumont, my sister-in-law.'

The butler returned after a moment and asked them to follow him. They were shown into a drawing-room which met with Catrina's instant approval and admiration. It was not because it was particularly grand, but an obvious attempt had been made to furnish the room in a style which suited its architecture, and apart from one plain rug of some animal fur, nothing detracted from the beauty of the tiled floor.

Seated in a carved ebonised armchair which was obviously Spanish, a distinguished-looking older man with hawklike features and silver hair had been reading a newspaper, probably brought by ship from Britain that day, and was hastily straightening his wig.

A woman was sitting at the pianoforte, playing the last notes of a ballad. Her lace cap did not completely hide her greying dark hair, and diamonds sparkled on her fingers as they moved over the keys.

She smiled as she turned her head and then rose, with her husband, to greet the visitors. The atmosphere in the room told Catrina that, in spite of the difference in their ranks and ages, General Ridgway and Dominic were on terms of personal friendship.

To Catrina's surprise, Mrs Ridgeway folded her in a warm embrace, and then said, 'You don't remember me, do you?'

'No . . .'

'Well, I suppose it is not to be wondered at. You were very small when last we met.'

Catrina studied her in some perplexity. There was something vaguely familiar about her, although she certainly had no conscious recollection of ever having seen Mrs Ridgeway before. Neither was there anything reminiscent of Lady Prudence about this woman, whose even features and deep-set blue eyes proclaimed the fact that she had once been a great beauty. Despite her warm embrace and welcoming smile, Catrina could not help suspecting that she was hiding tension of some kind.

'My goodness!' General Ridgeway boomed, taking Catrina's hands in his. 'Who would ever have thought you would grow up to be such a beauty!'

She smiled mechanically, and turned back to his wife. 'Mrs Ridgeway,' she asked tensely, '*are* you the daughter of Lady Prudence Welles?'

'Indeed I am.' The woman gave her a puzzled, questioning look. 'But you must know that, my dear.'

'I did not know it. Until this evening, I had no knowledge of your existence.'

A look of pain crossed Mrs Ridgeway's face. 'She . . . never even mentioned me? She wiped me so completely from her life . . .?'

Catrina heard Dominic make an angry sound. He obviously believed that she was inflicting pain with a deliberate lie. But then, he had already made it clear that he would believe *anything* of her.

She ignored him, and addressed Mrs Ridgeway again. 'I am very sorry to tell you,' Catrina said gently, 'that your mother has died. It was very peaceful, while she slept.'

Mrs Ridgeway bowed her head. 'I guessed, as soon as the butler announced your name, that she must have died. You would not have left her alone, to come here.'

'Let us all sit down,' the General said, taking his wife

tenderly by the arm and leading her to a sofa.

This really was a most peculiar, baffling and uncomfortable position in which to find herself, Catrina thought. She cleared her throat, and addressed Mrs Ridgeway again. 'Your—Your mother left her estate to me.'

'I am glad,' the woman responded quietly.

'Did you know that she was very wealthy?'

'I did not know the extent of her fortune, but I do not begrudge you a penny of it.'

'Mrs Ridgeway,' Catrina asked abruptly. 'Why did my parents give me away to your mother?'

The woman stood up and drifted about the room, straightening ornaments unnecessarily. 'You were—a difficult child,' she said, echoing Dominic's earlier comment. 'Moving about constantly with your father's regiment unsettled you, and there was a gap in my mother's life after I'd . . . after I'd left to be married, so she offered to bring you up. Mary Beaumont—your mother—and I were lifelong friends, and that is how Lady Prudence came to be your godmother. It seemed a most satisfactory solution all round.'

'Satisfactory!' Catrina cried passionately, unable to stop herself. 'The arrangement was not in any way satisfactory to me! Lady Prudence . . .'

'That will do, Miss Beaumont!' Dominic snapped.

'No, it will not!' Catrina cried. 'I have a right to be heard, too! I cannot believe that I was difficult! I know only that I was utterly wretched and unhappy as a small child living with my godmother! I remember begging my parents to take me away!'

Mrs Ridgeway made a muffled excuse and fled from the room. Catrina sighed, her anger burnt out. 'I'm sorry I distressed your wife, General Ridgeway. I should not have let her know that I was so unhappy with her mother.'

'No, indeed you should not!' Dominic looked as if he were contemplating carrying out his threat to wring Catrina's neck there and then. 'We are leaving, Miss Beaumont,' he added.

'Please don't,' General Ridgeway said. 'Alice would be far more distressed if you were to leave now. Give her a while to recover her composure. What has really upset her is the fact that her mother not only refused to mend the quarrel between them, but that she denied Alice's very existence to the end.'

If he knew the reason for the quarrel between mother and daughter, Catrina thought, he clearly considered it to be a family matter, for he did not enlarge upon it, and she did not feel bold enough to question him.

He gave her an indulgent smile. '*You* may not believe that you were ever a difficult child, my dear, but you clearly have a strong character. I believe that your parents had your material welfare at heart as well, you know. They must have been aware that Lady Prudence meant to provide for you, and your father was not a rich man. He worked his way up through the ranks . . .'

'Lady Prudence practised the most stringent economies,' Catrina interrupted in a colourless voice. 'She never gave the appearance that she had anything more than a decaying old house to leave.'

'A miser, was she? Very rich people often are. You may depend on it that your parents knew the true state of affairs.'

Catrina was silent. Her parents had neither known nor cared, but she could not prove it, and she felt it would be useless to argue the point.

She heard Dominic say sardonically, 'I believe *you* had a shrewd suspicion of the true state of affairs, Miss Beaumont, and that was why you refused to leave your godmother when you grew older.'

'I did not refuse to leave her! I was constantly writing to my parents, begging them to allow me to leave!'

'They would have refused for your own sake,' General Ridgeway said. 'Old people are unpredictable, and Lady Prudence might well have changed her will in favour of some charity if you had been allowed to leave her.'

Catrina was about to launch into a passionate description of her life with Lady Prudence, but at that moment Mrs Ridgeway returned to the room.

Dominic sprang up and went to her, taking her hands in his. 'I am so sorry you have been put to such distress . . .' he began.

She gave him a watery smile, and silenced him with a shake of her head. She turned to Catrina. 'Forgive me for my rudeness. I daresay my mother became—difficult—

towards the end. Old people often do.'

Catrina allowed that understatement to pass. There was no point in distressing the woman further. Instead, she said, 'I want to share my inheritance with you. Indeed, I don't believe Lady Prudence knew the extent of her own wealth. She had succeeded in deluding herself that she was almost a pauper.'

'My dear child,' Alice Ridgeway said quietly, 'I do not want, or need, any part of your inheritance. My husband is a man of means, and we have no children whose future needs providing for. You deserve the money my mother left you, because you must have been a great comfort to her in her loneliness.'

A note of pleading entered her voice. 'Go back to England and enjoy your inheritance, and try to forgive your parents. They did what they thought was best, however it may have seemed to you.'

Her meaning was only too clear to Catrina. Her own presence in Gibraltar was an embarrassment: she asked too many unanswerable questions and made too many damaging accusations. She threatened disruption in a society which was already facing the imminent and greater disruption of war.

Dominic had obviously understood Mrs Ridgeway's meaning, too, for he said with emphasis, 'Miss Beaumont will be taking the first available passage back to England.'

'That may not be for some weeks,' General Ridgeway told them. 'All vessels which were seaworthy sailed today, to carry the many passengers who wished to leave. We shall have to wait for the supply ships to arrive from England, and then make the turn-around voyage.'

'The child must be got to safety!' There was something shrill and almost bordering on hysteria in Alice Ridgeway's voice as she appealed to her husband. 'John, you have influence! You must contrive some way . . .'

'Calm yourself, my dear.' He patted her shoulder. 'The latest news from our spies is that the Spaniards will not blockade the Bay until they have completed their works on the *Linea* . . .'

He broke off to explain to Catrina, 'I fear we sadly neglected Gibraltar's defences in the past. In 1727 the

Spaniards built a wall along the coast, supposedly to control smuggling. Later they extended it and added redoubts, or forts, to house their batteries, and this *Linea* of theirs straddles part of the isthmus which connects us to the mainland.'

He continued cheerfully, 'If I know the Dons, they'll take forever to complete their works and mount their batteries, because of course every man jack of them downs tools each day for the siesta, war or not. In the meantime, we don't intend them to interfere with our planned activities. There is the Governor's Gala next week, Dominic. You will have to attend, of course, but I know Millicent will be unable to accompany you. So bring your beautiful sister-in-law in her place, and in the meantime show her the sights.'

'Very well, sir,' Dominic returned woodenly.

Alice Ridgeway looked as if she were about to cry again, obviously at the unwelcome thought of having Catrina on the Rock for weeks to come. Dominic put his arm about her shoulders and kissed her cheek before they left, and General Ridgeway shook Catrina's hand warmly.

As they walked home together along the cobbled road in the moonlight, Dominic broke the silence. His voice did not remind her remotely of brown velvet now; instead it was like cracked ice.

'You are even more cunning than I had imagined. You gained John Ridgeway's approval with your oh-so-affecting offer to share your inheritance with his wife. But you had made quite sure that Alice would not dream of accepting, by first claiming that her mother had denied her very existence to the end!'

Catrina gritted her teeth and ignored his insults. 'There is some connection,' she said grimly, 'between Lady Prudence's quarrel with her daughter and my being given to be brought up by her. And I mean to find out what it is before I leave Gibraltar!'

'You mean that you intend making more trouble!'

'If necessary.'

'I'll stop you,' he promised in a dangerous tone. 'Even if I have to use unscrupulous means.'

'Be careful, Dominic,' she said recklessly, 'that I do not make trouble for *you*.'

He laughed contemptuously. 'What possible trouble could you make for me?'

'I should have thought that was obvious! I could tell Millicent that I saw and overheard you taking leave of your mistress!'

'I am reasonably certain that Millicent knows,' he returned carelessly.

'What an unprincipled devil you are! Does she also know that you are already looking for someone to replace your mistress?'

'She would have to be very stupid not to have guessed.'

Catrina caught her breath at his cold, uncaring shamelessness. 'You may not scruple to have Millicent hurt!' she flung at him. 'But judging by the insults you have heaped upon me, you are not indifferent to what society thinks. How would your fellow-officers and their wives react, do you imagine, if I were to make it known that you offered *me* the vacant post as your mistress?'

He stopped in his tracks. Uttering a violent sound, he spun her round. His hands encircled her throat, and she thought she had gone too far, that this time he really would strangle her! Instead, his hands were suddenly cupping her face, just as they had done in her dream that afternoon, and she could feel his warm breath on her face as he bent his head.

Her heart was beating tumultuously as she waited for his kiss. No man had ever kissed her before, but she knew intuitively what it would be like. Mindlessly, blotting out everything and everyone else from her consciousness, she parted her lips.

His mouth was a fraction of an inch from her own when he put her away with a savagely muttered oath, and strode off ahead of her towards the house where his wife and daughter were asleep. He had already disappeared from sight by the time she entered through the front door, which was being held open for her by one of the servants.

Catrina picked up a branch of candles and sought her room. No, she amended to herself as she gazed about her, *Millicent's room.* She began to prepare for bed and then sat down by the dressing-table to brush her hair.

She paused for a moment, peering closer at her reflection,

arrested by something which flickered on the periphery of her mind. It was gone almost as swiftly as it had slipped into her consciousness, and she dismissed it.

CHAPTER FOUR

CATRINA AWOKE WITH a start as a gong sounded somewhere in the house. Strong sunlight was creeping into the room through the gaps between the shutters of the window, creating a striped pattern on the tiled floor.

It was not surprising that she had overslept, for she had tossed and turned for a long time after going to bed, and when she did doze off, her dreams had been haunted by Dominic. One in particular had been vivid enough for her to remember it in detail. She was standing outside a house, her arms hugged about her breasts, and staring through a window into an unfamiliar room. A fire crackled in the hearth, and Lucy stood warming her hands by it. On a sofa Millicent nursed an infant. Some way beyond them, Dominic stood locked in a passionate embrace with a beautiful girl. The two groups were totally oblivious of one another, as if an invisible wall separated them.

As the fierce, biting wind which had been lashing Catrina turned into a blizzard, she knocked on the window and cried to be let in. Dominic released the beautiful stranger and gave her a cold glance. Millicent transferred the baby to her shoulder and leant forward, taking a handbell from the table and ringing it. Everyone went on with what they had been doing and then a serving-maid entered and drew the blinds, shutting Catrina out completely.

She rose from the bed, shaking her head in an effort to banish the dream. The jug of water which a servant had brought while she slept had grown tepid, but she felt herself too unwelcome a guest to ring for a fresh supply. After washing quickly, she twisted her hair up into a Grecian knot, from which tendrils escaped to frame her face. Then she searched through her trunks for her most sober morning gown, black and white striped cambric, and she draped a fichu of white muslin about her shoulders.

A passing serving-maid directed her to the morning-room, where breakfast was laid out on a refectory table. Catrina had deliberately made her way there slowly, in the hope that Dominic would have broken his fast and already left upon his military duties. Instead, she watched from the shadows of the doorway, her heart thudding, for far from making a hasty meal he was engaged upon the task of carving a joint of cold sirloin. Millicent was seated at the table, watching him.

She looked even more dishevelled this morning than she had the day before. Her hair gave no indication of having been brushed at all, and she had simply bundled as much of it as she could inside a white lace cap, which was none too clean. And even though she was in mourning for their parents, surely there was no need for her to wear such frumpish modes? Judging by the bodice of her gown, it might have been designed for a dowager.

Dominic regarded his wife with a blank expression, seeming not to notice what she looked like, for all he said was, 'You should try to eat some of this beef.'

'The very sight of it turns my stomach!'

'May I suggest that you try to overcome your own queasiness, and think of the baby . . .'

'The baby!' Millicent's voice was low-pitched, but that did not disguise the note of hysteria which it held. 'All you care about is the wretched baby! I only pray that this time the infant will prove to be a boy, for I cannot endure the thought of being made to repeat the whole dreadful nightmare once again!'

Catrina then deemed it prudent to make her presence known. She coughed discreetly, and approached the table. 'Good morning. I am so sorry that I'm late.'

She avoided looking at Dominic as she spoke, but helped herself instead to bacon and scrambled eggs from a covered silver dish after she had sat down. There was hot chocolate for the ladies and a tankard of ale for Dominic, but Millicent made no attempt to eat or drink anything. Catrina wondered why she had troubled to come to the breakfast table at all. Was she perhaps, in a pathetic way, trying to gain her husband's attention and sympathy by underlining the wretchedness to which her pregnancy reduced her? Was that the only way she could think of in which to fight for him?

He spoke suddenly, addressing Catrina without looking up. 'A note was brought round for me from General Ridgeway early this morning. I have been excused duties so that I may escort you and show you the town, Miss Beaumont.'

His tone made it clear that he viewed the task with the utmost distaste. Stung, Catrina retorted, 'You do not need to escort me anywhere, Captain Ross. This morning I intend to hire a gharry, for I wish to visit the graves of my parents.'

He gave her a brief, grim look. 'General Ridgeway may be a personal friend, but he is also my commanding officer, and he wishes me to escort you. And knowing your taste for making trouble with ostentatious displays, it is as well that I should keep an eye on you.'

She shot him a blazing glance, but addressed her sister. 'Perhaps, Millicent, it might be wise if you were to accompany us as a chaperon.'

'What nonsense! Why should any tongues wag if you are seen together without a chaperon? There could be no impropriety in your being alone with my husband!'

Catrina thought of Dominic's hands cupping her face, and of his mouth almost touching hers, and her heart beat so stormily that she feared Millicent would hear it. She forced a mocking note into her voice. 'It is your husband's reputation I am thinking of. His sense of propriety has been greatly outraged by the fact that I did not arrive wearing mourning crape, and I know he would hate anyone to leap to the conclusion that I am more than his sister-in-law.'

Millicent looked bewildered, and Dominic said in a flint-like voice, 'You may be sure, Miss Beaumont, that my behaviour will be such that no one will be in doubt that I am dutifully showing my wife's sister the sights!'

'In other words, you will not hide your distaste and your reluctance!' Catrina turned to Millicent. 'You will have realised that your husband and I do not find one another's company convivial, so you really would be doing us a service by accompanying us. Besides, I feel that some fresh air would do you good.'

Before Millicent could reply, Dominic said in that neutral

tone which he always seemed to employ towards his wife, 'Millicent prefers to suffer the torments of her pregnancy within these walls.' He rose. 'Let us get this excursion over with! I shall have the gharry brought to the front of the house.'

After he had gone, Catrina considered for a moment questioning her sister about the obvious unhappiness of her marriage. But she sensed that she would be answered with a rebuff, and, besides, there was something of personal importance to her upon which she needed to be enlightened.

'Millicent, have *you* always known that Mrs Ridgeway was Lady Prudence's daughter?'

'Yes, naturally I have.'

'Why did you never mention her existence on the occasions when you visited the house in Belgravia with Mother and Father?'

'Did I not?' Millicent shrugged. 'I don't recall. If I didn't mention her, it was probably because there was too much else to talk about at the time.'

Yes, Catrina thought with remembered bitterness, her present pity for her sister temporarily evaporating. There were the parties which our parents arranged for you, the gifts they bought you, the new gowns and bonnets which you could not wait to describe to me in great and gloating detail . . .

'In any event,' Millicent went on, 'I scarcely thought of her as Lady Prudence's daughter. She was just Aunt Alice, Mama's dearest friend. And *you* must have known of her existence, surely!'

'I did not, until yesterday. Do you know why Lady Prudence quarrelled with Alice?' Catrina asked.

'No. The matter was never discussed in my presence.'

'Were you ever told the real reason why I was given away to Lady Prudence?'

'Mama said you were a most difficult child,' Millicent repeated the by now familiar vindication. 'I dare say that was the reason why she and Papa found it impossible to love you.'

For a moment the wretchedness had left her sister's face and Catrina was reminded of the old, gloating, triumphant

Millicent. Shrugging the memory away, Catrina excused herself.

In her room, she took from a hat-box a black bonnet trimmed with white satin ribbons and two white silk roses inside its shallow poke. She tied the ribbons underneath her chin, pulled on a pair of white gloves and selected a parasol of white and black stripes that matched her gown.

When she emerged from the house, Dominic was waiting for her. He was standing by a gharry, above which a fringed canopy fluttered, and a nimble-looking pony was hitched to the shaft.

As she walked towards him, Catrina was sharply conscious of everything about Dominic, from his Hessian boots, his tightly-fitting buckskins and the cut-away coat which skimmed his waist, to the dark hair beneath his hat which stirred in the breeze.

'Don't you ever wear a wig, or powder your hair?' she asked him impulsively.

That one dark eyebrow shot into the air in a characteristic fashion. 'The sight of my natural hair offends you?'

She flushed. 'Don't be absurd!'

'To answer your question—I can see no reason why I should follow the absurd custom which pertains here on the Rock of covering the hair in flour. *Or* why I should wear a cumbersome wig merely to ape fashion.' He added tauntingly, 'But fashion is something for which *you*, I am sure, would gladly suffer!'

She glared at him. 'If we are to trade insults, Captain Ross, let me tell you that I have been quite horrified at the change which marriage to you has made in my sister. I remember her as being very pretty, and fastidious about her appearance, whereas now . . .'

'Hold your tongue!' he snapped. 'I have no intention of discussing Millicent with you!'

'I am quite sure you have not! You would far sooner vilify and condemn me! What a monstrous hypocrite you are! You told me in so many words that Millicent knew you had a mistress, and that you are seeking to replace her. You do not show an ounce of sympathy for her unhappiness or the misery to which her condition reduces her, and yet you are very concerned that your fellow-officers should not learn that you had made me a proposition!'

'Listen, you stupid little baggage!' he exploded. 'It is not the fact that I made you a proposition that I wish to conceal! It is the fact that, unknowingly, I made such a proposition to *my wife's sister*! Now be quiet, for I am fast reaching the point where I won't be answerable for my actions!'

Something in his voice warned her that it might, indeed, be wise to lapse into silence. She sat back, and listened to the bo'suns' pipes sounding from the direction of one of the bays.

As Dominic steered the pony towards the town's main street, the sky was suddenly darkened as if a heavy black storm-cloud were racing across it. Catrina uttered an involuntary exclamation. It was no cloud, but a huge swarm of enormous dark birds.

'Black kites,' she heard Dominic explain, his voice passionless now, as if he were punctiliously performing the role of her guide which had been thrust upon him.

'But so many of them,' she observed, taking her cue from him.

'They are birds of prey, using the upcurrents for soaring on their way to migration.'

Catrina shivered. There had been something sinister in the sight; almost as if it presaged the hostilities which were to come.

Then she gave her attention to more mundane matters. In spite of the many British imports such as inn-signs, a pillory and an official whipping-post for public floggings, there was something ineradicably foreign about the place.

When she mentioned this thought to Dominic, he said shortly, 'Many different nations have stamped their mark on Gibraltar. Jews from the Barbary Coast, Moors, Genoese, Portuguese and, of course, the Spaniards.'

In the many cobbled side-alleys off the main street she could see a jumble of Moorish and Spanish-style old houses with porticos and bright shutters, and sometimes small plazas in which ragged, swarthy urchins played.

Women in stuff gowns kilted above their ankles, their feet clad in sturdy boots, were emerging from or entering the huddled old houses, carrying bundles or baskets. Men who, from their dress and their weather-beaten appearance, were probably fishermen in normal times, were engaged in boarding up windows of the mean houses, in a pathetic attempt at turning them into fortresses. Outside open-fronted shops Jewish merchants were doing a roaring trade, and now Catrina understood the significance of the women with their bundles and baskets. They were stockpiling provisions and other commodities. Catrina could almost smell the tension and suppressed panic in the air, and only by gazing at the batteries and cannon with which the entire place bristled was she able to resist becoming infected by it herself.

'Everyone seems to be expecting an imminent attack,' she commented.

Dominic shrugged. 'At the moment, we are safe enough from land attack. After the Spaniards built their *Linea*, our north-pointing batteries were improved and a morass was dug on our side of the isthmus to prevent an invasion. The Inundation, as it is called, was dug to a depth of two feet below water-mark, and dotted with deeper pits to drown anyone foolhardly enough to try and cross it. When the Dons have completed their works, they will be unable to do more than take wild pot-shots at us from the isthmus.'

'We are reasonably safe, then, from land attack?'

'*We,* Miss Beaumont?' he mocked. 'By the time the fighting starts you will be back in England, dazzling the young blades of Society with your wealth and your beauty . . .'

'Do you think me beautiful, Dominic?' she taunted softly, and immediately regretted the reckless impulse.

He glanced at her from beneath half-lowered lashes, and a small muscle jerked beside his mouth. 'Let us talk about the war, Miss Beaumont,' he said in a colourless voice. 'The main weakness in our defence lies to the sea.'

My sister's husband, Catrina told herself. A man who treats her with a cold indifference which is almost worse than cruelty. Why do I keep forgetting it, and allow myself to be so disturbed by him?

Aloud, she said, 'I would have thought, from my first glimpse of the Rock, that it was quite impregnable from the sea.'

'Perhaps. But Gibraltar suffers from two great handicaps. Virtually our only fresh water supply comes from the rainfall, and as you can see, the rocky mass predominates. That leaves only a small area of soil capable of raising foodstuffs for the garrison and the townspeople.'

'So that you rely almost totally upon supplies being brought in by ship.'

'Precisely. We shall have to fight to prevent the Spanish and French from blockading the Bay. The devil of it is that our warships will have to be shared between the action taking place in America, and an attempt to scatter any blockading vessels here.'

'Have we no friendly allies?'

Dominic's shrug indicated scant optimism as he replied, 'The Moors have agreed to run supplies from the Barbary Coast to Gibraltar.'

'Do you realise,' Catrina asked impulsively, 'that for at least five minutes we have neither quarrelled nor insulted one another?'

He glanced at her, his eyes holding a glint of amusement, and his lips flickering at the corners. 'Perhaps we had better confine our conversations to the topic of war.'

She gazed about her, at a church spire which might have been pointing into the sky anywhere above a British town, but as they drew closer to the building she realised that it could not have been more unlike an English church. The approach to it was through a long colonnade of trees.

'The Church of Santa Maria la Coronada,' Dominic explained. 'Commonly known as St Mary the Crowned. It was once a mosque, built on the foundations of a temple. The Catholic sovereigns, Ferdinand and Isabella, ordered the conversion of the mosque into a church. These trees forming the colonnade, although they no longer bear fruit in any quantity, are orange trees. The colonnade is known as the Patio de los Naranjes. I am afraid that when our troops first took Gibraltar in 1704, they behaved atrociously, and all but this church was sacked and looted. A brave priest stayed behind to guard Santa Maria, and out of respect for his courage he and his church were spared. Would you like to see the interior?'

'Very much.'

He stopped the gharry, and they walked along the colonnade. 'It is still used by the Catholic community,' he told her. 'The rest of us worship in the King's Chapel inside the Convent.'

'Convent?'

'The Governor's residence is still known as the Convent. But because Governor Eliott cannot bear the noise of the bells, they were removed from the tower, and we are called to worship by the beating of drums.'

They had entered the church now, but as they walked round, Catrina found she could not concentrate. Instead she was vividly imagining the sound of drumbeats summoning friends and relations and fellow-officers to the wedding of Millicent and Dominic four years ago. If only those drums had been beating for herself, with his tall figure by her side, *she* would not have allowed things to come to the pass they had in such a short time . . .

She shook her head. Dear God, even inside a place of worship she was beset by sinful thoughts!

'I'll show you the slab bearing the royal arms of Ferdinand and Isabella,' she heard Dominic say.

'Thank you,' she replied. 'But I have seen enough for the moment, and I wish to visit my parents' graves.'

He led the way to the door, and neither of them spoke again until he reined in the pony to halt the gharry as they reached the military cemetery. He jumped lightly from his seat, and held out a helping hand to Catrina, for here the cobbles were broken and uneven. She pretended not to see it, afraid of any physical contact between them, and gathered her skirts to step from the vehicle.

The heel of her boot caught in a loose cobble, and she lurched forward. He was just in time to catch her before she fell to the ground. For an instant he held her, so that she could hear the rapid beating of his heart against her cheek and feel his breath stirring the tendrils of hair which framed her face. Then, almost as if the touch of her had contaminated him, he pushed her away, and strode towards the graves.

Catrina asked quietly, when he had pointed out the graves where her parents lay side by side, 'Would you mind very much leaving me alone for a while?'

She watched him walk back to the gharry, and then she knelt between the graves of the people whose name she bore, whose love for one another had resulted in her own birth and who had yet given her away so callously. Sighing deeply, she untied the satin bow of her bonnet and lifted it from her head. Then, very carefully, she removed the two white silk roses from inside it, and laid one on each of the graves.

Retying the bonnet upon her head she walked back to the gharry, her eyes bright with unshed tears.

'Very affecting, Miss Beaumont,' Dominic said in a hard voice. 'But a small sacrifice to make, after all. I'm sure you have any number of fripperies among your trunks with which to replace the roses in your bonnet.'

She sensed that, in some obscure way, he was punishing her for that moment when she had tripped and forced him again to catch her in his arms.

'Shall we talk about the war again?' she asked quietly. 'What preparations have the British been making?'

He uttered a harsh laugh. 'Yes, let us talk about the war. I assure you that the British have not been idle. Willis's battery on the north face of the Rock is being strengthened with several well-gunned works, and our lines have been extended into a very formidable obstacle to any assault which may be mounted along the narrow sands of the isthmus.'

Catrina could not help reflecting, as the morning progressed, that the peace between herself and Dominic continued to be as false and precarious as the apparent peace existing between Britain and her two enemies.

Sometimes they used the gharry, and at others Dominic left both pony and vehicle in the charge of street urchins in exchange for a few coins, while he and Catrina continued on foot, climbing winding steps hacked out of the rock. As he pointed to the uncompromising precipices which frowned down upon them, brooding and hostile, topped by towers and flags, he said,

'Up there are Sugar Loaf Point and Mount Misery, our look-out posts. Sugar Loaf Point is the highest accessible peak of the crest. It means an arduous climb, but I am sure you would wish to see it, and I am equally sure that General

Ridgeway will continue to relieve me of my proper duties in order that I may provide amusement for you.'

She stared steadily at him, recognising that the statement had been a taunting challenge which he had no expectation of her accepting.

'I should certainly like to climb to Sugar Loaf Point,' she said.

Something flickered in his eyes, and she realised that it was a conflicting expression of reluctant admiration and chagrin. 'I shall arrange it,' was all he said.

A fresh-faced officer who had been overseeing a working party of troops toiling at the defences came walking towards them at that moment. He was regarding Catrina with an undisguised and almost impertinent admiration that brought a flush to her cheeks. But it was Dominic he addressed, slapping him on the shoulder.

'Ross, you sly, lucky dog! You stole a march on all of us who saw Violet's lovely new recruit . . .'

'Take back that remark,' Dominic demanded with deadly menace, 'and apologise!'

'Now look, dear boy!'

'Take it back!' Dominic repeated between his teeth.

'The devil I will!'

With frozen horror, Catrina heard Dominic say, 'Name your seconds, Price!'

'This is madness!' Catrina cried. 'I will not be fought over!' She turned to Dominic's brother-officer. 'You have made a mistake, Please allow me to introduce myself. I am Catrina Beaumont, the sister of Captain Ross's wife.'

A deep flush of dismay suffused the officer's face. 'Captain Henry Price, at your service, ma'am,' he mumbled automatically, and added in a rush, 'I do beg your pardon. And yours too, Ross.'

Catrina glanced at Dominic's implacable face, and said quickly, 'Perhaps I had better explain, Captain Price. I made the voyage from England on board *Oriole*, and I came ashore in company with Violet. I was dreadfully seasick almost from the moment the vessel left England, and Violet, who had been standing by the rail with me, helped me to my cabin. She cared for me throughout the voyage with the utmost dedication.'

She looked defiantly at Dominic again. 'I was not aware of Violet's profession, but even if I had been, I would certainly not have spurned her after what she had done for me. Why, I could not even have dressed myself, let alone stepped ashore, without her help and support.'

'I understand, ma'am,' Captain Price said. 'Violet has ever had a kind heart.' He glanced at Dominic, and extended his hand. 'Shall we forget the whole sorry misunderstanding, and shake on it?'

His expression still grim, Dominic accepted the proffered hand and then swept Catrina away.

'I am sorry that such a scene should have occurred,' she said in a low voice. 'But, really, you cannot offer to fight a duel with *everyone* who chanced to see me step ashore with Violet!'

'Don't flatter yourself,' he interrupted brusquely. 'It was not for your sake that I was prepared to fight, but Millicent's. Your reputation would reflect on her.'

'Oh, you do have an amazing code of honour!' Catrina flung at him. 'You neglect your wife; you betray her with other women; you are quite unmoved by her physical suffering—but let anyone besmirch her family name and you are ready to take up pistol or sword! I must remember to tell Millicent; I am sure she will be truly moved!'

He grabbed hold of Catrina's wrists, his hands bruising her flesh. 'You will keep out of matters concerning my wife and myself!'

'I don't believe I have ever met anyone I despised more than you!' Catrina cried furiously.

'The feeling, Miss Beaumont, is entirely mutual!' He dropped her wrists and turned away. 'I am heartily tired of squiring you about the place. We will return home now, in time for luncheon.'

CHAPTER FIVE

THEY HAD BEEN driving along the cobbled streets for some minutes when Catrina broke the silence. 'Whether you choose to believe it or not, I told Captain Price the truth about myself and Violet. My arrival in Gibraltar was not the deliberately engineered act of malice of which you have accused me.'

He glanced at her, and said in a clipped voice, 'Sea-sick or not, you were presumably in possession of your senses. With your parents so recently dead, you must have been aware that by wearing such a revealing gown, and allowing your face to be powdered and painted, you would cause scandalous comment.'

Since Millicent had allowed him to believe that she had written to her sister with news of their parents' death, Catrina offered no defence. Millicent had enough to contend with in her marriage, without arousing her husband's anger over the issue.

Catrina gave him a defiant look. 'Since my parents did not want me when they were alive, my behaviour after their death would have been a matter of complete indifference to them.'

She could see his jaw hardening. 'So you are persisting with that fiction!'

'Oh, believe what you like!' she snapped, and lapsed into a silence which lasted until they had reached home.

The maid-servant who met them at the door informed them that Millicent was entertaining a guest, Mrs Dinah Forest, who would be joining them for luncheon.

'I am glad to hear that Millicent appears to have at least one friend,' Catrina remarked pointedly, before hurrying to her room to tidy herself.

Her gown was still quite fresh and she decided against changing it, but merely removed the muslin fichu, leaving her throat and shoulders uncovered. She took off her bonnet and set her coiffure to rights; then she made her way to the drawing-room.

The first thing she noticed was that not even the arrival of a guest had moved Millicent to exert herself to do something about her appearance. As for Dominic, he lounged in a chair, his long legs stretched out in front of him, but he rose almost immediately to make her a formal bow. She guessed that he had been forced into this gesture of politeness because of the presence of a guest, and in return she dropped him a mocking curtsy.

'Miss Beaumont,' he said in an expressionless voice, 'allow me to present you to Mrs Forest.'

For the first time Catrina gave her attention to the guest. Dinah Forest could not have been older than twenty-five or thereabouts. She was small and slight, with round blue eyes beneath arched brows, which lent her a look of startled innocence, and her fair hair, which had been powdered so that it appeared almost flaxen, was arranged in artless ringlets. Her blue taffeta gown showed her small rounded breasts and tiny waist off to perfection, and in one hand she held a fan of painted chicken-skin mounted on carved ivory which she fluttered coyly. Indeed, were it not for her lace cap, which Catrina knew was a formal token of maturity, she would have mistaken the woman for a young girl.

'How do you do, Miss Beaumont,' she was greeted in a gushing tone. 'Welcome to Gibraltar! I am sure your visit will do a great deal to cheer poor dear Millicent's low spirits.'

Catrina blinked. Was Dinah Forest malicious, or merely silly? It was obvious to even the most casual eye that Catrina's visit had done nothing whatever to improve Millicent's spirits.

'I am happy to meet you, Mrs Forest,' Catrina responded politely. Making conversation, she went on, 'Is your husband, too, under the command of General Ridgeway?'

'My husband, alas, is dead.' Dinah cast her eyes downwards.

'Dinah was married by proxy to a naval officer,' Dominic put in. 'She was sailing from England to join him here in Gibraltar when his ship foundered in a freak storm and he was drowned.'

'That really is most tragic,' Catrina murmured.

Dinah gave a brave little smile. 'Life must go on. I have come to terms with my loss, and at least I still have dear John and Alice, not to mention all my good friends. John Ridgeway is my cousin, you see, and the only family I have in the world.'

Catrina could think of no adequate comment to make, and Dinah did not seem to expect one, for she addressed Dominic, obviously continuing a conversation which had been interrupted, peeping at him over her fan as she spoke.

'As I've said, I know it was unwise to dance more than once with the man, but I gave him absolutely no encouragement, and now he is bombarding me with the most ridiculous love-tokens. As his fellow-officer, dear Dominic, you will rid me of his unwelcome attentions, won't you?'

'Yes, Dinah, I'll get you out of yet another of your scrapes,' he returned indulgently.

She fluttered both her eyelashes and her fan at him, and Catrina recognised, with sudden insight, that behind the girlish silliness there was determination, and that this young woman was setting her cap at Dominic. In such a small place, everyone must be aware that he had had a mistress who had departed the day before, and Dinah was clearly offering herself as a replacement.

'By the by,' Dinah addressed Dominic again, 'you *will* be escorting me to the Governor's Gala next week, won't you?'

She had spoken with such transparently assumed casualness that Catrina immediately knew that this was one of her chief reasons for having called. Telling herself that she was doing it for Millicent's sake, Catrina interposed,

'Oh dear, I do hope my arrival has not made things awkward for anyone, but I understood from General Ridgeway that *I* was to accompany Dominic to the Governor's Gala.'

She could see the muscles of his face tauten at the thought of escorting her to the function. But when he spoke his voice was light, and gave no indication of his feelings. 'Sorry, Dinah. But you, of all people, will not be short of an escort. Choose one from among your many admirers.'

Catrina was not deceived by the good grace with which

Dinah seemed to accept the situation and to go on talking animatedly about other matters. Angry compassion coursed through her as she studied her sister. There she sat in her chair, unkempt and unnecessarily unattractive, totally ignored while Dinah was flagrantly flirting with Dominic.

I'll take Millicent in hand this very afternoon, Catrina told herself. I shall bully her and force her to see that no man is likely to be won back by guilt and pity. She must stop wearing her wretchedness on her sleeve, and make an effort to appear attractive and cheerful.

A small, inner voice of honesty told Catrina that her anger was not altogether on Millicent's behalf. For reasons which she preferred not to examine too closely, she herself could not endure the thought of a possible affair between Dominic and Dinah.

In an attempt to escape from the voice of truth, she addressed Dinah in a conversational tone. 'I am surprised that General Ridgeway has such a very young cousin, Mrs Forest.'

'Oh, I am his second cousin.' Dinah gave a tinkling laugh. 'You have quite swept poor John off his feet, Miss Beaumont! If he did not so obviously adore Alice, she might have had cause for concern. He has always had a weakness for Titian hair.' Again that bell-like laugh rang out. 'I dare say it does not even occur to him that the Egyptians have, for centuries, been able to create that colour with the use of henna and that we have learnt our tricks from them!'

So the playful little kitten had sharp claws, Catrina thought grimly. She smiled. 'It is quite surprising, is it not, Mrs Forest, just how many little female tricks even the most intelligent of men are totally unaware of!'

Dinah returned her smile, but each knew that she had taken the measure of the other.

The gong sounded then, and they went in to luncheon. Millicent looked with distaste at the table, at one end of which stood a ham flanked by some capons, and at the other several dishes of vegetables. She merely picked at a little breast of fowl, which at least gained her a moment of Dominic's attention, for he urged her to eat something more substantial. But she was not allowed to occupy the stage for long, because Dinah claimed that she, too, had always had the appetite of a bird.

'Indeed,' she added, drawing Dominic's attention to her slender wrists by lifting her arms so that her flounced sleeves dropped to her elbows, 'I have often been compared to a bird by some silly love-struck man or other.'

Yes, a vulture, Catrina thought, while aloud, she said, 'The point is that Millicent needs proper nourishment.'

'The very sight of all this food makes me feel queasy!' Millicent rose. 'You will have to excuse me, please. Dinah, I know that I need not stand on ceremony with you.'

'Indeed not, dear Millie. I, too, shall have to leave after the meal, and I'm sure Dominic will lend me his strong arm and escort me home.'

Catrina watched with less than enchantment as the two of them left. Then she went to Millicent's room and knocked on the door. Receiving no reply, she pushed open the door. Millicent was not there, and Catrina was about to turn away when she noticed that the deep drawer of the side-table by the bed had been pulled out at a crooked angle. On a purely instinctive reflex, because she had been conditioned for years to create order out of chaos, Catrina went to shut the drawer properly.

The reason why it was difficult to shut in a hurry became only too clear. It housed a large tin of sweetmeats, sugared fruits and ratafia biscuits and squares of marchpane, all mixed up together.

Catrina did not attempt to shut the drawer after all but left the room, deep in troubled thought. She made another disturbing discovery a few minutes later. Having decided, with some reluctance, that she ought to become acquainted with her small niece, she made her way to the nursery. But even before she reached it she could hear Millicent and the child laughing as they obviously played some kind of game together.

The usually fretful, unhappy Millicent *laughing*! While, in Dominic's presence, she gave every indication of keeping her daughter at arm's length.

Catrina went to her room, and after staring unseeingly out to sea for a while she took out her diary and began to put her thoughts on paper:

My sister loathes, to a quite unnatural degree, the state of pregnancy. I wonder if it might not be the case that Dominic had first begun to stray when my sister was expecting Lucy, and that the only revenge my sister can inflict on him is to pretend to reject the child when he is present.

But whatever the truth is, Millicent's attitude must be very confusing and perhaps even damaging to Lucy. One moment she is being fussed over affectionately by her mother; the next she is publicly ignored and dismissed.

Catrina read through what she had written, and then put her diary away with a sigh. For the sake of everyone concerned she would have to try to force a discussion with Millicent, and make her see the folly of her actions.

But there were no opportunities, in the days which followed, for Catrina to have a frank and intimate talk with Millicent, for not only did her sister's attitude discourage intimate conversation, but Dominic continued to follow General Ridgeway's instructions to show her the sights.

He took care, however, that they should not be alone again. A private soldier belonging to his regiment accompanied them, and drove the conveyance when she was taken to see the Land Port Gate at the British side of the isthmus. They trundled along steep rocky slopes surrounded by bare rock-faces, gullies and precipices. Such soil as there was was dry and obviously unfruitful, and there were few trees or shrubs apart from the ubiquitous palmettos. Only on the neutral ground of the isthmus, between the British defences and the Spanish *Linea*, could garden produce be grown.

The Gate itself Catrina found impressive. Narrow and sheltered, it was built of heavy stone, and its approach was by a road raised on arches. Several bastions and an old Moorish castle commanded the morass, or Inundation, of which Dominic had previously told her. Between the Inundation and the sea was a wide ditch fenced in by steel-pointed palisades. Beyond this rose a sheer stone wall topped by embrasures filled with the mouths of cannon.

Dominic, his voice coolly impersonal, explained the defensive and offensive significance of everything she saw, and she shuddered as her mind translated all these facts into the harsh reality that, before long, people would be killing—or being killed.

Catrina felt a growing depression settling upon her spirits. It was a depression which she could not confide to anyone, and so she poured her heart out to her diary in her spare time:

> I should never have come here, and now I wish only to leave. I find myself watching Dominic when he is not aware of it—the way in which his eyelashes curl quite absurdly for a man with such a strong face; the curve of his mouth; the strength of his hands which I long to have touch me, and I am filled with bitter shame. Then I think of poor Millicent, and to the shame is added guilt and self-disgust.
>
> On my first evening here I threatened Dominic that I would do everything in my power to discover why Mother and Father gave me away to Lady Prudence. What an empty threat that was! I still feel the whole matter was somehow bound up with the quarrel between Lady Prudence and her daughter Alice, for Mrs Ridgeway could not conceal her agitation at the thought of my continued presence in Gibraltar.
>
> Everyone assumes—or pretends to assume—that I charmed General John Ridgeway so completely that he has placed one of his officers at my disposal as a courier and guide—and this at a time of appoaching war! What nonsense! Dominic was meant to divert me and occupy my time, so that I would not ask awkward questions of mutual friends.

Then she locked the diary away and sat by the window, gazing out to sea. Even the sight of the sun sinking in the west, changing the limestone bastions of the Rock from white to pink and turning the water to flame, failed to lift her spirits.

That evening, when Millicent went through her now-familiar charade of picking at a morsel of food and then rejecting it, Catrina had to restrain herself from uttering a sound of pity at the futility of her sister's campaign. Again,

Millicent rose halfway through the meal with the excuse that her head ached and that she felt bilious.

With the air of a man goaded beyond endurance, Dominic scraped his chair back harshly. 'You are punishing yourself and our child!' he told his wife. 'You have lost any power to punish *me* !'

Millicent flushed deeply. 'I—don't know what you mean. I feel unwell . . .' She hurried from the room.

Catrina too, jumped from her chair and began to follow her sister, but Dominic stepped into her path.

'Leave her alone! She will not wish you to discover her secret—that she satisfies her hunger with sweetmeats.'

'You—You know . . .?'

'Of course I know! I am not a fool. I would ignore her games, were I not concerned for my child she is carrying, and who needs proper nourishment!'

'You really are the most insensitive and cruel man I have ever encountered!' Catrina cried angrily. 'It has not even struck you, has it, that Millicent toys with her food at table because that is the *only* way *she* is able to get any attention from *you*!'

Disconcertingly, he threw back his head with a crack of harsh, unamused laughter. 'You, Miss Beaumont, are an expert on marital matters, of course,' he taunted. 'You have seen so much of it, after all, in your life as the cosseted god-daughter of a wealthy widow! I bow to your . . .'

At that moment they were interrupted by a serving-girl, who entered without troubling to knock. Sullenly, she offered Dominic a visiting-card resting on a silver tray. He took it and examined it.

'General Ridgeway and his wife are here,' he told Catrina with a frown. 'They wish to speak to us.'

She followed him as he led the way to the drawing-room, into which she found the General and his wife had been shown. Catrina curtsied to each in turn, and General Ridgeway kissed her hand with charming gallantry.

When everyone was seated, Alice Ridgeway looked intently at Catrina and said, 'I have come to tell the truth. Rather than have you discover some distorted version, I wanted to tell you the real reason why your parents gave you away to my mother.'

CHAPTER SIX

HAVING STATED the reason for their visit, Alice Ridgeway seemed strangely reluctant to begin her explanation. 'How is poor dear Millicent?'

'She has not long since retired to her room,' Dominic said. 'She will not have had time, yet, to disrobe for bed. I'll go and tell her that you are here.'

'No, leave her in peace, Dominic. What I have to say will only distress her.' Alice slipped her hand inside the General's, as if for moral support. But still she hesitated, apparently trying to marshal her thoughts.

Catrina studied the couple. In some indefinable way they resembled one another; not physically, but in gestures and certain facial expressions. It was as if, after long years of closeness and devotion, they had each acquired mirror-image qualities of the other. But physically, there was something about Alice Ridgeway that still nagged at Catrina's mind.

'Miss Beaumont,' the older woman spoke abruptly. 'Catrina—I have learnt from my husband that you tried to tell him, the other night, about your life with Lady Prudence, but that he made light of what you said.'

'I did not want to cause you more anguish, my love,' General Ridgeway put in gruffly.

She gave him a look of deep tenderness and then glanced at Catrina again. 'Please tell me exactly what your life was like.'

'Do you really think it would be wise?' Catrina asked quietly. 'She was your mother, when all is said and done.'

Pain shifted across Alice's face. 'Pray do not think of that. I wish to know how she used you.'

'Very well.' Catrina made her voice as expressionless as she could, and allowed none of her banked-down bitterness to show as she cast her mind back to those bleak, cheerless years with her godmother.

'From the beginning, I remember being in the care of servants. I was confined first to the nursery and later to the schoolroom, and I seldom saw Lady Prudence at all, but I sensed that she did not like me. Until I was fifteen, I had a series of governesses. But Lady Prudence was never able to keep staff for long; she would force them to wait, sometimes for months, for their wages. Not surprisingly, they left as soon as they had received their money and looked for other posts. As time went on, Lady Prudence ceased to replace servants who had left, and naturally those who remained resented the extra work piled on their shoulders, so they, too, left her service. Lady Prudence said that money was short. She engaged only three new replacements, and they *did* stay with her, accepting lower than average wages and putting up with the fact that they were made to wait for their money. They knew that no one else would have employed them, you see, and at least they were receiving their keep. The cook was a slattern addicted to gin; there was a doddering old man who was meant to cope with both the garden and the heavy work about the house, and the general maid was half-witted. The house fell more and more into disrepair and chaos. If Lady Prudence had ever had friends or relatives she must have quarrelled with them all, for we never entertained, and no one ever visited . . .'

'Almost as one,' Alice Ridgeway put in quietly, 'all our friends and relatives sided with me in our quarrel, and that of course only increased Mother's bitterness. But please go on.'

'Lady Prudence required me to wait upon her at all hours of the day and night,' Catrina recounted. 'I fetched and carried for her; if she could not sleep—which was often the case—I had to read to her. I did her sewing and her laundry. When some ancient garment disintegrated in the wash, she blamed me. I don't recall her buying any new clothes in all the time I lived with her.'

'What about your own clothes?' Alice Ridgeway asked the question as if the answer were important; perhaps because she understood, as a woman, that clothes mattered a great deal to any female.

Catrina shrugged. 'I bought cast-off clothes for a few

pennies, and made them over for myself. Lady Prudence said it did not matter what I looked like, as no one of account ever saw me, which was indeed the case.'

'If all this is true,' Dominic put in, his voice hard, 'why did you not write and tell your parents?'

She gazed steadily at him. 'I did. They also saw for themselves what my life was like on the few occasions when they visited us. No matter how hard I tried, I could never please Lady Prudence!'

'Poor child, poor child,' General Ridgeway murmured, while his wife bit her lip and cast her eyes downwards.

'You believe all this, sir?' Dominic asked with insulting incredulity.

Catrina glanced at him, and something in his expression told her that he *wanted* to continue thinking ill of her. He did not wish his preconceived prejudices to be overset. Was he the kind of man who could not bear to be proved wrong? She would not have thought so.

'I have no doubt,' Dominic went on, 'that the old lady did become somewhat eccentric towards the end, but as for the rest of the story—it sounds like gross exaggeration to me! If Lady Prudence had disliked her god-daughter, and treated her so shabbily, why should she have left her fortune to her?'

'I assumed it was because there simply wasn't anyone else to whom she might have left it,' Catrina answered him. 'Because of the isolated life we lived, and because she never mentioned her existence, I was unaware that Lady Prudence had a daughter of her own. She was not the kind of woman who would have considered benefiting charities, or the church, and, as I have already said, I believe she did not realise the extent of her wealth.'

'If she had disliked you,' Dominic persisted, 'why should she have been willing to bring you up in the first place?'

'I can answer that question,' Alice Ridgeway interposed in a quiet voice. Catrina noticed that she was clutching her husband's hand tightly; as if she were holding on to a sheet-anchor.

At that moment a Genoese maid ushered Dinah Forest into the room. No one had heard the front door-knocker sounding, and the maid's sullen attitude explained why she had not troubled to announce the visitor beforehand.

Catrina wanted to burst into tears of rage. She had to restrain herself from launching a physical attack on that girlish-looking woman who was regarding them all with an artless smile that made it clear that she did not for one moment imagine that her presence might be an unwelcome intrusion.

After one brief glance, Dinah ignored Catrina. She peeped through the feathers of her fan at Dominic, and then addressed the Ridgeways.

'That awful Major Seymour called on me, and the only way I could decently rid myself of him was to pretend that I was expected at your home. He escorted me, and then I learnt from Hobson that you had gone out.'

She pouted prettily. 'I could have asked the good Hobson to see me home again, but I suddenly felt lonely and I knew I would only sink into a fit of the blue-devils when I was alone. So I asked Hobson to walk with me that I might join you.'

General Ridgeway gave her a half-indulgent, half-anxious look. It was obvious that he regarded her as something in the light of a daughter. 'Well, my dear,' he said, 'Alice and I have often begged you to make your home with us instead of rattling about alone in that house of yours.'

Catrina noticed the fleeting look which crossed Mrs Ridgeway's face, and felt a sudden kinship with her. It was clear that she, too, had no illusions about her husband's second cousin.

'Dear John,' Dinah said earnestly. 'You and Alice are kindness itself, but I would not dream of imposing myself on you as a permanent fixture.'

The conversation, perforce, became general after that, and Catrina knew that she would have to wait in an agony of suspense to learn why she had been given away to Lady Prudence.

Some while later, General Ridgeway consulted his gold hunter, and told his wife, 'My dear, it is time we took our leave. Dinah, we will give you escort as far as your home.'

'Oh, but it is out of your way!' she protested. 'I'm sure Dominic would not mind seeing me safely home.' She glanced at him coyly from beneath her lashes as she spoke.

'No, I don't mind. In fact, I would welcome the opportunity to stretch my legs.'

Catrina went to bed after they had all gone, and although she listened almost obsessively for Dominic's return, he was either so quiet that she did not hear him, or else he was spending a very long time with Dinah Forest.

The next day was Sunday, and Catrina awoke to the sound of church bells. They would be coming from Santa Maria la Coronada, pealing for the Catholic community. A cold breakfast had been brought to her room on a tray, obviously so that the Genoese maid would be able to attend early Mass.

After she had eaten and washed, Catrina put on a robe and carried the tray into the kitchen. On her way back, she heard Dominic addressing his wife in that neutral, controlled manner which he adopted towards her.

' . . . insist that you attend Church as usual, Millicent.'

'Why should you care whether I go or not?' Her sister's muffled voice reached Catrina.

If Millicent had been hoping for some kind of personal reassurance, she must have felt stricken by his reply. 'I care about Lucy! She deserves some kind of normality. I won't have people feeling sorry for her because her mother behaves like a hermit and wallows in her own twisted kind of self-martyrdom!'

Shaking her head angrily, Catrina hurried out of earshot, back to her own room. She tried to forget what she had overheard and concentrated instead on looking through her wardrobe to decide what to wear. Everyone would know who she was, and would be talking about the fact that she was not mourning her parents. Let them think what they liked! In the end she decided on a foaming white muslin worn over a blue petticoat, the skirts of the gown spread over a hoop. A blue sash round her waist matched the underskirt. The bodice was cut fashionably low across the bosom and trimmed with flounces edged in blue. A plain white bonnet, adorned only with sprays of silk forget-me-nots, a pair of white kid gloves and a blue parasol completed her ensemble.

She could not have presented a greater contrast to Millicent in her unrelieved black gown that had been designed for someone far older than her twenty-one years. With sudden insight, Catrina realised that her sister was wearing the gowns their mother must have had made for herself after the death of their father.

'Millicent,' Catrina offered impulsively, 'I am quite clever with a needle, you know, and it would not take me a moment to stitch a softening white fichu to the bodice of that gown . . .'

'I am perfectly happy with the gown as it is,' her sister told her coldly.

Catrina bit her lip. 'I am only trying to help! I am not blind or deaf.'

'I don't know what you mean, and I require no help from you!'

At that moment Dominic came to join them. He looked magnificent in dress uniform, with its gold-braided red jacket cut to emphasise the breadth of his chest and shoulders and the narrowness of his waist. He was holding Lucy by the hand, and since all the servants were at Mass, it seemed obvious that he must have dressed the child in readiness for church.

'Ooh, Aunt Catrina is *pretty*!' Lucy cried, clapping her hands. 'Papa, is she not?'

He flicked a glance in Catrina's direction and said curtly, 'Indeed. Shall we go? The gharry is waiting.'

Millicent complained several times about the jolting of the vehicle, and that the heat of the morning was worsening her headache. If she had hoped for sympathy from her husband she was doomed to disappointment, for he continued to stare straight ahead of him as he drove.

Long before they reached the church, they could hear the drumbeats. The Governor's Residence, which housed the church, was an impressive sight.

As Dominic had told Catrina, it had formerly been a Franciscan convent, and its origins were plainly visible. 'How old is it?' she wanted to know, staring at the building which had acquired a beautiful yellow patina over the centuries.

'About two to three hundred years. If you look back, you'll be able to see right across the town and over the Bay of Algeciras.'

'Really,' Millicent protested, 'this is not a sight-seeing expedition! Let us hurry and get inside out of this heat!'

Catrina did not like to ask further questions and increase her sister's discomfort, even though she would dearly have wished to know the name of an enormous tree which cast its shade over the large, handsome square in front of the convent. Apart from the tree, a fountain also aroused her curiosity, and the square itself appeared to be an official parade ground. This morning one end of it was occupied by the uniformed drummers who were summoning the Protestant community to worship.

After the service inside the King's Chapel, General Ridgeway introduced Catrina to Governor George Augustus Eliott, a somewhat austere man. She was also introduced to a great many other people, most of whose names she failed to remember, but all of whom regarded her with covert curiosity.

Everyone had congregated in the square. Dinah was there, like an exotic dragonfly, dressed in a gown of multi-coloured pastels and flitting from group to group, but always making sure that Dominic would see how gay and effervescent and sought-after she was, and always returning to his side.

General Ridgeway's attention was demanded by a fellow senior officer who wished to speak to him about the latest news received from their spies, but before joining him, the General handed Catrina over to his wife.

Alice's smile was uncertain and a little anxious. She began to make small talk as they wandered about the court.

'The water in that fountain is said to be the finest in the world,' she explained. 'It is brought by an aqueduct from a hill outside the town.'

'How interesting. What is the name of this huge tree?'

'It is a Dragon Tree, and is said to be almost a thousand years old.'

'Quite amazing,' Catrina observed politely. Had Mrs Ridgeway changed her mind about disclosing the reason why she herself had been given away to Lady Prudence? If so, the devil take Dinah for interrupting . . .

Uncannily, Mrs Ridgeway chose to turn the conversation to Dinah at that moment. 'My husband's cousin is in good spirits this morning, I see.'

'Yes.' Catrina caught Alice's eyes, and added impulsively, 'You do not like her either, do you?'

Alice sighed. 'To my husband, she takes the place of the child we were never able to have, but I confess that she irritates me with her girlish ways. John tried to persuade her to leave for the safety of England and stay with friends, but she declared herself far too devoted to him to think of herself at a time like this. The truth is,' she added drily, 'that she enjoys herself far too much here, being the teasing coquette and playing with the affections of vulnerable, lonely young officers. That is also the reason why she has not married again.'

The truth is, Catrina corrected mentally, that Dinah wants Dominic.

She could easily pick out his tall, impressive figure from among the crowd, and her heart twisted with pain and hopeless desolation as she added to herself, But surely not a fraction as much as I want him—even while I hate him for what he is doing to my sister . . .

Catrina was about to ask Alice bluntly to continue the explanations upon which she had been about to embark the evening before, when Henry Price and two fellow-officers joined them, and shortly afterwards Alice moved away.

Catrina only half-listened to the three young men's compliments upon her appearance, and no one seemed to be in any hurry to leave the square outside the Convent. Perambulation between various groups appeared to be a social custom, a time when invitations were issued and accepted.

An officer was interrupted in mid-sentence by Dominic. 'We are leaving,' he informed Catrina shortly. 'We have been invited to luncheon by the Ridgeways.'

Her heart jerked. So, at last, Alice would be continuing with her explanations.

But in that Catrina found she was wrong, for apart from themselves, Dinah, two other married couples and a pair of young officers had also been invited to the Ridgeways' residence, where the staff had laid out a cold collation over which Hobson presided.

To Catrina, it was a frustrating, unsettling afternoon. The

men gathered in groups to discuss defensive strategy, and speculated upon the waiting game which the Spanish and the French were playing with them. The women discussed the forthcoming Gala to be held at the Convent, fashion in general and the shortcomings of their Genoese servants. Everyone agreed that the latter had become unco-operative and sullen, almost as if the British were to blame for the war which France and Spain had forced upon them.

Catrina was pleased to see that Millicent, for once, seemed happy—or as close to that state as it was possible for her to feel in the circumstances. One of the other wives in the party was also pregnant, and the two of them were engrossed in trading symptoms and complaints. Catrina had also noticed that, unobtrusively, her sister had made a very good lunch. It was obviously because Dominic, seated some distance away, had been deep in conversation with the people on either side of him and would not have spared her any attention if she *had* picked at her food.

Afterwards, Millicent also enjoyed showing off Lucy. 'Come, dearest, recite your rhyme to the ladies. The one I have been teaching you. "Little Miss Muffet . . ." ' she prompted.

In spite of her own instinctive, shamed prejudice, Catrina could not help admitting to herself that the child made a pretty picture in her blue tabby dress worn over satin petticoats. She clasped her hands in front of her and lisped the first two lines, then she faltered, her mouth working. 'I've forgotten the rest, Mama!'

Catrina was the only one who did not join in consoling the child, and assuring her that she was clever to have remembered as much as she had.

After tea, when Lucy had been put to bed for a nap, the adults played checkers, and Catrina's frustration grew. At last it was time for everyone to leave, and it was still as if last night had never been; as if the Ridgeways had never arrived at the house with Alice's announcement that she had come to tell Catrina the truth about herself.

When the guests began to disperse, Dominic announced that it was time for them to leave also. Catrina was not surprised at the marked change in Millicent as soon as they were on their way home.

'What a long, exhausting day it has been,' she sighed. 'It has taken a toll of my strength.'

'I want you to hold me, Mama!' Lucy grizzled.

'You are not a baby!' Millicent snapped at her, and foiled the child's attempt to climb on her lap.

Dominic concentrated on driving, but Catrina saw his mouth setting at this rejection of their daughter by her mother. Could *this* be why Millicent treated the child as she did when Dominic was present? Because it was the only way she could get a reaction of any kind from him?

The servants evidently had Sundays free, for the house was quiet. Only Lucy's nanny was there, to take the fretful child off to the nursery and prepare her for bed.

'I, too, intend retiring early,' Millicent announced. 'I am sure there would be cold food in the pantry if either of you is hungry.'

She left the room, and Catrina found herself alone with Dominic. She looked at him and glanced away. 'Would you like me to find something for you in the pantry?' she offered.

'No, thank you.'

'In that case, I shall say goodnight . . .'

'Don't go,' he interrupted her. 'It has been arranged that you and I are to return to the Ridgeways' house. This time we shall not be disturbed. Please fetch a cloak.'

Trembling with eagerness, Catrina hurried to obey. The sun was setting, its reflecting rays turning the Rock to fire and making it seem more menacing than ever. The bells of Santa Maria were ringing for the evening Mass, and townspeople dressed in their best clothes were streaming towards it.

Catrina and Dominic found the Ridgeways awaiting them. Alice looked more tense than she had the evening before, and it was clear that the enforced delay in her explanations had been as great a strain to her as it had been to Catrina, even though she had succeeded admirably in concealing it during the day.

She wasted little time in commencing her story. 'When John and I became betrothed,' she said as soon as they were all seated, 'my father was still alive, and both my parents were happy about the match. But while John was abroad with the regiment, my father died quite suddenly, and everything changed. When Mother had recovered from her first shock and grief, she demanded that I break off my engagement. She said my place was now with her, and that I should remain unmarried so that I might be a comfort to her in her old age. She claimed I owed it to her, and that it would be grossly selfish of me to go ahead with my marriage to John and accompany him wherever the regiment sent him, leaving her alone in England. I felt sorry for her, but I considered it quite unreasonable of her to expect me to sacrifice the whole of my life to her . . .'

'But that is precisely how Lady Prudence would have behaved!' Catrina interposed. 'It was totally in character!'

'I did not realise it at the time. One tends not to see one's parents as they really are. To me it was a great shock when Mother issued her ultimatum. If I refused to give up all thoughts of marriage, she said, I was to leave her house.' Alice shook her head. 'I could not believe that she really meant it. I thought my father's death had temporarily affected her mind. But I left the house, hoping she would come to her senses, and I took refuge with my life-long friend, Mary Beaumont. *Your* mother, my dear Catrina. Mary had been married for some months to a junior officer who had recently been posted abroad to serve under John, and she was expecting her first child when I arrived at her rented lodgings. She had a truly wretched time of her pregnancy, and we were able to give one another mutual comfort. I was present at your birth, Catrina, and it was an extremely difficult one.'

Alice fell silent. It was obvious that talking about the past was painful to her, and her husband rose, pouring a glass of canary wine which he handed to her. Catrina accepted one too, and when Dominic and the General were nursing tumblers containing something stronger, Mrs Ridgeway took up her story again.

'Your mother was wretchedly ill for some time after your birth, Catrina. A wet-nurse cared for you. I—I am afraid it is quite true; she *did* reject you.' A pleading note entered her voice. 'Please try hard to understand. Because she seldom saw you at all during the first weeks of your life, she was never able to form a maternal attachment to you. Your very existence was a constant reminder to her of the pain and suffering she had borne.'

'So she rejected me right from the start,' Catrina said with bitterness. 'I used to believe that it was Millicent's birth which caused them to turn against me, perhaps because she was more appealing than I . . .'

'No. You were a very beautiful baby, but Mary simply could not feel for you as she ought to have done. You represented to her months of illness and almost unbearable pain.'

'My father suffered no illness or pain,' Catrina said rawly, 'and yet he felt no more for me than she did!'

'He was abroad when you were born, and did not see you until you were a few months old. It is difficult enough for a man to feel emotionally close to a young baby in normal circumstances—unless, perhaps, it is a longed-for son and heir. Because your mother left you in the care of servants and paid you little attention, your father absorbed and reflected her attitude.'

Alice addressed Dominic. '*You* will be able to bear me out. Did you take pleasure in Lucy during the first months of her life?'

'I—felt uncomfortable with her. She seemed forever to be crying, and I disliked picking her up because I feared that I would either drop her or that she would be sick over my uniform. I could not agree with the general view, either, that she was beautiful. To me she was singularly ugly. But I did begin to find her interesting and enchanting as she grew older, and I cannot believe that Rodney Beaumont did not find his own first-born so as *she* grew out of infancy.'

'He did not,' Alice said flatly, 'because he seldom saw her. When she no longer required a wet-nurse, Mary engaged a nursemaid for her and she was kept in the background.'

'How did Lady Prudence come to be my godmother?' Catrina wanted to know. 'Surely she must have resented my mother for having given you sanctuary, Mrs Ridgeway?'

'She promised, when Mary was first married and long before our quarrel, that she would be godmother to her first child. I hoped it would help to heal the breach between my mother and myself. She ignored me completely during the christening, however. She made some barbed remarks to the effect that perhaps one day her god-daughter would show her more devotion and respect than her own flesh and blood had done, and then she left. It was the last time I ever saw her.'

Alice sighed. 'John and I were married shortly afterwards, and a few months later we all left for North America, where your father and John were to fight under General Wolfe in the Battle of Quebec. Once again, Mary was expecting a child, but this time she bloomed with radiant good health, and Millicent's birth was an easy one. Your mother felt quite differently towards her, and because she spent so much time with the baby your father was able to follow her progress from infant to toddler, and he formed a normal affection for her. Not unnaturally, Catrina, you became jealous, and you showed this in your enmity towards Millicent, slapping and pinching her. When you were three years old your parents felt that you had best be separated from your sister until you were both older. Your mother wrote to Lady Prudence and asked whether she would take you in. She agreed, and since your mother did not wish to be separated from Millicent, it was decided that I should travel to England with you. We also hoped that if I arrived at my mother's house with you, the quarrel between us might at last be healed. But she refused even to see me, and I left you with servants when I arrived.'

'Why did Lady Prudence agree to take me in, Mrs Ridgeway?'

'But don't you see? You were to become the comfort and support in her lonely old age which I had refused to be.'

'A comfort! She did not even like me!'

Alice's shoulders drooped unhappily. 'I believe the shock of my father's death, followed so closely by the anger and bitterness she felt towards me, affected her mind. From what you have told us, she certainly became very peculiar. I believe she must have made that will in your favour when you first went to live with her, chiefly as a final punishment meant for me, and then she gradually deteriorated mentally as she came to realise that devotion could not be bought or gained by force.'

It was Dominic who broke the long silence. 'What I cannot understand is that Rodney and Mary Beaumont should have left their daughter to such a fate! Good God, I knew them well! They were kind, decent people!'

'But they were unable to love Catrina, and they were deeply ashamed of that fact,' Alice said. 'So while they made infrequent duty visits to her they closed their eyes to the reality of the situation, and persuaded themselves that things were not nearly as bad as they seemed.'

A clock struck the hour, and Dominic said, 'It is getting late, and you are looking quite drained, Alice. I think it is time we took our leave.'

Catrina nodded, and stood up. Alice rose too, and held out her hand. 'I am so sorry for what you were made to suffer at the hands of my mother. And if there is anything I could do to compensate . . .'

'Thank you. You are very kind.'

'As I said on the first night we met—try to forgive your parents. In their own way, they suffered too.'

Catrina nodded bleakly. *Their* way of suffering could not have involved more than a passing pang of troubled conscience, quickly shrugged off.

Both Dominic and Catrina were silent and preoccupied as they walked back. When they entered the house, he went into the drawing-room and poured a glass of brandy for himself. Catrina followed him into the room, for she had earlier noticed a history of Gibraltar among the books in the glass-fronted case, and instinct told her that she would find sleep elusive.

She had picked up a branch of candles and was about the repair to her bedroom with the book when Dominic's quiet voice stopped her.

'Please stay a moment. There is something I wish to ask you.'

Catrina set the book and the candles down, but remained standing. They faced one another.

'Did Millicent write and inform you of your parents' death, Catrina?'

It was the first time he had ever called her by her name, and the sound of it uttered in his low and slightly husky voice sent a long, trembling weakness through her which she tried desperately to suppress. She did not answer his question, but there had been no need for her to do so.

'I see.' He nodded grimly.

Catrina leapt to Millicent's defence. 'The death of our parents, coming so swiftly the one after the other, must have devastated her. It is no wonder that she forgot.'

'She allowed me to go on thinking, however, that you arrived in Gibraltar in the full knowledge that your parents were dead!'

'Can you blame her?' Catrina demanded. 'I have watched the pitiful attempts she makes to gain a spark of interest or sympathy from you! She would hardly wish to add . . .'

He interrupted with a crack of harsh laughter. 'You mistake the matter entirely! Millicent does not want sympathy or interest from me. She wishes me to feel guilty!'

Catrina opened her mouth to argue, and closed it again. What he had said might well be true. Millicent's behaviour *could* be construed as that of a woman who wished to punish her faithless husband for her state of pregnancy—particularly when she knew that all he cared about was that she should produce a son for him.

'And do you feel guilty?' Catrina demanded.

'Not in the least,' he replied with a brazenness that almost took her breath away.

'Do you have any love left for my sister?' Catrina asked after a moment.

'I have gone as far in discussing our marriage as I intend to. Now, I have to make you an apology, and it is not something which I find easy to do.'

'You would have preferred to go on despising me,' Catrina said with sudden insight.

'Prejudice can often provide a most effective defence,' he returned enigmatically. He moved towards her. 'I was less than welcoming when you arrived. May I offer you a belated welcome now, Catrina.'

He held out his hand, and she took it. He studied her, one dark eyebrow raised and a half-smile playing about his lips. 'If we are to wipe the slate clean, then you have just stepped ashore after your voyage. I have come to meet you. How could I be expected to welcome my wife's sister?'

'Not by offering her the position of the mistress from whom you had just parted!' Catrina retorted impulsively.

'Indeed not!' His eyes mocked her. 'I would have taken care not to be seen with her. And when I met you I would have planted a brotherly kiss on your cheek—like this.'

He placed an arm about her and brushed his lips against her cheek. She felt the pressure of his arm increasing, and his mouth travelled to hers. At the last moment his head jerked up sharply, and they stood motionless, staring at one another.

His eyes were nakedly revealing, his defences down, the cast of his mouth hungry. She felt herself caught up in the same intense undercurrent which, by one word or gesture from her, would threaten to sweep both of them away. But there were only dangerous rocks awaiting them, she reminded herself.

'You have welcomed me to Gibraltar most properly, Dominic,' she said in a crisp voice, and took a step backwards, so that they were no longer almost touching. 'And the slate has been wiped clean.'

'Has it? I wonder . . .' He lifted her hand and touched it to his mouth. 'You and I will always know that I had meant that proposition I made to you, and that I wish you had turned out to be anyone in the world other than my wife's sister.'

He dropped her hand, and moved away. She watched as he drank his brandy in one gulp before striding to the door. When he had reached it, he turned.

'By the way, Surgeon Major Peters has examined Millicent several times, and declares her to be in excellent health. She has been prescribed potions for the headaches and the billious attacks of which she complains, and the fact that she takes neither speaks for itself. Also, she has been told that the actual birth is likely to be as easy, as quick and uncomplicated as Lucy's was.'

He gave Catrina a brilliant, mocking smile. 'So don't waste too much sympathy on Millicent, will you?'

CHAPTER SEVEN

IT TOOK A FEW moments before Catrina felt able to follow Dominic from the room. The candle-light guttered, throwing grotesque shadows, as she held the branch aloft.

She undressed, and lay in bed, and tried not to dwell on that highly-charged scene between them, but to concentrate on something else instead. For a while she went over in her mind the story Alice Ridgeway had told her. A good deal was clear to her now. Once having rejected her, her parents would not have been able to claim her again even if they had wished to do so. They had told everyone that she herself refused to leave her doting godmother, so how could they have explained away her sudden change of mind? And how could they have trusted her not to tell everyone the truth—that she had been abandoned and neglected for years?

But they had *not* wanted to claim her. She had failed to fit into their domestic circle when she was small, and she would have been an even bigger misfit as a young woman. So they had told themselves that her life with Lady Prudence was not really as bad as it seemed, and as Catrina insisted it was. They had shut their eyes and gone away again and forgotten her, and when her letters arrived to remind them, they had persuaded themselves that she was exaggerating the misery of her life. And they had poured out all their love on Millicent, who continued to live with them after she was married . . .

That thought led her full circle to Dominic again. In desperation, Catrina lit the candles and reached for the book she had taken from the case.

In ancient times, she read, Gibraltar was known as Calpe, the European side of the Pillars of Hercules, the African one being Abyla. If she had stopped there, Catrina might have fallen asleep. But as she read on, to the capture of the

Rock by the Arab conqueror Tarik ibn Zaid, her imagination was caught and held. The mass had been named Jebel Tarik, or Mount Tarik, and Gibraltar had become its corrupted form. How different the Rock must have been under the rule of Tarik ibn Zaid in the sixth century! She read of marbled mosques, of houses with arcades and courts and beautifully fountained gardens, of vineyards and orange groves, and of minarets from which the worshippers of Islam had been called to prayer.

Today, instead of vineyards and lush orange groves there were batteries and cannon and forts and redoubts, and men like Dominic were preparing to defend the Rock from yet another attempt at its capture.

It was no use. Everything led her back to Dominic. Catrina put the book away and snuffed out the candles, and tried again to go to sleep. But she was more wide awake than ever.

She turned her thoughts to Millicent. Dominic's statement that she was exaggerating the miseries of her pregnancy had, Catrina felt, been intended to convey information of another kind to herself. And yet she had heard her sister talk about 'the dreadful nightmare' which she sought at all costs to avoid repeating.

It must be that she could not endure the distortion of her slim body during pregnancy. She would loathe the sight of her thickening waist, and the growing heaviness of her breasts. And she would also be terrified, with each pregnancy, that its end might leave her with a matronly figure, her youthful slenderness lost for ever.

So, with an exaggerated view of her own ugliness, she made no attempt to look after her appearance; she neglected her hair and her skin and deliberately chose garments which she no doubt told herself her grotesque body deserved. And instead of trying to understand and reassure her, Dominic had simply turned to a mistress. Sighing, Catrina drifted into sleep.

She awoke, what seemed like minutes later, to the sound of uproar in the house. But the uproar was not confined to the house alone; it was echoed in the streets outside. Catrina jumped out of bed and ran to the window, flinging the shutters wide.

Where the Bay had contained only a few watchful Spanish ships before, it was now crowded with vessels, all flying the enemy flag, and even as Catrina stood by the window, others were manoeuvring into position to join them.

She washed hastily in the cold water left in the jug from the day before, and dressed in the first gown which came to hand. Then she hurried from her room.

The servants were rushing about aimlessly, wringing their hands, arguing shrilly or rending the air with noisy weeping. Millicent, looking dishevelled in a robe which covered her nightgown, was trying without success to restore order among them. Lucy clung to her robe, sobbing.

Dominic came in from outside at that moment. He looked grim-faced and preoccupied. He barked a few commands at the servants, who quietened down and slunk away. Picking Lucy up in his arms and cradling her to his chest, he summed up the situation.

'The Spanish fooled us. They diverted our attention to their works on the *Linea*, making us believe that they intended combining a land attack with a blockade. It was no such thing.'

'What on earth is happening, Dominic?' Millicent demanded plaintively. 'I could get no sense out of the servants, and my head . . .'

'You have obviously not looked outside. The Spanish have been planning from the beginning to starve us out. While we have been waiting for them to fire their first shots, they have been biding their time, and during the night their fleet slipped into the Bay.'

He set Lucy upon her feet. 'Run along to the nursery now, love. Nanny will be getting your breakfast.' He turned to the two sisters. 'I shall have to report for duty immediately. Catrina, could you take stock of the food supplies and other household needs at our disposal? The strictest economy will have to be practised from now on, for it is clear that our supply ships are not likely to get through the blockade.'

She nodded. 'But have you broken your fast?'

'I helped myself to some bread and cheese and a jug of ale.' He was heading for the door even as he spoke, urgency in every line of his body.

Millicent began to cry. 'What are we to do?'

'I shall tell you the first thing we are to do!' Catrina said vigorously, taking her sister's arm and forcing her towards her bedroom. Millicent sank weakly into a chair, and Catrina stood over her.

'You heard what Dominic said! Food will become scarce. I am going to confiscate your hoard of sweetmeats, Millicent, for we may all have need of them before long, and you may now drop the pretence of picking at your meals, for there will soon be precious little to pick at!'

Millicent ceased crying, and raised a shocked, bloated face. 'You . . . How did you . . .? You haven't told Dominic?'

'No.' It would have been unnecessarily cruel to tell her that Dominic had found out for himself. 'But, from now on,' Catrina continued, 'you will share any rations we have; you will allow me to dress your hair properly and refurbish your dreadful gowns, and you will accept that you are not ugly and repellent merely because you are pregnant . . .'

Millicent began to laugh hysterically, rocking back and forth in her chair. 'You—You think—I *mind* being ugly?'

Catrina stared at her. 'Is that not what has been behind your behaviour? I thought you hated the loss of your figure . . .'

'Let me tell you—I would give heartfelt thanks—if I were permanently shaped like a sideshow freak! I wish Dominic—to feel such repugnance for me—that he will never want to touch me again!'

Catrina knelt on the floor, and imprisoned her sister's hands inside her own. 'What on earth do you mean?'

Millicent cried wildly, 'Oh, you don't realise how lucky you are, Catrina, being a spinster! I know it is a disgrace to be on the shelf, and that everyone pities an old maid, but—Oh God—you have no conception of what being married entails!'

Catrina caught her lower lip between her teeth. 'I always assumed,' she said after a moment, 'that it entails two people living together in love, creating a family . . .'

'*Love!*' Millicent spat the word out. 'Mama tried to warn me, but I did not understand . . . I thought love meant Dominic kissing my hand, and whispering endearments in my ear, and—and *respecting* me! But it is not like that at all, Catrina! Men are animals; they wish only to do dirty, disgusting, loathsome things to one's body!'

'Not—Dominic,' Catrina said faintly.

'All of them! On the first night of our marriage, when I learnt what Dominic expected me to allow myself to be subjected to, I threatened to scream the house down. Thank God, we were forced to begin married life here because the house which the army was preparing for us was not yet ready. Well, when I realised what Dominic intended towards me, I flatly refused to move out of here, because I knew that only the presence of Papa and Mama stood between me and his bestiality.'

Catrina shaded her face with her hand. She had only the vaguest notion of what passed between a man and a woman when they were married, but all her own responses to Dominic had been instinctive and completely unafraid. Why, the very thought of him produced a strange pain in her loins and a thundering of the blood in her veins.

'Millicent,' she said gently. 'If *all* women felt as you do, the human race would die out . . .'

'But that is nature's trap, don't you see? All girls imagine how their marriage will be. They see themselves sitting by the looking-glass in a beautiful silk nightshift, brushing their hair by candle-light while their husband looks on adoringly. And then he puts his arm round her, and leads her to the bed, where he kisses her gently and strokes her cheeks and tells her that she is the most wonderful creature on earth.'

Millicent gave a bitter laugh. 'But when they discover the reality, the—the gross, revolting, depraved behaviour they are expected to endure, they enter into a conspiracy of silence. They are too ashamed to talk about it. Mama was ashamed when she tried to explain to me how it would be. She said I must look upon it as a duty, which all but a handful of unnatural, corrupt women abhorred, but I did not understand until later what she meant.'

Catrina bit her lip. 'You said—you threatened to scream the house down if Dominic . . .'

'Yes, and that stopped him. Oh, he tried again and again on the nights that followed. He tried with sly, cunning little tricks, pretending that he only wished to hold me in his arms and caress me, but when it came to it, he still wanted to—put me through that dreadful nightmare of bestiality.'

That dreadful nightmare.

'But you had Lucy . . .' Catrina began.

'Oh, yes!' Remembered revulsion twisted Millicent's face. 'We had been married for several months when Mama and Papa visited the Ridgeways one evening, and all the servants had gone home. Dominic sat in the drawing-room drinking. I was peacefully in bed, reading, when he came in and—forced me to . . .'

She looked away. 'He tried to win my forgiveness the following morning. He said it would be different next time, if only I would allow him to teach me . . . As if he had not already taught me how utterly abhorrent it was! I made it clear there would be no "next time," and fortunately I discovered some weeks later that I was expecting a child. I asked Mama, and she agreed that it would be wise for us to occupy separate bedrooms until after the birth. That connecting door was put in, and he occupied the room next door.'

'And—the second time? Did he get drunk then, also?'

Millicent shook her head. 'He was quite sober, and very impersonal and practical. He said he wanted a son, that it would be over very quickly, and that it was a necessary duty we both had to perform because he *had* to have a son. His family is quite wealthy, you know, with estates in England, and he is the only son. He entered the army against their wishes, and he said he owed it to them to leave at least one male heir in case anything should happen to him. So I had to agree. But it was—quite horrible. Worse even than the first time, for he—broke his promise that it would be over quickly, and tried all his old tricks, touching and kissing me in ways . . . Oh, I can't bring myself to go into the sickening details.'

Her face crumpled. 'And it was all for nothing, for I did not conceive, so I had to go through it several more times. If this baby should be another girl, he will expect me to endure it yet again. Oh, why could Lucy not have been a boy?'

Catrina was silent. So much had just been explained. Millicent wished to become so physically repellent to Dominic that he would not want to touch her again, even for the sake of an heir. And could her treatment of Lucy in his presence be anything other than a way of saying to him—If I continue to bear you one daughter after another, I shall reject them?

'Come,' Catrina said at last, gently. 'Let me help you back to bed. You are clearly not in a fit state to be about. And afterwards I shall bring your breakfast in to you—a proper breakfast! Has it occurred to you, Millicent, that if you continue to eat the wrong food you might damage this baby, so that even if it should be a boy he might be too sickly to live?'

It clearly had not occurred to Millicent, for alarm sprang into her eyes, and she allowed herself to be led back to bed.

Catrina's mind was a chaotic whirlpool as she set about tasks which, until today, had not existed for her in this household. Her first priority was breakfast of scrambled eggs and hot chocolate for Millicent, and she was forced to prepare the meal herself, because the Genoese cook was almost half-witted with fright at the state of siege which they had awakened to that morning. With grim humour, she recalled the many occasions in London when the gin-sodden cook had been unable to prepare a meal, and she had had to do so instead. At least life with Lady Prudence had prepared her for many contingencies.

She herself carried the breakfast in to her sister, but it was a very different Millicent who received her. Speaking in a stony voice, she said, 'If you repeat one word of what I have told you, Catrina, I shall deny it. You would not be believed in any case, for no wife would speak of such matters, and to a spinster at that. *I* should not have spoken of them.'

'I shall keep it to myself,' Catrina promised quietly.

'You will do more than that! You will dismiss it from your mind, for—for it was not true. I was not myself. The shock of the blockade affected my mind.'

Catrina understood: Millicent, the favoured sister, the privileged one, could not bear to be pitied by the family outcast. She merely nodded, and left to make a detailed inventory of stored foodstuffs and other provisions, but in spite of Millicent's defiant command, her mind was preoccupied by what her sister had earlier told her.

A conspiracy of silence existed between married women, Millicent had said, but all except a few unnatural, corrupt females shared her sister's feelings. Catrina frowned to herself as she thought of Alice Ridgeway. She and the General seemed so genuinely devoted to one another. But then, of course, they were old, and passion would have died in John Ridgeway long ago, so that their love was now based on companionship.

But Dinah Forest had been married, and if ever a woman wanted a man, Dinah wanted Dominic! Then Catrina remembered that Dinah had been married by proxy, and had never shared a bed with her husband. She, too, was still in that state of unreal romantic dreams which Millicent had described.

Catrina's frown deepened. She had never conjured up an imaginary scene such as Millicent had so vividly depicted. During her years of bondage to Lady Prudence she had longed for some man, any man, to rescue her and make her his wife. But she had dreamt of nothing more than that he should provide her with a home which did not smell of dust and mildew, and that he should bring a little gaiety into her life and not complain incessantly about her shortcomings, the way Lady Prudence had done.

Hitherto, he had been a faceless, shadowy figure. Not until she'd first caught sight of Dominic standing by the waterfront had her senses been stirred by a man, real or imaginary. And she had certainly never thought of him watching her brushing her hair by candle-light. She had thought of his hands and his mouth . . . Flushing, she shook her head and forced herself grimly to concentrate on the inventory she was taking instead of on her sinful fantasies about Dominic.

The sound of distant cannon-fire reached her, and she ran to the window. Out at sea a Moorish vessel was trying to enter the Bay, and Spanish ships were harassing it, firing warning shots and forcing it to turn back. Catrina guessed that it was a sight which would be repeated many times until the British warships could arrive to engage the blockading Spaniards in battle.

Mindful of the inventory she had taken, Catrina told the cook to prepare only one course for lunch, a simple dish of roast beef served with cabbage. Fresh provisions, subject to deterioration, would have to be used up first, and everything which would keep was to be rationed.

Dominic was preoccupied when he arrived home, and did not seem to notice that Millicent was no longer picking at her food. Neither did he notice that Catrina spoke to him in a strained voice and did not meet his eyes.

'Do you think the blockade is likely to last for an appreciable time?' she asked.

'Yes, I do.' His tone was grim.

'In that case,' Catrina said, 'I don't see how we are to feed ourselves and the many servants for the duration.'

Dominic frowned. 'The Governor is putting military staff on basic rations, but that will not extend to their families, or to their servants. You are suggesting that we should get rid of some of the servants?'

Catrina nodded. 'I have been questioning them this morning. All but three have families in the town who could help to feed them. I think we should keep only these three. One can act as general maid, one as laundress and parlour-maid, and one can help in the kitchen. I think the cook should go. Apart from the fact that she has two sons who are fishermen, I also believe she has been pilfering. I have been going through the household receipts, and there is not as much flour or sugar left as there ought to be.'

Millicent put in sharply, 'I am not allowing Lucy's nanny to be dismissed! And if the cook goes, who is to prepare our meals?'

'I would take over the cooking,' Catrina said, 'with the help of the present scullery-maid, Gina. And of course Lucy's nanny must stay. I don't suppose she has anywhere else to go, in any case.'

Dominic nodded slowly. 'If you are indeed prepared to take over the cooking, Catrina, then I agree with your suggestions. I shall tell the servants myself. They will not starve, because most of them have relatives who are fishermen or own shops. It has already become clear that the shopkeepers have been anticipating this present situation, and have been stockpiling supplies, no doubt in the hope of profiteering. And our guns are making sure that the Spaniards remain clear of Rosia, Camp and Little Bays, so that the fishermen will be able to continue putting out their lines.'

Catrina studied him covertly as he spoke, her mind on what Millicent had told her. She tried to picture that scene on their wedding night, and to share her sister's disgust, but instead she was seized by a pounding excitement which shamed her deeply.

You don't know what it is like, she told herself. Millicent does. In your own way, you are clouding the reality with romantic fantasies.

During the following days, Catrina could not help reflecting wryly on the way things had changed since the siege. Instead of preparing for the Governor's Gala, which had of course been cancelled, she imagined that each service household must be experiencing domestic convulsions similar to their own.

Catrina was kept busy in the kitchen, and she did not find Gina of much help. One of the girl's duties was to go very early to one of the three bays still in use and buy fish, on which she contrived to spend most of the morning, so that Catrina found herself coping not only with the cooking, but with much of the cleaning as well.

The dismissal of the other servants had caused great resentment, for those involved as well as for the ones who had been kept on, as they now had to work harder than before. They expressed their feelings in a demonstration of slowness and pretended stupidity, and Lucy's nanny openly displayed her wrath as she banged about in the kitchen, washing up the nursery dishes or collecting cleaning materials to scrub its floors.

Catrina felt a vast relief when the first Sunday dawned, for the resentful Genoese servants would be absent from the house, and lunch would be cold, having been prepared the day before.

When she dressed for the church service, she searched through the jewellery case for her sapphire brooch to pin her lace fichu about her shoulders. It was not there. She bit her lip, and decided to say nothing about it for the moment. During the remainder of the week she thought long and hard about the matter. It must have been stolen by one of the dismissed servants before leaving the house. Although the brooch was valuable, Catrina could not envisage it ever being found again. The stones had probably been prised out of their setting and sold separately and the remaining gold melted down. In the end she decided to keep its loss to herself. Even if the thief were caught, the brooch would not be restored to her, and Catrina could not bear the thought of anyone being sent to gaol because of herself.

Just over a fortnight after the blockade had started, she was woken by what seemed uncannily like an echo of the events of the morning which had first heralded it. A great deal of noise was coming from outside. Catrina yawned, and padded to the window. People were streaming towards the harbour, but all she could see were the usual Spanish vessels blockading the Bay.

Something of importance must have occurred, however. She pulled on a robe and went into the kitchen. Gina would have left earlier to buy fish, but there was no sign of the other servants either. They had obviously rushed out to investigate the cause of the excitement.

Catrina carried water to her room, washed, dressed and pinned up her hair. Then she entered Millicent's room, and found her still asleep. Catrina tried to rouse her without success. Her sister had probably taken a sleeping-draught the evening before; something she had been doing increasingly of late, she suspected.

In the morning-room, the table had not been laid for breakfast, which would have to wait in any case until the servants returned. So Catrina cut slices of cold beef for herself in the kitchen, and washed them down with water before she left the house to find the source of all the excitement.

When one was not encumbered with boxes and trunks, it was an easy enough walk to the harbour, although Catrina did not so much walk there as find herself being driven willy-nilly by the press of jostling people. A Dutch vessel had succeeded in slipping through the blockade, bringing supplies, and people were hurrying to bid for whatever cargo she was carrying.

Catrina decided to turn back, as she had brought no money with her. She was fighting against the tide of people streaming towards the waterfront when she suddenly encountered a familiar figure.

'*Violet!*' Catrina stared at the pert, pretty girl who was now soberly dressed in a gown of brown holland, and whose face was innocent of powder and rouge.

A guilty flush stained Violet's cheeks. 'Oh, ducks! I didn't think as how we'd be likely to run into each other . . .'

'But whatever happened to you? I thought you were safely back in England!'

'It weren't for want of trying, love!' Violet returned with feeling. 'Look, I know a place where we can talk, away from all this mob.'

She allowed Violet to take her arm and steer her through the crowd towards one of the side-alleys. A deserted wooden seat stood in one of the small plazas, and they sat down with the morning sun beating down on them. In her haste, Catrina had neglected to put on a bonnet, and she shaded her face with her hand as she regarded Violet. 'Tell me what happened.'

'Well, ducks, you're prob'ly thinking I stole that money what you give me for my fare home, and in a manner of speaking you're right. But it weren't meant that way. The truth of it is that I couldn't get a passage back home for love nor money.'

She gave her old, infectious chuckle. 'And I tried offering both, believe me! But all the ships was chock-full with passengers, and there I was, stranded. I didn't know what to do. There ain't any places for my sort to go to now the whore-house has been closed down. Been turned into a munitions-store,' she explained resignedly. 'A proper mess I was in, love, with no more ships due to sail for weeks. And then I ran into Eddie Blake.'

'Who is he?'

'He *was* an old friend.' Violet gave her a half-shamed, half-defiant glance. 'An old customer, you're thinking, and you're right. But he ain't a bad sort, Eddie. Serves with one of the foot regiments, he does. Well, the long and the short of it is, ducks, that he offered to marry me. But only if I handed over that money you give me as a dowry.'

'Oh, Violet, surely you didn't think I would begrudge you the use of the money in any way you wished!'

'To be honest, dear, it weren't what I *wished* as much as the devil driving. I handed over the money, and the knot was tied, and I'm living in married quarters in the barracks.'

Catrina was about to congratulate her, and ask her whether she was happy, when Violet continued, 'When I heard this morning there was a Dutch ship in, and that the Spanish'll not stop her leaving now she's got through their blockade, I hurried to see about a passage for meself. If there *had* been one, I'd have got that money back off Eddie if I'd had to take a knife to him. But it weren't no use. Others had got there before me, and all the berths are taken.'

'So you obviously regret having married Eddie . . .'

Violet shrugged philosophically. 'As I said, he ain't a bad sort, but I'd rather have me freedom. I have to dress what he calls respectable, and he made me sell all my clothes and buy *this* kind of horror.' She tweaked the skirt of her holland gown with an expression of disgust, and added fiercely, 'He won't never make me part with that silk gown you give me, though!'

Catrina regarded her, and felt the colour sweeping into her cheeks. Violet was not only a married woman, but she had made a profession of the act which filled Millicent with such disgust.

'Violet,' she murmured hesitantly, 'what—what is it like—you know—being married? I mean, in—in bed.'

'Thinking of getting hitched, love?' Violet asked with surprise.

'Oh, no!' Catrina said hastily. 'It is just . . . I wondered . . .'

'A job of work, that's how I look on it, love. In the old days, it were better than skivvying. Now, if I gives Eddie what he wants, he lets me off having to polish his buttons and clean his boots. I hates doing them!'

She giggled. 'I generally thinks of something else while he's at it—like how I can lay me hands on a nice piece of fish for supper, say, and before you know where you are, it's over.'

'I see.' So, even to Violet, who had embraced it as a means of making her living, the act of love was something to be endured while it lasted and made more bearable by filling her mind with unrelated thoughts.

'Now tell me, ducks, how you've been getting on,' Violet asked.

'I . . . Well, I discovered that my parents had died, and I was to have returned to England as soon as the supply ships arrived. Now, of course, I shall have to wait until the British Navy have broken the blockade.'

'I am sorry, love. About your parents, I mean. You had all that miserable sea-sickness for nothing.'

'That's right,' Catrina agreed bleakly. The sea-sickness, and so much more besides . . . She stood up. 'I'd better go now. I left the house without telling anyone, and I'll have been missed by now. I dare say I'll see you again, Violet, before I'm finally able to leave for England.'

Catrina hurried away, back to the main street which was now thronged with people returning from the harbour. She was pushing her way through them when a hand descended on her arm, and she looked into Dominic's face.

It wore a strained expression. 'I suppose you know that a Dutch vessel slipped through the blockade,' he said. 'I hurried to secure a passage for you. You'll have no difficulty in getting to England from Holland.'

'I—see.'

His jawline was hard. 'It is best this way.'

'Yes. Gina should be able to cope with simple cooking.'

He nodded. 'As soon as we arrive home, you must pack. The Dutch ship will sail again as soon as she has finished unloading her cargo and taken on fresh water.'

Neither of them spoke again as they walked on, but many inconsequential thoughts slipped into her mind. She would never climb to Sugar Loaf Point with him after all; she would not know for months—perhaps years—whether Millicent's baby was a boy or a girl, and whether she was having to endure 'that dreadful nightmare' again . . .

They were about to pass the Church of Santa Maria when Dominic suddenly pulled her inside the shelter of the colonnade.

'I—cannot let you go without saying goodbye.' His voice was more husky than usual, and his silver-grey eyes were shadowed with pain. 'We may never see one another again . . .'

'No.' She had begun to tremble.

His arms enclosed her, drawing her towards him. She had dressed hurriedly that morning, forgoing stays and hoops, and had simply thrown a concealing shawl over her low-cut gown.

The shawl fell to the ground and she was moulded against him, his hands moving over the contours of her body, his mouth at her breast. An unfamiliar hardness in his loins pressed against her and sent a wild, leaping flame through her, and when his mouth fastened on hers, a little moan rose in her throat. Without thought, acting only on some primeval instinct, her hands began to explore the mysteries of his body, and in response his mouth invaded hers with a ferocious hunger which ought to have disgusted her, but which merely awakened a white-hot passion such as she had never before dreamt existed.

Then he put her away from him suddenly, almost forcibly, and uttered a hoarse sound. She could not bear to look at him, and see the disgust in his eyes. She began to run, and heard him coming after her, but she succeeded in losing him in the crowd.

She was one of that handful of unnatural, corrupt women their mother had told Millicent about! She was as much an animal as her sister had stated men to be. She would have been ready to lie down with him there, in the open and in broad daylight.

And, dear God, the last thing she would have had on her mind was a nice piece of fish for supper! She was even baser than Violet, who at least had the virtue of merely enduring such depraved behaviour instead of responding to it and wanting more. The sooner she left on the Dutch vessel, the better . . .

Dominic caught up with her just as she was entering the house. Millicent flew at them, her face puffy, her hair disarranged. She was in a state bordering on hysteria.

'They've gone!' she cried. 'Every one of them! Took all their belongings and disappeared!'

'Who, Millicent?' Dominic demanded, going to her and shaking her lightly by the shoulders in an effort to calm her.

She shook off his hands and stared wildly at them. 'The *servants* have gone!'

'You must be mistaken,' Dominic told her. 'They have nowhere else to go.'

The truth suddenly struck Catrina as several things slotted into place. 'Yes, they have,' she said, without looking at Dominic. 'Gina would have left the house early this morning as usual to buy fish. She saw the Dutch vessel, and she secured passages for herself and the other servants, and then crept back to alert them and to pack. I dare say they'll make their way to a safe port, from where they can join their relatives.'

'Nonsense!' Dominic said impatiently. 'I paid your passage on that ship, Catrina, and I know precisely what the Dutch captain is demanding. The servants could never have afforded the money!'

'They could. My sapphire brooch was stolen; I said nothing, for I suspected the thief was one of the servants who had been dismissed. But it must have been Gina or one of her friends, with just such an eventuality in mind as a ship getting through the blockade.'

Millicent was wringing her hands, and sobbing hysterically. 'How—How can I possibly cope—in my condition—and with Catrina leaving as well? All the work—the cooking and cleaning—and Lucy to be looked after . . .'

Catrina still did not glance at Dominic as she went to her sister, taking her hand. 'You won't have to cope alone. I'll be here to help you for as long as I'm needed.'

CHAPTER EIGHT

In a sense, the chaos with which she had to contend that first morning was a welcome diversion as far as Catrina was concerned, because it forced her to concentrate on matters other than the memory of her own debasement.

Lucy came wandering into the room, weeping, and still wearing her nightshift. 'Go back to the nursery,' Millicent ordered automatically. 'Nanny will . . .' She stopped, her mouth working as she remembered that there was no longer a nanny to care for the child.

Dominic swung his daughter into his arms and strode towards the nursery with her, and Catrina hurried into the kitchen to cook porridge with the oatmeal which had been set to soak the previous evening.

As she made chocolate, which consisted more of water than of anything else, she was suddenly reminded of the presents she had brought with her for her family, and which had not yet been unpacked. Among them was chocolate and tea and sugared fruits. They had best be left where they were, as emergency supplies. She carried the tray containing the breakfast into the morning-room, and Dominic sprang up to take it from her. She gazed beyond him.

Lucy sat beside her mother at the table, perched on a chair upon which two extra cushions had been piled. 'I'm to eat with the grown-ups, Aunt Catrina!' she announced excitedly.

Catrina gave her a mechanical smile, and wished that the child did not look so hauntingly like the Millicent of her own early memories. She also wished that she had not learnt the circumstances in which Lucy had been conceived.

Hastily she thrust that thought aside, and announced, 'I'm afraid there is only porridge for breakfast. I thought the cold beef had best be saved for luncheon.'

Millicent nodded, and spooned porridge into plates.

'Dominic says we shall not be able to replace the servants, Catrina. Money has become of so little value that they will now work only for food or other supplies. Since no vessels are able to get through the blockade . . .'

'The Dutch vessel got through!' Catrina exclaimed, perceiving a glimmer of hope. She might yet be able to sail away from Gibraltar, from Dominic and the memory of her own shame . . .

But Dominic shook his head. 'The Dutch vessel carried only animal feed. A valuable enough cargo, but it will not relieve our immediate needs. The main problem about trying to recruit replacement servants from among the townspeople is that they all have families and dependants, and therefore they will certainly pilfer from our small supplies to help to feed them.'

'I see . . .'

Millicent went on after a moment, 'Dominic thinks we should close some of the rooms in the house now that we are to manage without servants. He suggests that we take all our meals in here from now on, and do without the dining-room, and also that the nursery should be closed.'

'Yes,' Catrina said. 'That would be sensible.'

Millicent gave her a calculating look. 'The problem is, where is Lucy to sleep if we close the nursery? She cannot share my room, for I need my rest, and she is in the habit of sometimes waking during the night. And of course, it would be out of the question for her to share Dominic's room.'

'She may share mine, of course,' Catrina said with a reluctance which she hoped she had succeeded in hiding.

The little girl clapped her hands. 'Oh, I shall like that! I shall like it far better than sleeping in a room with Nanny! She snored!' Her mind darted from one subject to another. 'I wish I still had my puppy. Mama said its hair made her sneeze, and we had to give it away.'

Millicent rose and said, 'I shall make a start on moving Lucy's clothes into your room, Catrina. You may come and help me, Lucy. And pray, why did you not tell your father when he dressed you that that is one of your Sunday pinafores?'

'I like it,' the child responded defiantly, scrambling from

the chair. 'Papa likes it too.'

'Well, it will have to be changed. Come along.'

Catrina stood up too, and began to stack the dirty dishes on a tray. To her agitated dismay, Dominic insisted on carrying it into the kitchen for her. As the door closed behind them, he said abruptly,

'I have no intention of apologising for what happened earlier.'

No, she thought with shame. You have no need to apologise, for I behaved even more badly than you. I cast aside all virtue and modesty and self-restraint . . .

His voice took on a rough edge. 'Grateful as I am to you for staying, I still wish to God that you were leaving on the Dutch vessel when she sails, so that I need never set eyes on you again.'

She understood perfectly. He had given way to the physical desire he had felt for her, but had been repelled by her response. And now, knowing his wife's sister to bc utterly without shame, he would have preferred not to harbour her under his roof.

But she made no reply. After he had gone, she plunged her hands into the hot water and began to wash the dishes with coarse soap. Her hair, so hastily pinned up earlier that morning, began to come adrift and she pushed it away from her face. The dishes washed and stacked, she cleaned and black-leaded the kitchen grate. Then she left to dust the furniture in the morning-room. Millicent entered with Lucy.

'We have finished moving the child's clothes out of the nursery,' she said, and added helpfully, 'I'll rearrange the ornaments in here, shall I?'

Catrina gave her a frowning look. 'Millicent, there is a great deal of work to be done, and rearranging ornaments is the least important of it all!'

'I know nothing of housework, or of cooking. And even if I knew how to tackle them, I could not perform heavy tasks in my condition.'

'True. But there are many things which you *could* learn to do. You might, for instance, polish the silver. The maids have been neglecting it quite disgracefully.'

'I have never polished silver . . .'

'It is easy. You simply dip a wet cloth in some wood-ash,

and rub it in well before removing it again with a clean, dry cloth.'

'Wood-ash!' Millicent shuddered.

'There is nothing particularly revolting about wood-ash. I shall rake out the grate and bring some in.'

'I want to help!' Lucy cried eagerly. 'May I have a cloth for myself, please, Aunt Catrina?'

Nodding, Catrina spread an old cover upon the table to protect it, and then collected the household silver and placed it in the centre. In the kitchen, she raked out the ashes from the grate and scooped the finest of it into two containers, and searched for cloths. She left Millicent and Lucy polishing the silver in the morning-room. The child, at least, was tackling the task with enthusiasm, kneeling on her cushions, her tongue caught between her teeth as she concentrated on what she was doing. But Millicent worked gingerly, with a look of disgust on her face as the wet wood-ash clung to her fingers.

Catrina went to make up the beds. She had to force herself to enter Dominic's room, and then she found it almost impossible to beat down the shameful thoughts which insisted on invading her mind as she shook out his pillow and straightened the sheet upon which he had spent the night.

When the front-door knocker banged, she left her task with relief to answer it. Dinah Forest stood on the step, looking as trim and girlish as ever in a rose-coloured morning gown. Catrina stood aside for her to enter. 'Millicent is in the morning-room,' she said.

'I really wished to see Dominic,' Dinah told her, but she walked towards the morning-room. She uttered a sound of astonishment at the sight of Millicent and Lucy polishing silver.

'Our servants have run off,' Millicent explained, tears rising to her eyes. 'We have no domestic help at all.'

Dinah shrugged, and said, 'At least you still have a home of your own. I had to let my servants go, for I could no longer feed them since I don't qualify for service rations. I have moved in with the Ridgeways. Dear Alice is kindness itself, but of course it's not the same, and their house is crammed with useless old family retainers from England.'

She paused for breath. 'I came to ask Dominic's advice about safeguarding my own house from looters now that it is unoccupied. But as he is not here . . .'

A thought had struck Catrina, and before Dinah could make her excuse to leave, she said, 'Mrs Forest, would you oblige me please by staying here until I return? I have an urgent errand to run, and I don't like to leave Millicent and Lucy alone.'

When Dinah gave her an arrogant, supercilious look which clearly indicated a refusal, Catrina added deliberately, 'I know Dominic would be most grateful to you.'

Without giving any of them a chance to react, she ran to her room and grabbed a shawl, and stopped only for long enough to push her hair underneath the first bonnet she could lay her hands upon. Then she left the house.

The atmosphere of tension was almost tangible in the cobbled streets of Gibraltar. Catrina thought it probably had something to do with people's frustration and sense of anti-climax because the Dutch vessel had brought in only animal feed, instead of supplies to alleviate their daily hardship.

How deceptively serene and beautiful the Spanish ships in the Bay looked, with their sails billowing in the breeze. But it only needed a glance at the first of the barracks which she had reached to underline the grim reality of their situation. Soldiers were marching and counter-marching in its square, and one of the sentries told Catrina,

'Try the Town Range Barracks, miss. You'll find Eddie's missus there.'

When she reached her destination another sentry, just going off duty, took her to the married quarters. Violet saw her and came to meet her with startled surprise.

Catrina had to struggle hard to hide her feelings of shock at the appalling conditions in which common soldiers and their families lived. Privacy was scant almost to the point of non-existence. Only blankets suspended around beds shielded each couple from the view of the others, and in the living area of the barrack room, harassed women were trying to cope with crying children and at the same time carry out such wifely tasks as sewing and preparing food. Catrina tried to ignore a noisy quarrel which had broken out between two of the women, one of whom was accusing the other of stealing rations.

She drew Violet aside, and said, 'There is a passage booked and paid for in my name on the Dutch vessel. I don't know when she is to sail, but I shall give you a note addressed to the captain, allowing you to take my place. I have been prevented by circumstances from leaving my sister.'

Violet gazed about her, and was silent for a long while. Then she sighed. 'You know, love, right till you made me that offer I thought I coulda done it—run out on poor old Eddie, I mean.'

'Are you saying that you now wish to go on staying in this place?'

'You think it's rough in married quarters? Well, let me tell you, ducks, it's a sight rougher in ordinary barracks for the troops as aren't married, and that's where Eddie'd have to move back to if I went. He ain't a bad sort, really he ain't,' she added defensively. 'I mean, how many men woulda married a whore, dowry or no dowry? Besides, I worry about him. He's had such a nasty hacking cough lately.'

Catrina interrupted her with a strangled little laugh. 'I ought to have known that running away was just a fantasy as far as you were concerned. You're still the same Violet who worried about me on *Oriole* and looked after me without a thought for yourself. You tell Eddie I think he is a very lucky man!'

Violet giggled self-consciously. 'I ain't no angel, so don't go thinking me one. It's just . . . If I left Eddie, I'd have to go whoring again, and believe me, ducks, that ain't no fun. Less even than living here with Eddie on low rations. You understand?'

'I do understand only too well. I have to go now, Violet. If there's ever anything I can do for you, you'll find me living with my sister and her husband, Captain Ross.'

Catrina kissed Violet's cheek, and gave the other women in the barrack room a friendly wave, and then she hurried home.

She had scarcely set foot inside the morning-room when Dinah Forest pulled on her gloves and prepared to leave.

Watching a pregnant woman and a child cleaning silver with wood-ash was clearly not something which afforded her any amusement.

Catrina said, 'Mrs Forest, there is a spare berth available and paid for on the Dutch vessel. I was to have sailed on it, but naturally I could not leave Millicent to manage alone when the servants fled. You are welcome to the berth if you want it.'

Dinah gave her tinkling, girlish laugh. 'And desert the sinking ship? Oh, no! I quite see why you wished to leave, but *I* am made of sterner stuff, Miss Beaumont!'

'As you please.'

When Catrina returned to the morning-room after having seen Dinah out, she found her sister crying soundlessly and trying to hide her tears from Lucy. Millicent had been polishing a knife and had cut her finger, and she was wiping the mixture of blood and wood-ash on a cloth with unobtrusive movements. The very lack of drama which she displayed in her wretchedness stirred Catrina to pity.

She put an arm about Millicent's shoulder, and said gently, 'You have done enough for now. Go and wash your hands, and lie down for a rest.'

Millicent gave her a grateful, tremulous smile and left the room. Catrina had expected Lucy to grow bored with the silver once her mother had gone, but the child remained where she was, working with total absorption if not with much thoroughness.

Catrina looked at the small girl, and in that moment she was no longer the ghost of three-year-old Millicent, gloatingly displaying her new possessions to her less-privileged sister. She was a child with wood-ash smeared across her cheeks and ingrained in her small hands; a child with an identity of her own.

She looked up with satisfaction. 'I have finished polishing everything, Aunt Catrina! What shall I do now?'

'Shall we tackle the floor together? I'll scrub, and you may go over it with a clean, dry cloth afterwards.'

They worked together, and when the tiled floor was clean and shining, they stood together and admired their handiwork. Catrina smiled at the little girl. 'Let us clean ourselves up. It will soon be time for luncheon.'

She carried hot water from the kitchen to the bedroom, with Lucy trotting after her. Millicent, she noticed, had simply piled her daughter's clothes upon the bed.

'After luncheon,' Catrina said, 'I'll clear out some drawers for your clothes. And we'll have to ask your father to move your bed in here.'

'Aunt Catrina,' Lucy whispered, 'could I—could I not sleep in your bed with you?'

Catrina stiffened involuntarily at the thought. In her clean pinafore, with her face and hands washed and her curls brushed, Lucy was Millicent's ghost once more.

Then the child disarmed her by adding in a low, shamed voice, 'Sometimes, when I wake up in the night, I think everyone in the world has gone away 'cept me. I didn't mind Nanny snoring then, 'cause it meant *she* was still there. But sometimes she forgot to snore, and then I cried and woke her up, and she slapped me. If I slept with you and I woke up, I could touch you and then I'd *know* everyone hadn't gone away.'

Catrina thought of her own lonely nights as a child in Lady Prudence's house, and how she had longed for someone to comfort her when she awakened from a frightening dream.

'Yes, Lucy,' she said gently. 'You may sleep with me. And if ever you should wake up and be afraid, you may wake me up too. I shan't slap you.'

Lucy slipped her hand inside Catrina's, and said, 'Oh, thank you! What shall I do to help you now?'

'You may set the cutlery out on the table for me. I am going to prepare luncheon.'

Then Dominic came home for his meal, looking tense and frustrated. Catrina guessed that boredom must be a problem for the officers as well for the ordinary soldiers and sailors. From what she had seen at the two barracks she had visited earlier, there was little to do except mark time and try in whatever ways they could to maintain morale, and Dominic's duties probably consisted of little more than drilling the troops under his command.

As they sat down to cold beef and pease-puddng, Catrina said, without looking at him, 'You must tell me, please, Dominic, the sum you paid for my passage on the Dutch vessel so that I may reimburse you.'

'I do not wish to be reimbursed,' he returned shortly.

'In that case, I brought with me from England some fine brandy. It was intended as a present for . . . Well, I wish you to have it.'

'I won't refuse your offer. Good brandy is worth far more than money. I could use it in bartering for food with one of the traders who has been hoarding supplies.'

Millicent shuddered. 'Who would ever have thought that we would be reduced to bartering, like serfs of old? Or that *tradesmen* would be able to drink good brandy while we have to worry about food supplies?'

'Papa,' Lucy changed the subject excitedly, 'I am to sleep in the same bed with Aunt Catrina!'

He made a muffled sound, which caused Catrina to glance at him. His eyes had narrowed to slits and his face was carved in harsh lines.

It could only be caused by revulsion, she thought with a sick feeling. He does not want his daughter exposed to someone like me . . . She was aware that he had pushed back his chair, and then he was excusing himself and in a moment could be heard leaving the house.

Millicent glanced with distaste at the dirty dishes on the table. 'I'm sure I could do a simple task like washing the dishes!'

Catrina gave her her head, but her sister proved to be more of an encumbrance as she stood in the kitchen later, laboriously engaged at the wash-tub.

'You have to work up a lather first with the soap, Millicent,' Catrina instructed as patiently as she could.

'It is disgustingly coarse, and it smells quite vile.'

'Nevertheless, it is all we have.'

Then Catrina had to show her how to rinse everything in clean water and make sure that she dried the crockery and cutlery properly. Catrina was itching with impatience at the time it all took, for she needed the kitchen tub in order to do the laundry. She had decided that it would be best to wash each day, rather than to allow things to pile up into unmanageable proportions.

'Millicent,' Catrina said at last. 'Leave the rest of the dishes to me. I think you had better take on the sewing and let me tackle everything else. I noticed that the hem of the tablecloth we used at luncheon has come unstitched. Why don't you work on that this afternoon?'

Millicent nodded gratefully. 'I shall take it to my room. And I could also put Lucy to bed for her afternoon nap. I am not totally useless, am I?'

Catrina patted her shoulder. 'Of course not.'

But it was less than the truth. As the days passed, Millicent pursued the only occupation her gentle upbringing had fitted her for—sewing a dainty seam—while Catrina dealt with the grinding day-to-day toil of keeping the house clean, of doing the laundry and preparing and cooking meals.

Lucy loyally dogged her footsteps, and set out each morning with her to buy fish at the harbour or purchase whatever was available from one of the stores.

There was something eerie and discomfiting about the town, Catrina felt, with the Rock looming ominously over it and the Spanish vessels anchored in the Bay. The few British ships which helplessly hugged the safe anchorage of the harbour only emphasised the vulnerability of their situation. The general atmosphere was claustrophobic and tense, the frustration felt by everyone made worse by the blowing of the Levanter.

Catrina had grown to dread the prevailing wind in the straits. It came in from the east in the warm Mediterranean and struck the sheer cliff-face of the Rock, where it rose to condense in a white cloud covering the summit like a tablecloth. It increased the humidity and produced a feeling of irritation in everyone, so that many fights broke out among the townspeople. Life was difficult enough, Catrina thought morosely, without forever having to make sure that she and Lucy were not trapped in one of those affrays.

The fishermen, who were able to provide their families with food, were among the few in Gibraltar to whom money still meant anything. Catrina would pay for the fish she had selected, barter one of her silk handkerchiefs for a supply of flour or whatever else might be obtainable, and then take Lucy's hand to return, drenched in perspiration from the wretched humidity, to tackle the tasks of the day.

One afternoon, when both Lucy and Millicent were taking

their usual nap and Catrina was in the kitchen, heating flat-irons on the fire and using them to press a pile of laundry, Dominic walked in unexpectedly. She did not look up, but her heart was beating tumultuously. She heard him sigh.

'Poor Catrina, everything has fallen on your shoulders, has it not?'

'Millicent does what she can to help, but . . .' she began defensively.

'But she was not brought up to face harsh reality. Her mother spoilt her and shielded her to an unnatural degree.' He moved, suddenly, and tilted Catrina's chin, forcing her to meet his silver gaze.

She placed the flat-iron upon its trivet, the blood drumming in her temples merely because he was touching her. 'I—don't know what you are talking about,' she said unsteadily. 'If you mean that Millicent was not brought up to iron laundry, as I was . . .'

'You may have considered yourself to be a Cinderella of a daughter,' he interrupted in a rough voice. 'But, believe me, you were fortunate! You escaped your mother's kind of crippling devotion. She arrested Millicent's development; she trapped her like a fly in amber so that she retained the emotional age of a child. She will always be a child. Her mother's little girl.'

'You are being unfair to Millicent, and insulting to me!' Catrina cried angrily. 'To call *me* fortunate! Millicent was properly brought up by my mother to be a lady. *I* was allowed to grow up, totally neglected, taught only how to be a domestic drudge. And . . .'

She stopped. She could not put into words the thought that had just come to her. *She* was the one whose development had been distorted and flawed by the lack of a devoted mother's teaching. There had been no one to instil into her the kinds of sensibilities that caused other women to shrink in repugnance from the attentions of men; no one to warn her that she must suppress and eradicate the shameless, degraded side of her nature.

'We won't quarrel over the matter,' Dominic said. 'I am very grateful, Catrina, for all your hard work. It may not be necessary for much longer. When the siege is over . . .' He stopped, as if he had said more than he had meant to.

Catrina moved to the fire to re-heat the flat-iron. 'I can see very little evidence of the siege coming to an end shortly. Nothing seems to be changing. The Spanish ships remain in the Bay. Are you hinting that British warships are on the way to scatter the Spanish from the Bay?'

'No.'

'Well, then . . . Nothing is changing, except for the worse. Lucy and I went to the town as usual this morning, but because we are all heartily sick of fish I tried to barter an expensive shawl in exchange for meat. I was told that there are only some forty-odd head of cattle left on the Rock, and they are not for sale by their owners at any price.'

'Things *will* be changing soon,' Dominic said definitely. 'I am not at liberty to tell you more than that. What I can tell you, however, is that Alice Ridgeway is sacrificing one of her chickens because it is Dinah's birthday, and we have been invited to dine there this evening.'

'Oh!' A flame of excitement shot through Catrina. Not only because of the rare treat of eating a meal she had not had to contrive herself, and one of chicken at that, but also because a social evening spent away from this house would break the claustrophobic monotony of the life they had been forced to lead.

'I had better leave the ironing in that case,' she went on, 'and prepare for dining out. Would you please wake Millicent and tell her about the invitation, while I see to Lucy?'

The child was entranced at the prospect ahead. 'I shall say please and thank you and not spill anything. What are you going to wear, Aunt Catrina? You have such pretty gowns.'

'Would you like to help me choose?'

'Oh, yes!'

A little later, when Lucy had made her choice, Catrina laughed recklessly. 'Very well—why not? I'll wear it!'

She knew that, for a small dinner party in a town under heavy siege, the gold satin gown worn over a petticoat of gold net was flamboyantly inappropriate, but she did not care. Lucy stared, open-mouthed, as Catrina added gold slippers and fastened her emerald pendant about her throat. Through her coppery curls she threaded a satin ribbon of matching emerald green.

'Oh, you look like a princess, Aunt Catrina!' Lucy exclaimed, finding her voice.

Catrina laughed, and shook out the skirts of her gown. She had become such a drudge of late that, by contrast, she did look like a princess. She looked precisely as she had meant to look.

Dominic said nothing when he saw her. Millicent, who was not in the best of humours, snapped, 'Don't you think you are a trifle over-dressed, Catrina?'

'Who cares if I am? The gown was Lucy's choice, and as for myself—I am tired of wearing a sacking apron! Tonight I intend to enjoy myself!'

She did enjoy herself. She enjoyed General Ridgeway's frank admiration and the look of envy and spite which crossed Dinah's pretty face and spoilt her usual facade of guilelessness as she said,

'My goodness, you do believe in putting everything you own on show, don't you?'

Catrina enjoyed, perhaps most of all, Alice Ridgeway's quiet response to Dinah's remark. 'I am honoured, my dear, that you should have taken so much trouble to dress up for the occasion. I am as thoroughly tired as you must be of all the gloom there has been about lately. Dinah has told me that you are without any servants of any kind. I have wanted to call on you, and the only reason why I have not done so is because I did not want to add any more work to your load.'

'*I* help, too, Aunt Alice,' Lucy said earnestly.

'Anyone would suppose,' Millicent put in crossly, 'that I do nothing!' She held her hands out for inspection. 'My fingers are like pin-cushions from all the mending and darning I have been doing!'

'It is a pity,' Dinah remarked sweetly, 'that Miss Beaumont has been unable to keep her gloves on all evening.'

The remark had the effect of causing everyone to glance at Catrina's hands, which were red and rough from the coarse soap and water in which they were constantly immersed. She felt herself flushing, and tried to hide her hands in the folds of her skirt.

Then she saw that Dominic's eyes were blazing. He moved

towards her, and made her a deep bow. He reached for her hands.

'They bear the evidence of all the hard work you have been doing for my family,' he said in a clear, carrying voice. 'And I kiss them in humble thanks!'

General Ridgeway applauded loudly as he raised her hands to his lips in turn, and Dinah moved away, her colour high.

Alice had dressed the dining table as prettily as she could, using her best silver candlesticks and a damask cloth. The chicken had been stuffed with a mixture of oatmeal and wild herbs to make it stretch as far as possible, and with it she served the inevitable boiled pease. But she had procured dried fruit from somewhere, and had saved all the eggs her hens had laid that week, so that there was a pudding to follow.

'That was a wonderful meal!' Catrina congratulated their hostess when the last of the dishes had been removed from the table.

Alice smiled faintly. 'Everything is relative, is it not? I looked through some old menu-cards earlier today, and I came across one for a modest little party given some two months ago. I could hardly believe that there had been fourteen courses, and that the menu had included such things as sweetbreads, collared pig and five other different kinds of meat!'

She rose. 'Shall we leave the men to their port?'

General Ridgeway and Dominic joined them later, and the evening only came to an end when Lucy began to yawn and rub her eyes.

As they were returning home, the child summed up the evening. 'I liked my first proper dinner party, with grown-ups. I was good, was I not, Mama?'

'You behaved as you had been brought up to behave,' Millicent said crushingly.

'You were *very* good, my love,' Dominic assured the child with warmth. 'I was proud of you.'

'I'm glad, Papa.' Lucy hesitated. 'If I go on being good, Papa, do you think I could have a puppy?'

'Now, Lucy,' Millicent said before he could reply. 'You have been told many times that you could not have another puppy, and why.'

Catrina allowed the conversation to wash around her, making no contribution herself. When they entered the house, Millicent said, 'I am most unusually sleepy. It must be because of the canary wine I drank this evening. You will have to excuse me, for I need to seek my bed.'

Lucy yawned. 'I am tired, too. I love sleeping with you, Aunt Catrina, because you're soft and warm. Will you tell me a story tonight? Tell one about a puppy.'

'We'll see.' Catrina took her hand and led her to their bedroom and put her to bed. The child, worn out by excitement and the lateness of the hour, fell asleep almost immediately, her plea for a story forgotten.

Catrina divested herself of the gold gown and underdress. She removed her hoops and stays, and thrust her arms inside the sleeves of a satin *peignoir*. Then she removed the pins from her hair and brushed it so that it fell in a copper-coloured curtain about her face to her shoulders.

Her mind had been over-stimulated by the conversation at the Ridgeways' home, and she knew that *she* would not be able to sleep yet. She decided to go and fetch a book from the drawing-room. She left the room quietly, carrying a single candle. The house was silent and in darkness. She pushed open the drawing-room door, and as she did so, the fitful light of the candle showed her that Dominic was slumped in a chair, his head resting on one hand while the other was curled round a glass of rum.

He turned his head and grinned at her, raising his glass. 'Well, Catrina?' His voice was dry and self-mocking. 'Don't you know it's dangerous to interrupt a man who is seriously intent upon getting foxed?'

She looked at him, biting her lip. He had prepared for bed and was wearing a braided robe, so what had sent him to the rum-bottle instead? 'You shouldn't sit here in the dark, Dominic,' she said. 'Why don't you finish your drink and go to bed?'

'Such sisterly concern!' he jeered. 'Well, to the devil with your advice—*sister*!'

She had almost no experience of men, and none at all of men in their cups, and she decided, warily, that she had better leave him to his own devices. She moved past him to reach the book-case.

He stretched out a hand, suddenly, and drew her roughly towards him. She stumbled and would have fallen but for his hard grasp on her arm. He stood up, and drew her against him.

'Would you like to know,' he demanded thickly, 'what drove me to the rum? It was something Lucy said.'

'Lucy?'

' "I love sleeping with you," ' he quoted, ' "because you're soft and warm." Dear God,' he ground out, burying his face in her hair. '*How* I envy Lucy the sharing of your bed!'

CHAPTER NINE

UNSTEADILY, CATRINA GROPED behind her and placed the candle she was still holding on the table. He had raised his head, and their eyes locked. A pulse began to beat insistently in her throat. She had thought he disliked her sharing her bed with Lucy in case she might contaminate his daughter with her own lack of moral decency, and all the time he had been jealous of the child!

He drew a long, ragged breath and released her. 'Go away, Catrina,' he growled. 'Leave me to my rum.'

Her limbs felt curiously heavy and languorous, and every nerve-end seemed to have acquired a life of its own. Without having drunk more than two glasses of canary wine throughout the evening, she felt as intoxicated as if she had been sitting in the dark with a bottle of rum for company.

'Don't send me away,' she whispered, moving towards him and watching his eyes darkening with desire. She lifted a hand, and gently moved her fingertips from his jaw to the base of his throat. She saw that his hair was clinging damply to his forehead, where perspiration had formed.

'For the love of God,' he ground out, 'get away from me, Catrina, before I . . .'

'I love you, Dominic,' she said simply.

A groan escaped him. 'If I were—halfway drunk before,' he muttered, 'you are accomplishing—what an entire barrel of rum could not do . . .'

'Dominic,' she said seriously, 'I was not brought up in a delicate way, and so I cannot help it if my love is without shame . . .'

He uttered a low, unsteady laugh. 'Yes, the one thing you lack is shame, is it not . . .' He shook his head in a blind gesture. Then he gripped her by the shoulders.

'Let me see you as you really are,' he said in a thick voice. 'As God made you. Without shame.'

She hesitated for only a fraction of a second. Then, recklessly, she shrugged her arms out of the sleeves of the *peignoir* so that it fell to the floor.

He moved slowly towards her. She gasped as his mouth travelled in a slow, burning trail from her throat to her breasts, taking each nipple softly between his lips while his hands explored her body. Then he picked her up and carried her to the sofa, and his tongue teased the places which all the servants who had cared for her had taught her were dirty and should be kept secret. But she did not feel dirty at all. Her whole being throbbed and pulsated, and as she twined her hands in his thick hair she whispered,

'I do love you, and I don't care . . .'

The words were cut off by his mouth fastening on hers, and she shuddered with delight at the incredible, undreamt-of intimacy of his probing tongue which seemed to be in perfect rhythm with his hands caressing and exploring her body. She felt as if she were drowning in love and never-before-experienced sensations.

He laughed deep in his throat, an exultant, reckless sound. 'Shameless, shameless Catrina . . . You remind me of a flower-bud, bursting open at the first touch of the sun . . .'

His mouth began to make its voyage of discovery of her body again, and she felt more like a river in full flood, hurtling towards an inevitable and glorious waterfall.

Her hands wrenched recklessly at the belt of his robe. He did not help her; his delight in her own body appeared to be enough for him for the moment as his questing mouth and caressing hands sent countless spasmodic impulses coursing through her body, so that she uttered a little cry of ecstasy.

'Animals!' Millicent's voice was almost unrecognisable as it cut through the air, and as Dominic pushed Catrina away a completely different simile slipped into her mind.

It was as if her sister had thrown cold water over a fire which had been about to rage out of control.

Catrina struggled to her feet. Millicent stood in the doorway, dressed for bed, the branch of candles in her hand showing her distorted face and her wild eyes. 'Filthy, disgusting, obscene *animals*! Both of . . .'

She stopped, and made a violently retching sound.

Dominic was hurrying towards her, but she raised her free hand, warding him off as if he were Satan himself. Then she was running, with Dominic after her, and as Catrina covered her own flushed, aroused body with the *peignoir*, she could hear Millicent vomiting in the slop-pail in her bedroom.

Now the shame which had been entirely missing before invaded Catrina. Oh, dear God, even allowing for her neglected upbringing, surely she could not be normal in the way other women were normal? She had offered herself to her own sister's husband, quite prepared to fill the vacant position as his mistress, and she had felt no spark of moral scruple as she did so. Why, even now, in the depths of her humiliation, one part of her mind was bitterly resenting Millicent's untimely appearance on the scene!

For once, she supposed, her sister must have refrained from taking laudanum. Millicent had drunk several glasses of canary wine at the Ridgeways' house, and as a result had felt sleepy enough to forgo the drug. But the unaccustomed rich food must have given her indigestion and she had probably been on her way to look for the powders prescribed for her when she had seen the light in the drawing-room.

In her own room, Catrina slipped into bed beside Lucy. What would happen now? She spent a restless night, and in the morning she responded mechanically to Lucy's innocent chatter. She washed both herself and the child, and then went into the kitchen to prepare the breakfast. Dominic entered and closed the door. He looked strained and haggard, as if he too had not had much sleep, but there was also a quality of remoteness about him.

Catrina glanced away from him, and said, 'If—If Millicent wishes it, I shall leave . . .'

'You have nowhere to go, and she would not be able to manage without you.' His voice was without expression. 'But what happened last night must never happen again.'

She nodded wordlessly.

'I do not defend my own behaviour in the least,' he went on. 'The fact that I had had too much to drink is no excuse. I should have turned my back on temptation.'

She felt herself cringing. 'I—I should have left you alone when you told me to . . .'

'Yes, Catrina,' he agreed sombrely. 'You must understand that men, even when they are quite sober, are likely to lose their heads if the woman concerned behaves without restraint.'

He had, she thought dully, been kind enough to call it restraint. What he had really meant was chastity, decency, virtue—all the things she appeared to lack.

'Last night,' he went on, 'you and I were only just prevented from committing a criminal action. It must not happen again. You must not provoke me. Do you understand?'

'I do,' Catrina managed.

'You spoke of love last night,' he continued, his voice taking on a brutal edge. 'I do not love you, and you—whatever your passionate nature might have tricked you into believing—do not love me. I am your sister's husband, and that is all I will ever be to you.'

All. The word beat through Catrina's mind like a dreary dirge after he had left the kitchen and she continued preparing the breakfast.

Millicent did not appear in the morning-room for the meal, and Catrina kept her breakfast hot for her. There was no need for the usual daily visit to the harbour and market, for the fish which had been bought the previous day had been well salted and wrapped in wet cloths, and would do for tonight's dinner.

Dominic had left the house, and Catrina was clearing up the morning-room with Lucy's help when Millicent entered. She looked ravaged and heavy-eyed. She swayed slightly as she approached the table, and Catrina went to her, putting out a helping hand.

'Don't—touch me,' Millicent mumbled, shrinking away.

Catrina bit hard on her lip, and went to fetch her sister's breakfast. 'Lucy, love,' she said, trying to make her voice normal and cheerful. 'Would you do something for me? I have left the dirty laundry on the kitchen floor. Would you please sort it into bundles of whites and coloured garments?'

The child nodded, and ran from the room. 'Millicent,' Catrina began when they were alone, 'I am very sorry . . .'

Millicent clapped her hands to her ears. 'You are only sorry that you were found out! Dear God, the look on your face last night as you . . . The very thought makes me heave! You were so depraved that you did not even think to snuff out the candle! I can understand, now, why Mama and Papa were never able to love you!'

Catrina sank into a chair. 'That is most unfair! I was scarcely older than Lucy when they gave me away. I was innocent . . .'

'You must have had it within you all the time, from the very beginning—this coarse brutishness. It must have shown itself in other ways.'

Catrina remained silent. Could Millicent possibly be right? Had the matter of her own upbringing been irrelevant? Could it be that even Alice Ridgeway had never guessed that the true reason why her parents had rejected her was because they had recognised her as a bad seed? Was there some way of telling, even at an early age?

Dominic had been charitable enough to describe her nature as being 'passionate'. But had her mother realised, even when Catrina was a little girl, that no matter what moral principles one might try to instil in her, she would grow into one of those few unnatural, corrupt women Millicent had been told about?

'I would leave if I could,' Catrina broke the silence, 'and if it were possible for you to manage without me.'

'You should never have come here in the first place! You should have stayed in London and prowled the back streets like an alley-cat! It's what you were clearly meant to be!'

Self-revulsion rose inside Catrina, and she could find no words with which to defend herself. After a while, she managed, 'If—If it gives you any comfort, Dominic was not to blame. He tried to send me away, but I . . .'

'Good God, do you think I am jealous, because he is my husband? Do you think I am so stupid that I don't know he has been satisfying his lust elsewhere?'

Catrina made an involuntary sound of desperate protest. That was something she could not bear; the thought that Dominic already had another mistress.

'I knew, of course,' Millicent went on in biting tones, 'that he would look around for another whore when she scuttled back to England and safety. I did not imagine for one moment that my own sister would offer herself, like a bitch in season, without even the usual motives of need or greed!'

Catrina allowed the insults to wash over her, for they were, after all, justified. Even though it altered nothing, she was taking comfort from the fact that Millicent had been talking about the pretty Irish girl whom Catrina had seen with Dominic on the waterfront when she arrived.

'You said—she returned to England. So you knew her identity . . .'

'Of course I did. She was my personal maid.'

Catrina stared at her sister. 'You did not mind?'

'*Mind?* I arranged it. She did it for my sake, because I asked it of her. But at least she and Dominic took care not to indulge in their activities under my nose!'

Catrina shook her head in disbelief. 'You—You procured your maid for Dominic? Did he know?'

'Of course he did not know! He thought she had allowed herself to be seduced because of his good looks and his manly presence. He did not realise that, for her, it was merely an extra duty.'

Catrina stood up. 'Millicent, I know that my behaviour last night was quite indefensible. But—I think—to ask your own maid to perform the functions of a wife is—is . . .'

'Is precisely the same as paying her to perform some other, equally repugnant task! And if you are thinking of telling Dominic that I paid her, Catrina, let me warn you—one word from me about the—the *bestial* scene I witnessed last night, and no decent person would ever acknowledge you again!'

'I would not dream of telling Dominic anything so humiliating to himself, and so shameful about you.'

'*Shameful!* You dare to talk to me about shame!' Millicent's face was contorted. 'I am forced to suffer you under my roof, Catrina. But I want as little contact with you as possible from now on!'

She was true to her word. She spoke to Catrina only when it became strictly necessary, and she spent much of her time in her room. Catrina reflected wryly that although the revulsion her sister felt for herself was perfectly genuine, Millicent was quite content to leave Lucy in her care. Like a child ignoring inconvenient facts, Millicent did not allow herself to think of the possibility of Lucy becoming corrupted by such close contact with someone she abhorred. It obviously did not suit her to have to care for the child herself.

Dominic now put in an appearance at the house only when he was forced to do so. He ate his meals hurriedly and departed again, and he found somewhere else to spend his evenings. Even when he was at home, Catrina found that he made a point of avoiding her eyes.

She immersed herself in the dreary day-to-day routine, but her mind was churning endlessly over everything that had happened. Dominic had said that they had been on the point of committing a criminal action. The thought continued to puzzle her, until she realised that it had been a simple slip of the tongue. In polite society, she knew, the euphemism for adultery was 'criminal conversation', more commonly referred to as 'crim con', and that was what he had meant.

Lucy was now her only solace. Catrina knew next to nothing about children, but it seemed to her that the little girl was far in advance of her years, and unusually intelligent. She was also intuitive, for at early dawn one morning she turned over in bed and took one of Catrina's hands between her own small ones.

'Why are you sad, Aunt Catrina?' she whispered.

Catrina had not even been aware that the child was awake, and she herself had been lying very still, her thoughts their usual jumble of despair and shame.

'I am not sad, Lucy. I woke early, and I was just thinking that today is Sunday, and that it was not worth trying to go back to sleep, because soon the bells of Santa Maria will start pealing for the early Mass . . .'

Her voice was drowned at that moment, not by the pealing of church bells, but by a cacophony of cannon shots and mortar firing.

The Spaniards must have crept from their lines on the isthmus, and they were attacking the town!

Catrina was trying to soothe the terrified Lucy, and at the same time dressing with haste. The noise had awakened even Millicent from her laudanum-induced sleep, for she ran into the room, looking wild-eyed.

'Dominic has not slept in his bed all night!' she cried. 'Heaven knows where he spent the night and with whom, but it seems we are to be left to the mercy of the Spaniards! They are probably invading even now! Oh, dear Jesus, what is to become of us?'

'Millicent!' Catrina said sharply. 'Control yourself! Stay here with Lucy while I see what I may discover.'

She hurried outside. The sun had not yet made its appearance, but even if it had it would have been obscured by the wreaths of smoke which hung in the air. It soon became apparent that the flames and flashes of discharge were not coming from the Spanish side after all, but from the Rock itself. The British were bombarding the *Linea*.

Catrina remembered that Dominic had said definitely, 'Things will change soon.' This must be what he had meant. By attacking the Spanish on land, the British were obviously hoping to send the blockading vessels out of the Bay, on their way to flank the isthmus instead to help to defend the lines.

Catrina went back inside the house to reassure Millicent and comfort Lucy and then, since further rest would have been impossible, she started cooking breakfast. Normal Sunday routine was abandoned. There was no question of going to church, and Catrina wondered what she could sacrifice for lunch, and whether Dominic would be sharing the meal with them. They had all been invited to a meal with the Ridgeways after the service, but those plans would obviously also have to be cancelled.

All morning the steady firing continued, the roaring and thundering echoing from the Rock as the British bombarded the Spanish lines. When Catrina looked out of the window, she saw that the town itself was deserted. Everyone had barricaded themselves inside their houses, afraid of being caught in any cross-fire.

But Alice Ridgeway and Dinah braved the possible danger and arrived shortly after noon to join Millicent and Catrina. They had brought a corner of boiled ham with them.

'Since you were to have joined us for luncheon,' Alice explained, 'I guessed you would not have made any provision for the meal.'

The strange silence from the Spanish *Linea* seemed

reassuring as they had lunch, but as the day wore on it became more and more disquieting. Why, Catrina wondered, did they not return the British fire?

Only towards the evening did the bombardment from the Rock slacken, and soon afterwards Dominic came home, looking tired and grim.

Dinah ran to him and clung to his arm. 'Oh, thank goodness you are safe!'

With uncharacteristic tartness, Alice said, 'Try not to make a bigger cake of yourself than usual, Dinah! Why should he not be safe? The Spaniards have not fired a single shot at our lines!'

'They were too cowardly to defend themselves against our brilliant attack!' Dinah crowed.

'It was scarcely brilliant,' Dominic corrected wryly. 'For all the ammunition we used and the energy we expended, we did little damage to the Spanish works.'

'Do you think they refrained from counter-attacking because it is Sunday?' Catrina asked.

He shrugged. 'Tomorrow will tell.'

But to everyone's astonishment and growing unease the Spaniards consistently refrained from retaliating, and although the bombardment continued from the Rock, it produced little in the way of results. Catrina, in common with other townspeople, began to take the bombardment for granted and did not allow it to interfere with the daily necessity of obtaining food. The unceasing noise and smoke and flames from the discharging guns had become a part of life, just as the blockading Spanish fleet in the Bay was a part of life.

Government rations for the military personnel had been drastically cut, so that she had to exercise all her ingenuity to contrive at least one proper meal a day. When rumours reached her that a privateer had succeeded in slipping through the blockade, and that its supplies had been snapped up by traders who were selling them at vastly inflated prices, she wrapped a pile of sovereigns inside a handkerchief and pushed it down the front of her bodice. To carry money about in a reticule was no longer safe; starvation had made thieves of many formerly honest citizens.

Flour was selling at the outrageous price of a shilling a

pound. When Catrina protested at the price, the merchant shrugged. 'Take it or leave it, lady. There's plenty others'll take it.'

She bit her lip, and turned away to retrieve her money from the front of her bodice. When the merchant saw the gleam of the sovereigns, an answering gleam entered his eyes.

'Tell you what, lady—I'll make you a good price if you take a barrel of flour. Fifteen sovereigns, and not a penny more. And I'd be robbing myself, the good God knows!'

He would, in fact, be profiteering, and both of them were aware of it. But, she argued with herself, flour was available at the moment, and tomorrow it might not be. She did have sufficient money with her to purchase a barrelful.

The merchant took advantage of her inward struggle. 'I'll throw in the hire of a gharry to take you and the flour and your lovely little daughter home. Hey, you,' he called to a passing gharry driver, before Catrina could react. 'I've a job of work for you!'

She gave in then, and a short while later she and Lucy were travelling on the gharry with the barrel. Their progress was slow, impeded by crowds surging along the cobbled street, and suddenly she realised why people had come out in droves.

Bread was being sold through grated doorways of the bakeries, with armed soldiers standing guard to break up the fights which were continually being started among people desperate for bread, and terrified that supplies might run out before they had the chance to reach the doorways.

Catrina caught sight of a familiar figure among the waiting crowds, and called to the driver to stop. She jumped from the gharry, and pushed her way through the mob.

'Violet! I am so glad to see you!'

'Hello, ducks.' Violet's voice was preoccupied. 'I must keep moving, see, or I'll lose my place . . .'

'I have flour; you are welcome to some of it. Come quickly, before the driver takes it into his head to put Lucy off and make away with the flour!'

As they pushed a path towards the vehicle, Catrina added with a frown, 'The only problem is, what are we to use as a container?'

A tired smile flickered over Violet's face. 'Me apron will do, love. Oh, yes, I knows it's a bit dirty! But hunger makes you so's you stop being too particular about things like that. But are you sure you can spare it?'

'Quite sure! Indeed, I'm ashamed, now, of having encouraged the profiteering by buying such a large stock at a ridiculous price. Climb aboard the gharry.'

Because she knew that the mob would have stormed them if they had seen flour being scooped from a whole barrelful of the precious stuff, Catrina told the driver of the gharry to pull into a quiet side-alley.

Violet removed her apron so that Catrina could scoop handfuls of flour into it. 'Hello, young 'un,' she greeted Lucy.

The child regarded her with large, serious blue eyes. 'Hello. My name is Lucy. What is yours?'

'It's Violet, love. You must be your Aunt Catrina's niece.'

'I am. I sleep in her bed at night, and I help her with the work. Do you have a little girl of your own, Violet?'

'Lord forbid!' Hastily, Violet amended, 'No, I ain't been blessed.' She glanced at Catrina, and protested, 'Stop! You're giving me too much! You give me enough already, what with the money and the silk gown and everything!'

'That's what friends are for,' Catrina returned lightly. She knotted the ends of the apron so that it formed a compact parcel. 'Tell me, Violet, how have things been with you in general?'

'Well, not counting the hellish noise we all live with, there's poor Eddie almost half-dead with tiredness every day. We're all on very short rations. I don't know what officers gets, but a common soldier don't get no more'n will keep his body and soul together, and he has to share that with his family. So you can think for yourself what it's like, with thieving of food going on, and fights breaking out because of it . . . There's many a soldier as is talking openly of deserting and surrendering to the Spaniards. I knows of two lads who tried to get to the *Linea* and fell over the edge of a high cliff instead, and was brought up later dead as mutton.'

She climbed from the gharry, and Catrina handed the flour down to her. Violet bade them goodbye and, with her precious parcel clutched firmly, she made her way back to the main street.

Compassion as well as fear moved Catrina to give the driver of the gharry some flour too, for which he used his hat as a receptacle. When they arrived home, the driver carried the flour into the house by the back door for her. She thanked him and gave him a coin, and then went into the morning-room, where she discovered that Alice Ridgeway and Dinah were visiting Millicent.

Hobson, the Ridgeways' butler, Catrina learnt, had that morning purchased oranges brought in by the privateer, and Alice had called with a gift of a dozen for Dominic's household. In exchange, Catrina filled a linen bag with flour and presented it to Alice.

'It is a pity that you could not have spent some of your wealth on tea or chocolate,' Millicent grumbled waspishly.

Catrina bit back the retort that her wealth, or at least such funds as she had brought to Gibraltar with her, were dwindling fast. Then she remembered about the supply of best tea she had brought with her from England.

'I did buy a little tea,' she lied now. It was best not to let Millicent know about the size of the supply. 'I'll go and make a brew.'

The tea was inside an airtight tin hidden in one of her trunks. Catrina took two sheets of notepaper, fashioned them into pokes and filled each with tea. One of them she intended to give to Alice.

After making the tea, Catrina carried a tray into the morning-room. She was in time to hear Lucy say excitedly,

' . . . a friend of Aunt Catrina's, and she spoke funny. Her name was Violet, and she lives in the barracks, where people fight over food, and she told about two soldiers who fell over a cliff and were found dead as mutton! *Dead as mutton*,' she repeated with ghoulish relish.

Millicent frowned at Catrina. 'What is the child talking about? How could you possibly have a friend who lives in the barracks, and speaks in such a vulgar manner?'

'We—I met her on board *Oriole*,' Catrina told her reluctantly.

'She sounds a most unsuitable friend!'

'Oh no, Mama,' Lucy put in earnestly. 'She is very pretty!

Not as pretty as Aunt Catrina, but she has black curls and eyes that sparkle . . .'

'That will do, Lucy!' Millicent said. She picked up the basket in which Alice had brought the oranges. 'Take this through into the drawing-room and arrange the fruit carefully in a bowl.'

When the child had left the room, Millicent addressed Catrina in a cold voice. 'I should prefer that you do not pursue this strange friendship of yours while you have Lucy in your company.'

Only the presence of Alice and Dinah prevented Catrina from pointing out tartly that, because of her sister's self-absorption and lethargy, Lucy had perforce to be in her company almost all the time.

Just then Dinah clapped her hands like a child who had suddenly solved a complicated puzzle. 'Just a minute! *Violet!* I was at a dinner party one evening, just after war was declared, and two of the junior officers became disgustingly inebriated. They claimed they were drowning their sorrows because of the closure of the—the . . .'

She blushed prettily. 'The house by the Casemates Barracks. They were comparing the charms of the various girls, and they both agreed that one named Violet would be most sorely missed. They became exceedingly boring as they talked about her black curls and her sparkling eyes. That could surely not have been your friend Violet?'

'Yes,' Catrina said, lifting her chin. 'That is my friend Violet. She cared for me like a mother when I was sea-sick throughout the voyage, and she is now respectably married to a soldier.'

Millicent gave her a look which said as clearly as words that she was not in the least surprised at her sister's choice of a whore as a friend. Catrina hoped that Alice had not intercepted that glance, and guessed what lay behind it. Let Dinah think what she liked about her, but Catrina had come to care about Alice's good opinion!

Whether she had understood the significance of Millicent's speaking glance or not, Alice changed the subject by talking about the difficulties facing the garrison and the townspeople.

That evening, when Dominic had taken himself off

elsewhere as usual, and Millicent had swallowed her laudanum and gone to bed and Catrina was facing another evening of loneliness, she turned to her diary for solace.

But she was finding it increasingly painful to write about her feelings for Dominic and her sense of disgust of herself, and so she confined herself to writing an account of the present situation in Gibraltar:

> Perhaps the greatest problem of all is the lowness of spirits. One can sense it everywhere one goes. The Spanish continue their strange refusal to answer the constant bombardment from the British, and their ships remain in the Bay.
>
> General Ridgeway has his own views about the Spaniards' policy of turning the other cheek. He says they are striving to destroy the confidence of our men completely by cocking a snook at us. Perhaps he is right. After all, the Spaniards know that our total strength is not above 7,000 men, while they vastly outnumber us.
>
> The fear which grips the town is not of the enemy, but of one's fellow-citizens. People are hungry, and there is a real feeling of terror that one might be murdered and robbed for the sake of a loaf of bread. The Governor does what he can to help matters.
>
> When the town's chief baker refused to go on producing bread on the pretence that he had no wood for his fires, Governor Eliott knew that the man's real motive was to hoard supplies until the poor people became desperate enough to pay hitherto undreamt-of sums for a loaf. He stepped in, and had twenty-nine of the baker's stock of sacks of flour seized, and made sure that it was distributed to the people.
>
> He has also banned the officers from following the silly fashion of powdering their wigs with flour. One of the first things that struck me about Dominic was that he scorned to wear a wig at all . . .

She stopped writing, and scored out the last sentence with unnecessary force. Then she dipped her quill into the ink again, and continued:

> The Governor is also trying to persuade as many people as are interested to create gardens, and grow the vegetables which have by now become almost a forgotten luxury. I understand there is approximately a mile of land on the isthmus which is British territory, and not in the line of fire. The soil is fertile there by all accounts, and cultivation should be relatively easy.

Catrina sprinkled sand on the page and put her diary away. As she slid into bed beside Lucy, she gave up the thought of applying for a plot of land on the isthmus. It was not the extra work which daunted her, or the problem of Lucy, for the child could have accompanied her as she tilled the soil. But taking up a garden would have meant leaving Millicent alone at home with no one to cope with the housework.

The following morning Catrina awoke to find that Lucy had caught a slight chill, and she made the tearful little girl stay in bed. There could be no question of herself going to the harbour as usual, for Millicent could not be counted on to wake up until mid-morning. There was a piece of salt pork left; that would have to do for dinner. Having reached her decision, Catrina threw herself into household tasks, breaking off frequently to attend to Lucy.

Millicent was totally unco-operative when she did rise, and Catrina acquainted her with news of her daughter's indisposition.

'The child has ever been prone to chills,' she said with a shrug. 'There is no need to make a fuss.'

Catrina gritted her teeth. 'I am not making a fuss. She needs someone to look in on her from time to time and to see that she drinks plenty of water . . .'

'Well, don't look to me,' Millicent interrupted shortly. 'I am not risking catching a chill from her in my condition.'

Catrina said nothing. It seemed to her that Millicent's earlier pretence at rejecting Lucy had turned into reality, for now her sister seldom had time for her little daughter. The day continued at a frantic pace, with Catrina fitting in the nursing and the amusing of Lucy. The child was given an early dinner and settled down for the night, and Catrina hurried into the kitchen again.

That evening she, Millicent and Dominic dined alone in strained silence. Lucy usually made meals bearable with her chatter. To the relief of all three of them, the front-door knocker banged, and Dominic rose. 'I am probably needed at the barracks,' he said.

But a few moments later he ushered in a weeping Violet. Pert, sparkling, pretty Violet had never looked utterly defeated like this before, and without even considering the matter, Catrina leapt from her chair and ran to gather the woman in her arms.

'Oh, Violet, whatever is the matter?'

'Violet!' Millicent echoed, rising too.

Catrina ignored her. 'Tell me what has happened.'

'You—You said I was to come to you, ducks, if ever—if ever I needed help,' Violet sobbed. 'And Lord knows, I needs it now—for I'm fair out my wits with worry . . .'

'Come and sit down,' Catrina urged, guiding her towards the table.

Millicent turned angrily on Dominic. 'Do you know who and what this woman is?' she demanded.

'I do.' His voice was without expression. He moved to the chiffonier and poured a generous amount of wine into a glass, offering it to Violet.

She expressed her thanks in a watery smile, and gulped the wine down. 'It—It's Eddie,' she told Catrina in a shamed whisper. 'Took me dowry—or what was left of it, and run off. Deserted. They're kicking me out of married quarters, and—I've nowhere to go.'

Catrina thought grimly of the miserable Eddie, for the sake of whom Violet had loyally sacrificed the chance of returning to England. She glanced over Violet's head at Dominic, a question in her eyes.

He nodded. 'She may stay here. Heaven knows, we have enough spare rooms in the house.'

'Have you taken leave of your senses?' Millicent almost screamed at him. 'I won't have her in my house—*I won't!*'

For once, Catrina could not help but sympathise with her sister. Dominic and Millicent were part of the army hierarchy: they moved in rigid circles where class barriers were insurmountable. For them to take a lowly-born woman who had been a known whore into their home would send waves of shock and condemnation through the regiment.

When Catrina had given Dominic that pleading look, it had simply been in the mute hope that the army might somehow come to Violet's rescue and allow her some rations and a roof over her head. It had never entered her mind that she should be invited to stay here.

Violet rose to leave, her shoulders drooping in defeat. Dominic stepped in her path, and addressed his wife.

'She stays. Whatever she may have been in the past, she is now an army wife. The fact that her husband has deserted her does not make her guilty of anything.'

Weeping, Millicent ran from the room, and they could hear the door of her bedroom slamming shut.

Dominic thrust a hand through his hair. 'Violet, go and fetch your possessions,' he ordered.

'I didn't want to make no trouble, sir,' she said miserably. 'It were just—I didn't know which way to turn . . .'

'Stop fretting. Go and collect your things from the barracks.'

When she had gone, Catrina said in an expressionless voice, 'People will talk, Dominic.'

'No, they won't. They'll merely think we were lucky enough to acquire a reliable English servant at last. Violet will be known to everyone as Mrs Blake, and without her powder and paint and gaudy clothes, no one will connect her with the girl who used to ply her trade in the house near the Casemates Barracks.'

'You think not? Both Dinah and Alice Ridgeway know who and what Violet is. How else did you suppose Millicent could have recognised her name instantly like that? *They* won't be fooled when they meet Mrs Blake!'

He frowned, and then said fiercely, 'I shall go immediately and make certain that both Dinah and Alice keep their mouths shut. Would you please prepare one of the servants' rooms for Violet in the meantime?'

Catrina stared at him. Why was Dominic so insistent that Violet should stay here?

The answer came to her like a sickening blow to the midriff. He was a man of passionate appetite, as she knew only too well. He must miss the comforting embraces of the mistress whom Millicent had procured for him, and who had fled to the safety of Britain. But Violet—pretty Violet . . .

'I see!' Catrina gave expression to her thoughts with a brittle laugh. 'We all know what Violet once was, and what she could easily be persuaded, through need, to be again! You want your own private whore under your roof, don't you, Dominic? Just as you once . . .'

She stopped. His eyes were narrow silver slits, and his strong face had paled beneath the tan, while his mouth was taut with rage. His hand came up with the speed of sheet lightning, and the next moment her head rocked back as he dealt her a stinging slap across the cheek.

Tears of anger and shock rose to her eyes and rolled down her cheeks. He made a strangled sound and put his arms round her in a gesture of contrition and comfort. All other emotion was instantly blotted out as she clung to him, moulding her body against his, and offering her mouth.

To have done anything else would have been like asking a moth to ignore a naked flame.

CHAPTER TEN

WITH HIS MOUTH a fraction of an inch from Catrina's, Dominic battled for control. God, was there ever a woman who made things so easy for a man, and at the same time so hard! Here she was, eager to abandon all restraint, leaving it to him alone to be strong if he could.

He should not have lost control and slapped her. He ought to have learnt by now to keep all emotion, even that of rage, in check where she was concerned. And now he would, somehow, have to salvage the situation and erect some kind of protective barrier behind which to retreat.

He saw the way in which it might be done, not only to withdraw from this present potentially dangerous situation, but, possibly, to diminish what she felt for him. Christ, why did she have to be *his wife's sister*?

She would never know what it cost him to release her, and take a step away from her, and say with apparent frankness, 'I am sorry I struck you, Catrina. I suppose I was enraged because you had guessed my true motives before I, myself, was even aware of them. I am married to a child-wife who wants to be adored from a distance. So—yes, I dare say it occurred to me that if Violet were agreeable . . .'

'*No!*' The word seemed to have been torn from Catrina.

He made his voice harsh and cold. 'Listen to me! Any relationship I may choose to have with Violet—or with anyone else for that matter—would be my own concern and would have nothing whatever to do with you!' He could not prevent his voice from softening somewhat. 'At least one of my motives for asking Violet to move in here concerned you, Catrina.'

'Don't be a hypocrite!'

'You fool, has it not crossed your mind that in two more months Millicent will give birth to our child? Even when she has recovered from her lying-in, can you imagine her doing more for the infant than feeding it?' He shook his head. 'All the extra work would fall on *your* shoulders. You need help, and Violet can provide it.'

He saw the relief leap into her eyes. She was totally transparent, without artifice or the cultivated façade employed by every other woman he had known. 'So *that* is why you want Violet here!' she exclaimed. 'Not because you . . .'

'Any other reason I may have,' he interrupted with deliberate brutality, 'is entirely my own affair. Go and prepare a room for Violet, and see if you can find uniforms left behind by the other servants which could be made to fit her. I'll be on my way to speak to Alice and Dinah about the matter.'

He left for the Ridgeways' house, and Catrina went to open up and air a room for Violet, her limbs heavy with despair. She remembered reading a novel to Lady Prudence once; it had concerned a young woman who suffered the pangs of unrequited love. *She* had sought solace by wearing a handkerchief belonging to her beloved inside her bodice against her heart, and had finally married a blind man whom she did not love, finding fulfilment in sacrificing her life to him.

Catrina knew that there was nothing so romantic or selfless about her own love for Dominic. It was fierce, and tempestuous, and utterly painful in its frustration. A bitter, scornful little laugh escaped her at the thought of purloining one of his handkerchiefs from the laundry and taking it to bed with her. She wanted *him*: his physical presence, his body twined about hers in what Millicent said was gross bestiality.

She shook her head fiercely as she laid out clean linen for Violet's bed. She would do everything in her power to prevent any relationship forming between the girl and Dominic. It would not surprise her in the least if Violet, too, had realised the implications behind Dominic's offer of sanctuary.

When Violet returned with her parcel of belongings, Catrina said bluntly, 'You once told me that whoring is preferable to skivvying. Well, Violet, if you are to stay here, it will be solely for the purpose of helping with the skivvying.'

'Look, love,' Violet said fervently. 'Right now I'd wear me fingers to the bone, scrubbing and cleaning for the devil hisself, if it meant a roof over me head and at least one meal a day!'

Catrina relaxed slightly. 'You will have to wear a servant's uniform, Violet, and answer to the name Blake, and—and make quite certain that you give my sister no cause for complaint of any kind.'

Violet touched her hand. 'I'll step very careful, love.'

Catrina expelled her breath in a soundless sigh. Violet had understood perfectly. 'I'll be sharing the work fairly with you,' she went on. 'Now, I suggest you put your things away in your room while I prepare a meal for you.'

She had, she told herself, made as certain as she was ever likely to that Violet would not become Dominic's mistress.

Later, she drew up a chair and joined Violet at the kitchen table, marvelling at her resilience. From the weeping, defeated creature she had been a few hours ago, she seemed to have bounced back to a resigned acceptance of fate. All the same, Catrina said,

'I'm very sorry about Eddie leaving you.'

'It ain't the leaving of *me* as I mind so much,' Violet retorted fiercely. 'It's the running off like a cowardly rat to surrender to the Dons!'

'Didn't he do or say anything to warn you of what he had in mind?'

'Oh, he did, right enough,' Violet returned bitterly. 'Only I were too stupid to see it! He says to me, he does, "Why don't them Papist devils answer our fire? What they got up their sleeves? I can't take this much longer, what with the worry, and being stuck on the blasted rock with them enemy ships in the bay, and short rations, and the kids keeping me awake nights, and all." And I just goes, "There, there, we're all in the same boat, love", never dreaming as how he were planning to climb out the boat and leg it to the enemy with me dowry!'

'By the sound of it, it seems that you are well rid of him,' Catrina commented.

Violet tilted her head in a thoughtful attitude. 'Well, he *were* someone of me own while it lasted, ducks,' she said at last. 'Husbands is different to clients, you see. You can be comfortable with a husband. You don't have to pretend all the time, see, or put on an act.'

Catrina was silent, reflecting on what marriage meant to different women. To Millicent, it was a trap which forced her to surrender to 'that dreadful nightmare'. To Violet, it meant someone to call her own and be comfortable with.

A giggle from Violet interrupted her thoughts. 'Speaking of putting on an act—I weren't so far off the mark when I first told you I was an actress! That's what I had to do, see, for me clients. Act, I mean.'

Catrina moved so that her face was in shadow. 'But you never once—found pleasure—with anyone?'

Violet shook her head. 'I always give value for money, mind! I never let on.'

Catrina thought of all the things Millicent had said. 'Did it ever make you feel like—like an animal?'

'Them feelings is for wives. A good thing too, 'cause no whore'd ever earn a crust otherwise!'

Catrina decided to change the subject then, and they discussed how the domestic tasks were to be divided between them. Soon afterwards they retired to bed.

In the morning, when Violet appeared dressed in her neat uniform, with her dark curls tucked discreetly away beneath a starched cap, it would have been difficult to guess at her previous occupation.

Even Lucy, who had shaken off her chill, failed to recognise her, and accepted that she was a new servant called Blake. But she did stare at her with a frown when she first heard Violet's voice.

'I've heard somebody else speak like you,' Lucy stated. 'I can't remember . . .'

'Lots of people speak like Mrs Blake,' Catrina put in swiftly. 'It simply means that she was born in London and grew up there.'

'*You* grew up in London, Aunt Catrina,' Lucy persisted.

'Your aunt's a lady, love,' Violet told her, 'while I ain't. That's where the difference lies, see.'

Catrina had to acknowledge that Violet's help was a blessing, but she found herself watching Dominic obsessively when the so-called new maid was in the room. He treated her with impersonal courtesy, however, and gradually Catrina relaxed. She could not help reflecting on the irony of the situation. Millicent's only concern was with what people would say if they realised Violet's true identity, while the sister-in-law who had no rights suffered the tortures of jealousy and suspicion.

Alice Ridgeway and Dinah called on them a few days later after Violet had been installed. When the 'maid' carried in a weak brew of their precious tea, Alice waited until she had withdrawn again and then said lightly, 'I'm glad, Catrina, that a reliable servant has at last been found to help you with the work.'

Whatever Alice really felt about the situation, Catrina had the strangest impression that Dinah secretly envied her her own friendship with a former whore, in spite of her barbed remarks in the past. *Dinah*, Catrina suspected, would not have sought to disguise the true facts. She would have taken a dramatic stand, and presented her case in a brave, defiant and girlishly passionate manner to the world.

'I don't know or care what the precise nature of her former profession might have been,' Catrina could almost hear her say. 'She has been good to me, and I shall stand by her!'

And all the men in the garrison would have applauded her courage and her loyalty, while the women would have seen through her, and yet been forced to remain silent for fear of being thought petty and vindictive.

Violet had her own opinions on both Alice and Dinah, and she voiced them to Catrina with her usual frankness.

'The one's sad and the other's frightened,' she said.

'Yes, well, Mrs Ridgeway's mother did quarrel with her, and pretended afterwards that she had never existed. I suppose that would have left its mark of sadness.'

'She's the one that's frightened,' Violet corrected.

Catrina stared at her. 'Nonsense! Alice Ridgeway is an army wife; it would take more than a state of siege and the never-ending sound of bombardment to frighten her!'

'Then it's something else as is frightening her. And why does she wear them ugly eye-glasses when she don't need them?'

Catrina frowned. Alice had, for some time now, taken to

wearing pince-nez, but even though it was true that she seemed to peer over the top of them most of the time, presumably she did need them, for she would not otherwise have worn such an unattractive device.

Catrina shrugged the subject of the eye-glasses aside as an irrelevance, and said, 'I don't agree with you. And as for Dinah Forest being *sad* . . .'

'I didn't mean tragic-sad. Pathetic-sad, that's what she is. She wants time to stand still. She don't want to grow old or lose her looks. She don't want life to be boring and everyday and dull. She wants to play-act and be queen of the dung-heap.'

There was a certain truth to that statement, but there was one obvious thing about Dinah which Violet appeared to have missed. 'She's in love with Captain Ross,' Catrina told her.

Violet snorted. 'Depends what you mean by love! He's the best-looking man around, so she wants him. And making up to a married man is exciting, like playing with fire. That's all.'

Catrina thought it advisable to talk about something else. 'Violet, you've never spoken about your family, except your parents. Have you brothers and sisters?'

'Two brothers; six sisters; all of 'em respectable, and poor as church mice with it,' Violet said drily. 'Me brothers share a costermonger's barrow; me sisters works as crossing-sweepers or in slop-shops, and one's a laundress.'

Catrina hesitated. 'What made *you* decide to . . .?'

'Well, now, love, I'm the eldest, see, so right from a nipper I has to share the one bedroom with Ma and Pa. And every night I has to listen to his grunting and groaning and panting, and Ma begging him to leave off, just for the once. As I watches her getting old afore her years, with a new baby every eleven months regular as clockwork, I says to myself—Vi, girl, any man as wants to put you through that night after night is gonna pay for the privilege, and not take it as his right!'

Catrina decided once again that the subject had best be changed. 'Violet, what are we to do about tonight's dinner? We have plenty of flour, but apart from the breakfast oatmeal, there is only a small amount of butter and some sugar left from Captain Ross's rations.'

'We should make sweet dumplings,' Violet suggested as she poured hot water from the cauldron on the fire into the tub to start on the laundry.

'Rather a stodgy meal!' Catrina racked her brains. This was the most trying period of all, being almost the end of the month, and just before the officers' rations were issued.

The last of the money she had brought with her from England was now exhausted, and Dominic was in a dilemma similar to her own. His private means, too, were deposited in a bank in England, and with no British ships able to slip through the blockade, it had been impossible for either of them to draw on their resources.

'I've just remembered!' Catrina exclaimed. 'I have some tea left!'

'Dratted fire needs stoking again,' Violet observed abstractedly, and made for the outside shed. At the door she paused. 'Tea would make the dumplings go down better.'

'I didn't mean that,' Catrina explained, when Violet returned. 'I'll take the tea, and sell it to one of the traders, or otherwise barter it for a piece of salt pork. Will you look after Lucy for me? Although I'll probably be back before she wakes from her afternoon nap.'

'A bit of salt pork'd be just another headache, love,' Violet said grimly, ' 'cause we couldn't cook it. We ain't hardly got no fuel left. It woulda lasted out till the month's end, but as you know, your sister has been wanting a fire in her room nights. There'll be just enough left for boiling dumplings, but the Lord knows how the breakfast porridge can be cooked in the morning.'

Catrina sighed. 'There's only one thing for it. I'll have to go down to the harbour and look for driftwood.'

'Seems like it. I'd go with you, but I'd best do all the washing I can while the hot water lasts.'

'One of us has to stay at home in any case to keep an eye on Lucy when she wakes. Violet, do you think I could borrow one of those holland gowns of yours? Collecting driftwood is bound to be a dirty business, and holland is too tough to be spoilt.'

'Help yourself, love. You'll find them in me room.'

The brown holland gown was too tight and too short for Catrina, but that could not be helped. She took a sack with her and set out for the harbour. No one paid attention to her as she began to scavenge for driftwood, and many others were engaged upon the same task. Her gown became increasingly wetter as she filled her sack, and her hair was coming down. She pushed it impatiently away from her face, aware that she was probably leaving a trail of dirt along her cheek.

Her sack was full, and she had begun to drag it away from the harbour when she became aware that a crowd had gathered and were excitedly staring to sea. She joined them, and followed their gaze.

A cutter was approaching the Bay, flying the British colours. The Spanish put out to sea with two ships of the line, a frigate and some galleys to intercept it. In an outrageously impudent move, the captain of the cutter lured the Spanish ships towards the Barbary coast, and then sailed across the bows of the enemy vessels and slipped neatly between them. Shots were fired but missed their target, and in a short while a tremendous cheer went up from the watching crowd as the cutter anchored safely in the harbour.

Catrina watched as the captain of the cutter stepped ashore. He was not in the least what she would have expected, for he would have looked far more at home in an elegant London drawing-room than on the high seas.

She judged his age to be about thirty, and he was quite magnificently dressed in a coat embroidered in gold and silver, with jewelled buckles on his shoes. He swept off his hat and acknowledged the applause of the crowd with a bow.

He wore no wig, which would have been surprising in so fashionable a gentleman were it not for the fact that his own hair was far more impressive than any wig would have been. It was tawny gold, the colour of a lion's mane, and arranged in carefully disordered locks which suggested that one of his crew doubled as a skilful valet. As he straightened and faced the crowd, Catrina saw that his eyes were blue and his features so regular that they would have been the envy of any woman.

He began to supervise the unloading of the vessel, which she noted was named *Arabella.* He did not take part in the work but stood fastidiously to one side, calling out commands to his crew as they brought the cargo ashore. When everything had been unloaded from the cutter, one of the crew began to auction the cargo, while the captain stood watchfully by.

A crowd of merchants, as well as servants of the more affluent officers, started the bidding, and Catrina drew a sharp breath as she listened to the prices being paid. She could not help looking enviously at such luxuries as cabbages, potatoes, oranges and cheese. What irony, that her own fortune was lying in the bank in London, so far out of her reach that she was unable to purchase as much as a cabbage!

The captain of the privateer noticed her, and moved towards her, grinning. He was missing nothing—from the wet holland gown that clung closely to her curves, to her hair which was tumbling untidily to her shoulders.

'Down on your luck, aren't you,' he observed.

'Like many, I am temporarily embarrassed,' she returned stiffly.

His eyebrows rose in amusement at what he obviously assumed to be false pride. 'Well,' he drawled, 'I am willing to cover your—ah—temporary embarrassment by offering you food and shelter. You are a pretty little thing, or would be when cleaned up and parted from that hideous gown. So, shall we shake hands on it?'

He extended his own, and she flushed as she realised the precise nature of the offer he had been making her. She turned away, dragging her sackful of driftwood behind her.

She had not gone far when he caught up with her, and took hold of her shoulder. 'Here, accept this with my compliments, and think over what I have said. I shall be putting up at the Queen's Head for the next day or so, and I shall expect a visit from you soon.'

He held out a small linen bag containing flour. If he had offered her a cabbage, she might have reacted differently. But the bribe of a small supply of flour, when flour was the one commodity they had no need of, increased her outrage, and she took it, flinging it at his head.

'If I ever acquire anything from you,' she said bitingly, 'I shall pay for it!'

He stood utterly still, covered from his magnificent hair to his richly-embroidered coat in his own flour. Catrina suddenly became aware that the crowd surrounding them had turned menacing. The man was obviously regarded by them as a hero, not only because he had slipped through the enemy ships but also because he had brought in much-needed supplies, even if they had been sold at vastly inflated prices. Their attitude made it quite plain that they were ready to avenge the insult she had offered him.

The man released the tension by uttering a laugh. 'You'd best know my name if you intend becoming a customer!' He swept her an exaggerated bow. 'I am Jake Farraday, at your service!'

CHAPTER ELEVEN

As SHE TOOK HOLD of her sack and dragged the driftwood home, Catrina wondered what would have happened if Jake Farraday had not decided to laugh off her rash action. He was obviously a vain man, and could not have taken kindly to being made to look ridiculous in public, and she had been lucky to escape from the scene unscathed.

When she had stacked the driftwood in the shed, and had washed and changed, she discovered that Dominic had come home early, and had brought Surgeon-Major Peters with him.

Catrina had met the physician, a fresh-faced middle-aged officer, on several occasions, and as she entered the morning-room she heard him say to Millicent, 'My dear Mrs Ross, you must cease taking laudanum altogether. Indeed, I want you to hand over your supplies to me.'

Catrina was glad that Dominic had taken the step of bringing Peters himself to speak to Millicent about the matter. But she realised its futility when Millicent said flatly,

'I *have* no supplies left.'

Catrina could see that the men believed her as little as she herself did, and that all three of them guessed Millicent's supply of laudanum had been well hidden. Dominic shrugged resignedly, and offered the physician a glass of wine. Catrina hoped the latter was not anticipating being invited to dinner, and decided to make the position clear in case that was what he had in mind. She said lightly,

'I am afraid we are reduced to sweet dumplings for dinner tonight, flavoured with a sprinkling of nutmeg. Tomorrow I'll see what I may contrive. A cutter named *Arabella* out-manoeuvred the Spanish fleet and slipped into harbour, and goods are available—at a price.'

'I can guess at the price Jake Farraday would put on his cargo!' Dominic returned grimly.

'You know him?'

'Everyone knows *of* him, Miss Beaumont,' Peters answered her. 'But no one would receive him, or claim friendship with him. He is an unscrupulous rogue and a profiteer.'

'A brave rogue, however,' Catrina commented, 'to have cocked a snook at the Spanish like that.'

Dominic's jaw-line hardened. 'He may be brave, but he is also devious and corrupt. And he would take any risk in pursuit of profit.'

'He really is beyond the pale,' Surgeon-Major Peters confirmed. 'He was once a naval officer, Miss Beaumont, but he was forced to resign his commission after a scandal.'

'What kind of scandal?' asked Catrina.

'There were rumours about several different matters. One concerned a sixteen-year-old girl, and another involved the suicide of a foolish young nobleman who was said to have lost a great deal of money to him. Nothing was ever proved, but it all added to the cloud he was under, and when he was caught cheating at cards, that put the seal on things. Somehow—no doubt by other dubious means—he acquired *Arabella* and embarked on a new career as a privateer.'

Surgeon-Major Peters finished his wine and stood up. He had clearly taken the hint about dinner. 'I must get back to the mess. I'll see myself out. Remember what I said about the laudanum, Mrs Ross!'

'I am tired of being treated like a child who tells lies!' Millicent erupted even before he was out of earshot. Catrina feared that she would work herself up into a fit of hysteria, and deliberately returned to the neutral subject of Jake Farraday.

'Apart from cheating at cards,' she argued, 'nothing has been proved against the man. Since he risks his life to land supplies, he cannot be altogether bad.'

Dominic gave her a long, level look. 'You seem very interested in Farraday. And there is nothing altruistic about what he does. He exploits the desperate needs of others.'

'Oh, but surely he could have chosen a less dangerous way of exploiting others?'

'He was limited to what he knows best—seamanship. After he was caught cheating at cards, all the gambling saloons were closed to him, and he needed some way of paying for his expensive tastes. Because he was never court-martialled or dismissed the service, he was able to obtain letters of marque.'

'What does that mean?'

'It means a commission from the government, authorising him to use *Arabella* as an armed vessel against hostile nations. But he employs those arms only in defence of his cargo, and therefore his profits!'

'Nevertheless,' Catrina said, 'I must confess that I found him—well, intriguing. I also think he could prove useful . . .'

Dominic's head jerked up and his dark brows drew together. 'You have met the man?'

'We had a—confrontation—at the harbour. It has occurred to me, Dominic, that he might be commissioned to sail for England and bring back a letter of credit for me from my bankers.'

'You are to have nothing whatever to do with him!' Dominic ordered sharply.

His high-handedness angered her. 'I don't see what harm . . .'

'You are an heiress, Catrina, and as soon as Farraday found that out, his predatory interest in you would be aroused. Keep away from him!'

She hid her growing anger behind a smile. 'Now I know that you are misjudging him! He believed me to be destitute, but that did not prevent him from showing an interest in me—predatory or otherwise!'

Dominic's jaw hardened, but before he could respond, Millicent contributed a spiteful barb. 'From all accounts, Catrina, it sounds as if you and Jake Farraday would deal very well together!'

At that moment Violet entered to announce that the sweet dumplings were ready, and Catrina rose to set the table for dinner. The subject of Jake Farraday was dropped, as Lucy joined them for the meal. They had just finished eating when the front-door knocker banged, and a moment later Violet entered the room.

'That hoity-toity butler, Hobson, brung you a note, sir,' she addressed Dominic, holding the sealed sheet of paper out to him.

Millicent uttered an exasperated sigh. 'You are supposed to carry it in on a silver tray, Blake!'

Violet winked surreptitiously at Catrina, and replied in a cheerful voice, 'Seems a lot of unnecessary malarky to me, ma'am. Me hands are clean.'

Dominic had broken the seal on the note, and had read it. 'It's from Dinah,' he announced. 'She is still anxious about possible looters getting inside her house. She wishes me to join her this evening and help her to check that everything has been made secure.'

'You can hardly refuse,' Millicent said without much interest.

'No.' He rose, and went to the bureau, dipping a quill into the container of ink before he wrote a reply. Cheerfully ignoring Millicent's orders about conveying it on a tray, Violet carried it in her hand to give it to the waiting Hobson.

Why, Catrina wondered sourly, had Dinah not asked her cousin, John Ridgeway, to check on the security of her house with her? This was surely another of Dinah's ploys to be alone with Dominic, but Millicent did not care enough to give the matter deep thought, while he . . .

A bitter conviction snaked into her mind. Dominic knew perfectly well why Dinah wished him to spend the evening alone with her in an empty house, and he was more than willing to do so. Perhaps the assignation had even been pre-arranged by the two of them, and that note of Dinah's had merely been for Millicent's benefit. Anger mixed with pain warred inside her. If she had been his wife, she would have been able to give vent to her feelings and so gained some relief. But, as he was forever reminding her, she was no more than his sister-in-law, with no rights to feelings of jealousy. That did not stop *him*, however, from dictating to her whom she might or might not consort with.

Catrina did her chores mechanically, helping Violet with the washing of the dinner dishes, and then putting Lucy to bed. As she worked, her rebellious rage and jealousy deepened. Dominic had already left to join Dinah, and she faced the prospect of wondering what was going on between them, and of waiting in helpless frustration and suspicion for him to return.

No, she would not! She reached the decision suddenly.

She would pay Dominic back by defying him. She would call on Jake Farraday at the Queen's Head.

Commissioning the man to bring back a letter of credit for her had been no more than a random thought to begin with. But Dominic's high-handed opposition, and now his assignation with Dinah, stiffened her resolve. It was ridiculous that she should have all that money lying idle in England and yet be unable to purchase so much as a cabbage! A letter of credit was clearly the answer, and Jake Farraday, so adept at slipping through the blockade, was the very man to deliver it to her.

She dressed carefully, choosing an aquamarine gown of silk brocade which she wore over an underskirt caught up and looped at intervals with clusters of pale-pink silk rosebuds. She smiled maliciously to herself, picturing Farraday's expression when he realised his mistake in taking her for a destitute waif who could be bought with a bag of flour.

With her hair dressed high on her head, and a few artless ringlets allowed to fall to her shoulders, she looked in at the sleeping Lucy before she let herself out of the house, intending to hail a gharry.

Then the thought suddenly struck her—What was the point in defying Dominic when he did not know that she was doing so? She nodded grimly to herself. She would go, first of all, to Dinah's house. She would tell Dominic that she was about to call on Jake Farraday whether he approved or not. He would be unable to stop her, and he could scarcely abandon Dinah and insist on accompanying her himself. It did not take long to reach Dinah's house. The night air was lit up, as usual, by the flames of the continual bombardment which the British aimed at the Spanish lines, but both sight and sounds had become so familiar that they barely registered in her consciousness.

The front door of Dinah's house had been reinforced with a grilled wrought-iron gate, Catrina found, and the windows had been protected with criss-cross bars of iron set in on the inside of the house. The place had been turned into a fortress and clearly did not warrant any security inspection. And yet a flickering light was moving behind one of the windows.

Her mouth set and determined, Catrina reached through the wrought-iron gate and banged the knocker on the front door. A moment later it was opened by Dominic, holding a branch of candles. He stared at her through the lacy pattern of the wrought iron.

'I don't want to disturb you and Dinah,' Catrina said sweetly. 'I simply broke my journey to tell you that I have decided, upon reflection, to commission Jake Farraday to sail to England on my behalf. I am on my way to speak to him now.'

She broke off as he made a guttural sound in his throat. The next moment the gate was jerked aside, and his hand fastened on her arm, pulling her inside the house.

'I told you to keep away from Farraday!' he said through his teeth.

'You have no right to dictate to me, Dominic! I am of age. And had you not better return to Dinah?'

'Be quiet!' he rasped. 'Dinah is not here.'

'Oh . . .' The word escaped her in a deflated sound.

'I could see no point in both of us examining the house, and so I insisted that she remained with the Ridgeways while I came to do so on my own.'

That, Catrina thought, must have displeased Dinah mightily. Dominic's hand was still clamped like a vice around her arm, and now he was drawing her inexorably inside the house. 'I have one more bedroom window to examine. You are not leaving my sight, Catrina. When I have done here, I shall take you home, and you will have nothing to do with Jake Farraday! Is that clear?'

She merely nodded, her rebellion fading. It was beginning to seem to her that Dominic was as needlessly jealous of her interest in Jake Farraday as she herself was of Dinah.

She watched as Dominic set the candle down so that he could test the effectiveness of the iron bars across the window. He grunted, and said, half to himself, 'Dinah was right to be concerned. There is one which is loose, and which could be prised away with some time and patience. I shall have to . . .'

His voice was lost in the sound of a tremendous blast, and just before the candles went out, Catrina stared in shock as the walls of the room began to move and bulge as if they were alive.

The next moment Dominic had thrown himself bodily at her, bringing her down with him on the floor. They had time only to wriggle underneath the bed before masonry crashed round them and its vibration struck the bed. Catrina sensed that the same thought was in both their minds. Would the bed be strong enough to withstand the falling rubble, or would they be crushed underneath it? At last the noise diminished, and settled down to a sporadic tinkling of glass and the sound of loose rubble sliding from the pile.

Catrina broke the silence between herself and Dominic. 'Are—Are we being fired on by the enemy?'

'I don't think so. It's more likely that someone on our side misjudged his range to a disastrous degree. Indeed, spirits are so low and discipline so difficult to enforce that I'm surprised it has not happened before.'

'We—We could have been killed!'

'Yes.'

The knowledge that they had been so close to death, and that they had escaped it, brought a sudden euphoric elation to Catrina. She raised herself slightly and found Dominic's mouth, and with a muttered sound he pulled her against him. The forces released inside her by his kiss, by his hands upon her body, were in their own way as violent as the blast which had ripped through the house. They clung together, locked in a need and a desire which they knew could never be satisfied.

He lifted his mouth from hers. 'Catrina—no! For the love of God, one of us has to be strong. *Don't always leave it to me to be that one!*'

'It won't go away, Dominic,' she whispered. 'This feeling won't go away . . .'

'Then you must fight it!'

She gave a long, tremulous sigh. 'I'm tired of fighting. We both came close to death. For all we know, we are doomed to be buried alive, with no one searching for us until it is too late. People have become used to the noise of blasting; they won't be aware that this house has been hit. So why not take what we can, while we can?'

He kissed her fiercely, and she sensed the mingled anger and passion churning inside him. 'You delude yourself.

Dinah and the Ridgeways know that I am in the house, and in the morning a rescue party will start digging us out.' He muttered an oath. 'And you, Catrina, must not be found with me! What excuse could we offer? No one would believe that we had not . . .'

She twined her arms about his neck, bringing his mouth close to hers again. 'Since they will believe it in any case, why *should* we not . . .'

'Sweet Jesus, I've never known a woman like you!' he exploded, desperation in his voice. 'Anyone else would have been hysterical in the circumstances; *you* offer me temptation instead!'

He put her away from him quite roughly, and she could hear him wriggling out from underneath the bed. Then he cursed as he obviously bumped into some débris. Cautiously, she, too, slid out from beneath the bed. In the moonlight through the broken window, she could see the devastation all around them. The doorway had disappeared behind fallen masonry, and she coughed as its dust entered her lungs.

'Get back underneath the bed!' Dominic commanded. 'I am going to try and dig through the débris to reach the window, and it will be dangerous.'

'Dominic, even if you reached the window, you would still have the iron bars blocking our escape!'

'One of the bars is loose, remember. If I could prise that from its setting, it might loosen the next one too, and then there might be enough space for you to wriggle through. It would be pointless to try and clear the door, since we don't know what kind of condition the rest of the house might be in. Now, get back underneath the shelter of the bed!'

She obeyed, knowing that he was not in a mood to be deflected from his course of action. She could hear him throwing lumps of masonry across the room as he cleared a path, grunting and cursing as he did so. Suddenly she heard him cease his efforts, and become still. Voices reached her from outside; the excited voices of Genoese servants returning to their homes after the completion of their duties. She wondered why Dominic did not try to seek help from those people who were inspecting the damage done to the house, and then she understood. He did not wish anyone to know that they were trapped inside, for then it would inevitably become publicly known that the two of them had been together when the disaster struck.

After a while she could hear the spectators moving on, their voices receding, and Dominic began to work on clearing a way to the window once more. Catrina, in spite of everything, felt herself dozing off in her uncomfortable position underneath the bed.

She was jolted to full wakefulness by a sound of triumph from Dominic. Then he was calling her to come out and join him. The bright moonlight streaming into the room showed her that he had cleared a channel to the window, and she followed it. The reason for his triumph became plain. The blast had ripped two of the iron bars from the window, leaving a gap.

'You'll be able to squeeze through that,' he said, removing the last of the jagged pieces of glass from the shattered window.

She eyed the gap, absently noting that it must be well after midnight, for the mortar blasting had stopped and the town was now quiet.

'I'll not get through that space!' Catrina objected.

'Yes, you will. You are small and slight enough. *I* could not get through it, but with my help you could wriggle your way to the outside.'

She shook her head. 'The panniers on my gown are padded, and they would get stuck in the gap. And—And my stays push my bosom upwards and keep it rigid, so that I would not have the flexibility to squeeze through . . .'

'Then take off your clothes,' Dominic ordered. 'I shall hand them to you after you have reached the outside.'

She hesitated for a moment, and then began to obey. As the bundle of clothing at her feet grew, she looked up, and in the moonlight she saw the desire flaring in his eyes.

She took a step towards him. He stood with his arms rigidly at his sides but as she pressed herself against him, he uttered a groan and slid his hands over the silky softness of her skin. Then he was on his knees, his hands moulding her breasts and his mouth everywhere, so that small explosions tore through her. She buried her hands in his hair and sank to her knees too, taking his face between her palms and offering him her parted lips.

A long shudder shook him as they clung together. Then he rose, pulling her to her feet. 'Damn you, damn you, damn you!' he said in a desperate monotone. 'Why did you have to come here tonight?'

She was about to tell him that she was glad she had come, that Fate must surely have ordained it, but the next moment he grabbed hold of her with something resembling frenzy and lifted her in his arms. Then he was pushing her through the gap in the iron railings, without any pretence at gentleness, in a way which made it clear that nothing mattered to him in that moment other than to rid himself of her physical presence.

She landed feet first among a pile of rubble, and he pushed her clothes out to her.

'Get dressed,' she heard his hoarse command. 'Go home, and try not to be seen.'

'Shall I—Shall I not try to summon help for you?'

'*No!* You must appear to have no knowledge of what happened! When it grows light, I shall attract someone's attention. Now go home—and hurry!'

As she walked swiftly along the quiet, deserted street a few minutes later, her body still aching with unfulfilled longing and pulsating in response to his kisses, the memory came to her of something Dominic had said.

'I have never known a woman like you . . .'

If she had needed further evidence that she was not made like other women, he had provided it for her tonight.

The destruction of Dinah's house and the fact that Dominic had had to be dug out from the rubble became the main topic of conversation the following day, and served to relieve the monotony of the siege and of the constant sound of bombardment. General Ridgeway had relieved Dominic of all duties for the day once he had been rescued, and had told him to go home and seek his bed. But after only a few hours' sleep he rose, and was in the morning-room with Millicent and Lucy when Catrina answered the front door to Dinah's knock.

Ignoring everyone else, Dinah launched herself at Dominic, clinging to him and sobbing. 'Oh, my dear, I am so sorry for what has happened! And my poor, poor house . . .'

'The army will compensate you for your losses,' he reassured her.

'You saved my life!' she declared dramatically. 'Some sixth sense must have warned you of what was to happen, and that was why you insisted on examining my house on your own!'

'I woke in the night,' Lucy announced suddenly, 'and Aunt Catrina was not there.'

Catrina felt a deep flush mounting her cheeks, and she hid it from the others by kneeling and burying her face in the child's hair. 'I—was unable to sleep, Lucy, and so I came to the morning-room to read.'

'Your wakeful night has certainly left its mark!' she heard Millicent's spiteful comment. 'You are looking quite haggard.'

Catrina rose and turned away. 'If you will excuse me, I must see what I may contrive for tonight's dinner if we are not to have sweet dumplings again.'

She salvaged the remainder of her precious supply of tea and slipped into the kitchen. 'I'm going to see if I can barter the tea for some meat or fish, Violet.'

'The best of luck, dear! I won't make up the kitchen fire till you gets back, to save on the fuel.'

Catrina left the house and began to make for the harbour, where traders had set up their stalls. Her tea procured her only a scrawny rabbit. She could not help looking about for Jake Farraday, but there was no sign of him, although *Arabella* was bobbing at her moorings. She returned to the house with the rabbit, and set about making pastry for a pie, while Violet skinned and cleaned the animal. Millicent, Catrina learnt, was lying down, while Dominic had taken Lucy out for a walk.

That evening Millicent prodded her dinner distastefully with her fork. 'If you had asked me, Catrina, I would have told you that I cannot eat rabbit.'

Catrina suppressed a sigh. Her sister, she felt certain, was deliberately being difficult and had probably been indulging in hoarded sweetmeats again. 'I'm afraid rabbit was all I could get.'

Millicent pushed her plate away. 'Well, I shall just have

to go without dinner.'

'Millicent,' Dominic said with weary patience, 'if this seige continues unbroken we shall all be forced to eat far worse things than rabbit. Try to overcome your prejudice.'

'No. I shall retire for the night, just as soon as Violet has had time to make up the fire in my room.'

Catrina bit her lip. 'Could you not do without a fire?'

'Am I to be denied a fire, as well as doing without dinner?' Tears of self-pity rose to Millicent's eyes.

'We have no firewood left,' Catrina explained. 'We are burning driftwood, and when that is finished, I shall have to go and collect more from the harbour.'

'No one asked you to come to Gibraltar in the first place, Catrina, and if you now resent having to share our hardship . . .'

'Be quiet, Millicent,' Dominic commanded with the air of a man close to the end of his tether.

'No, I shall not be quiet! This is *my* house! It came to us from *my* parents, and if I want to have a fire in every room, I shall have them!'

Dominic scraped his chair back. Catrina drew her breath in sharply as she saw the expression with which he was regarding his wife. It held repugnance and revulsion and something very like loathing. Without offering an excuse, he left the room, and a short while later he could be heard slamming out of the house.

Violet entered to clear away the plates, and Millicent said with emphasis, 'Leave that and go and make up a good fire in my room, Blake.'

Catrina lifted Lucy from her chair and took her to their room to prepare her for bed. The child must have understood a good deal of that scene during dinner, for she seemed subdued.

She knelt down in her nightgown to say her prayers. 'Please God, bless Papa and Mama and Aunt Catrina and Blake. Please let me have a puppy, and forgive me for not being a boy. Amen.'

Catrina tucked her into bed, and said quietly, 'Why did you ask God to forgive you for not being a boy?'

The child stared at her over the edge of the bedcovers. 'Mama was crying this morning, and when I asked her if she had a pain, she pushed me away and said, "May God forgive you for not being a boy." So I thought I should ask Him, 'cause I don't want to be cast into 'ternal darkness.'

Catrina's mouth set grimly. 'You have nothing to ask forgiveness for. God *meant* you to be a beautiful little girl! Now go to sleep, Lucy, and don't worry about being cast into eternal darkness.'

She kissed the child, and left the night-light burning as she let herself out of the room. In the kitchen, Violet was washing dishes, and Catrina picked up a cloth to dry them.

'Me and you,' Violet said resignedly, 'will have to trot backwards and forwards to the harbour for driftwood tomorrow. Your sister made a big fuss tonight over her fire. She wouldn't have it no other way than I should stack a heap of wood on the hearth so's she could stoke the fire later if need be, even though she saw to it that I had a roaring furnace going. It ain't possible for her to need that much wood during the night, but she said it was to stay there.'

Catrina said nothing. Millicent, she thought, must be very unhappy to be so spiteful. It was only because she knew that her sister had been forced to scavenge for the wood that she was insisting on using it with such profligacy.

Catrina and Violet retired to bed too as soon as their work in the kitchen was done. Both were exhausted: Violet after the exertions of the day, and Catrina because of the sleep she had missed the previous night. She sank into oblivion almost as soon as she had crept into bed beside Lucy.

She was awakened by a hand shaking her shoulder. 'Love,' Violet's urgent voice reached her through the drowsy mists of her mind. 'Get up, quick!'

'What's wrong? What time is it, Violet?'

'Close on midnight. Come on, ducks, up with you! Something's caught light in your sister's room, and she's locked the door!'

Catrina was wide awake now, but alarm made her stupid and slow as she pulled on a wrap. 'Dominic—where is he?'

'He ain't home yet. Hurry, now!'

There was a pungent smell of burning coming from Millicent's room. Catrina tried the door, but as Violet had said, it was locked. She ran into Dominic's deserted bedroom and tried the communicating door but that, too, was locked from the other side.

Catrina hurried back to Violet, and together they hammered on Millicent's door.

Breathlessly, Violet said, 'I think what happened was, a piece of burning wood fell out the fireplace and set light to the pile on the hearth. Why don't your sister wake up?'

'Oh God . . .' Catrina clapped her hand to her forehead. 'I suppose she must have taken laudanum again! The doctor came and told her it would harm the baby, but I suspected she'd hoarded some. *Millicent, wake up!*'

But the only sound they could hear, above the crackling of burning wood and other materials, were stertorous snores coming from the room.

'Violet,' Catrina said urgently, 'come with me, and hold the candles. The window is barred. I'll have to search in the shed for an axe to break down the door.'

They hurried outside, but a fierce wind was blowing, and the candles went out. Stumbling and tripping several times in the dark, they reached the shed and groped for an axe or anything else which might have been used for smashing Millicent's door.

By the time they had found an axe and had hurried back inside, smoke was curling underneath Millicent's door and a fierce crackling came from inside. They could hear the sound of glass exploding.

As Catrina lifted up the axe, Lucy came stumbling into the corridor, barefoot and crying. 'What—What's happening, Aunt Catrina? I heard noises, and I was frightened . . .'

Amid the chaos in her mind, a voice of common sense told Catrina that the child should be removed from the house. 'Wrap Lucy in a blanket,' she told Violet, 'and take her to the Ridgeways'.'

Violet nodded. 'I'll raise the alarm on the way, and send help. But, love, don't hope for nothing. I reckon the smoke will have done for your poor sister by now.'

'No!' In a frenzy, Catrina began to attack the door with the axe, only half aware that Violet had hurried Lucy away. The door was solid, and her efforts with the axe seemed to make no impression upon it. The heat from inside the room

was so intense by now that the paint on the door was blistering, and choking smoke curled into the corridor from beneath it.

Suddenly there were noises other than the sound of the battering. Dominic, his face gaunt and stricken, grabbed the axe from Catrina's grasp and began to attack the door. General Ridgeway was there too, saying urgently,

'Dominic, we must wait for reinforcements and an adequate supply of water! If you break down the door, the fire will rage out of control!'

Dominic seemed not to have heard him. Catrina felt totally unreal, as if she were caught up in a grotesque dream. She had no sense of personal danger, and she ignored General Ridgeway when he said, 'Get out, my dear! Quickly!'

The house seemed to be filled with people: soldiers and Genoese men who ran along the corridor with wet sacks, coughing as the smoke entered their lungs. The Ridgeways' butler was also there, carrying pails of water. Catrina heard a crash as the door finally succumbed to the onslaught, and the next moment a huge tongue of flame mixed with black smoke leapt out into the corridor. General Ridgeway shouted a command to the soldiers, and several of them ran to restrain Dominic. The struggling men were etched against a background of leaping flames.

'Catrina, get out of here!' General Ridgeway bellowed.

Horror filled her mind completely. She blundered along the smoke-shrouded corridor, and found herself standing in her bedroom. She was aware of holding something in her hands but was quite unaware of what it was or how she came to be holding it. Then a soldier appeared and grabbed her arm, forcing her through the smoke and the heat and the noise until she found herself breathing in the night air.

A crowd of onlookers stood outside, and some of them spoke to her, but their remarks did not penetrate the frozen horror of her mind. She moved like a sleep-walker through the darkened streets, the soldier still gripping her arm.

Lights were flickering through the windows of one house, and Catrina registered the fact that it was the Ridgeway house, and that she was being led to its front door. Then it opened and Alice was there, drawing her inside the house.

'Let's go into the kitchen,' Alice said. 'It's warm in there; Violet has been making up the stove.'

'Lucy . . .' Catrina muttered.

'I've put her to bed.'

Catrina looked down at the tissue-wrapped package in her hands, the thing that her fragmented mind had compelled her to rescue before she would allow herself to be driven from the burning house.

It was the length of pale-blue watered silk she had brought from England as a present for Millicent.

'Dominic spent the evening here,' she heard Alice say. 'He was just preparing to leave when Violet arrived with Lucy.'

Numbly, Catrina entered the kitchen in her wake. Violet was busy at the stove, but she left what she was doing and came to Catrina, folding her in an embrace. 'Your sister can't have suffered, love,' she murmured.

A long shudder tore through Catrina. She moved away from Violet and looked down at the parcel of watered silk still clutched in her hand. *Millicent was dead.*

She had died because spite had prompted her to order that the driftwood so laboriously harvested should be piled up in her grate. She had died because she had locked both the entrances to her room. She had locked them from long habit, to keep out the husband whose attentions filled her with such revulsion. She had died because her obsessive fear that her second baby might also be a girl had driven her to seek oblivion in laudanum. She had died like the spoilt, selfish, frightened child Dominic had said she was. But even though Catrina's mind acknowledged all this, she still felt racked by a sense that she had failed her sister.

Violet poured hot water into a bowl so that Catrina could wash off the soot with which she was grimed, and Alice excused herself and went out of the room. She returned with a bundle of clothing.

'There is a gown and undergarments for each of you,' she explained. 'They probably won't fit, but they'll do for the moment.'

They changed there in the kitchen, and afterwards sat down at the table to drink hot water faintly flavoured with chocolate and sweetened with sugar. Catrina tried to rouse herself from the burden of guilt and grief which threatened to crush her.

'Where is Dinah?'

'Asleep,' Alice answered. 'She went to bed just before Violet arrived with Lucy, and I thought it best not to awaken her.'

Dawn had begun to streak the sky, heralding the end of that terrible, disastrous night. A short while later, Dominic and General Ridgeway and Hobson arrived at the house, all three rimed with smoke and soot. Dominic looked gaunt and haggard, his eyes blank and fixed in an unfocusing look.

'We could do nothing to save the house,' General Ridgeway said heavily. 'I ordered the men to salvage clothes and bedding and food supplies and anything else they could. They hurled the stuff clear of the fire, but when they went to collect them afterwards, they discovered they had been taken. Looted by the onlookers, damn their souls!'

He glanced at Dominic, who had slumped into a chair and was staring fixedly ahead of him. General Ridgeway lowered his voice. 'I have ordered that a watch should be kept over the ruins; when they have cooled sufficiently they will be searched for . . .' He stopped.

. . .for the remains of Millicent and her dead, unborn baby. The unfinished sentence hung in the air and beat through Catrina's brain.

Alice rose and went to Dominic, placing her hand on his shoulder in mute sympathy. He looked at her as if she were a complete stranger whom he had never seen before.

She sighed. 'I think you men should get cleaned up. Hobson, get some rest afterwards. I shall wake Cook and ask her to prepare breakfast, and then I must contrive to find rooms for everyone.'

'Not for me, ma'am,' Violet interrupted with quiet dignity. 'There ain't no place for me here, and I knows it. By all accounts, you've enough servants and old retainers cluttering up the house as it is. And leaving everything else aside, there's no call for you to have to stretch rations to feed one more mouth than needs be. I'll make out; I always do.'

Dinah came stumbling into the room at that moment,

looking tousled and sleepy and wrapped in a feather-trimmed robe. 'What on earth is going on? Why is everyone in the kitchen? I heard voices . . .'

Alice told her briefly what had happened. She ran to Dominic, and flung her arms about him. 'Oh, you poor dear! Poor Millicent! And the poor little baby!'

He pushed her away from him so that she almost lost her balance and fell, and then he walked blindly out of the room and out of the house.

'Well, really!' Dinah said, tears rushing to her eyes. 'I only . . .'

'You only behaved as you always do!' Alice snapped. 'I'm surprised you did not add that you knew how he felt, because you too have had your house destroyed!'

'Now, my dear,' General Ridgeway chided his wife as Dinah began to weep in earnest. 'We are all tired and overwrought. This has been a great tragedy, a terrible thing.'

Catrina rose and walked numbly from the room, still clutching the parcel of silk to her. Outside, everything was bathed in the rose-and-pearl light of dawn, and the blackened, smouldering ruins of the house showed up starkly. Two armed soldiers kept guard at each end of it. Where the front door had been, Dominic stood alone, his head bowed. Catrina moved towards him.

'Dominic?'

'I should never have married her,' he said tonelessly, without looking up. 'She was a child who wanted to remain a child. If I had not married her, she would be alive still.'

Catrina sighed. 'I suppose it must be natural for grief to take the form of guilt . . .'

He turned, gripping her by the shoulders. His eyes were stark and tortured. 'My guilt is that I cannot grieve for her as I ought to! At the end, I had nothing left to give her. No love, no patience, no respect, no sympathy. Only a kind of disgusted pity. Can you understand the hell of not being able to mourn the death of my wife?'

'Come away from here,' Catrina urged. 'You are punishing yourself too harshly.'

But it was not until the sun had risen that he agreed to leave, and they walked in silence to the Ridgeways' house.

They were met by Alice. 'Catrina, dear,' she said apologetically, 'we simply won't be able to heat all the bedrooms when the colder weather settles in, and I wondered if you would mind sharing Dinah's room?'

'I won't, but she might! Particularly as Lucy will insist on sharing my bed.'

Alice's lips tightened. 'Dinah will have to accept the situation gracefully. I'll have the servants move an extra bed into her room. Go and rest when you have breakfasted. When Lucy wakes up, I'll take care of her.'

Mechanically Catrina allowed herself to be escorted, a while later, to the room she was to share with Dinah. She lay down, fully clothed, the parcel of watered silk clasped to her.

'Where is Violet?' she wanted to know.

'Resting,' Alice said. 'Try to rest also.'

But grief overcame her and she wept for poor, unhappy, lost Millicent. At last she fell into a heavy doze, and awoke to find Violet sitting beside her bed.

'I come to say goodbye, dear,' she announced quietly.

Catrina sat up. 'Where will you go?'

Violet said seriously, 'The way I looks at it, love—we was all given one talent in life, something as'll help us to survive. The only talent I got was to act the whore. So that's what I'll be doing again.'

'Oh, Violet, no! Even if you were to go back to that life, you could not survive! Not in a besieged town, where every spare penny has to go on food . . .'

'I'm making for the *Linea*, ducks,' Violet interrupted. 'The Spanish has money and food in plenty.'

'You couldn't! Not—the enemy . . .'

'I don't like it any more'n you do. But there's one consolation. The Dons'll be good customers. Their women, even the ones as are near-starving, rarely goes on the streets. Too scared of eternal damnation, see. So I'll not have much competition.'

'Violet, there must be some other way out for you—there must!'

Violet hesitated, and then dropped her voice to a whisper. 'Listen, dear, I'm telling you something as you must keep strictly to yourself. General Ridgeway and me, we had a little talk earlier on. He knows the way I feel about Eddie deserting. To make up for it, I wants to do my little bit for Britain. So I won't just be selling my body to the Dons. I'll be keeping me eyes skinned, and slipping back across the isthmus to report the enemy movements.'

'You mean—you are going to act as a spy?'

'That's right.'

Catrina thought of something. 'Violet, you'll be in terrible danger! Not only in danger of being found out by the Spaniards, but their lines are being bombarded by us every day and well into the night, and you could easily be killed by British gunfire!'

'I knows that, love. General Ridgeway made no bones about it.'

'And still you mean to go?'

Violet nodded. 'I shouldn't've told you any of this, but I didn't want you to think too badly of me.'

'How could I think badly of you? I'm proud to have had you as a friend! And—And I want you to accept this.'

Violet took the parcel from her and unwrapped the tissue paper. She stared at the blue watered silk. 'It's lovely! It'd make a beautiful gown. But I can't take it, dear. You'll have need of it yourself, now all your clothes has either been burnt or been stolen by them thieving, heartless pigs!'

Catrina shuddered. If she had to spend the rest of her days in rags, she could not have worn a gown made of the silk. Just as her reasons for choosing it in the first place had been confused, so her motives in rescuing it from the fire were too complex for her to understand.

'Take it,' she told Violet, 'and have it made up into a gown, and wear it in memory of a poor, spoilt little girl who never learnt to grow up.'

CHAPTER TWELVE

MILLICENT'S REMAINS were buried near the graves of her mother and father, and Catrina tried to settle down to living with the Ridgeways. Theoretically, Dominic lived there too, but he was seldom at home, and the General explained that he was volunteering for any extra duties.

'It's Dominic's way of coming to terms with grief,' he said. 'If hard work helps him, we shouldn't interfere.'

On the rare occasions when Dominic was at home, Dinah made a point of gushing over Lucy, which left the child bewildered and uneasy, and which appeared to be totally lost on Dominic, for he seemed not to notice. He looked strained and haggard and totally withdrawn.

Lucy asked surprisingly few questions about her mother. Catrina thought she understood a good deal of what had happened, but was afraid to put her thoughts into words. For herself, after the first shock and grief of her sister's death had begun to dull, life in the Ridgeway household was uneasy, and matters were not improved by Dinah's thinly-veiled hostility.

One of the first things Alice had done had been to organise, from among the other officer's wives, a collection of clothes which could be made over for Catrina and Lucy.

'I should have been only too pleased to sacrifice some of my gowns to Miss Beaumont,' Dinah said, her eyes very round and wide and innocent, 'if I weren't such a poor little scrap of a thing, while *she* is quite statuesque. I do so envy large females!'

Even though the officers' wives had offered their donations willingly and generously, Dinah succeeded in making Catrina feel that she was an object of charity.

'Beggars can't be choosers,' she would say when Catrina chanced to remark on the difficulties of making over a particular gown. Worst of all were her hints that Catrina contributed nothing towards the daily food supplies. Apart from the rations received by General Ridgeway and Dominic, both Dinah and Alice sold items of jewellery to the merchants and were able to buy extra food at inflated prices. Even the British servants, under Hobson's directions, spent their free time in staking out fishing-lines from the beaches of the three bays which were not menaced by the Spanish. Catrina was made painfully aware of the fact that she was a liability.

She had begged writing materials from Alice, and poured out her feelings in the new diary which she was keeping:

> I don't belong here; I fulfil no function other than that of caring for Lucy, and I miss dear Violet sorely. More and more, I realise what a friend she was to me. If only there was something practical I could do to earn my keep in the household . . .

She stopped writing as a sudden thought struck her, and she hurried to General Ridgeway's study. He smiled when she entered after knocking. 'Oh, it's you, Catrina. I thought Dominic might have decided to come home before midnight for once.'

'Lucy is in danger of forgetting what her father looks like,' she commented.

'He is being driven by demons. Give him time to recover. Did you wish to speak to me about anything in particular?'

'I wanted to ask you, sir, whether there are still plots available on the isthmus. For, if so, I should very much like to take one up and grow vegetables for the household.'

'I believe I could secure a plot for you. And no doubt Dinah would be happy to care for Lucy while you are gardening.'

Only the fondest of relatives, Catrina thought, could have been so taken in by Dinah's sporadic flurries of attention towards the child. The thought of her being happy to care for Lucy was quite ludicrous.

'I would take Lucy with me to the isthmus each day,' Catrina said diplomatically. 'She would enjoy scratching in the soil.'

'Very well. But you won't see any return for your efforts until the spring. It is too late in the year for most vegetables,

I understand.'

'At least I could prepare the ground, ready for sowing,' Catrina said.

Only two days later she learnt that she had been allotted a piece of ground on the isthmus, and she and Lucy set out to begin working on it. While Lucy cleared the land of small stones, Catrina began the digging. Even though no vegetables could be sown yet, the making of the garden gave her something to do, and best of all it took her away from the house.

Lucy had grown more firmly attached to Catrina since Millicent's death. As they worked together on the vegetable plot one morning, she asked anxiously, 'Aunt Catrina, don't you think God is greedy?'

'Why, love?'

'Well—first of all he took Grandpapa and Grandmama to be angels. And then he took Mama. Aunt Catrina . . .'

'Yes, Lucy?'

'If you were ever so slightly wicked, God would not want *you* for an angel, would he?'

Catrina reached for the child. 'Nothing is going to happen to me, my love!'

Lucy's fearful gaze searched her face. 'All the same, it might be safer to be a little wicked. If both of us said something wicked, God would want us to be sorry before he took us for his angels.' She paused. '*My* something wicked is—I hate Mrs Forest.'

'One shouldn't hate people, Lucy . . .' Catrina began.

'But you hate her too,' the child said with perfect understanding. 'So now God will wait until we're sorry for hating her before he'll want either of us for his angels. You won't be sorry for a long time, will you, Aunt Catrina?'

'I never said I hated her,' Catrina demurred. She kissed the little girl. 'Stop worrying. Oh, look!' she cried, glad of a diversion with which to turn the child's gloomy thoughts. A young puppy was scampering towards them, and then became side-tracked and started chasing its own tail.

Lucy ran to it, and picked it up. 'Aunt Catrina, may I keep it? Please, may I?'

'I'm afraid not, Lucy. It must belong to someone else.'

But the puppy appeared again the next day, and it wolfed

down so eagerly the extra slice of bread that Lucy had brought with her in the hope of seeing it again that Catrina decided it must be a stray. That evening, after the child had been put to bed, Catrina told the others about it, and added, 'If no one at the gardens claims it, or knows to whom it belongs, may we bring the puppy home for Lucy?'

'That is really something Dominic ought to decide,' General Ridgeway said.

'He is never here.' Catrina could not keep the bleak note out of her voice, and covered it by adding, 'A puppy would help to make up to Lucy for her father's neglect.'

'John, you will have to speak to Dominic!' Alice told her husband. 'He cannot go on burying himself in work to the exclusion of everything else!'

'I agree,' Dinah put in. 'Even when he is here, he is too tired to take an interest in anything.'

'Very well,' the General gave in. 'I shall order him to stop volunteering for extra duties.'

'I'm sure Dominic wouldn't object to Lucy keeping the puppy,' Catrina returned to the original subject under discussion, 'provided you agreed to give it a home.'

'Of course the child may keep the puppy,' Alice said warmly. 'I know she has hankered after one. You have no objections, have you, John?'

'None at all.'

But Dinah said, 'Of course, I do understand that the poor little girl needs something of her own to love now that her Mama has been taken away from her so cruelly, and there is no one more devoted to dogs than I am. But, all the same, it does not seem to have occurred to anyone else that it would be one more useless mouth to feed.' Her gaze was resting on Catrina.

Catrina flushed. 'I would share my ration with the pup.'

Alice made an angry sound. 'There are always scraps of food which have to be thrown out, and bones to be picked clean. The puppy may be given a home without undue sacrifices from anyone!'

That night, when they prepared for bed in the room which they shared with Lucy, Dinah allowed her claws to show fully.

'For someone who has no right to be here at all, you take

a good deal upon yourself! The pup will whine to be let in here at night, and I shall have to put up with its noise and smell, as well as having to share my room with you and the child! I shall be overjoyed when the first of Admiral Rodney's convoys arrives, and the two of you are shipped back to England!'

'*You* have no intention of returning home?' Catrina enquired politely.

'And miss all the excitement and the fun of seeing the Spanish beaten? Oh no!'

'I take it you mean the excitement and the fun of battle, of killing and seeing people being killed?'

'Of course! I have not endured the dreadful boredom and hardship of the siege thus far, just to be cheated of the climax when the enemy are crushed!'

Catrina studied her, remembering what Violet had said of her. 'Why did you choose to get married by proxy? I mean, most girls would have waited until they could join their betrothed before the altar.'

'I am not *most girls*!' Dinah's eyes shone with an intense glitter. 'Being married by proxy was quite one of the most exciting things that ever happened to me! I was the talk of London society. Everyone remarked on what a brave, sad little figure I cut, standing before the altar alone and repeating my vows, while my bridegroom was doing the same many, many miles away!'

And I'll lay odds, Catrina thought drily, that you revelled equally in your dramatic bereavement and widowhood before the marriage could be consummated. It was true what Violet had said. Dinah saw life as a vast stage, with herself playing the heroine in each act.

The next day, Catrina enquired of the other gardeners on the strip of land along the isthmus, but no one laid claim to the puppy.

'I think it was abandoned by its owner,' one of the men told her. 'It comes here because someone generally takes pity on it and feeds it.'

'Well, Lucy,' Catrina said with a smile. 'It seems that the puppy is now yours.'

The little girl clutched the animal to her, unable to speak for a moment. 'I'll call it Tim,' she whispered at last.

The two became inseparable after that, much to Dinah's disgust, for the puppy invariably succeeded in sneaking into the room at night and sleeping at Lucy's feet.

Even though General Ridgeway had ordered Dominic to stop taking on extra duties, nothing changed very much. He spent one evening at home, looking tortured and restless and taking little part in the conversation. Dinah had specially changed into a pretty gown of blue sprigged muslin, and was insinuating herself into a game Lucy was playing with the puppy, but she might as well not have bothered for all the interest it aroused in Dominic. After that evening, the frenzied activities into which he flung himself kept him away from home just as often as hard work had done. There were rumours about hard drinking and reckless wagers with fellow-officers, and when he and several of his men missed one of the field-days, the whisper went out that he risked being court-martialled.

The field-days were held with the main purpose of relieving tension and boredom among the troops, for discontent was increasing in the garrison as each passing day brought no sign of Admiral Rodney's relieving fleet. As Catrina stood with Alice and Dinah and Lucy to watch the ceremony, she tried to suppress her bewildered anxiety over Dominic's behaviour by concentrating, instead, on the glamour and the pomp of the occasion.

In the courtyard outside the Convent each regiment was reviewed in turn. The Governor inspected the rows of red-coats standing stiffly to attention, interspersed with halberded sergeants and officers bearing swords. Then he turned ceremonially towards the mounted field-officers to take the salute.

The regiments had just marched away to their alarm posts, accompanied by volleys of parapet fire, when Dominic came riding into the courtyard. He looked dishevelled but strangely triumphant, his eyes glittering with a feverish brightness. He dismounted, and approached the Governor with a salute.

They did not learn until later in the day what had happened. 'We kept it quiet,' General Ridgeway told them, 'but the army had almost no feed left for the horses. What little grazing there is cannot support all the animals. We faced the prospect of having to slaughter them, which would not only have been a calamitous loss in itself, but it would have been totally demoralising to the troops.'

'But what has that to do with Dominic?' Alice broke in.

'I'm coming to that, my dear. Dominic knew from his contact with Vi— . . . from reports by our spies that the enemy were expecting supply wagons loaded with animal feed. He suggested that he and volunteers among his men should sneak into the *Linea*, attack the drivers and guards of the supply wagons from ambush, and seize them. They did this successfully and drove the wagons right through the enemy's ranks. The Spaniards were taken so much by surprise that they did not begin to fire at them until Dominic and his men had almost reached the no-man's land on the isthmus.'

'Oh, how splendidly brave!' Dinah exclaimed. 'But why did you not tell us where Dominic was, and why?'

'Because the raid was strictly unofficial. If it had failed, he would have had to be charged with absenting himself from his post.'

'And, presumably,' Catrina said slowly, 'if he and his men had been killed in the attempt, it would have been assumed that they had deserted, and the army would have done nothing to set the record straight.'

'But they weren't killed,' General Ridgeway said, 'and so there is no need to look on the black side.'

Catrina did not pursue the subject, but her thoughts were troubled and confused. Dominic's action had undoubtedly been brave and had saved a potentially disastrous situation, but it had also been totally reckless and indifferent to the possible consequences. Was it a coincidence that all these reckless pursuits of his kept him from spending time at home? There was no reason why he should wish to avoid the Ridgeways or Dinah, so he must be avoiding Catrina herself. Was it all somehow tied up with his feeling of guilt over Millicent's death? She could find no answers to any of these questions, and she went on bleakly with daily life, while Dominic continued to make himself conspicuous by his absence from home and by the devil-may-care escapades which reached them in the form of rumours.

* * *

Winter was setting in upon the Rock, and Lucy caught one of her chills. 'You will have to stay in bed today,' Catrina told her. 'Aunt Alice will take care of you while I'm working on the garden.'

In truth, there was no real point in Catrina going to the isthmus at all. The ground had been dug over and the clumps of soil broken down, and there was little left to be done until spring. But she liked the company of the other gardeners, and at least being there and needlessly raking over the soil gave her the illusion of being busy and useful.

Suddenly shots rang out, and a shell embedded itself in the earth close by. In the confusion, everyone thought it was a badly-aimed shot from the British side, and then they saw the flashes of fire from the direction of the *Linea*, and more shells exploded around them.

'The Spaniards have opened fire on us!' someone shouted. 'Take cover!'

Everyone scrambled towards a near-by ditch and lay down inside it. The firing continued remorselessly, and when Catrina lifted her head slightly she saw that the gardens had been destroyed. Winter crops had been blasted out of the ground, and great holes had appeared in the previously neatly tilled rows.

'The Spaniards are quite determined to starve us out by any means at their disposal,' someone said bitterly.

'All our work has been for nothing,' another gardener agreed. 'We had better wait until it grows dark before we venture home, for it would not surprise me in the least if the Dons took it into their heads to mow us down as they have mown down our vegetables.'

Catrina was profoundly glad that circumstances had prevented Lucy from having to share the long and frightening vigil, but she also mourned the loss of the garden which was to have been her refuge and her contribution towards the household's food supplies.

Once again her diary became her only solace.

> The winter rains and the increasing shortage of food add to the general tension, and there have been more desertions among the troops. But Spanish soldiers are deserting also, and giving themselves up to the British,

> and there is some comfort to be gained from the stories they have to tell.
>
> The enemy are experiencing difficulties of their own, mainly from outbreaks of fever, and from the flooding of their trenches caused by the rain. I cannot help thinking of Violet, however, and this prevents me from sharing wholeheartedly in the general rejoicing at the news of the enemy's misfortunes.
>
> Dominic's behaviour continues to puzzle and worry me. Lucy asked me last evening, in all seriousness, 'Where does Papa live now, and why does he not visit us?' He is said to be spending a good deal of time in the Tower of London inn. It is in the charge of a widow, I understand; a half-Portuguese who is said to allow officers unlimited credit for gambling, and I am told that card-games are played there throughout the night. Certainly, he seldom troubles to come home.

Catrina sighed, staring in front of her. Then she continued her entry in her diary:

> Christmas will soon be upon us, and it promises to be a dismal time. I wonder if we shall even have something more to put on the table than the wretched pease-pudding which is now our staple diet.

But in that she later found herself proved wrong. A short while before Christmas the blockading Spaniards allowed a Moorish vessel to get through, and Catrina stood with Alice, Lucy and Hobson and watched as a few live cattle were landed.

'My goodness!' Alice sighed. 'They are little more than skin and bone, poor beasts. They have clearly been at sea for too long.'

Indeed, several of the cattle died almost immediately after staggering on to dry land. Even so, bidding for the carcasses was brisk, and Alice acquired a piece of meat which was to be saved for Christmas dinner.

They were about to leave with their purchases when Catrina froze. Standing a short distance away among the crowd was Dominic, his arm about a young woman as he said something to her. Although not in the first flush of youth, she was exotically beautiful, with hair so black that it shone with a bluish sheen, and dark, flashing eyes. Her face was skilfully painted and powdered, and her red gown displayed her voluptuous curves.

Through a chaos of shock and disbelief, Catrina tried to think coherently. Lucy must not see her father, for the first time in so many days and weeks, all but embracing a strange woman in public. Yet their party would have to pass the couple, and there was no way in which Dominic with his tall, uniformed figure and his flamboyant companion in her scarlet gown could have been missed in the crowd.

Alice whispered, 'Who on earth could she be?'

Hobson answered her in a low, expressionless voice. 'Her name is Marisol Lomax, madam, and she is the landlady of the Tower of London inn.'

Catrina drew a painful breath. So it was not drink or gambling which had been luring Dominic to the inn for entire nights at a time. She heard Alice mutter angrily, 'I shall have to tell him to remove himself and his doxy from sight so that we may pass.'

'Please,' Catrina said quickly, 'let me go and tell him.' She was plunging through the crowd even before Alice could reply.

Dominic and his companion were so engrossed in one another that they did not see her immediately and she stood there, studying him with anger and a devastating sense of betrayal. He was free now, so why was he ignoring her so completely and sharing his nights and his embraces with this brash, beautiful innkeeper?

He turned his head away from the woman, and saw Catrina. He was not in the least put out, and he did not release his companion. 'Yes, Catrina?' he asked in a remote voice.

She tried to keep her own voice neutral. 'May I speak to you for a moment in private, Dominic?'

'Can it not keep until later?'

'No, it cannot.'

He shrugged, and addressed his companion. 'Excuse me for a moment, Marisol, while I find out what is troubling my sister.'

As Catrina forged a path for herself towards the edge of the crowd she swallowed against a painful lump in her throat. Why had he gone out of his way to describe her, falsely, as his sister?

They had reached the outskirts of the crowd. 'Well, Catrina?' he enquired politely.

She could no longer control her seething emotions. 'No, Dominic, it is far from *well*! For months your behaviour has been atrocious! You insult the Ridgeways by treating their home as a convenient place in which to sleep when the occasional mood takes you. You expose yourself to reckless, foolish risks without a thought for anyone, and you seem to have forgotten . . .'

'Mind your own business, Catrina!' he snapped. 'I am not answerable to you or to anyone else when it comes to my private life!'

'I grant you, no one could stop you from flaunting your mistress for all to see!' she said bitingly. 'It may interest you to know, however, that Lucy is among the crowd with Alice, and the child was about to clap eyes on you embracing the woman in public! Lucy, who has not seen you for weeks on end, who believes that you no longer live under the same roof, and who wonders why you have not been to visit her!'

The anger in his eyes had faded. He said defensively, 'As far as Marisol Lomax is concerned, at least, my behaviour has not been entirely what it seemed. She . . .' He stopped, and after a moment's hesitation he went on, 'Keep this to yourself, Catrina. She is not half-Portuguese as she pretends, but half-Spanish, and it has been suspected for some time that she is spying for the enemy. She encourages soldiers to patronise her inn by extending credit to them, and any information they can be persuaded to let drop while in their cups is conveyed to the Spaniards. I was asked to cultivate a relationship with her and obtain evidence of her activities.'

'And, naturally,' Catrina said scathingly, 'you were the obvious candidate for the task, for it fits very well with the reputation you have been building for yourself!'

Renewed anger flared in his eyes. 'I have tried to explain the situation to you, and I'm damned if I'll justify myself further!'

'Perhaps you would care to justify yourself to Lucy!

Explain to her why, when she has already lost her mother, she is also being deprived of her father's love and attention! Tell her why your new reckless, rackety mode of living is so much more important than her happiness!'

A stricken look had entered Dominic's eyes. 'I have not been considering Lucy,' he admitted. 'But I shall mend my ways, Catrina.' He touched her hand briefly. 'Please go and distract the child's attention while I remove Marisol from the scene.'

A short while later, as Lucy skipped along beside Hobson ahead of them, Alice asked, 'What did Dominic say when you asked him about flaunting that woman in public?'

'He told me to mind my own business.' It was, Catrina thought, at least half the truth. 'However,' she added reassuringly, 'he did promise to consider Lucy in future.'

Alice sighed. 'I wish the year of mourning for Millicent was over, so that he might marry again. A wife would soon curb his excesses.'

Catrina's heart turned over. How she, too, wished the months would hurry by, for she sensed that Dominic would not even discuss marriage with her until a full year had passed.

She said lightly, 'At least Dominic has not kicked over *all* the traces, and rushed into marriage with someone like Marisol Lomax!'

'Oh, no, my dear!' Alice exclaimed with conviction. 'Even in the worst excess of folly Dominic would never dream of marrying someone like that! When it comes to choosing a wife, a man looks for someone who is virtuous, modest and reserved. The Lomax woman can scarcely be said to possess those qualities!'

Only two days later, everyone in Gibraltar learned precisely what qualities Marisol Lomax did possess, for she was arrested and charged with spying for the enemy. And, true to his word, Dominic began to spend his free time at home.

Dinah, Catrina observed sourly, lost no opportunity after that to manoeuvre matters in such a way that she and Dominic and Lucy formed a threesome. She did it very cleverly by wooing Lucy, knowing that Dominic, in his new penitent mood, would wish to spend time with his daughter.

On Christmas morning Dinah presented the child with one of her own exquisite handkerchiefs, and Lucy was so astonished and overwhelmed at receiving such a magnificent and grown-up gift that she forgot she had disliked the woman. Just as they were all about to leave for the Christmas morning service, Dinah produced a scarlet ribbon which she tied in Lucy's hair, and inside the gharry she continued to fuss with the bows, retying them in the child's curls, appearing so absorbed in Lucy that she ended up by sitting between the child and her father during the service.

After the Christmas lunch Dinah produced a surprise present of a dog-lead for Tim, and suggested that they christen it by taking the pup for a walk. Naturally, Dominic elected to go as well.

On the morning of New Year's Eve, Alice announced, 'Come what may, I mean to have some gaiety with which to usher in the New Year. Dinah, you and I will call separately on all the officer's wives, and invite them to a party here tonight!'

'And where, my love,' General Ridgeway asked with a rueful smile, 'are we to obtain the means of feeding them and quenching their thirst?'

'Everyone will be asked to contribute something. And John, I should like you to organise a military band for the provision of music, because I intend that there shall be dancing!'

All the officers and their wives entered into the spirit of the planned festivities. Jealously hoarded bottles of brandy and rum were sacrificed, and the women arrived with various dishes which they or their servants had prepared during the day.

Catrina sat that evening and watched Dominic dancing with Dinah. The latter was magnificently gowned in lemon-yellow silk and old lace, and she made an entrancing picture as she circled gracefully round him. Their hands were held high in the air, and they were smiling at one another.

Catrina stifled a pang of jealousy, and told herself not to be so absurd. Dominic had not invited *her* to dance, because he was aware that such frivolous pastimes had not figured at all in her life with Lady Prudence, and so she would not know any dance steps. He did not wish to embarrass her by drawing attention to the fact.

Simultaneously, all the clocks in the house struck twelve. Couples left the dance-floor, and Catrina joined everyone else in raising her glass in a toast to a new year and a new decade.

'Damnation to the enemy!' someone cried.

'Peace and prosperity!' General Ridgeway amended. 'A happy New Year, everyone!'

People had just drained their glasses when Dominic took Dinah by the arm and led her to the centre of the room. Catrina stared at them in bemusement, thinking that perhaps they were about to take the lead in some kind of customary ritual New Year dance. But Dominic began to speak, and as she listened to him, she grew numb with total disbelief and shock.

'There is something which I wish to tell all of you. In the normal, conventional way I would not be speaking of the matter at all at this stage. However, I am aware that my reckless and often disreputable behaviour during the past months may well cause anyone with whom I associate particularly the embarrassment of being gossiped about. Because I don't want there to be any misunderstandings, I decided to take you all into my confidence. I owe my late wife's memory the respect of a full year's mourning and there will be no formal announcement until that time has passed. But I wanted you to know, meanwhile, that an understanding exists between myself and Dinah Forest and that, at a suitable time in the future, we shall be betrothed.'

His words reverberated chaotically in Catrina's ears. It was all a joke. A grotesque, cruel, wholly unfunny joke! Then she looked at Dinah, her arm linked through Dominic's, a triumphant light in her eyes which even the exaggerated demureness of her smile could not cancel.

As she listened to the murmurs of sympathetic understanding from the guests, Catrina's stricken glance fell upon the empty glass from which she had so recently drunk a toast. The new year of 1780 was only minutes old, and whatever might happen during its course could not, for herself, possibly be as utterly devastating as its birth had been.

CHAPTER THIRTEEN

CATRINA COULD NOT sleep. There were still at least two hours to be endured before dawn and she knew, from recently-acquired bitter experience, that those two final sleepless hours would drag her spirits down to the lowest pit of despair. Quietly, careful not to disturb either Lucy or Dinah, she crept out of bed and wrapped a shawl around her. Then she groped for her diary and a candle and padded soundlessly from the room.

In the drawing-room, by the light of the single candle, she sat down to commit to her diary the anguished question which had been churning in her brain since Dominic made his public announcement.

> Why, why, *why?* I thought he loved me as I love him! I thought he was offering a kind of penance to Millicent's memory by avoiding me, but I never doubted for a moment that when he ceased to be haunted by her death we would be free to love one another. Why have his feelings changed towards me?
>
> He behaves as if there had never been anything between us in the past. Dinah is always by his side when he is not on duty. I cannot believe that he loves her, and it is not only my own pain and despair which leads me to this conclusion. He treats her with such stilted correctness. If she ever wishes that he would do more than merely kiss her fingertips, she does not show it. Neither of them ever schemes to be alone together, and God knows, I watch them obsessively enough to be aware if they did.

The writing on the page blurred before her eyes, and the light from the candle turned tears to prisms of colour. She dashed them away, and picked up her quill again.

Dinah will glory in the role of the blithe spirit who is bringing happiness back to a man whose first wife died dramatically in a fire. But when the novelty of that has worn off, what other part would there be in which to fulfil her need for play-acting, for being the heroine? She would not settle for the dull routine of wife and mother. She would want constant new drama, and because life does not consist solely of dramatic situations she will create them herself.

And what of poor Lucy? Already Dinah is becoming bored with the attention she has been showering on the child of late, and she now ignores her when Dominic is not present. Lucy has been bewildered by . . .

Catrina dropped the quill as a hellish noise suddenly erupted outside. It was the sound of exploding shells and the blast of cannon. Why, she wondered irately, had the British decided to resume their firing on the *Linea* at this unearthly hour of the morning?

The noise had awakened the household, and she could hear running footsteps and male voices shouting. She gathered up her diary and writing-materials and prepared to return to the bedroom, for Lucy would be frightened by the noise coming at such an unaccustomed hour.

In the corridor she almost collided with Dominic. His coat-buttons were unfastened and his hair was awry, as if he had dressed in a great hurry. She looked at him in the light of her candle, yearning to touch him.

'Put on warm clothing, and see that Dinah and Lucy do the same. Then leave the house and make for the gulleys in the rocks as quickly as you can!' he said urgently.

'But—But why . . .?'

'Because Gibraltar is under attack,' he answered tersely. 'It's enemy fire you are hearing. Now hurry and do as I say!'

For the next few minutes the household was in a state of pandemonium almost equalling that taking place in the beleaguered town. Catrina grabbed the first gown which came to hand, and when she had pulled it over her head she thrust Lucy's arms into the sleeves of her smock. Dinah was dressing, too, but choosing her best gown of sapphire-blue velvet and her furs, and stopping to collect some of her jewellery in case the house should be destroyed.

Moments later the three of them joined Alice and the female servants. Through the window they could see a trail of fire streaking through the air, and a moment later came the sickening crump of a building being hit. They fled as they were, joining a stream of other women, children and servants.

They cowered, cold and hungry and frightened, in a gulley and listened to the ferocious blasting. The smell of gunpowder was heavy in their nostrils and it was impossible to see what damage was being done to the town, for it was wrapped in a dark pall of smoke. At one o'clock, the Spaniards ceased their attack. The British continued firing, but when there was no response from the enemy they, too, slackened off and stopped.

Alice began to laugh, helplessly and with a faint note of hysteria in the sound. 'The—The siesta! They are observing their usual custom, even in the middle of battle!'

The laughter spread, relieving the tension that had been gripping all of them. Then something occurred to Catrina, and she silenced them urgently. 'If the Spaniards mean to cling slavishly to their siesta, then they will begin firing on us again at five o'clock. We have four hours in which to hurry home—if there are still homes left standing!'

Feverishly, everyone began to stream back to the town. There were gaps, like wounds in the landscape, where homes had been blasted into heaps of rubble, but the Ridgeway residence was intact. Catrina helped to collect blankets and rations while Alice and the servants prepared a hasty meal. Dinah was packing up her gowns to carry them to safety.

Shortly after four, they began to make their way back to the shelter of the rocks, everyone carrying emergency supplies. Hobson and the other male servants elected to go and help the militia in any way they could, and the women and children were left alone in the gulleys. The Spaniards resumed their fire precisely at five o'clock, and continued well into the night.

Catrina huddled beneath a blanket, with one arm about Lucy, who was cuddling Tim to herself. The rocks were sharp and cold and offered no comfort, and the gulleys themselves were overcrowded now that women had brought so many belongings to them. Children wept with fear and discomfort and cold, and their distracted mothers tried to soothe them. Other women quarrelled over the ownership of space in the gulleys. Sleep was quite impossible.

Those twenty-four hours set the pattern of their lives for what came to seem like an eternity. The only respite they had came during the siesta period. They saw nothing at all of the men, and the constant anxiety that a husband, a father, a son or a lover might have become a casualty added to the general tension.

During an ugly quarrel among the women in the gulley one morning, Alice said with quiet desperation, 'I am almost driven to returning home, and taking the risk of being blasted by the enemy's fire.'

Lucy began to weep. 'I want to go home too. I hate it here!'

'Oh, be quiet!' Dinah exclaimed irritably. 'And we'll have to get rid of that dog of yours. He takes up too much space, and he smells.'

'Tim does *not* smell!'

'Come, Lucy,' Catrina interceded, 'you and I will take Tim for a walk. I should like to find a stream in which to have a proper wash. Do you think Tim might be clever enough to smell out water?'

'I'm sure he is clever enough for *anything*!' Lucy stopped crying, and they left the noisy, overcrowded gulley.

Catrina had not really expected to be successful, but Tim streaked off unerringly towards a place where water was dripping from an overhanging rock. It came, clearly, from a depression higher up that had been filled by recent rains.

'I told you he was clever enough to find water!' Lucy crowed as the pup lapped thirstily at the wet rock.

'Yes, he is quite brilliant,' Catrina answered absently. She had just spied, half-hidden away by vegetation, what appeared to be a cow-byre, and went to investigate.

Almost overgrown with palmettos, it was built of stone and must obviously have served as a dwelling for the cowherd as well, for there was a chimney in one corner. Close by it was a rough crag in the rocks which opened up into a shallow cave. It would make an ideal sheltering-place, Catrina decided. And what bliss it would be to escape from the tense, quarrelsome, noisy crowd of women in the gulleys!

She would say nothing about it at present, she decided, but would secretly prepare the cow-byre for habitation. When it was ready, she would tell Alice and Dinah and their servants about it, so that they could make for it unobtrusively each afternoon before the Spanish resumed their firing.

'Let us keep this as our secret spot, shall we?' Catrina suggested to Lucy. 'Just for the present.'

The child nodded. 'Only you and me and Tim will know about it.'

But that afternoon the bombardment from the Spanish lines suddenly stopped well before the normal siesta time. In their gulleys in the rocks, service wives and townspeople exchanged puzzled, anxious glances.

A tense half-hour passed. 'Do you think,' Catrina said to Alice, 'that we should go home?'

Alice considered for a moment. 'The cease-fire may be a trick, Catrina. It may well be that the Spaniards are hoping we shall do precisely what you have suggested, so that they pick us off and demoralise our troops by inflicting heavy civilian casualties.'

The waiting continued. Then a jubilant sound of laughter and singing reached them, and as they raised their heads above the gulleys, they were amazed to see several British soldiers and officers hurrying towards them. When Catrina scrambled out to find out what was happening, she noticed Dominic was among the men. Without thinking, overwhelmed by the sight of him after so many anxious, uncertain days and nights, she sped towards him. He was laughing as he caught her in his arms. His uniform was crumpled and stained with gunpowder and his face was covered in the stubble of several days' growth of beard, while the dark hollows around his eyes bore witness to the fact that he had had no rest for a long while. But in spite of it all there was an air of euphoria about him, and it was shared by the laughing, cheering, embracing crowd which surrounded them.

At that moment, Catrina did not care about the cause of

all this joy. Dominic's arms were about her for the first time in months, and she could feel the beat of his heart against her cheek. She raised herself on tiptoe and laid her mouth against his. Just for an instant his lips parted in response and his arms tightened about her. Then, deliberately, he moved his head, brushing her cheek with his mouth before setting her aside. She followed slowly as he plunged through the crowd towards Alice and Dinah and Lucy. When he had embraced all of them, and had swung Lucy on to his shoulders, Dominic told them what had happened.

'An English brig got safely into the New Mole, and brought news that Admiral Rodney is on his way with a large British convoy. The Spaniards obviously received the news at the same time as we did, for their blockading fleet left the Bay for the open sea to engage the convoy. Since we are in sight of relief from the sea, there is no longer any point in the Spaniards firing on us from the *Linea*.'

'It is safe for us to go home?' Alice asked.

'Perfectly safe. Moreover, the brig which got into the New Mole is said to have brought flour and other food supplies.' With Lucy still perched on his shoulders, Dominic moved to Dinah's side and took her arm. 'Come, my dear, let us go down to the harbour and watch the cargo being brought ashore.'

The battered town went wild with joy as more and more of Admiral Rodney's warships arrived, bringing not only supplies of every kind but also captured Spanish warships. Free wine was distributed to the cheering crowd who lined the walls of the fortress to watch the arrival of the victorious British convoy.

When Admiral Rodney himself was known to be entering the Bay in HMS *Sandwich* at the head of the remainder of the British fleet, Catrina asked Alice to keep an eye on Lucy while she herself joined the throng waiting near the waterfront.

For a while she forgot her personal misery as she became caught up in the euphoric mood of Gibraltar's inhabitants. To everyone in the garrison town, accustomed for so long to the hated, humiliating sight of Spanish ships blockading the Bay, it was intensely satisfying to see, in their place, the vessels of Rodney's victorious fleet, and the steady unloading of all manner of supplies. But without a doubt, Catrina reflected, the biggest joy of all was the sight of the many captured Spanish vessels.

She allowed herself to be carried along with the tide of people streaming down to the wharves and the moles. As well as the official cargoes there would be supplies sent by relatives and friends from England; there would be letters and newspapers. Catrina had her own reason for anxiously awaiting the unloading of parcels and mail from home. Mr Stanmore, the lawyer who handled her affairs, would have kept abreast with the news of what had been happening in Gibraltar. He would have sent her food supplies and money.

Instead, she discovered there was only one letter for her, addressed in an unfamiliar hand. She broke the seal, and read its contents with growing dismay:

> Dear Miss Beaumont,
>
> I regret to inform you that my father has died suddenly, cut off in his prime by a seizure. As his only son and heir I shall be stepping into his professional shoes and I should be very happy to act for you in the future. If it is your desire that I should do so, would you please send me official notification, for without such a letter of authority I may not transact any business on your behalf. I anticipate your favourable reply, and in the meantime I remain your humble servant,
>
> Godfrey Stanmore.

Catrina returned slowly to the Ridgeways' home, her thoughts anxiously preoccupied. It would be some weeks before any of the British ships could leave Gibraltar with her reply to Mr Stanmore's son, and heaven only knew how many weeks or months after that before another ship brought a response to it. In the meantime, she would be entirely without funds.

Everyone but herself, it seemed once again, had cause for celebration. Hobson had also returned from the waterfront a while ago, and Alice reported with satisfaction, 'Several crates have arrived for us from England, sent by John's sisters! There is a cured ham, and live chickens, and so many different kinds of sweetmeats that . . .' She broke off. 'Is anything troubling you, Catrina?'

In silence, Catrina held out her letter. As Alice finished reading it, something flashed across her face; an indefinable expression which seemed to be compounded of relief and regret. 'You will have to return to England when the fleet sails.'

'I could not even do that! I am quite unable to pay my passage home!' Catrina gave a bitter little laugh.

'It would not be necessary for you to pay your passage home. Governor Eliott has issued a decree to the effect that all civilians and service wives who are unable to lay in twelve months' provisions are to take ship for England when the fleet leaves.' She sighed. 'I am afraid the poor old family retainers will have to be shipped home too, whatever their wishes may be in the matter.'

But I shall not leave, Catrina thought with the defiance of despair. Dominic loved me once, and I shall do everything in my power to make him love me again. He is not officially betrothed yet to Dinah.

Later that afternoon Dominic and General Ridgeway returned home for their first respite since the bombardment had started and the British fleet had made its subsequent victorious appearance in the Bay. Both of them looked exhausted, but their mood was elated.

Dinah claimed Dominic's attention immediately. 'My love, there are to be parties on board many of the ships in the harbour, and almost everyone is going! I know you are tired, but it would be too tame if we were not to put in an appearance at one of them!'

'I want to go to a party too, Papa!' Lucy put in.

'So you shall,' Alice told her. 'Mrs Brockway is giving a belated birthday tea for her little daughter, and all officers' children have been invited. The Brockways are, at the same time, putting on a musical *soirée* and buffet supper for adults.'

Dinah wrinkled her nose. 'The Brockways are so dull! A ship-board party sounds like much more fun! Do let us go to one, Dominic!'

He nodded with no great show of enthusiasm, but Dinah

was satisfied, and she left the room to select what she intended to wear.

General Ridgeway announced that he meant to take a nap, and Alice insisted that Lucy, too, should have a nap before the birthday party.

'Since Dinah will doubtless be primping and preening in the bedroom all afternoon, the child had best sleep in my bed,' she said. 'Come along, Lucy.'

For the first time in a very long while, Catrina found herself completely alone with Dominic. But he was already on his feet, and the mask of politeness which he wore told her that he was about to excuse himself and leave the room.

She stepped into his path. 'Dominic, what have I done?' she asked quietly.

'I don't have the faintest idea what you are talking about!'

'Don't you? You have announced that you intend becoming engaged to Dinah. You avoid me, and when you are forced to be in my presence you treat me like a distant stranger . . .'

'Good God!' he exploded, his knuckles showing white as he clenched his hands into fists. 'Are you never satisfied? You read me a lecture upon my wild behaviour; you reviled me about the reputation I was gaining for myself and you reminded me of the duty I owed to Lucy! So I reformed, and I announced that I was to marry a woman who is beyond reproach . . .'

'But you do not love her, do you?'

'What has that to say to anything? I loved Millicent once. Now keep out of my affairs, Catrina. And, what is more important, keep out of my way!' He strode to the door, and turned. 'I hear that you will be forced to take ship for England. Thank God for that!'

She sank into a chair, racked by a pain which was almost physical in its intensity. He could not have made himself more clear. He had decided to marry a woman who was 'beyond reproach'. What was it that Alice had once said? 'When it comes to choosing a wife, a man looks for someone who is virtuous, modest and reserved.'

In sick despair, Catrina stared in front of her. How careful he had been, since Millicent's death had set him free, to give her no encouragement at all. Everything about his behaviour had been saying, You were a delightful, desirable diversion while I was trapped in an unhappy marriage. But now everything has changed, and I need a wife who is beyond reproach.

Anger, humiliation and rebellion warred with the pain which Catrina was feeling. She would not conveniently disappear from his life! She would *not*. She would stay, and haunt Dominic, and be a thorn in his side. If she could have nothing else, she would have revenge.

Later, she found Alice had prepared Lucy for the birthday tea-party and sent her to the Brockways' home escorted by Hobson. In the bedroom which they shared, Catrina watched Dinah prepare for the ship-board parties. The girl was wearing her most becoming gown of a satin underdress beneath flowing pale blue gauze. When she had finished arranging her elaborate fair curls, and powdered them to lighten them even further, she moved away from the dressing-table and gave Catrina a bright smile.

'I am leaving now, so you will be able to attend to your own toilette in peace.'

But Catrina did not sit down before the mirror when Dinah had swept out. Instead, perversely probing the wound, she hovered in the doorway and watched as Dominic came to meet Dinah. How splendid he looked in his gold-braided dress uniform, with his wide shoulders and narrow waist and his breeches fitting tightly to his thighs. No wonder Dinah's smile was possessive as she tucked her hand into his arm.

Catrina turned away, and began to get ready for the far less exciting *soirée* and buffet supper the Brockways were giving. There was not a great deal for her to choose from among her made-over gowns. Not that it mattered overmuch what she wore, she thought wretchedly, and chose a flowered muslin. At the last moment the thought of spending the evening in the company of people who had cause for happiness and celebration, and of having to pretend to the same emotions, proved too much for her. She went to find Alice, and made her apologies.

'I have a wretched headache, and I'll be poor company. Please explain to the Brockways.'

'I am sorry, my dear. Go and lie down, and I shall ask

Cook to send supper to your room.'

'No, that will not be necessary. I'll have something on a tray in the drawing-room.'

After the Ridgeways had left, Catrina picked at her supper. The meal should have been a greatly relished treat after the meagre rations of the past months, and yet she scarcely tasted it. From outside in the town came the sounds of revelry, making her feel more desolate than ever.

The house itself was oppressively quiet. She suspected that the servants had also been unable to resist the urge to mingle with happy, celebrating crowds. It had, after all, been a mistake to isolate herself like this with her own misery. Ought she, perhaps, to go and join the Brockways' party after all, and explain that her headache had vanished?

Half-decided, she went to the bedroom and picked up a drab-coloured cloak that had been donated to her by one of the officers' wives and which had seen better days. She draped herself in it and slipped outside. The streets were all but empty. The crowds had poured into inns and taverns and private houses to continue their celebrating. Catrina abandoned the notion of joining the Brockways' party and wandered, instead, towards the harbour.

The British vessels were gently rocking at anchor and were gay with the sound of music and laughter. They were brightly lit with flambeaux, and she was standing in the circle of light which they cast upon the jetty when she heard footsteps behind her. She turned swiftly.

A tall figure loomed up out of the darkness and came purposefully towards her. It flashed through her mind that she had been an utter fool to come out alone on a night like this, when the British fleet was in and their crew would be seeking adventure. When there was so much noise going on, the screams of a lone female would be completely drowned . . .

Jake Farraday had been emerging from the Queen's Head when he had seen the girl wrapped in her drab cloak passing by. He would not have given her a second thought had it not been that something about her had stirred a memory. Something about the tilt of her head and the way she carried herself . . .

Then it had come back to him. He had offered her a gift of a bag of flour once, and she had thrown it at his head. He had questioned the crowd at the waterfront about her, and had learnt that her name was Catrina Beaumont, and that she was an heiress whose money was temporarily out of her reach in England.

An heiress! And now here she was crossing his path again, as reckless and foolhardy as ever. He had been invited to the party being held on board HMS *Venturer*. In the present circumstances, his specialised knowledge of the local sea conditions made him too valuable for the officers of the British Navy to ostracise him as they usually did.

Catrina turned at the sound of his footsteps. The hood of her cloak slipped slightly, revealing the rich dark-red hair he remembered. He moved into the circle of light thrown by the flambeaux, and swept her a mocking bow. 'No longer quite so temporarily embarrassed, I trust?'

'What? Oh . . . Of course! Jake Farraday!'

'How gratifying that you should remember my name! Particularly,' he added with a note of feigned reproach, 'since I waited in vain for you at the Queen's Head.'

Catrina's lips twisted in a painful grimace as she remembered how she had, in truth, set out to meet him at the Queen's Head that night, with the main object of punishing Dominic. And it had ended with the two of them trapped inside Dinah's house, in a scene between them which must have given Dominic yet one more reason for deciding that she was not a fit person to be his wife.

Catrina's attention returned to the present. 'Indeed, Mr Farraday, I am as financially embarrassed—in a temporary way—as when we first met. Tell me, will you be setting sail for Britain soon?'

'Looking for a free berth, Miss Beaumont? Unfortunately, I ply between here and the Barbary coast, or the Portuguese harbours. But if you have some urgent reason for getting away from here, I am happy to place myself and *Arabella* at your disposal.'

'I had hoped that you might be willing to undertake a commission to bring something for me from England.'

He was silent, considering. Her fortune was obviously still tied up at home. A voyage to England would involve a loss of profit to himself, but on the other hand it would earn him a debt of gratitude from her. On second thoughts, the fortune had best remain where it was for the moment, since the lack of it rendered her more vulnerable, and that suggested several interesting possibilities.

'Unfortunately,' he said at last with mock-sorrow, 'I am *persona non grata* in most British ports. I am sure you will have been told what a shocking character I am, Miss Beaumont.'

Disappointment that he, too, had failed her caused Catrina to turn waspish. 'I have, but at least I did not think you lacked courage as well! You have returned to Gibraltar now that it is safe to do so, but where were you when people were near to starving, and desperate enough to pay your extortionate prices?'

'Alas, I was wounded in the chest during a skirmish with a French vessel. And instead of castigating me, Miss Beaumont, will you not show some compassion and come with me to my lodgings, and give me your honest opinion as to whether the scar has ruined my manly beauty for ever?'

In spite of herself, a laugh escaped her. He might be a rogue, as Dominic had said, but he was undeniably entertaining in an outrageous way.

Jake Farraday hid a smile of satisfaction. He had been exactly right in the approach he adopted towards her. He added smoothly, 'But I dare say you have a prior engagement. You are obviously about to join one of the parties on board ship.'

'No. I—I merely came out for a walk.'

'As I have also. But now that we are both here, Miss Beaumont, shall we not join in the revels together? Shall we go aboard *Venturer*?'

Recklessness swept through Catrina. For a few minutes in what had been a wretched, desolate day he had cheered her spirits, and she could not bear the thought of returning alone to an empty house. 'I'll go with you.'

He caught her hands in his. 'You are a wench after my own heart!'

'I am *not* a wench!'

'I beg your pardon, ma'am,' he mocked. 'Shall we go?'

Her recklessness evaporated before a sudden rush of misgiving. He was as magnificently dressed as he had been on the first occasion when they had met, and would not look out of place among the invited guests, while she certainly would.

'I . . . My gown is not suitable . . .' she began.

'You disappoint me, Miss Beaumont. I had not thought you would be faint-hearted enough to cry off on such a trivial excuse!'

'I am *not* crying off!'

He tucked her arm inside his own and began to lead her towards the gang-bridge, and she was committed.

She was relieved to find that the crush on board *Venturer* was so great that no one challenged them. Coolly, Jake Farraday announced their names to the officer who was receiving the guests, and they were welcomed aboard. As Catrina handed her cloak to a seaman it suddenly struck her that Farraday had known her name when they met this evening, and yet she could not remember having told him who she was at the time of their first encounter. But she must have done so, she decided, and forgot the matter as she allowed him to steer her towards a table where food and drink were being dispensed.

A Naval band was playing, and at one end of the deck people were dancing. Jake Farraday set his glass down and held out a hand to Catrina.

'Shall we join them?'

'I cannot dance,' she admitted.

'You amaze me, Miss Beaumont! You are quite beautiful, and yet no one has ever taught you a simple social accomplishment like that! Well, *I* shall teach you to dance!'

She shook her head. 'The steps look far too complicated.'

'Hmm . . .' He stared for a moment at the lines of men and women weaving and twirling, touching hands briefly before reforming in a dextrous pattern. 'Wait here, Miss Beaumont,' he said at last, and thrust his way through the throng towards the band.

This time Catrina noticed that heads, particularly female ones, turned to watch him. He was, she thought, not a man who would escape notice for long.

The music came to an end, and the dancers clapped and

returned to their seats. Jake Farraday had reached Catrina's side again when the band struck up once more, but this time it was music played at a completely different tempo.

'We shall try this one,' Farraday said briskly. She found his arm about her waist, one of her hands clasped in his, and she was drawn against his chest.

'You are making a public spectacle of me!' she whispered fiercely. 'Let me go at once—this is no dance . . .'

'Indeed it is. One—two—one, two, three . . . No, don't look at your feet. Just allow your body to relax, and follow my steps.'

Involuntarily, she found herself moving in time with him and with the music, and she felt his lips brushing her cheek. 'This is called a waltz,' he explained. 'It is a new dance.'

For the first time, she allowed her attention to be diverted from the newly-mastered intricacies of the dance steps, and she realised that they were the only couple on the floor. 'Do they not know the steps?' she enquired.

'I dare say not.' Jake Farraday's arm tightened about her waist. He felt stirring inside him a desire for this girl which his jaded sexual appetite had almost forgotten. She amused him; she excited him, and she was an heiress. Here was the kind of challenge which he relished!

As he whirled her around, Catrina realised that something was very wrong. Some of the elegant guests were watching them with outraged expressions while others had ostentatiously turned their backs upon them. She realised that Dinah and Dominic were among those watching, and her heart gave a jerk as she recognised the fury in his eyes.

A senior Naval officer was saying something to the musicians, and they stopped playing abruptly. Her face flaming, Catrina waited for the officer to approach them and order them to leave the ship. Instead, the band struck up a lively tune and this time couples rose and took up positions for the formation of a more conventional, restrained dance.

'The party has become tedious,' she heard Farraday say lightly. 'Shall we seek entertainment elsewhere?'

'Please—Please let us leave.' As they threaded their way through the dancers, Catrina found herself being studiously ignored by the women and boldly appraised by the men.

Suddenly she felt her arm grabbed from behind, and then she was whirled about, and staring into Dominic's blazing eyes. Dinah stood beside him, a prim look about her mouth.

'I don't know how you could have done such a thing, Catrina!' she exclaimed. 'Why, even in London there are only a few hostesses who are risquée enough to allow the waltz to be danced!'

'Oh, mind your own business!' Catrina snapped, close to tears.

'Come,' Dominic ground out. 'I am taking you home.'

'The lady,' Farraday interrupted languidly, 'is with me.'

'The lady,' Dominic snarled, 'is a member of my family, and if you ever pass so much as the time of day with her again I shall knock you senseless!'

Jake swept Catrina a bow. 'My regrets, Miss Beaumont. I had forgotten how very provincial and prudish English society is. For the moment I am at a disadvantage, for I have a great aversion to being knocked down. But I do hope we shall meet again.'

'Indeed we shall!' Catrina replied, anger and defiance breaking through her sense of humiliation. 'I know where you may be reached!'

Dominic took her arm in a hard grip, and said through gritted teeth, 'You are leaving. I am taking you home this minute!'

'*That* would please Dinah!' Catrina said nastily, glancing at the other girl. 'I fancy she had not expected her evening to be cut so short!'

'No, I did not,' Dinah muttered resentfully. 'Someone else could be asked to take Catrina home, Dominic.'

'Harry Price will be glad to look after you while I am away,' he told Dinah shortly. 'I shall return as soon as I can.'

Then his hand was on Catrina's arm, pulling her inexorably through the crowd, to retrieve her cloak. He maintained an ominous silence until they had reached the darkened street, and then he raged at her,

'What did you think you were about, attending the party with Farraday? And dancing in that manner with him? Do you realise the kind of reputation he has? Apart from the fact that he is as likely to run guns to the Spaniards as he is to break through the blockade and bring in food, he is known to be a man who would ruin a woman with as little compunction as . . .'

'He could not ruin me, Dominic,' she interrupted quietly. 'I am beyond that.'

He stopped in his tracks. 'What the devil does *that* mean?'

'You know what it means. You have said yourself that I am not like other women. I am not repelled by the thought of a man. By the thought of . . . Oh, do not pretend to be stupid! I am not modest or virtuous or reserved. Millicent said that I had the depraved appetites of an animal, and she was right.'

He took hold of her shoulders, and shook her. 'What nonsense is this? How could you believe in Millicent's distorted views?'

'It was not only Millicent who made me realise that I am without shame. I learnt from Violet that men expect their wives to be disgusted by their attentions, and—and you yourself admitted that the reason you have decided to marry Dinah is because she is beyond reproach. I am certainly not that!' Her voice blurred with tears.

He pulled her into his arms, and a groaning sound escaped him. 'You fool, Catrina! In their different ways, both Violet and Millicent filled your head with warped travesties of the truth! Believe me, you are exactly what any normal man would want in a woman!'

'But—But you wouldn't wish to marry me . . .'

'Dear God in heaven, there is nothing I wish more! I wish it so desperately that I have been driven half out of my mind! But surely you know, Catrina, that you are forbidden to me? Surely you know that I cannot marry you—*ever*?'

CHAPTER FOURTEEN

CATRINA BROKE LOOSE and began to run, instinct alone taking her in the direction of the Ridgeways' house, pushing her way past revellers who tried to obstruct her. She could hear Dominic cursing as he followed her, but she was nimbler than he at weaving through the dancing, inebriated crowds who had spilled into the streets.

Catrina found the sounds of revelry coming from everywhere almost indecent and wholly incongruous in her own emotional state. People were celebrating, while she herself felt bereaved and betrayed. Dominic had been lying. He must have been lying. How could he be forbidden to marry her?

The Ridgeways' house was in sight now, and she could hear someone—Alice, presumably—playing the pianoforte in the drawing-room. She and the General must have left the Brockways early so that Lucy could be put to bed. Only now did Dominic catch up with Catrina, and he took her arm.

No one saw or heard them as they entered by the side door. Still holding her arm, Dominic forced Catrina towards his room. He closed its door firmly behind them, and lit candles.

'Sit down, Catrina,' he ordered. His dark hair was dishevelled, and his face wore a taut, unsmiling look.

She perched on the edge of the bed and watched him numbly. He himself remained standing some distance away, as if he were afraid of being tempted to touch her—and so ruin whatever other lies he intended telling her.

'Catrina,' he began, 'did you really not know that a marriage between us would never be possible?'

'I don't believe you!'

'Then ask any minister of the Church, or any representative of the law.' His voice roughened. 'What do you think caused my demented behaviour during those months after Millicent's death? I faced a new refinement of torture. I was ready to start living once more; I was free to love again and to marry again, but it could never be you. I could not come to terms with the fact, and so I began to pursue a life of wild, reckless excess. When you forced me to realise that my behaviour was harming Lucy, I decided to accept the only solution open to me. I asked Dinah to marry me.'

'But *why*? Why Dinah? Why not me?'

He sighed. 'Have you understood nothing I have been saying? Has no one ever told you that a man is legally prohibited from marrying—or having sexual connection with—his wife's sister?'

Cartina stared at him. 'But Millicent is dead . . .'

'That alters nothing. The prohibition is based upon biblical law, and in the eyes of the law I shall always be your brother. That is what the term "brother-in-law" means. I thought you knew that.'

She shook her head, and sat in shattered silence for a moment. 'I—assumed you did not consider me fit to be your wife,' she muttered at last.

He looked down at her, his face harsh with pain. 'As your brother, there is at least one service I can render you. You learnt all you know about married love from Millicent and from Violet, and both of them had twisted views upon the subject. Millicent was over-fastidious by nature, and your mother sheltered her from the realities of life. She taught Millicent to be ashamed of her own body. Your sister thought marriage meant that I should place her on a pedestal and worship her upon some purely spiritual plane. Nothing I did or said could convince her that physical love was not dirty and disgusting. And as for Violet—love never entered into her experience. She performed a mechanical service in return for money, and any views on marriage she gained from those of her clients who had wives were bound to be distorted. We live in a society in which marriages are arranged, and some of them are bound to be unhappy. It is from that kind of marriage that Violet would have drawn her clients.'

In the depths of her own pain, Catrina experienced an overwhelming desire to inflict pain too. 'You are saying that

I am quite normal, Dominic. And yet—I love you, but when Jake Farraday held me in his arms and danced with me, and his mouth brushed my cheek, I felt *something*. I wanted him to kiss me. Would you call that normal, too?'

She watched as his eyes narrowed to slits and his face took on a gaunt look. But she felt no triumph at the knowledge that her truthful admission had struck him to the heart.

He stooped, and took her hands in his, drawing her to her feet. 'I would call it unfortunate and dangerous, but entirely normal,' he said rawly. 'Jake Farraday is a devious, cold-blooded scoundrel, but he has good looks and charm, and you responded to that. You are a warm and passionate woman, and whomever you marry will be a very fortunate man one day.'

She shook her head, tears coursing down her cheeks. 'I shall not marry . . .'

'You will. You must. Do not waste your life, Catrina, because of me.'

'Since we cannot marry, I would rather be your mistress than someone else's wife!'

He released her hands and moved away from her. He folded his arms across his chest and looked at her, his expression harsh, stark lines carved about his mouth. 'You have still not fully understood, have you? Anything of that nature between us would be termed incest. You *do* know what that means, don't you?'

'I don't care!' Catrina cried wildly. 'No one need know! You could end your unofficial engagement to Dinah, and you and I and Lucy could live together. As her aunt, what could be more natural than that I should care for her?'

A muscle jerked in Dominic's cheek. 'Even if I were prepared to consider such a thing, the world would not be fooled. But I am *not* prepared to consider it. I am your brother, and responsible for your welfare, both moral and physical.'

He moved towards the door, and stopped. The guttering candle-light etched his face in dour lines. 'And, as your brother, I am ordering you to return to England. Be prepared to leave when that fleet sails, Catrina.'

All but one of the candles went out as he slammed the

door behind him. She remained there in his room, knowing that he was returning to Dinah.

Her brother! How could fate have been so pitiless? Why should some old commandment forced upon the children of Israel and incorporated into modern law have the power to wreck her own life?

She sprawled upon the bed, sobbing, her fists beating an impotent tattoo on the pillows. Dimly, she heard the door opening, and then Alice was seated beside her, stroking her hair.

'Poor child. Poor Catrina,' she murmured. 'I wondered where you had disappeared to. And then I heard a door slamming with force, and I went to investigate. I spoke to Dominic, and he told me . . .'

'It isn't fair!' Catrina cried passionately, sitting up and hugging her arms about her breast.

Alice sighed. 'Life seldom is fair. We all assumed you understood the situation. It has been obvious to everyone—well, to myself and John, at any rate—how you felt about Dominic. And that is why you must return to England. You must forget him.'

It was as pointless as telling her that she would have to cut off her right arm. Catrina shook her head blindly, and rose.

'I'm—going to bed. I don't wish to be awake when Dinah . . .' She was unable to go on, but Alice's expression told her that she understood.

Catrina let herself quietly into the shared bedroom, and undressed by the light of a single candle so that Lucy would not be disturbed. She slid into bed beside the child, and willed herself desperately to fall asleep. But thoughts scurried through her brain like trapped insects, and there was no comfort to be found in any of them.

Even the knowledge that she was not the flawed, base creature she had imagined herself to be brought a torment of its own. For that meant that Dinah would not automatically recoil from Dominic's advances, as she had believed. She would welcome them, and perhaps even invite them, and it was a thought which Catrina could scarcely contemplate without wanting to scream.

Almost as if her own anguish had somehow communicated itself to the child by her side, Lucy began to sob in her sleep. Catrina gathered her in her arms, and woke her gently.

Lucy clung to her. 'I dreamt—I dreamt God had taken you to be one of his angels,' she whimpered.

'It *was* only a dream. Go back to sleep.'

'Aunt Catrina—you won't leave me, will you?'

'I promise I won't leave Gibraltar,' Catrina said recklessly, and in that moment she knew that she had never reconciled herself to the thought of leaving. Remaining in Gibraltar, and being near Dominic in the tormenting knowledge that he was forever forbidden to her would be hard enough. But going away, and trying to forget his very existence, would be impossible.

Lucy went back to sleep, but Catrina was still wide awake when she heard whispering voices in the corridor outside, and a few moments later Dinah slipped into the room, carrying a candle.

Catrina tried to feign sleep, but Dinah was not fooled. 'I hope you realise what a scandal you caused,' she whispered balefully, 'arriving uninvited on *Venturer* in the company of that card-sharp and profiteer! And dancing with him the way you did! No one will acknowledge you after this!'

Catrina ignored her, and a while later she fell into a restless, dream-haunted doze from which she awakened fitfully throughout the remainder of the night. She rose early the next morning, before anyone else in the house was awake. Her plans had been forged during the night, and now she let herself quietly out of the house.

She wandered, undisturbed, through the ruins of the houses which had been hit during the Spaniards' bombardment of the town. Catrina guessed that the townspeople had looted most of the remaining items after the owners had salvaged what they could, but even so she found that by searching through the rubble she was able to harvest a few necessities. One ruined dwelling yielded a dust-covered palliasse; another several blankets hidden beneath the wreckage of what had been a wooden chest. She also unearthed some cooking-pots.

Catrina manhandled the palliasse so that it sat sideways upon one of the blankets; then she piled the rest of the articles on top of the palliasse and dragged all of it to the cow-byre she had discovered.

She returned to the house just in time to wash hastily and change her gown before joining the others at breakfast. Lucy gave her a reproachful look. 'I woke up, and you weren't there, Aunt Catrina.'

Smiling at the child, avoiding the eyes of everyone else, Catrina said, 'I couldn't sleep, so I rose early and went for a walk. I went further than I had intended to.'

Her explanation was accepted in silence. Dominic and General Ridgeway left for their duties, and Alice announced that she and Hobson intended to spend the morning at the harbour, bidding for supplies to last the household the regulation twelve months. Dinah expressed the intention of joining them to do the same, and gave Catrina a sidelong look.

'*You* had better pack. No one knows precisely when the fleet will be sailing.'

Lucy dogged Catrina's footsteps suspiciously. 'What did Mrs Forest mean about packing, Aunt Catrina? You promised you wouldn't leave!'

'And I'll keep my promise, love. See, I am not packing?'

But she did continue to pack her belongings unobtrusively, and in her spare time she kept her diary up to date:

> The weather is bad, with a good deal of rain and heavy winds. It has put my mind at rest about one important thing. The cow-byre is quite weatherproof and does not let in the rain. Also, I have been able to place every utensil I have salvaged in position below the near-by rock, which is a catchment area for the rain, and I shall be assured of a water supply when I move in.

One evening Catrina was alone as usual. The servants had retired; Dinah and Alice had accompanied General Ridgeway to a function at the Convent and Lucy had been put to bed. In spite of all her reassurances, the child still sensed that Catrina was preparing to leave, and she had become even more clinging of late. She lay in bed, rigid and unrelaxed, her eyes wide open.

'Go to sleep, Lucy,' Catrina urged.

'As soon as I'm asleep, you'll go away.'

Catrina sighed. If only the child were a little older, and could be trusted with an adult confidence. But regrettable though it was, the little girl had to display genuine distress when Catrina's disappearance was discovered, for otherwise the adults would worm the truth out of her almost at once.

'Look,' Catrina said. 'I'll get undressed for bed, shall I? I could hardly go anywhere in my night-shift.'

Lucy said nothing, but her face relaxed slightly. Catrina slipped behind the screen and changed into a transparent chemise of pale blue batiste. She shrugged her arms into the sleeves of a woollen wrap, and returned to Lucy's side.

'Your hair is still pinned up,' the child pointed out relentlessly.

Catrina shrugged, and moved to the dressing-table, pulling the pins from her hair and allowing it to fall to her shoulders.

'*Now* will you go to sleep, Lucy?'

The child nodded, and closed her eyes. Catrina snuffed out all but one candle and sat down to confide her plans to her diary.

> I have found that wild leeks grow in abundance not far from the cow-byre, and they could be made into a broth. The harbour will provide me with driftwood so that I may build fires. But I could not live indefinitely on a diet of wild leeks, and so I must think of some way of making provision for the future.

She sprinkled sand over the page and closed her diary. She could tell, from Lucy's breathing, that the child was asleep. The long-case clock in the hall struck seven times. What a ridiculous hour at which to be sitting in the near-dark, and dressed for bed! But if she were to get dressed again in this dim light she might make so much noise that Lucy would wake up again, and then it would be almost impossible to persuade the child to go back to sleep.

She would, she decided, carry her clothes into Alice's room and dress in there. She felt sure her hostess would not mind if she borrowed some of her pins with which to put her hair up again. She slipped quietly out of the room, and almost collided with Dominic. Her heart gave a painful jerk.

'I thought you were on duty tonight,' she murmured.

'I was. I am. I slipped away.'

'Hush! For goodness' sake don't wake Lucy!'

'I have to talk to you, Catrina.'

'Not here. I'm going to Alice's room, to dress. I'll be in the drawing-room afterwards.'

'I can't wait as long as that. I have to return to my post.' He hesitated. 'We'd better go to my room.'

She nodded, and followed him. As he held open the door for her, he asked, 'What is the reason for all the dressing and undressing at this time of the evening?'

'Lucy,' she said, and explained what had happened. She placed her clothes on a chair and watched as he lit branches of candles. 'What did you want to talk to me about, Dominic?'

He looked away from her. 'News has just reached me that the fleet is sailing in the morning, Catrina. I knew I would be unlikely to have another chance to say goodbye.'

'Oh . . .'

'I also wanted to ask you to . . . Well, to tell some kind of soothing lie to Lucy. You have spent more time with the child than anyone. You'll know how best to soften the blow.' He placed his arms about her, quite dispassionately, and brushed her cheek with his mouth. 'Farewell, my dear sister. I hope life will be good to you in the future.'

She twisted away from him. 'Dominic, you can say it as often as you like, but I am *not* your sister! I do not feel like your sister, any more than you feel like a brother towards me.'

'You have said enough, Catrina.' His voice was cold. 'You must come to terms with reality, as I have done. I feel exactly as a brother towards you now.'

'Do you, indeed!' Reckless anger tore through her. He believed he was saying farewell to her for ever. Did he really imagine she would be comforted, in the months and years ahead, by such a lie?

Deliberately she shrugged her arms out of the woollen wrap and stood before him clad only in her chemise. Beads of perspiration gathered on his brow as his gaze slowly raked her body, and he thrust a hand through his hair. 'Damn you, Catrina,' he grated, 'cover yourself!'

'But I am your sister, Dominic,' she taunted. 'And since you feel as a brother towards me now, why should I not dress in here? Please hand me my stays.'

He stooped, and grabbed up the wrap and moved towards her. As he flung it over her head to cover her shoulders she took a step towards him and the impetus of the violence with which he had slung the wrap around her made her fall against him.

'Is—Is this brotherly behaviour, Dominic?'

With a hopeless, muttered oath, he dropped the wrap and gathered her to him, his hands moving over the transparent chemise with feverish hunger while his mouth sought hers.

She felt herself lifted in his arms, but he did not remove his mouth from hers. Then she was lying on his bed, with his body stretched out beside her and he was kissing her throat while his hands slid beneath the chemise to caress her, sending that sweet, painful pounding through her loins. He felt her fumbling at the buttons of his tunic, and the sudden reminder that he was in uniform, that he was officially on duty and had left a junior officer in charge during his absence, brought him to his senses. His hands grew still upon her body and a long, hopeless shudder shook him.

He had tried, for so long now, to condition himself to the fact that she could never be more than a sister to him. If only their parting could have been dispassionate, with each of them maintaining a tacit lie, acceptance of the way things were might have become possible in the future. He might truly have come to think of her fondly as his sister. But she had torn aside the façade he had been trying so painfully to erect, and neither of them was any better off for it.

He heaved himself from the bed, and stood looking down at her. His voice was bleak as he said, 'For what it is worth, Catrina, you have made your point. But it has changed nothing. It has merely given each of us one more memory to try and blot out during the years to come. We shall never meet again. Goodbye.'

Then he was gone. She lay there for a while, weeping,

and then rose. She ignored her hoops and stays, and dressed in the remainder of her outer garments. Her night-shift felt uncomfortable worn over them, but it was necessary to put it on, for the frills on its shoulders and around its wrists must be visible to Dinah in case she should glance in the direction of the other bed when she came in later.

It no longer seemed a ridiculous hour at which to retire for the night, because she had to be awake early. Catrina returned to the other bedroom and slid quietly in beside Lucy. Against all her expectations, she fell asleep soon afterwards.

She awakened with a start to hear a clock chime five somewhere in the house. She could tell, by their even breathing, that both Dinah and Lucy were fast asleep. She slipped cautiously out of bed, and pulled her night-chemise over her head. After she had removed the bundle which she had made of her clothes from underneath the bed, she went into the kitchen and purloined a loaf of bread. Then she left the house.

When she reached the cow-byre she remembered, uneasily, that Lucy knew of the existence of the place. She could only hope that the child had forgotten about it, and would not mention it when the search for her inevitably began.

But no one approached the hiding-place. She ate a breakfast of bread and water, and then killed time by gathering wild leeks for a later meal. Afterwards she explored the terrain, mindful of the need to provide for herself. Once the fleet had sailed it might be impossible for her to be sent back to England, but she did not imagine that her act of defiance would go unpunished by the Governor. She would, therefore, have to remain in hiding.

When she judged it to be time, Catrina covered her gown with her drab cloak, and pulled the hood well over her hair. Then she went down to mingle with the crowd which was watching the sailing of the British fleet.

Catrina noticed that Admiral Rodney had left some vessels behind in the sheltered anchorages around the New Mole, but ominously, the Spaniards fired alarm guns and several rockets from the watch-towers along the coast as they witnessed the departure of the fleet. It was only too obvious that a renewed siege would soon be keeping

Gibraltar in a strangle-hold once more.

'So,' a mocking voice drawled behind Catrina. 'We meet again, Miss Beaumont.'

She turned, and looked into Jake Farraday's smiling blue eyes. 'I trust,' he went on, 'that your angry relative will not, once again, arrive from out of the blue and carry out his threat to knock me down! This coat was far too expensive to be made to suffer such a fate. What is he to you, may I ask?'

'He is—my brother,' she answered, her mouth twisting.

'Is he, indeed?' Farraday pursed his lips. A brother, and such a violent, domineering, possessive one at that, would be a decided complication. But he made his voice light. 'Tell me, does this brother of yours habitually keep you locked up in a cellar?'

Catrina stared at him. 'What a ridiculous question!'

'Well, you have a decided air of the fugitive about you. I spotted you only because I was looking out for you. I watched you for some time, and you took pains to be as unobtrusive as possible, besides hiding your face away beneath the hood of that remarkably ugly cloak you are wearing.'

'If it comes to that,' Catrina retorted, '*you* have been taking pains to keep in the background! I came to the waterfront with the express purpose of seeing you . . .'

'Indeed? How very flattering! If you did not see me before, it was because I did not wish to subject my coat to the press of the unwashed mob. I do hope it was for the sake of my manly beauty that you were seeking me, Miss Beaumont!'

She ignored the remark. 'You were quite right; I *am* a fugitive. I was meant to have sailed with the fleet, but I went into hiding instead. I defied the Governor's decree that only those who could lay in twelve months' supplies were to remain in Gibraltar, but I have no doubt that if I came out of hiding I would be placed on the next vessel leaving for England.'

He stroked his chin. 'What is the terrible fate which awaits you in England?'

The fate of never seeing Dominic again . . . Aloud, she said, 'I have a fortune waiting for me in England, but I choose, for personal reasons, to remain in Gibraltar.'

'A fortune, is it?' He showed his teeth in a grin of mocking disbelief.

'Yes,' she confirmed coolly, and slipped her hand inside the pocket of her cloak to reassure herself that the letter written by Mr Stanmore's son was still there.

Jake Farraday was watching her with speculation. It was clear to him that the person she was really defying was her brother. But at this stage, he decided, he would not delve too deeply into her personal life. 'Why have you been confiding in me, Miss Beaumont?' he asked. 'Has it occurred to you that I could so easily use the information that you are a fugitive to force you into becoming my mistress? I am quite capable of demanding blackmail, you know.'

'I have no doubt of that at all! But let me assure you, rather than give in to such a demand I would vastly prefer to be taken into custody and transported back to England on the next vessel! In any case, I believe you would be far more interested in money than in making me your mistress.'

He laughed. 'Well, I don't talk business in public. If you have a proposition to put to me, you will have to accompany me to my lodgings so that we can talk in civilised comfort.'

She gave him a long, assessing look. 'If you are thinking of me as easy prey, Mr Farraday, because I am in a vulnerable position, let me assure you of one thing—I would slit your throat before I allowed you to lay one finger on me!'

'What a bloodthirsty young woman you are!' He sighed with mock resignation. 'And tavern-maids are so careless; they *will* leave such things as fruit-knives lying about. So be at ease, Miss Beaumont. I have far too much respect for this fine coat of mine to risk a drop of gore being spilt upon it.'

He offered her his arm. 'Shall we repair to my lodgings?'

'Just remember,' Catrina said steadily, 'I am going with you to discuss business—and nothing more!'

He shuddered with feigned horror. 'Pray, Miss Beaumont, no more threats, or my nerves will be far too unsteady to discuss business of any kind!'

She hid a smile as she allowed him to steer her through what remained of the crowd. He had succeeded, with his nonsense, in lifting her depressed spirits. All the same, she did not underestimate him, and she resolved to be on her guard once they had reached his lodgings.

CHAPTER FIFTEEN

CATRINA HAD NEVER been inside a tavern before, and she had vaguely imagined entering a squalid tap-room filled with men in various stages of inebriation. The reality could not have been more reassuringly different. The Queen's Head was no drinking den for rough and dissipated wretches. Its floors were polished and scattered with rugs, and brass-work gleamed in the glow of a cheerful fire burning in an enormous grate. Some half-dozen off-duty officers, both naval and army, were seated at tables and drinking ale while playing cards, and behind the bar the landlord was polishing pewter tankards.

Jake Farraday whisked her rapidly through the public room towards an interior door, calling to the landlord over his shoulder, 'Send in breakfast for two, if you please.'

She found herself inside a small parlour, furnished with a comfortable-looking upholstered sofa at one end, a small table and four chairs, and a sideboard of carved oak. A fire had been lit in the grate of this room also, and the entire effect was welcoming and reassuring.

'This is my private parlour, Miss Beaumont,' Jake Farraday said. 'We shall not be disturbed while we discuss business over breakfast.'

She flushed. 'If it is your intention to try and place me under an obligation by offering me charity . . .'

'Seducing a young woman by offering her breakfast is not my style at all!' He laughed. 'The truth is that I am hungry, and I do not choose to eat alone. I have been at the harbour since dawn, anxiously awaiting the departure of the fleet. They may have done wonders for the townspeople's spirits, but they were totally disastrous when it came to the fortunes of a humble privateer!'

Two serving-girls entered with laden trays which they placed upon the sideboard. From inside its cupboards a crisply starched tablecloth was produced, as well as crockery and cutlery, and after bobbing respectful curtsies, the girls laid the table and set the covered dishes with their delicious-smelling contents upon it. Gratefully Catrina helped herself to bacon and scrambled eggs while Jake Farraday carved slices of cold ham for himself.

She gave him a direct look. 'So my calculations were correct. You have a full cargo on board *Arabella*, and you have been anxious for the fleet to leave so that the Spaniards may blockade the Bay again. Once they have done so, you will be able to sell your cargo at your usual profiteering prices.'

He shook his head at her in pretended sorrow. 'How unfortunate that you should read me so well! I can see that I shall never appear a hero in your eyes!'

She allowed herself a faint smile, and then concentrated on the business in hand. 'As I told you at the harbour, I have a fortune in London which I am unable to lay my hands upon at present. But if I gave you a promissory note, would you be prepared to let me have supplies from your cargo on credit?'

He took a draught of ale, and set his tankard down. 'Assuming that I have such an unloaded cargo on board *Arabella*, what proof can you offer that your credit is good?'

She reached into the pocket of her cloak and handed him the letter from Mr Stanmore's son, which he read carefully.

'What manner of goods do you want, and how much?' he asked.

'Ten pounds of flour, four pounds of sugar; eight pounds of oatmeal and the same of pease. At the prices you charge, I have calculated that the total cost would be in the region of six sovereigns. I also . . .'

'Ten sovereigns,' he corrected coolly.

'But that is outrageous!'

He shrugged. 'You are not in a position to bargain, are you, my dear Miss Beaumont?'

Catrina bit her lip. 'That is gross profiteering, and you know it! Very well—ten sovereigns, but only if the price includes vegetable seeds. I am sure you must have brought some on *Arabella* in order to take advantage of the sowing season.'

'Vegetable seeds!' he echoed, astonished. 'Even were you not a fugitive, what earthly good would they do you? No one who has land of any size available is likely to allow you, or anyone else, the use of it!'

'I know that. I have thought about the matter, and I intend creating an artificial garden. I shall gather soil from wherever I may find it, and spread it upon a flat rocky ledge. When I have obtained a sufficient depth I mean to sow vegetable seeds and sell my crops in the market-place.' She smiled at him. 'I shall take a leaf out of your book, Mr Farraday, and charge whatever exorbitant sums the market will bear!'

He threw back his head and roared with laughter. 'Miss Beaumont, you are altogether beyond price! By God, I am going to enjoy doing business with you! Ten sovereigns it is, then, to include a selection of vegetable seeds.'

He picked up the hand-bell which stood on the corner of the table, and a moment later his summons was answered by the two parlour-maids.

'Bring me writing-materials when you have cleared the table,' Jake Farraday commanded.

The dishes were whisked away, and notepaper, ink, a selection of quills and a small box of fine sand set out in their place. Jake Farraday began to write with extravagant flourishes of the quill. Already he could see a way of bending this extraordinary, challenging girl to his will!

When he had sprinkled sand over the page, he handed it to Catrina. Her frown deepened as she read what he had written. 'This is nothing short of usury!' she stammered, outraged. 'You propose to charge monthly compounded interest on the capital sum at the rate of 50 per cent!'

His blue eyes gleamed at her. 'I am prepared to waive all interest whatever—in exchange for one kiss.'

Very deliberately, she reached for the quill and dipped it into the ink. Then she signed her name to the document. He would have been disappointed in her if she had not done so.

She handed the promissory note back to him, and stood up. 'If you will now escort me to *Arabella*, Mr Farraday, I shall collect my supplies.'

He folded the note and tucked it inside the pocket of his coat, then also rose. 'After you, Miss Beaumont.'

She moved towards the door, and he followed. He reached across her to open it and on a sudden impulse she turned, placing her hands on his shoulders and tilting back her head to offer him her lips.

He hid his surprise. Instinct told him that this was not a capitulation but a sudden whim, and he placed the utmost restraint upon himself as he explored her mouth with a subtle blend of practised skill and gentle sensuality.

Then he released her, and began to reach inside his pocket for the promissory note. She grabbed his wrist, and said fiercely, 'Oh no! The rate of interest remains as stated! My favours may be freely given when I choose to do so, but they cannot be bought!'

'A pity,' he murmured. 'A very great pity. For rather more than that one kiss, I would have been prepared to waive the entire debt. You would not—er—choose to give freely whatever else may not be bought?'

She turned away, her colour high, and opened the door before he could do so. The landlord bade them a courteous good morning as they left the tavern.

Outside, Catrina strove to bring matters between them back to a purely businesslike plane. She said crisply, 'You are far too conspicuous a figure for me to walk beside you now that the crowd has thinned. Please lead the way, and I shall follow you at a distance.'

He nodded and began to thread his way towards the waterfront. As she walked along in his wake, Catrina tried to analyse her feelings about that kiss, and also her motives for having offered it. It would have been hypocritical to deny to herself that she had enjoyed it. It had not swept her along on a explosive tide of longing and desire, the way Dominic's kisses had always done. But on a purely physical level she had found pleasure in it, and the knowledge shamed and confused her.

'You are a warm and passionate woman,' Dominic's words returned to her, 'and you responded to his good looks and his charm . . .'

She sighed. At the time, she had told herself that her impulse to offer Jake Farraday her mouth had been to punish him for his suggestion that her kisses could be bought. But was the truth not, instead, that she had wished to punish *Dominic* in some obscure way?

She abandoned the complex puzzle when she caught up with Farraday at the spot where *Arabella* lay moored. He gave instructions to his crew, and within a few minutes the supplies she was buying from him on credit had been weighed and poured into linen bags. Then everything was packed inside a sack.

'You cannot possibly carry that,' Jake told her. 'I shall deliver it for you.'

'Thank you,' she returned drily. 'but I do not trust you an inch. I have no intention of letting you know where my hiding-place is.'

He shook his head sadly. 'Such a suspicious nature . . . But you still cannot carry such a heavy load through the town without attracting attention. And that is the last thing you wish to do, I imagine?'

She gazed thoughtfully at his crew, mentally acknowledging the logic of his statement. Her glance fell upon an elderly man with an honest and rather simple face.

'If I may borrow the services of that gentleman,' she told Farraday, 'I would be grateful to both of you.'

'Rawlings,' Jake called to the man. 'Carry this sack for the lady.'

'Ay, sir.' The sack was easily lifted upon the broad shoulder of Rawlings.

Catrina looked at Jake Farraday. 'I very much hope to repay you in full, the next time *Arabella* arrives in the Bay. I trust you realise, however, how grossly unfair it would be if I were to be in a position to repay you long before your return, and the exorbitant monthly interest goes on accruing through no fault of my own!'

'I shall rely entirely on your word, Miss Beaumont. If you tell me that you are in a position to repay me at a particular date, I shall accept it without question.' His eyes mocked her. 'And I hope your conscience will smite you when you compare your own lack of faith in me with *my* utter confidence in your trustworthiness!'

Her lips twitched. She could not help being amused and intrigued by this contradictory man. She held out her hand to him. 'Until we meet again, Mr Farraday.'

Then she turned away, and began to walk along the crowded street, glancing over her shoulder every few minutes to ensure that Rawlings was following her with the sackful of provisions. When they had reached one of the gulleys in the rocks where the townspeople had sheltered during the

Spanish bombardment, she told Rawlings, 'Thank you. You may set the load down now.'

His kindly eyes wore a worried look. ' 'T'ain't a fitting place for you to be left, miss.'

'Oh, I shall do very well here,' she replied airily, indicating a sheet of canvas which someone had abandoned when the Spaniards ceased firing on the town. 'I shall construct a tent for myself, and be quite snug.'

'Begging your pardon, miss, but are you on the run from the law?'

'In a manner of speaking, yes. You see, I was ordered to sail to England with the fleet today, and I decided to go into hiding instead.'

He hesitated, and then withdrew from his pocket a grubby piece of linen. He untied the knot which held it together, and picked out one of three sovereigns which it contained. 'Take it, miss—to help out, like,' he said gruffly.

Tears stung her eyes at this unexpected generosity from a stranger, and one who could obviously ill afford it at that. 'Thank you, Rawlings, but I cannot possibly take it. I would guess it is part of your life's savings. I do appreciate the thought very much, but I shall manage very well. Please do not feel anxious about me.'

He shook his head doubtfully and retied the piece of cloth around the coins. Then, with several backward glances at her, he walked away.

It had been a busy night for Dominic and many other officers and men. There were countless tasks which needed to be completed in time for the sailing of the fleet; despatches had to be written, inventories had to be prepared, showing the military supplies which it was expected would be required by the time another relieving convoy arrived. But even when his duties had been completed, he had delayed going home. He had stood by the window of the officers' mess and looked down at the waterfront where the fleet were preparing to sail, his thoughts bleak. Only when the last of the ships was being carried away by the wind and the tide did he square his shoulders, and leave for home.

As he entered the drawing-room, Lucy threw herself at him. 'She—She broke her promise, Papa! She said—Aunt Catrina said—she would not leave me, but she has!'

He picked the child up in his arms. 'Aunt Catrina could not help it, Lucy. The army ordered her to leave . . .'

He was interrupted by a crack of brittle laughter from Dinah. 'You think she obeyed the army, Dominic? She has left, but not by any orders, and not with the fleet!'

'What do you mean?' He set Lucy down on the floor, and Tim bounded over to her, licking the tears from her cheeks in a gesture of comfort.

It was Alice who answered him quietly. 'When the household rose this morning, Catrina was nowhere to be found. I looked inside the trunk in the bedroom, and found it to be empty. At the same time we discovered that her clothes had gone.'

Anxiety mixed with anger coursed through Dominic. 'Where could she have gone? And how could she hope to subsist, with no money and no food?'

'More to the point,' Dinah put in acidly. 'how is poor John to explain her actions to the Governor? She has placed him in an intolerable position!'

'Does General Ridgeway know what has happened?' Dominic demanded.

Alice nodded. 'He is, at the moment, organising a search of all the ruined buildings in Gibraltar to see if she is hiding in one of them.'

A deeply repugnant and alarming thought struck Dominic, and without explanation he hurried from the room and left the house. Catrina was no fool, and she would not have taken this step unless she expected to be able to survive, and therefore she would have needed help from someone. There was only one person Dominic could think of to whom she might have gone for help.

It did not take long to reach the Queen's Head. 'Jake Farraday puts up here when he is on the Rock,' he addressed the landlord. 'I want to see him.'

'He went out about an hour since, Captain, and has not returned.'

'Did he have a young lady with him?'

The landlord made a deprecating gesture. 'Mr Farraday is a gentleman who likes ladies, and they like him. Some call on him from time to time when he stays here, but I don't take account of their comings and goings.'

'You would have noticed the particular young lady I am

enquiring about, and remembered her. She has copper-coloured hair and green eyes. Has she been here this morning?' Dominic demanded roughly.

'I am sure I couldn't say, Captain. I don't notice, in particular, the things that don't concern me. She is most certainly not here now.'

Dominic left the inn and hurried instead to the waterfront in search of *Arabella*'s mooring. He found Jake Farraday on the quay, in conversation with an elderly man who appeared to be a member of his crew.

Dominic approached Farraday, who dismissed his crew member and held out a hand. 'Good morning, Beaumont.'

Dominic ignored the offered hand. 'My name is not Beaumont. I am Captain Ross. Where is Miss Beaumont?'

Jake studied him. A step-brother, perhaps? If so, he was an unusually possessive one. Catrina must be fond of him to wish to stay in Gibraltar, although it was difficult to see why. Aloud, Jake said smoothly, 'I take it Miss Beaumont has disappeared? How very worrying that must be for her family and friends. But why should you assume that I . . .'

'Don't try to play games with me, Farraday,' Dominic cut him short in an ominous voice. 'I intend boarding your cutter and carrying out a search.'

Jake coloured angrily. 'You have no authority to do so!'

'I could very easily obtain the necessary authority after the event. I have only to explain that I needed to act immediately, and without giving you the opportunity to dispose of evidence.'

'You are talking nonsense, and you have no grounds for searching my cutter!'

'My official grounds,' Dominic interrupted bluntly, 'will be that I suspected you of having abducted Miss Beaumont, and of keeping her confined on board your vessel.'

'Why on earth should I do such a thing? I assure you, I have no need to *abduct* young ladies. Those who go with me, do so willingly, even eagerly.'

'Like a certain sixteen-year-old girl who ran away from home to sail with you to Ireland?' Dominic's voice was deceptively mild. 'It is known that her brothers went after you, for they were seen removing her from *Arabella* in Dublin Bay. Months later her brothers returned alone to England, and the family have always refused to speak of what became of her. Some say you had corrupted her so thoroughly that she turned whore in the streets of Dublin. Others maintain that she entered a nunnery because she could not face normal life after what you had done to her. Yet others insist that her mind had been unhinged and that she has been confined in an Irish asylum ever since.'

'Gossip,' Farraday said airily. 'But how dull a man must be if he attracts no gossip at all!'

Dominic grabbed hold of the revers of Farraday's embroidered coat. With his face close to the other man's, he said through clenched teeth, 'I am boarding your cutter. Try to stop me if you dare!'

He flung Farraday aside with contemptuous force, and mounted the gang-plank. Jake Farraday busied himself by smoothing the ruffled revers of his coat, his face a mask. He made no attempt to stop Dominic.

Catrina had waited until Rawlings was completely out of sight before she dragged the sackful of provisions to the cow-byre. She stood in the doorway, surveying the place which was intended to be her home from now on.

She had cleaned it out as well as she could, but it was still austere and bleak. The walls were of rough stone, and the floor of earth. Apart from the household utensils she had scavenged from among ruined dwellings, and the palliasse and bedding, there were no other home comforts.

She sighed, and then shrugged. She did not intend to spend much time inside the place; it would shelter her when it rained, and be a roof over her head at night. Otherwise, her days would be fully occupied in the struggle for self-sufficiency. She had already earmarked the spot where she intended to create her artificial garden. It was a flat, rocky ledge of substantial breadth and length. Dauntingly substantial, when she considered the quantity of soil that would be needed to build it up to a sufficient depth for a garden.

Then she straightened her shoulders. The sooner she started, the sooner her task would be completed. Armed with a dish and a soup-ladle, she left the cow-byre and went outside. It was frustrating, back-breaking work, digging soil with the handle of the soup-ladle from between rocks and anywhere else she could find it; scooping it into the dish and then carrying it to the ledge where it seemed to mock her with its inadequacy.

At mid-afternoon, she was forced to stop digging out soil, for the sound of voices reached her. Retreating swiftly towards the cow-byre, she peeped out from behind the shelter of the palmettos. Soldiers were searching the gulleys in which the service wives and townspeople had sheltered during the bombardment of the town, and they could only be searching for herself.

By the following morning, she realised they must have called off the search, and she went to work once more. Pushing the hair away from her forehead, she picked up the empty dish and the soup-ladle and went in search of more soil.

At times she had to roll heavy boulders away; if she was lucky there was soil underneath, but more often than not, when she had succeeded in shifting a boulder, it was to find only solid rock underneath.

But while her days were full and busy, Catrina found the hours of darkness almost unendurable in their loneliness. Most evenings she slipped down to the Ridgeways' house in the hope of catching a glimpse of Dominic. A few times, when Hobson delayed fastening the shutters, she could see inside the drawing-room. Alice would be playing the pianoforte, her husband would be relaxing on a sofa, while Dominic and Dinah would be sitting on the floor, playing with Lucy and Tim.

Catrina did not know which was worse; these glimpses of domestic closeness which made her feel shut out, or the evenings when she haunted the outside of the house like a pathetic ghost and could only guess at what went on behind the closed shutters.

Only one thing was certain. After that brief search for her by the soldiers, no one cared where she had gone, or whether she was alive and safe.

While she continued doggedly with the task of building up layers of soil on the rocky ledge, she became dimly aware that Spanish vessels had again slipped into the Bay, resuming the siege. The knowledge spurred her to renewed effort, and she conserved her food supplies wherever she could, making wild leeks her staple diet.

At last, after almost two weeks of grinding, unremitting toil, she judged that the level of soil on the ledge had reached sufficient depth for the sowing of seeds. She put them in in orderly rows; cabbages at the back, followed by carrots, parsnips and turnips. She marked the rows with small pebbles, and laboured at her task for an entire day, making sure that the seeds were sown evenly.

Almost as if Nature were blessing her handiwork, it began to rain as soon as Catrina had finished her task. She felt tired but contented, and for once she did not experience the need to seek solace by creeping down to the Ridgeways' house in the hope of being able to peep through the window. She scarcely had the energy to do more than stew some wild leeks for her dinner before she thankfully sought her bed.

When she awoke, sunlight was slanting through the gaps round the ill-fitting door, and she smiled with satisfaction. Sunshine after a shower was just what her seeds needed to speed germination. She was humming a tune to herself as she went to look at her garden. The sound died in her throat, and then she sank to her knees and began to sob with hopeless despair and rage, her fists beating the ground.

The garden over which she had laboured so long had been completely destroyed. The ledge was almost bare, and at the foot of one end of it lay a soggy mass of mud and pebbles, all of it swept away, along with her precious seeds, by the night's rain.

Slowly, she felt her fighting spirit beginning to return. She would *not* give in. On examining the ledge that had held her garden, too late, she could see the obvious mistake she had made. The soil should have been packed differently, instead of merely following the natural contours of the rock. She tried to assess the situation. If, as seemed probable, the whole waterlogged mass of soil had slid off the ledge in one fell swoop, the seeds must be at the bottom of the pile.

She went to fetch the soup-ladle and started to work. Carefully and painstakingly she ladled the mud back on the ledge, scooping it from the top of the pile and sloping it this time to resist slipping in the rain. She worked without letting up or pausing even to break her fast.

When the last of the mud had been evenly spread along the ledge, she took a dish and began to search for small rocks with which to build a retaining wall round her garden, embedding them in the wet mud. It was dusk by the time she had finished, and now there was nothing more to do but wait and hope.

After that, she rose from her palliasse each morning, and before starting the usual daily search for wild leeks, she examined her rebuilt garden. Each morning an arid expanse of soil mocked her. Nothing was sprouting, in spite of the fact that she kept the soil moist.

She hoarded her food supplies even more jealously than before. The spring weather had caused dandelions to send out their leaves in even the most inhospitable terrain; a mere half-inch gap between two immovable rocks was sufficient space for their tenacious roots. She began to harvest the leaves, having read that they could be cooked like greens, and found them quite palatable. If she pulled up the remaining wild leeks and allowed none to go to seed, there would be no harvest from that quarter again. And, for all she knew, the beginning of next autumn might find her still here, relying on wild leeks for nourishment. Certainly, no one else gave any sign of caring whether she survived or not.

Dominic leant against a rock, watching through his field-glasses as Catrina gathered dandelion leaves. His heart contracted with hopeless love and compassion, and admiration for her refusal to admit defeat. He had been watching her for several days, taking his field-glasses out with him at every moment he could spare. He had been saying goodnight to Lucy one evening when the child had begun, as usual, to talk about Catrina. While recalling tearfully some of the things they used to do together, Lucy had said something about a 'secret place.'

Dominic had questioned her, gently at first but with growing impotence and frustration as Lucy kept insisting, 'It's a secret, Papa. I promised Aunt Catrina I wouldn't tell. Only her and me and Tim were to know about it.'

Dominic had given up trying to question his daughter, and had thought hard about the matter instead. The 'secret place' had most probably been discovered at the time when the civilians were hiding among the rocks while the enemy bombarded the town. Therefore this place, whatever it was, must be within a reasonable distance from the gulleys.

He had begun his vigil with the field-glasses from a high

point among the rocks, and a few days after a downpour of heavy rain he had seen her for the first time. Having followed her unobtrusively, he had seen her disappear among a growth of palmettos. Later, when he knew that she was elsewhere, he had gone to investigate the spot and had seen the cow-byre, but had not been able to bring himself to enter it. The knowledge that she was living alone in a place like that, hiding like a criminal and scavenging for food, had brought a tight constriction to his throat and he had blundered away blindly.

His dilemma was that if she were forced to leave the byre, she would almost certainly be taken into custody, for General Ridgeway was still very angry with her. What John Ridgeway found hard to forgive was the distress and anxiety Catrina had caused Alice, who somehow seemed to feel that she ought to have been able to prevent her disappearance.

So, if Dominic forced her to leave the cow-byre, she would almost certainly be kept in confinement, probably in a room in the Convent, until the first ship was able to get through the blockade and sail for England. She would be physically comfortable and well fed, and the worst that could happen to her as a prisoner would be boredom. And yet he hesitated to do such a thing to her.

Today he had brought with him rice and flour and salt fish, which he had been able to buy. He waited until Catrina, in her search for dandelion leaves, had wandered far enough away from her shelter, and then hurried towards it with the bagful of provisions. He placed it inside the byre and looked around him, taking in the few crude furnishings, and his mouth tightened.

Somehow she would have to be rescued from this place, and an alternative found to having her locked away. He could confide in Alice, he decided. She could use her influence with General Ridgeway to soften his attitude towards Catrina, so that an acceptable compromise might be arrived at.

Catrina's eyes filled with tears when she found the bagful of provisions inside the byre. 'Lucy,' she said aloud.

The child must have remembered about the cow-byre, and told Dominic. Only he could have brought the food. She understood perfectly why he had deposited it there in secret. He had known that if he had offered it in person she would have refused to accept it, and then he would have had no alternative but to force her to leave her hiding-place and submit to whatever punishment the Governor might mete out. Far more than the practical value of the food, it was tremendously cheering to the spirits to know that Dominic was aware of where she was, and that he cared. She no longer felt so alone.

A few nights later it rained again. Catrina listened to the sound on the roof of the cow-byre, and hope rose inside her. Perhaps this was the fillip her vegetable seeds had been needing. The water she had been sprinkling on them each day could not have been nearly enough. But, in the morning, there was no sign of growth anywhere on the ledge. Uttering curses she had not even been aware that she knew, she grabbed a sharply pointed sliver of rock and drew it viciously through one end of her barren garden, churning up the soil. She was about to turn away, to give full expression to her despair in a bout of weeping, when something caught her attention, and she peered closer into the depths of the disturbed soil.

A wild whoop of joy escaped her. They were the pale sprouts of germinated seeds! She had, it seemed, calculated wrongly when she had rebuilt her garden. The seeds had not been at the bottom of the pile of mud which had slid from the rock, but near the top, and they had been germinating uselessly, too deeply buried in the soil for their tiny leaves to reach the surface.

For the third time, Catrina set to work to rebuild her garden completely. She worked on an area of roughly six square inches at a time, carefully scooping up the soil, picking out the germinated seeds, and replanting them on the surface. She had no way of knowing which seedlings belonged to which vegetables, but it no longer seemed to matter. Haphazardly or not, they would at last be growing.

The task occupied two days. On the third morning she was examining her handiwork, talking lovingly to the seedlings as if they were her children, and noting with joy that already some green leaves had unfurled. Sounds reached her, and then came the excited barking of a dog. She turned, her heart thudding, and watched as Dominic approached with Lucy and Tim.

The child broke away and ran to Catrina, hurling herself at her. 'You promised you would not leave me, and then you did!'

'I'm sorry, love. I had no choice.'

Dominic's eyes met Catrina's over Lucy's head. They were totally revealing in their hunger and longing, and a muscle tensed beside his mouth. She thought, forlornly, that it was a good thing Lucy was present, for she would not otherwise have been able to restrain herself from going to him and clinging to him in her own loneliness and need.

'You are coming home with us, Catrina,' Dominic went on. 'General Ridgeway is no longer angry with you, and he has had an audience with the Governor on your behalf. He explained to the Governor that you did not wish to leave your only relatives, your niece and—your brother.'

She flinched from those last two words as if they had been physical blows. 'The Governor was sympathetic when he was told that your mother, your father and your sister had all died in Gibraltar, and that you have no one elsewhere in the world,' he continued. 'He has agreed that you may remain in General Ridgeway's custody until such time as a passage can be arranged for you to England.'

She looked steadily at him. 'The Rock is under close blockade by the Spanish again. That means that service rations must have been cut once more, with no supply ships getting in. I refuse to be a burden, an extra charge upon the household, a "useless mouth." It was my decision not to sail with the fleet, and since I cannot contribute to my keep, I intend fending for myself.'

'And how will you do that?' he asked roughly. 'I know you have been subsisting on wild leeks and dandelion leaves, but you cannot hope to do so for ever!'

'I shall not have to. Look!' She turned, indicating her garden. 'Those tiny plants, Dominic, are carrots and cabbages and parsnips and turnips!'

'Where did you obtain vegetable seeds? From Jake Farraday?' he demanded.

'Yes.'

'So I was right,' Dominic said sombrely. 'You did turn to him for help. And no doubt he knows where you are hiding . . .' His voice roughened. 'You are to leave this place, Catrina, and have nothing more to do with Farraday!'

'I shall not leave, Dominic! And as for Jake Farraday . . . In the first place, he does not know where I am, and in the second, I could not have managed without his help. As well as vegetable seeds, he supplied me with basic necessities.'

Dominic gripped her arms. 'You fool, Catrina! Farraday does not give anything for nothing! He will expect, and demand, payment in some form or another!'

'He has not given me the supplies. I bought them from him.'

'And where did you get the money?' Dominic demanded.

'I . . . Well, he allowed me credit.'

Dominic's face hardened. 'I shall repay him myself, the next time he arrives in Gibraltar. How much did he charge you for the supplies?'

'Ten sovereigns,' she said, deciding not to mention the extortionate interest rate of 50 per cent compounded monthly. 'And I will certainly not allow you to repay it, Dominic! It is *my* debt!'

'Catrina,' he said tensely, 'you do not know the kind of man you are dealing with. He does nothing without an ulterior motive. He will use this debt you owe him to lure you into a trap.'

She was silent, debating whether to tell him after all about the interest rate, and that Farraday's only ulterior motive was to make as high a profit as possible. From the depths of her despair, she flung at him, 'Jake Farraday might be a rogue, but if he loved a woman he wouldn't care *what* society or the law said!'

'Lucy,' Dominic said tersely, 'take Tim for a run.' He gripped Catrina's arm and guided her inside the byre.

He pulled her into his arms with the sound of a man driven beyond endurance. Then his mouth was on hers, hungrily demanding, her body crushed to him, and the old sweet pain invaded her. He took a step away from her, and cupped her breasts for a moment, allowing his fingers to trace their curves through the thin muslin of her gown. Then he dropped his arms to his sides.

'Do you know what we have just done, Catrina?' he asked in a low voice. 'We have committed an act for which society would pillory you, and for which I would be drummed out of the army in disgrace. It is not just a question of what people would say. If I were to make you my mistress, as you want me to, we would be committing incest. Because in the eyes of the law and of the Church, you are my sister.'

They could hear Lucy and Tim approaching. Dominic moved towards the door of the cow-byre. 'Accept it, and for the love of God, go home to England on the next available vessel!' Then he was gone, and Catrina could hear Lucy's weeping as he forced the child to accompany him.

Even if Catrina had been prepared to leave on the next available vessel, she could see from her high vantage-point that none got through the close blockade of the Spanish ships, and she knew that military rations would have been cut yet again, and that food was at a premium. The thought made her spend every spare minute in tending her garden. Some scrawny bullocks grazed in a scrub-grown area some distance away, and she set off each day to collect dung for fertiliser.

Dominic visited her several times, always chaperoned by either Lucy or Alice Ridgeway, and tried to persuade her to leave her shelter and return to the house.

But apart from everything else, she knew that she could not have borne the sight of Dinah, officially and triumphantly betrothed to Dominic.

'For the dozenth time, I will not leave!' Catrina told him. 'And please take back the pease and the oatmeal you have brought; I do not need them!' She glanced at Alice, who had arrived with Dominic, and added, 'Thank you for the thought, but I know that it must have been a considerable sacrifice to make from the household rations . . .'

'Look at you!' Dominic interrupted, before Alice could reply. 'You are nothing but skin and bone! Your gown is little more than rags, and your face and arms have been burnt by the sun so that they are the colour of a labourer's.'

'And I smell of the cattle-dung I have just been collecting,' she finished for him with a sour laugh. 'Well, go back to Dinah. She must form a reassuringly feminine contrast with me! And stop worrying about me, both you and Alice!'

'I do worry about you!' He gripped her by the shoulders. 'Your vegetables are not nearly ready yet for harvesting, and you cannot go on subsisting on dandelion leaves!'

'I don't. I still have some of the provisions I acquired from Jake Farraday.'

She saw Dominic's face darkening at the mention of

Farraday's name, and in retaliation she taunted bitterly, 'When will your marriage to Dinah be taking place? Have you set the date for the happy day?'

'We are delaying our marriage until the enemy have been beaten,' he replied brusquely.

'If I know Dinah, what she would really like best of all is for you to be mortally wounded, so that she may cut a dramatic and sorrowful figure by marrying you on your death-bed!'

Dominic cursed under his breath, but Alice gave Catrina a look which said that she was in total agreement with her. A while later they left, taking with them the rations which Catrina had refused to accept.

These visits were merely interludes in her life, while she was anxiously watching over her garden, pouncing on every stray weed. She made several trips to the waterfront to collect seaweed, which she spread round the plants as a mulch.

Frugally as she was living, the day inevitably came when she had used up the last of the supplies bought on credit from Jake Farraday. Now she was forced to subsist on dandelion leaves, and she could feel herself growing weaker and more lethargic by the day. It was an omen that her luck was about to change, she was sure, when she happened upon a clutch of bird's eggs. She gathered all but two of them, and that evening her supper of stewed dandelion leaves was supplemented by the extra nourishment provided by the eggs.

The next day the Spaniards broke their long silence, and began to fire on the town once more. Catrina watched as people fled in panic to the rocks, but they returned home when it became clear that the firing was to be merely sporadic. It continued occasionally during the passing days, and she became hungrier and weaker. Worry also bedevilled her, for it had not rained for some time, and while she had a small amount of drinking-water left, she was concerned about her vegetables.

One morning when she woke to blazing sunshine once more, she suddenly remembered about the bullocks grazing in the scrub. Their owners would have made provision for them to be watered, and the beasts would not miss the small amount of the precious liquid which would make all the difference to her vegetables. Collecting her cooking-pots, she set off for the place where the bullocks grazed. When she had only a short distance to go, cannon shot suddenly rang out, almost deafening her, and instinctively she fell to the ground, cradling her arms protectively about her head. The firing stopped as suddenly as it had started, and when she rose, she saw that one of the bullocks had been hit. The others had taken to their heels and scattered. The beast was dead, and although she did not know who its owner was, in any event he was not likely to discover the loss until the carcass had been savaged and spoilt by predatory birds and stray dogs, so she felt morally justified in claiming it.

She hurried back to the cow-byre and collected a sharp knife, a blanket and the sack in which Jake Farraday had packed the supplies he had sold her. Then she hastened back to the dead animal. She could not, she told herself as she resolutely forced down nausea, afford to be squeamish. Trying to make her mind a blank, she hacked away, filling the sack with lumps of meat. Before she dragged the full sack back to the byre, she covered the remainder of the carcass with the blanket to keep off the flies. Her legs ached and trembled; she was covered in blood and her arms felt like lead by the time she had transferred most of the meat to the cow-byre. Even then she could not afford a breathing-space, for the air was sultry, and the meat would go bad.

She spent the remainder of the day dragging the meat by the sackload to the nearest market-place. She had no shortage of customers among the merchants and the servants of the more affluent officers, none of whom troubled to ask questions. Everyone was eager to buy, no matter where the meat had come from. She took a leaf out of Jake Farraday's book, and sold to the highest bidders, telling herself that she could not indulge in the luxury of being charitable. At last there was nothing left but the bullock's head. 'What offers?' she called, holding it aloft by the horns.

'Fifteen shillings!'

'A sovereign!'

Catrina listened as the bidding rose, and suddenly her glance fell upon Dinah standing on the edge of the crowd. She was charmingly dressed as always, in pale yellow muslin, and shading her face with a matching parasol. But there was no mistaking the horror and revulsion in her eyes as she gazed back at Catrina.

For a moment deaf to the voices of the bidders, Catrina assessed herself as she must be appearing to Dinah. Her ragged gown and her stick-like arms were covered in blood, and her hair was falling in disorder around her sun-browned face.

She re-collected herself. 'Sold to the gentleman over there for four sovereigns!'

It was an extortionate price, and she knew it. So, by her look of disgust, did Dinah, who turned away. Catrina knew that Dominic and the Ridgeways would not be spared a single detail about her appearance, and about her rapacity.

She shrugged, and sighed tiredly, and picked up the sack which now contained more sovereigns than she had hoped to see again for a long time. She was so exhausted as she returned to the cow-byre that she staggered like a man in drink, and as if to reward her efforts of the day, a sudden rainstorm burst, soaking her to the skin.

A weary little moan of gratitude escaped her. Her vegetables had been saved, and she would be in time to place her cooking-pots along their catchment area below the overhanging rock. Best of all, a piece of fillet steak was waiting to be cooked on the fire. It was still raining by the time she had devoured the meat. She would have liked to collapse on the palliasse and fall into a sleep of total exhaustion, but full advantage had to be taken of the rain, since there was no knowing how long it would be before the next downpour.

Catrina removed all her clothes, and picked up a precious piece of soap. She had found it hidden underneath the palliasse one day after Alice had called with Dominic, and it was one item of charity which she could not bring herself to refuse.

She stepped outside, and began to lather herself from her hair to the soles of her feet, and then she allowed the rain to rinse her clean. As she tossed the hair away from her race and rubbed water from her eyes, she became aware that a dark shape had loomed up out of the murk of rain and dusk, and was standing utterly still.

The sudden shock, after a day of almost superhuman toil, proved too much and she found everything spinning round her, pulling her down with its impetus into darkness. When she regained consciousness, she discovered that she was lying on the palliasse, covered with blankets, her wet hair spread out clumsily. In the light from the fire she could see Dominic kneeling beside her and watching her.

'I—could not find anything with which to dry you,' he said unevenly, 'and so I used my coat.'

'I hope it has not been ruined.' How formal she sounded, in view of the intimate service he had performed for her.

He shrugged impatiently, dismissing the importance of his coat. 'Dinah told us that she saw you today. How did you come by that meat?'

'I suppose the truth is that I stole it,' she answered thoughtfully.

She told him what had happened, and when she had finished he made a sound which was a mixture of anger, amusement and admiration.

'And to think that I once accused you of being nothing but a frivolous fashion-plate! And now, Catrina—now you are a fugitive, living in a cow-byre, dressed in rags. You are a thief and a profiteer and—and—*Oh God, I love you so . . .*'

She reached up, curling her arms about his neck and urging him towards the palliasse. She thrust the blanket aside and with a muffled sound he began to move his hands over her skin, while his mouth sought hers.

'Poor, emaciated, starved little body,' he murmured, lifting his head.

'Yes. I am sorry. I have lost whatever figure I once possessed. I have become scrawny and ugly . . .'

Her words ended in a gasp as he began to move his mouth in a slow, lingering trail over her body, making it very clear that he wanted her body, making it very clear that he wanted her in spite of her lack of curves, and sending the blood coursing in an answering surge throughout her being.

She fastened her hands in his hair. 'Stay with me tonight,' she whispered.

A long shudder shook him, and she sensed that he was on the point of capitulation. She made her voice soft and supplicating. 'Dominic, I am bone-weary. I shall probably fall asleep in a matter of moments. All I ask is that you should stay with me, and share the palliasse, so that for one night at least I won't feel so alone.'

He kissed her mouth, slowly and lingeringly. Then he said with laughter in his voice, 'If you are capable of cutting up a stolen bullock carcass and dragging it in sackfuls to the market, Catrina, then you are more than capable of sealing the day by using all your wiles to seduce me!' The laughter left his voice, and he ended on a bleak note. 'Into committing an act which is forbidden between us.'

He took the blanket and covered her with it, and then stood up. 'Catrina, you must have made sufficient money today to enable you to buy the supplies you'll need to render your stay in Gibraltar lawful. Come home tomorrow, and leave this god-forsaken place!'

'I cannot leave my garden. I have to harvest and sell my vegetables in order to repay Jake Farraday what I owe him.'

'How can that be? He extended you credit of ten sovereigns, and you must have earned more than that today!'

'The ten sovereigns represent only the capital sum,' she confessed. 'I have to pay, in addition, a monthly compounded interest of 50 per cent.'

'The rapacious Shylock!' But there was relief mixed with the disgust in Dominic's voice. 'So that was why he was so willing to extend you credit! Well, *I* shall repay him!'

'No! I have told you before; it is my debt and I shall repay it.'

'It would need only one word from me as to where you obtained the meat you sold today,' he growled threateningly, 'and you would be taken to the Convent and held there while the matter is investigated.'

'You will not betray me, however,' she murmured. 'Not even if you believe it to be for my own good.'

He cursed under his breath and turned to the door, slamming it behind him with force as he left the cow-byre.

CHAPTER SIXTEEN

THE DAY ON WHICH she had butchered and sold the carcass of the bullock marked the beginning of Catrina's period of prosperity. Her life-style continued to be frugal, but she was able to buy basic supplies, and as her body filled out again and her energy returned, she tackled the hard work of harvesting the first of her vegetable crop and selling it in the market.

She forced herself to be hard-headed and shrewd. Nothing was priced in advance, but was allowed to find its own value, and prices were high. Frequently she had to force herself to refrain from stopping the crazy bidding. Most people had not seen fresh vegetables for months, and even loose cabbage-leaves commanded an inflated price.

One morning Catrina was engaged in building the now bare patches in her garden to a deeper level so that the soil could sustain the growth of autumn vegetables. It could not be long before Jake Farraday found his audacious way through the blockade again, and he was sure to bring more seeds with him.

She heard the sound of weeping, and turned. Lucy, dragging a blanket along by her free hand and trying to restrain Tim on his leash with the other, was approaching. The child was covered in dust, and there was a bruise on her forehead.

Catrina ran to her, and gathered her in her arms. 'What has happened to you, love? How did you come to be hurt?'

'Tim—pulled me over,' she sobbed. 'Tim and me have run away.'

Catrina fetched water to bathe the bruise, and Tim, who had slipped his leash, was bounding around her in excited circles. He was no longer a puppy, Catrina realised, and it also came to her how much Lucy had grown.

Lucy had stopped crying, but she looked up with tear-drenched eyes. 'Tim and me have come to stay with you.'

'My love,' Catrina said helplessly, 'you can't stay here. Just think how sad your Papa would be if you did.'

'Mrs Forest won't be sad! I *hate* her, Aunt Catrina! I hate her millions more than I did before. And she hates me too.'

'Oh, Lucy, dear, I'm sure that's not true!'

'Yes, it is! When she brushes my hair she pulls it on purpose, and she washes me in cold water, and when I cry she pinches me.'

Catrina stifled a sigh. Obviously Dinah had had to assume responsibility for Lucy in her new position as Dominic's betrothed, and she resented it. There was nothing dramatic about it; no way in which she herself could be cast as heroine. So she vented her resentment on the child.

Her own circumstances, also, had changed. She had sufficient money, now, with which to repay Jake the capital sum he had lent her plus the interest accrued to date, and he had promised to take her word regarding the total of that interest. She also had enough left over to buy the amount of supplies laid down by the Governor.

On the other hand, there was her garden and its remaining crops. It was true that it was well-hidden from sight behind the growth of palmettos, and she had always taken infinite pains to cover her tracks each time she returned home from the market, so it was unlikely that anyone would find it and steal her vegetables. But there were the natural predators to be thought of; the birds who would denude it of every bit of growth if she were not there to frighten them away.

Catrina frowned deeply. Every instinct rejected the thought of returning to the Ridgeway's house, and living under the same roof with Dinah and Dominic. And yet, there was Lucy to be thought of . . .

'You can't stay here,' she told the child, making up her mind, 'so I'll go back and stay with you instead, and look after you.'

Lucy's joy was muted, and she made it clear that she would have preferred to share the cow-byre with Catrina and Tim. But she cheered up when Catrina said,

'First, you must help me to make a scarecrow.'

The task occupied an hour. The dry seaweed which had once done duty as a mulch was stuffed into the sleeves of Catrina's most ragged gown, and a palmetto sapling was cut for it to be mounted upon. Catrina embedded it in a patch of bare soil, and made it secure by piling two rocks against it. As an added precaution, she tore up her muslin gown and used the material to cover her vegetables and protect them from those birds not frightened away by the scarecrow.

She made a parcel of the remainder of her few clothes, collected her hoard of money, and set off with Tim and Lucy for the Ridgeways' house. A mixed reception greeted her. Neither of the men was at home, but Alice said warmly, 'I'm glad you've left that awful place! I've been worried about you. It has become known that you have made a good deal of money by your own enterprising efforts, and you could so easily have been attacked and robbed.'

But even as she said it, Catrina received an impression that Alice was not entirely happy about her return. In an odd way, she seemed to struggle between relief and fear. Suddenly she wondered why Violet had said Alice was afraid. She puzzled about it for a moment, and then realised the cause of the woman's fear. Alice had always been aware of the feeling between Catrina and Dominic, and had been afraid of the consequences. And now she was obviously once again afraid that living under the same roof might lead to a dangerous situation. Dominic was betrothed to Dinah, she must be arguing, but what if the feeling between him and his sister-in-law led to an explosion of passion which would plunge everyone into scandal?

Then Dinah entered the room, and her eyes narrowed when she saw Catrina, and they became slits when Alice explained that Catrina had decided to return to the house for good.

'I dare say we shall be ostracised from now on by anyone of account! After the way you have been behaving . . .'

'I returned for Lucy's sake,' Catrina interrupted shortly. 'I am sure you will be pleased to have her taken off your hands.'

'She is a difficult child, but I have done my best for her.' Dinah's voice was sullen, but there was relief in her eyes. She could not hide from Catrina that she would more than welcome the chance of being rid of responsibility for Lucy. 'I suppose you must be as rich as Midas now,' she added spitefully.

'I have more than enough for my immediate needs,' Catrina said. It struck her suddenly that Dinah was jealous of her, and not for any of the more obvious reasons.

I have done something, Catrina thought, which Dinah herself would have gloried in having to her credit. I have survived and prospered by my own efforts. Dinah would have hated the physical work involved, but how she would have revelled in the role of gallant little female who had pitted her wits against adversity!

Alice stood up. 'I dare say you would appreciate a hot bath. I shall instruct Hobson to have the kitchen fire stoked.'

Despite her faded, shabby gown, Catrina felt almost civilised by the time the two men arrived home that evening. Dominic hid his reaction at seeing her behind a totally wooden expression, but General Ridgeway hugged her warmly.

'So glad you have done the sensible thing at last, my dear! Now, we must take steps to regularise your legal position . . .'

Catrina freed herself, and picked up her heavy reticule. 'I have the money here, General, with which to pay for the supplies I need to have. Would you please arrange to have them bought for me from government stocks?'

'Delighted, delighted! My word, your enterprising spirit puts many of us to shame!'

Catrina smiled. 'Thank you. On a more practical level, I shall be able to supply the household with fresh vegetables.'

Dinah obviously decided that Catrina had been the centre of attention for too long, because she approached General Ridgeway and slipped her arm through his.

'I have been sprucing up my best gown for the Governor's dinner, John. In my modest way, I hope to be a credit to you and to darling Dominic.' She gave Catrina a slyly complacent glance. 'The King's birthday is to be celebrated on the 4th of June, followed by a formal dinner at the Convent. What a shame that you will have to miss it.'

'There is no reason why Catrina should not attend the dinner, now that she is no longer a fugitive from justice,' General Ridgeway put in. 'I could obtain an invitation for her.'

'Dear John, setting aside the fact that at this late stage it would be impossible to find a partner for her, she has been living like a gipsy for so long that her clothes have come to resemble those of a gipsy, too.' Dinah cast a malicious look at Catrina. 'And for all the money she has acquired with her profiteering and other dubious practices, it would be impossible for her to come by a suitable gown for the occasion. There is not a yard of fabric to be bought in the town!'

'I have no wish to attend the Governor's dinner!' Catrina cut short Dinah's gloating.

Mentally, she acknowledged that the statement had been far short of the truth. Catrina told herself that she would always have been less than human if she had not longed for the excitement of a social occasion after all the dreary privations she had endured. But what she came to hate most of all, in the days that followed, was Dinah's continual harping on the fact that she would have to miss all the fun. To get away from her, Catrina took Lucy and Tim with her and spent every spare moment working on her garden.

It was from there that she noticed a crowd gathering on the waterfront, and when she looked out over the Bay she could see a cutter playing a dangerous cat-and-mouse game with the blockading Spanish ships before she slipped successfully into the harbour. A smile curved her lips. Surely only Jake Farraday would have the audacity to goad the enemy instead of trying to sneak into the harbour by stealth!

She called Lucy and Tim, and hurried home. 'I have a business matter to attend to,' she told Alice. 'Would you mind keeping an eye on Lucy while I'm away?'

'No, but . . .' Alice stopped, looking troubled. 'This business matter—would it involve a meeting with Jake Farraday? I have just heard that his cutter has been spotted, taunting the Spanish fleet.'

'He made it safely into the harbour. And yes, I have to meet him, in order to repay the money he lent me,'

'Do you think it is wise—or—safe—to meet him alone?'

Catrina smiled. 'We will scarcely be alone. The waterfront is crowded with people. As soon as I have gained his attention I shall repay my debt to him.' She touched Alice's shoulder. 'Please do not be concerned about me.'

She washed, and changed into the best of the few gowns she still possessed, and when she had dressed her hair to her own satisfaction she left the house and made for the waterfront. But the main street was so crowded that she decided to make a détour by using some of the side alleys. There were many gaps in the rows of houses, a legacy of the Spanish bombardment. One upper storey had been sheared off, but what remained was still occupied. An old Genoese woman sat by the open window, stitching at something in a metal frame. She smiled and beckoned to Catrina, resting the frame in her lap. From a small table in front of the window she picked up several lace handkerchiefs, displaying them hopefully.

Catrina shook her head, and smiled to soften her refusal to buy. She noticed that the room, crammed with heavy pieces of furniture, had perforce to do duty as bedroom and living-room as well as working premises, for apart from a table and chairs there was an enormous tester bed in the background, covered with ivory lace which had probably been made by the old woman many years ago.

Catrina walked on, reflecting with pity on the plight of the Genoese woman. Who, in a besieged garrison town where everyone's preoccupation was with food, would be likely to spend money on lace handkerchiefs?

Then she dismissed the matter from her mind. She had reached the edge of the crowd, who were bidding for Jake's cargo. She could not even see him through the press of people, and in the meantime the hot sun was beating down upon her. She was also acutely conscious of her reticule stuffed with sovereigns. It would be only too easy for someone to attack her from behind and make off with it.

She thought for a moment, and turned away, towards the Queen's Head. Once, only the most dire of emergencies would have given her the courage to enter a tavern on her own, but her months of surviving by her own efforts had given her a self-assurance and a sense of her own worth, and she knew that this was being communicated to the landlord as she approached the bar with her head held high, looking neither to left nor to right.

'Do you keep lodgings in reserve for Mr Jake Farraday whenever he arrives in the harbour?' she wanted to know.

'Indeed I do, ma'am,' the landlord replied respectfully.

'I need to see him on a matter of business. I should like to wait for him in his private parlour, if you please.'

'Certainly, ma'am!' The landlord hurried to usher her

inside the parlour. 'Would you care for some refreshment while you wait?'

'No, thank you. Just tell Mr Farraday, when he arrives, that Miss Beaumont is here and anxious to discharge her obligations towards him.'

She did not have long to wait. He entered the room, his clothes as fashionable and immaculate as always, and she guessed that he must have sold only a small part of his cargo, saving the remainder until shortages had forced the prices even higher.

'Miss Beaumont!' He stopped, and lifted her gloved hands, bringing them to his lips. Then he sat down beside her on the sofa, hiding his thoughts behind a smile.

He was surprised at the pleasure it gave him to see her again. He would not deny that the pleasure was enhanced by what he had discovered about her while he was away from Gibraltar. Using the promissory note which she had given him as a guide, he had written a letter to her man of business in London, whose name and address he had carefully memorised. After making a vague reference to a previous letter, he had written:

> I would be obliged if you would give me a summary of the value of my assets, as I am considering making a certain investment. Because of the difficulties of communication between Gibraltar and Britain, I am arranging for this letter to be taken to Portugal, where it will be sent to England *via* the Lisbon packet. Please forward your reply to the offices of the Lisbon packet and address it in care of Mr Farraday, who will deliver it to me in Gibraltar.

He had signed Catrina's name to the letter.

The reply had greatly exceeded his expectations. Catrina Beaumont was a very considerable heiress indeed. But he would have to be careful to keep up the pretence that he believed her to have greatly exaggerated the size of her fortune in England.

'You have, of course,' he said, his eyes glinting at her, 'come to tell me that you cannot discharge your debt?'

'On the contrary.' She lifted her reticule and spilt its contents out on the sofa between them. 'There are your original ten sovereigns. And the remainder, although out of all proportion to the amount of the capital sum, is probably less than you had hoped the accrued compound interest would be. But you did say that you would take my word as to the length of time which would elapse before I was able to repay you in full. You see, I was able to steal a bullock carcass and cut it up and sell it . . .'

'You—did what?' He stared at her with lively interest and a touch of disbelief.

She told him what had happened, and how she had successfully established her garden, and several times he interrupted her tale with gusts of laughter.

'You are quite priceless, Miss Beaumont!' he told her when she had finished. He counted out several of the sovereigns and held them out to her. 'You did not really believe that I would demand compound interest at the rate of 50 per cent from anyone, did you? Five per cent is what I normally charge.'

'Then why did you quote me such an extortionate rate?' she demanded indignantly.

'I did not expect you to be able to meet your obligations, and I meant to demand payment in kind.'

'You really are the most unprincipled rogue!' Catrina cried.

He quirked a lazy eyebrow at her. 'So my friends continually reassure me. It is a comfort to know that my reputation remains intact.'

She could not help laughing. 'I shall be very careful before I do business with you again, Mr Farraday!' she said, and rose.

His hand encircled her wrist. 'Please stay, and join me for luncheon.'

'Well . . .' She hesitated. He was good company; he amused her, and if possible she would like to get even with him for having tricked her into working so much harder to earn the false rate of interest he had demanded. 'Very well.'

He rang for the parlour-maids and ordered luncheon, and when the covers had been laid he and Catrina moved towards the table.

The meal consisted of dressed crab, a fricassee of eggs, and roast loin of pork, and Catrina reflected that Jake Farraday must pay very well indeed for his lodgings to enable the landlord to offer such luxuries. She pointed with amusement at a dish of buttered cabbage.

'I believe I grew that!'

He looked intently at her. 'I know why *I* come to Gibraltar again and again. But you laboured like a slave for the privilege of being able to stay on this beseiged, hard-pressed, and often starving Rock. Why?'

She busied herself with cutting up a slice of roast pork. 'I have no friends or family in England. And I do have relatives here—remember? My—brother . . .'

'Who cared so little for you that he allowed you to fend for yourself?'

She did not look up. 'He cared to the extent that he wished to force me to return to England, and safety. I was the one who refused to go. And—he is my brother-in-law. Millicent, my late sister, was his wife. Their little girl, Lucy, is my niece, my only living blood-kin, and she was one of the reasons why I wished to stay in Gibraltar.'

She looked up, and found Jake Farraday appraising her. 'Has your brother-in-law remarried?' he asked.

'No, but he is betrothed and will do so.'

'You do not like your future sister-in-law, do you?' he observed shrewdly.

Catrina started to protest, and then shrugged. 'She is a very irritating, shallow woman. At the moment she is being more tiresome than usual, because the King's birthday dinner is soon to be held, and she likes to harp upon the fact that I shall not be able to go because I lack both a suitable gown and an escort.'

Jake Farraday studied her. 'What brought you to Gibraltar in the first instance?'

'I came to see my parents and my sister. I had grown up with my godmother, Lady Prudence Welles, and after her death I discovered that she had left me a fortune. Yes, there really is a fortune, whether you believe it or not!'

He smiled. 'If I find it difficult to believe, Miss Beaumont, it is because you have never struck me as the kind of young lady who enjoyed a sheltered, privileged upbringing. Such a genteel young woman would never have stolen a bullock carcass. She would sooner have starved in gentle refinement!'

Catrina laughed. 'You are right, I suppose. The truth is

that I was not brought up to privilege. Lady Prudence was a miser and the extent of her wealth came as a compete surprise. But for some reason she had left me everything in her will, so I decided to visit my family, whom I had not seen for years. When I arrived I found not only that my parents were dead, but that war had been declared.'

His silence spurred her into going on. 'One way and another, I found myself trapped here. My sister was expecting another baby, and then her Genoese servants deserted her, and she could not be left . . .'

'What happened to your sister?'

'She died in a fire. It started in her locked bedroom and it was impossible to reach her before the fire took hold on the rest of the house.'

'I see. And where are you living now?'

'At the home of General Ridgeway. His wife, Alice, is the daughter of Lady Prudence, but I never knew of her existence until I came here. The old woman quarrelled with her many years ago and had cut her completely out of her life.' Catrina paused. 'We have been talking about me all this time. Now tell me about yourself.'

'Surely you know all there is to be known about me,' he countered, his tone light. 'I am the black sheep of an otherwise respectable family. If I want something, I take it, and if it is not to be had easily I scheme to get it. I turn every possible situation to my own advantage, and I consider no one but myself. If I cannot win fairly, then I cheat.'

'No one can be as black as you paint yourself!'

'No?' His mouth curved in a smile.

'You run the gauntlet of the enemy ships in order to bring supplies to the beleaguered people of Gibraltar . . .'

'For a profit,' he reminded her. 'Don't forget the extortionate prices I demand!'

'As to that, I suppose your crew demand high wages in return for the danger to which they are exposed in breaking the blockade. And since there is always the possibility that your cutter might be damaged or even destroyed, I imagine you have to build up a capital sum on which to fall back if the worst happens.'

'Oh dear, Miss Beaumont,' he lamented, 'you are confounding me utterly! Are you determined not to allow me to cling to even a shred of my bad reputation?'

She grimaced at him. 'Last but not least, Mr Farraday, you refused to accept the accrued interest which I was quite prepared to pay you.'

'You forget my ulterior motive!' he pleaded. 'I hoped to make you my mistress!'

Smilingly shaking her head at him, Catrina rose. 'Thank you for the luncheon, Mr Farraday. And don't work quite so hard at fostering your bad reputation!'

He had stood up too, and she offered him her hand. As he looked down at it, he told himself that the interview had gone very well indeed. With a mixture of audacity, blunt truth and nonsense, he had succeeded in disarming her.

He lifted up her hand, making a show of examining its calloused roughness and the traces of soil which remained stubbornly ingrained around her fingernails. 'Damn me!' he exclaimed. 'To take one penny-piece from you would put me to shame! Take back the money, Miss Beaumont. You owe me nothing!'

'I shall certainly not take it back! I always pay my debts.'

'In that case—how would you like to turn the tables on this future sister-in-law of yours, who delights in taunting you with the fact that you cannot attend the King's birthday dinner?'

Catrina stared at him, startled. 'What do you mean?'

'If you can procure a suitable gown, I would gladly offer myself as an escort.'

'But—I'm sorry; I don't wish to sound offensive, but from what I have been told you are unlikely to receive an invitation to the dinner, and it is one occasion which even you would not be able to attend uninvited.'

He made a cynical sound. 'Miss Beaumont, there are more ways of opening doors than you imagine. If I were to offer the bulk of the of the food supplies among the *Arabella*'s cargo to the Governor so that it may be served at the King's birthday dinner, I guarantee that an invitation will be extended to me, and to whomever I might choose as a partner.'

She frowned at him in perplexity. 'But why should you wish to make such a financial sacrifice for the sake of a mere social event?'

'For the pleasure of escorting you, of course. And perhaps also for the pleasure of seeing the outrage on the faces of the other guests. Procure the gown, Miss Beaumont, and I shall procure an invitation to the dinner for myself and a partner. I promise you that.'

Excitement was quickening inside her. It had been such a long time since there had been any gaiety in her life at all, and he really made it sound possible.

'You know,' she said, 'I have a feeling that there is another reason altogether why you wish to obtain an invitation to such an illustrious event. You are no longer quite as amused by your bad reputation as you pretend to be, and you wish society to acknowledge that all those rumours about you were highly exaggerated. So what better way to start than by donating so much of your cargo for the celebration of the King's birthday?'

'Oh, Miss Beaumont, pray stop! I cannot bear all these virtues you insist on laying at my door!'

She laughed, and he brought her hand to his lips. He kept his head bent over her hand for far longer than necessary, so that she would not see the triumph and excitement in his eyes. It had been a long time since he had encountered a quarry so worthy of himself!

Catrina turned aside when he released her hand, and picked up her gloves and reticule. He escorted her out of the tavern.

'I shall call for you at the home of General Ridgeway on the afternoon of the fourth of June, the King's birthday,' he said. 'Until then, goodbye, Miss Beaumont.'

Catrina was thoughtful as she walked away. Dominic, she knew with certainty, would never allow her to attend the King's birthday dinner with Jake Farraday. But Dominic, she told herself defiantly, would not be allowed to know until it was too late for him to do anything about it!

After she had walked back along the main street for a while she turned into a side alley, and searched until she had found the house where the old Genoese woman made lace handkerchiefs in the window.

The woman recognised her, and greeted her with a hopeful smile. 'You like? You buy?' she entreated, picking up some of her handkerchiefs and holding them out to Catrina.

'No, not those. But would you sell me the counterpane and the draperies of the bed?'

The woman stared at her in astonishment. '*Vecchio!* Old!

Not new, not *bello*—like these . . .' She indicated the handkerchiefs.

'But that is what I want. I'll pay you three sovereigns for the lace.'

The woman's eyes widened, and she shook her head, not in refusal but in amazement at Catrina's folly. 'I sell,' the woman agreed.

Catrina glanced at the delicate work which had gone into fashioning the handkerchiefs. The old woman's hands were still nimble, her fingers full of skill. 'Tell me,' Catrina asked, 'are you able to do ordinary sewing, as well as making lace?'

'Oh, *si, si*!'

Catrina smiled. The old woman would transform the lace from her bed into a gown which would cause Dinah to bite her tongue with envy. But, most of all, and ultimately profitless though it might be, Catrina wanted Dominic to see her once again looking as beautiful and desirable as she could contrive.

CHAPTER SEVENTEEN

EVEN THOUGH SHE spent long hours in the house of the Genoese woman each day, being measured and fitted for the lace dress, Catrina had no means of knowing whether or not Jake would really succeed in obtaining an invitation to the King's birthday dinner.

Then, one afternoon during the last week in May, General Ridgeway remarked, 'The King's dinner promises to be a surprisingly lavish affair this year. It was thought we would have to rely on salt pork as the main course, and with nothing but rum with which to toast His Majesty. But it appears that an anonymous benefactor has donated sides of bacon, several casks of port wine and sufficient flour and dried fruits with which to bake a cake in the King's honour.'

Catrina shaded her face with her hand so that her expression would not be visible. So Jake's donation had been accepted, and he had obtained the invitation he had wanted. The fact that the donor was to remain anonymous did not surprise her. None of the Governor's aides would like it to be known that such blatant trading had taken place.

'It's such a pity that poor Catrina will not be able to be there,' Dinah put in smugly.

Dominic gave her a hard look. 'If you were to lend Catrina a gown, I think Colonel Frampton could be prevailed upon to attend as her partner.'

'Colonel Frampton is sixty,' Alice exclaimed. 'And such a crushing bore that everyone is relieved his gout keeps him from attending most functions!'

Catrina stood up. 'I have no wish to attend the dinner in a borrowed gown, escorted by a gouty old bore. I shall be quite content to spend the evening with a book.'

She left Lucy playing with Tim in the courtyard under the watchful eyes of the servants, and on the pretext that she was going to tend her garden, she visited the Genoese woman and collected her finished gown. On her return she entered the house by a side door and hid the gown inside one of thc unused bedrooms.

On the morning of the King's birthday everyone rose early for the usual celebrations, and made their way to join the crowds.

A gun was fired in salute for each year of His Majesty's age, followed by a *feu-de-joie* from the guns of the troops in the garrison.

There was a disciplined drill by the red-coats, and the air was filled with the flashes and flames and clouds of smoke coming from the muskets of the troops of the various regiments. The enemy, who could so easily have disrupted the day, goodnaturedly allowed matters to proceed, and the glint of their spy-glasses could be seen both from the ships in the Bay and from their lines on the isthmus as they watched the ceremony.

But even though she enjoyed the spectacle, Catrina was preoccupied with the dilemma which faced her. After some thought she decided that she would have to take Alice into her confidence. She drew the older woman aside.

'I have a problem,' Catrina said in a low voice. 'I am to attend the dinner after all, but I need to get ready and leave the house before the rest of you do so, for if I did not, Dominic would stop me.'

Alice frowned. 'How could you attend the dinner? And why on earth would Dominic stop you?'

'Because my escort is to be Jake Farraday.'

'Oh . . .' Alice looked at her with deeply troubled eyes.

'He is not nearly as black as he is painted,' Catrina defended. 'Most of those who speak ill of him do not know him at all. I have learnt to know him quite well.' As Alice continued to look unconvinced, Catrina tried another tactic more likely to evoke her sympathy. 'Besides, after Dinah's gibes and malicious taunts I really do want to attend the dinner, instead of having her describe it to me afterwards in gloating detail.'

'Yes, she has been more than usually insufferable! But what will you wear, my dear?'

Catrina smiled with pleasure. 'Oh, just wait until you see my gown! I shall tell you later how I contrived to come by it. But for the moment, I face a dilemma. The dinner is due to start this afternoon, and in about an hour or so the rest of you will be returning to the house to prepare for it. I have to be ready and on my way before then. If I left Lucy with you now, would you ask your maid to look after her later, and put her to bed?'

'I suppose so,' Alice agreed reluctantly. 'I cannot like all this subterfuge, however . . .'

'It is entirely necessary if you wish to prevent an ugly scene. Dominic would have to restrain himself in the Governor's presence, whether he likes it or not. Now, you will look after Lucy for me, won't you, so that I may hurry home and get ready? If anyone should miss me, tell them that I have gone to water my garden.'

'Very well,' Alice sighed.

Catrina melted away through the crowd, and when she arrived home she wrote a note to Jake Farraday, asking him to call for her within the hour. She asked the impassive Hobson to have it delivered to him at the Queen's Head, and then she hurried to prepare for the King's dinner which was to be held in the garden of the Franciscan Convent.

When she took her gown from its hiding-place, she could not suppress an exclamation of renewed joy at the sight of it. The Genoese woman had followed a sketch she herself had supplied, and had created a finished product of stunning magnificence. Cut low across the bosom, it fitted tightly at the waist and then clung in slim, graceful lines to the white satin underdress which Catrina had resurrected and refurbished to wear with it.

She dressed her hair in a classic Grecian style, and the last lock had just been pinned into place when a maid knocked on the bedroom door and told her that Jake Farraday had arrived. He looked magnificent in a coat made of cloth-of-gold, with white stockings which reached to his knees, and the heels of his shoes were studded with jewels.

He raised a quizzing-glass and studied Catrina. 'You look quite breath-taking, Miss Beaumont. If we were not at war with France, I would have hazarded a guess that you had sent to Paris for that gown!'

She grinned. 'It was made by an old Genoese woman, using a counterpane and draperies taken from her bed.'

He threw back his head with a roar of laughter. 'You are

unique, Miss Beaumont—a complete original!'

'Thank you. Shall we go? I take it you have a gharry waiting, for you would not have exposed that magnificent coat to the rubbing of shoulders with the crowds.'

'Yes, I have a gharry waiting.' He raised an eyebrow at her. 'But the dinner will not be starting for some time. Why did you send for me to collect you so early?'

Her lips flickered in a smile. 'Because I wished to save you from being knocked down.'

'I see. Your brother-in-law, who threatened to knock me senseless if I ever approached you again! I comfort myself with the thought that he would not dare to do so in the Governor's presence. If he is due to arrive home at any moment, by all means let us leave. We shall kill time by going for a drive.'

He helped her into the gharry and took his place by her side, and then gave instructions to the driver. Soon they had left the town's cobbled streets, and the powerful, sure-footed mule picked its way along a track towards high ground, where Jake ordered the driver to stop.

They could look across the Bay, with its mass of billowing sails belonging to the Spanish and French blockading vessels, an ever-present reminder that the inhabitants of Gibraltar were imprisoned on the Rock.

'I shall have to leave again quite soon, at any moment,' Jake Farraday broke the silence. 'There is a cargo to be picked up in Lisbon.' He turned to her, and took her hands in his. *'Rise up, my love, my fair one, and come away.'*

She had recognised the quotation, and its ambiguity made it impossible for her to know how to respond. She could feel a flush mounting her cheeks. He went on with a light laugh, 'Think what a team you and I would make, breaking blockades, sailing the seas in search of adventure . . .'

His eyes were glinting with the familiar mocking laughter, and with relief she treated the suggestion as the joke it obviously was. 'I would be totally unsuited in any such team, Mr Farraday, for I suffer most dreadfully from sea-sickness!'

'And the thought of turning my own hands, about which I am inordinately vain, to the creation of artificial gardens quite makes me shudder.' He smiled. 'I think it is time that we started for the Convent.'

Her heart was thumping with a mixture of excitement and trepidation as they approached the Governor's residence. The gardens had been set out with long lines of tables, and most of the other guests were already seated when Catrina and Jake Farraday were shown to their places.

Dominic was sitting beside Dinah. His eyes blazed and his mouth was a thin, white slit as he watched Catrina move slowly on the arm of Jake Farraday. Conscious as she was of Dominic, she could not help noticing the sensation they were causing among the other guests. There was scarcely a woman present who did not steal admiring glances at Jake, and scarcely a man who regarded him with anything but distaste and deep disapproval.

But she would have had to be blind and stupid not to have known that she was claiming a fair share of the attention. She knew that she looked radiant in her simple but stunningly beautiful gown, and that for a very long time now no one present had seen her in anything but worn, drab gowns, frequently made filthy by her labours and by the scarcity of water in which to wash them. She was glorying in the contrast, and in the petulant jealousy and chagrin of Dinah's expression. The only shadow cast over the occasion was the smouldering rage in Dominic's eyes.

She and Jake sat down, and convention demanded that they converse with the people seated on either side of them. She listened with amusement as he set out to charm the lady on his right, and gave only half her attention to the elderly officer beside her.

Not until the long formal dinner came to an end, and the King's health had been drunk, could the guests mingle freely, and Catrina found Dominic by her side. Jake was being monopolised by several young women.

'How dared you?' Dominic rasped, sweeping her out of earshot behind the Dragon Tree.

'How dared I *what*? Accept an invitation, and enjoy myself, in the same way as you are doing?'

'You know damned well what I mean!' His hands were on her upper arms, bruising the flesh. 'All the sly plotting and scheming, the air of resignation because you were unable to attend the dinner, while you knew you would be doing so with that contemptible rodent! By God, to think I was sitting there before you arrived, thinking of you, imagining you at home, lonely and wretched . . .'

He shook her so violently that her head jerked back. 'Farraday gave you this gown, did he not? He is not exactly known for his selfless generosity! What did you have to do to earn it, Catrina?'

'Dominic, you are going too far!'

'Not nearly as far as you must have gone! What did you promise him, Catrina, in exchange?'

'The gown,' she said quietly, 'was previously a counterpane and bed draperies which I bought for a few sovereigns from a Genoese woman, who made it up for me. It is quite unforgivable of you to suggest . . .'

'What do you expect me to do—apologise?' He laughed angrily. 'You are damned lucky, both of you, that the occasion forces me to restrain myself, for otherwise I would have broken every bone in his body and dragged you home by force!'

'You have no right, Dominic, to dictate to me as to . . .'

'Indeed I have.' The anger had left him suddenly, and he added in a bleak voice 'I am your brother. The law says so. The law gives me the right and the duty to protect you against predators like Farraday. Why did you behave in this underhanded way, Catrina?'

'I—wanted you to see me looking pretty,' she said unsteadily. 'It is not very much, is it? But it is all . . . All I can ever . . .'

A tortured sound escaped him, and he moved towards her. 'It is worse for me, Catrina, when you look beautiful as you do today. For I see, reflected in the eyes of other men, thoughts which I am forced to conceal.' He placed his palms against her cheeks and looked down at her with an expression of hopeless anguish.

Footfalls sounded close to them, and Dominic removed one hand from her face and produced a handkerchief. He tilted her head back and pretended to be removing something from her eye, and his mouth was twisted in bitter, cynical lines at the necessity for such deception.

Someone claimed Dominic's attention, and Jake approached Catrina. 'I am sorry to cut the occasion short, Miss Beaumont, but the wind is changing direction, and sailing conditions are in my favour. The Spaniards will be assuming we are all busy celebrating His Majesty's birthday.

I wish to slip away while their vigilance is relaxed.'

'I am quite ready to leave,' she told him. 'Let us make our excuses to our host.'

To her relief, Dominic did not see them leaving the garden of the Convent and driving away in a hired gharry. When they reached the Ridgeways' residence Farraday escorted Catrina to the door, and in the darkness he caught her hands in his.

'Did you think I was joking, earlier, when I quoted the Song of Solomon to you?'

'What? Oh . . . *"Rise up, my fair one, my love, and come away."* You—You *were* joking, were you not?'

'No. I have never before asked a woman to marry me, and because I could not think of suitable words of my own I borrowed from Solomon.' He gave an embarrassed laugh, and went on, 'And since sea-sickness plagues you, and I couldn't contemplate earning our daily crust by gardening, I suggest we make our home in London. I have quite a small fortune of my own put by . . .'

'Oh dear,' she interrupted him, close to tears. 'Mr Farraday—I wish you had not—I am so sorry . . . I cannot.'

He was glad that the darkness concealed his rage from her. It was true that he had never before considered asking a woman to marry him, and to be rejected, after all the planning and calculation he had put into the matter, was almost more than he could bear.

'Please,' she faltered, 'do not imagine it is because you—because of what people say about you. I don't believe any of it. The reason I cannot marry you, why I cannot marry anyone, is because I love a man who—who is unable to marry me because . . .'

'You don't have to search for an elaborate lie, Catrina.' He was in control of himself once more. Softly, he quoted, *'How fair is thy love, my sister, my spouse! How much better is thy love than wine!'*

She drew an uneven breath. 'You—are fond of quoting King Solomon . . .'

'He knew so many of the right words. And they are right, are they not? You and your—brother.' He pulled her against him suddenly, and sought her mouth, and because she felt that she owed him something she allowed him to kiss her.

It was only when she felt his hands move to her breasts that she pushed him away. 'Please, Jake—don't.'

'Do you intend denying yourself to all other men, Catrina, because the law forbids you to have the one you want? I could make you forget him, and I warn you—I have not admitted defeat. When I want something I never give up, and I want you—by fair means or foul.'

He added on such a matter-of-fact note that the scene between them might never have taken place, 'Those vegetable seeds you wanted will be delivered to you by messenger in the morning.'

She was grateful to be able to take her cue from him. 'Thank you. If you will wait a moment, I shall fetch the money to pay for them.'

'The seeds are a gift,' he cut her short. Then he swept her a bow, and returned to the gharry.

Catrina went to bed early, before the others returned from the Convent, but she did not fall asleep for a long while. Attending the dinner had been an exercise in foolishness, she decided. All it had achieved had been to encourage Jake Farraday to propose to her. Even though he had taken it very well, he must have been hurt by her rejection.

The inevitable inquest into her behaviour took place over breakfast the following morning. She had been expecting it, and had braced herself for it.

'I suppose you know,' Dinah said waspishly, 'that you made a perfect spectacle of yourself, arriving at the Governor's reception on the arm of a notorious rogue! People will be talking for weeks!'

Catrina had a shrewd suspicion that Dinah would have given much to have done precisely what she herself had done, and so claimed everyone's attention.

'It is all a storm in a teacup,' General Ridgeway commented. 'Catrina looked beautiful, and as for Jake Farraday, he behaved impeccably. Indeed, we have him to thank for the excellence and the variety of the food served at the dinner, for I have discovered that he donated it all from the cargo of *Arabella*.'

Dominic's head jerked up at the news, and he stared at Catrina. But it was Dinah who put into words what he was probably thinking.

'I wonder what Catrina promised him in exchange for

such generosity! He would never have done it out of kindness, for he is known to be a ruthless profiteer! When people find out about it, tongues really will wag!'

But if people talked, they did not do so for long. Just two nights later everyone in Gibraltar awakened to the sound of gunfire and the sound of drums beating the alarm. Catrina dressed quickly, and found warm clothes for Lucy. Dinah had run out of the room, covered in a wrap. She came back, searching feverishly through her wardrobe.

'The garrison has rushed to arms,' she reported, 'and Dominic and John have hurried to their command posts.'

Alice entered at that moment, fully dressed in outdoor clothing. 'It seems the Spaniards have launched a surprise attack on the British ships which Admiral Rodney left anchored in the Bay. John said we were to leave the house, in case of yet more unpredictable behaviour on the part of the enemy.'

Everyone was dressed and ready to go when it was discovered that Tim had disappeared, and Lucy refused to leave without him. A search was mounted by the servants, while Catrina tried to persuade Lucy that the dog would be safe.

'Oh, for heaven's sake!' Dinah burst out. 'Are we to risk our lives for the wretched dog? I, for one, am not staying to be blown up if the house should be shelled!'

'You've always hated Tim!' Lucy accused tearfully. 'You—You hope he is dead!'

But at that moment Hobson arrived from outside, with the errant Tim on the leash. Lucy flung herself at her pet, and moments later they all left the house to join the crowd who were watching the situation in readiness for flight if the enemy changed their tactics.

A fresh wind was blowing, and the night should have been dark and cloudy, but the whole scene was lit up by the fury of the hitherto uprecedented attack.

The leading Spanish ship in the Bay, Catrina saw with trepidation, was so close to the anchored British vessels that several fireworks and flammable substances were easily thrown aboard HMS *Enterprise*. Nine other enemy ships, which Alice explained to her were freighted with combustibles, were drifting towards the British vessels at anchor. They could hear the British squadron and the near-by batteries opening fire, and the scene became one of rolling clouds of smoke, pierced with flames from the Spanish fire-ships themselves, with their tall masts and sails burning.

Dominic's tall figure was suddenly clearly visible against the background of burning ships. He was at the water's edge, moving among the fishing-boats beached there, and he appeared to be issuing orders of some kind.

'Papa!' Lucy cried from her vantage-point on Hobson's shoulders.

'Let us move closer to the waterfront,' Alice suggested. 'Then we may find out what is happening.'

They pushed a path through the crowd. Now Catrina could see that fishing-boats were being prepared for launching by groups of sailors and civilians. As Lucy called out to him, Dominic became aware of their approach and thrust his way toward them.

'The Navy needs help,' he said. 'Somehow those burning ships must be forced to alter course. I am organising a force of sailors and volunteer fishermen to go out to them and attempt the task.'

'You . . .' Catrina moistened her lips. 'You are not going with them, are you?'

'Yes. As soon as the convoy has been made ready.'

She closed her eyes briefly. Stored between the decks of the fire-ships, Alice had explained to her earlier, were powder barrels. At any moment the heat generated by the fires could cause them to explode, blowing everyone in their neighbourhood to perdition.

'You will be a hero,' Dinah said ecstatically. 'Oh, Dominic, you make me so proud of you!'

'Do I?' His voice was colourless. 'I am glad.'

He moved to where Catrina was standing beside Hobson and Lucy. He took the child from the butler and kissed her, and handed her back to Hobson again.

He looked at Catrina. 'If anything should happen . . .' he began, and she thought he meant to make a veiled plea that she should look after Lucy. Instead, he mouthed soundlessly, 'I love you.'

Then he turned and plunged back to the water's edge again, and a few minutes later they watched as the convoy of fishing-boats and other small craft began to put out into the Bay, with Dominic and a crew of sailors in the lead.

Catrina strained her eyes in an agony of fear and suspense. Grappling-hooks were thrown, aimed at the blazing ships. Several times they failed to find their target. But at last, with nerve-tearing slowness, the convoy succeeded in grappling the fire-ships and began towing them away from the British vessels.

The sky was just lightening with dawn when a tremendous cheer convulsed the crowd. The fiercely burning vessels could be seen safely beached where the inevitable explosions could do no harm, and the convoy of small boats was returning. Catrina let her breath out in a long sigh. Dominic was safe, and the enemy's raid had failed.

'There will be a plentiful supply of firewood from the wrecks of the enemy vessels,' Alice commented with satisfaction. 'As soon as the fires have been put out, I shall send Hobson and the other servants to gather as much as they can.'

But Gibraltar's mood of elation did not last long. Catrina recorded subsequent events in her diary:

> No doubt in revenge for the failure of their raid, the enemy have intensified their close blockade of the Bay. The Emperor of Morocco has allowed himself to be bribed by the promise of Spanish gold, and he announced that he would give no further protection to British ships in Morocco's waters. As a result, we hear that several vessels laden with stores for Gibraltar, waiting for a favourable wind before they braved the blockade, have been seized by the Spanish.

As matters grew steadily worse, Catrina felt too heart-sick to write about them in her diary. Living through them was bad enough in itself.

Food supplies, already pitifully short, reached famine point. Bread was no longer being baked for public sale at any price. In a further attempt to force the British to their knees, the Spanish deployed their gunboats against the boats of the fishermen which until now had been regularly putting out under the shadow of the Rock, so that even fish became virtually unattainable.

One afternoon Catrina returned home after working on her garden. She carried some loose cabbage-leaves in a pail, and held Lucy's hand in her free one while Tim scampered impatiently ahead and returned again and again, as if to hurry them along.

When they arrived at the house Alice said in a restrained voice, 'Lucy, dear, take the cabbage-leaves through to the kitchen, and ask Hobson for a bone for Tim. He has one saved for him.'

After Lucy and the dog had left them, Dinah burst out, 'That is sheer lunacy, Alice! You can only be thinking of the bone which was left over after the last of the meat had been sliced from it at luncheon. It would have made a nourishing stock . . .'

'Tim is to have it,' Alice interrupted with quiet finality. 'The Governor has ordered all dogs in Gibraltar to be destroyed. The scarce rations can no longer be shared with household pets.'

Catrina sank into a chair. 'It will break Lucy's heart,' she muttered.

Through the window they could see Lucy playing with Tim in the small courtyard at the side of the house. As they watched, a Genoese woman in rags peeped through the grilled gate of the courtyard. She carried a baby in her arms, and two more children were holding on to her skirts. A few minutes after she had disappeared from the gate, Hobson entered.

'There is a Genoese woman with three children at the back door, madam,' he told Alice, staring fiercely into space. 'She wishes to know if she might have Tim.'

Catrina and Alice exchanged stricken glances. 'We'll go and speak to her,' Alice told the butler.

The woman was gaunt-faced and hollow-eyed, and her two elder children looked to be no more than skin and bone, while the baby in her arms was crying in obvious hunger.

With downcast eyes, the woman repeated her request for the dog. There was no doubt at all why she wanted Tim.

Torn between pity, revulsion and despair, Catrina nodded to Alice, and went to Lucy.

'Come and help me carry water to my garden,' she said, deliberately curt. She felt unable to meet the child's eyes.

'No, leave Tim behind for once. You know how boisterous he is. He will only upset the water.'

As they left the house, with Lucy carrying a small pail and concentrating hard on not spilling any of it, the sound of Tim's protesting howl followed them. Catrina almost spilled her own pail of water because she was blinded by the tears which she dared not allow Lucy to see.

CHAPTER EIGHTEEN

THE WEATHER TURNED hot, sticky and oppressive, and apart from the hardships they had to suffer, the people of Gibraltar were bedevilled by the claustrophobic monotony of the siege.

'Aunt Catrina,' Lucy asked for the dozenth time. 'Why do you 'spose Tim ran away?'

'I don't know, love. Perhaps—Perhaps he met a lady dog, and went to live with her.'

'Aunt Catrina, I've looked and looked, and I haven't seen *any* other dogs in the town.'

In desperation, Catrina said, 'Well—maybe they all decided to take to the wild. After all, there has not been much to eat lately, and they thought they would do better, hunting rabbits and things.'

'*I* think,' Lucy said bleakly, 'God was greedy again, and he took Tim to be a dog-angel.'

'Lucy, love, when the war is over, I'll make sure that you get another puppy . . .'

'It won't be the same.'

Catrina tried to shut her mind to the child's voice by thinking her own thoughts. Since money had become virtually useless, there being nothing to buy with it, there was little point in selling her vegetables. The household might as well be fed with them while they lasted, and she was also experimenting with ways of drying them.

She completed her harvesting, and such vegetables as they could not use themselves or exchange for other food supplies she tried to dry. She cut carrots and parsnips and cabbage-leaves into strips, and spread them out on a cotton sheet. Winter was upon them, and the sun had lost much of its heat. Although the rains had not yet started, there was a good deal of moisture in the air, so that by the end of a week, her carefully prepared vegetables had rotted.

Dinah, predictably, rubbed salt into the wounds of her

failure. 'You should have continued your profiteering,' she taunted. 'Your friend, Jake Farraday, slipped into the harbour this morning, after fighting off three Spanish gunboats. I hear he has been selling potatoes at more than a shilling a pound, and herrings at four sovereigns a barrel. If you had not chosen to rot your vegetables, you could have sold them instead and been in a position to afford such luxuries.'

So Jake was in Gibraltar . . . Catrina caught Dominic's gaze upon her, and decided it would be best not to see Jake. She had no money with which to buy any of his cargo, and if he really meant to continue pressing her to marry him, it was wiser not to encourage him.

But she had reckoned without Jake himself, she discovered the following morning. The household was eating their breakfast of severely rationed oatmeal porridge when the front-door knocker sounded, and moments later Hobson entered, carrying a hamper.

'A gharry-driver delivered this, madam,' he addressed Alice. 'He said it was a gift to the Ridgeway household from Mr Jake Farraday.'

Dominic scraped his chair back. 'Detain the driver!'

'He has already left, sir. He did not appear to wish for a reward.'

Alice began to unpack the hamper. It contained a whole ham and a cheese, together with some dozen oranges, two bottles of rum and one of port wine.

Alice stared helplessly at the provisions, and then exclaimed, 'There is a letter at the bottom, addressed to Catrina!' She picked it up and handed it across the table.

Catrina would have preferred to read the note later, in private, but Dinah's smile was challenging her. She broke the seal, hoping that her expression would not betray her if Jake had made some disconcerting reference to their last conversation.

But the note merely said:

> My dear Miss Beaumont, I believe I forgot to thank you for your delightful company on the occasion of the King's birthday dinner. I hope this small gift may do something to compensate for my oversight, and do something to make Christmas a joyful one for yourself

and your family and friends.

There were no pockets to her gown, and so she pushed the note down her bodice instead. She looked up, into Dominic's angry, suspicious eyes.

'The hamper must be sent back to the man,' he said curtly.

'A pity, but there it is.' General Ridgeway was eyeing the bottles of rum and port wine wistfully.

Catrina swept them all a frowning glance. 'Sending the hamper back would be a cruel slap in the face to Mr Farraday!'

'My dear,' Alice said, 'you must see why we cannot accept it. At the prices Mr Farraday charges, these things would have fetched at least fifteen sovereigns. Until the next relief convoy arrives with some of our funds from England, we are so hard pressed that we could scarcely raise that sum between us. Keeping the hamper would not only be a matter of accepting charity, but also . . .'

'Jake Farraday meant it kindly,' Catrina defended.

'However he meant it,' Dominic said shortly. 'It must go back.'

'My dear Dominic,' Dinah pointed out sweetly, 'the hamper would not have been sent at all if it had not been for Catrina, and presumably she did something to earn it, so it is for her, surely, to decide whether or not it should go back?'

'If Catrina earned it,' Alice put in testily, 'she did so by seeing good in a man whom everyone else condemns!' She turned to Catrina. 'It is not because of Mr Farraday's reputation that the hamper should be returned. If he had sent you, personally, a boxful of sweetmeats, it would have been a different matter, Catrina. But he is not even acquainted with any of the rest of us! I cannot think what moved him to send us such an expensive gift.'

'Perhaps,' Dominic put in, 'that note the man sent to Catrina could throw light on the matter.'

Catrina shrugged impatiently. 'He merely thanked me for my company on the occasion of the King's birthday dinner, and hoped the contents of the hamper would give us a little joy at Christmas. And I,' she added defiantly, 'will not allow his feelings to be hurt by sending his gift back!'

'Personally,' Dinah said, 'I feel that ham would be a vast improvement on salt fish for Christmas dinner.' She added maliciously, 'I think we should simply count ourselves lucky that Catrina is such a *particular* friend of Jake Farraday!'

Dominic rose, and without a further word left the house. General Ridgeway pushed his chair back too, and addressed Alice. 'I shall leave it to your good sense, my dear, to decide what is to be done.'

When the three women were alone together, Alice said, 'Catrina, please consider. Mr Farraday's reference to Christmas would make it quite impossible for us *not* to invite him to share the day with us if we were to accept his gift.'

'Would that be so terrible? Whatever people may say of him, he *does* know how to behave in polite society, and his conversation is always amusing and interesting.'

'Catrina, one would normally invite only intimate friends to share one's Christmas!'

'Perhaps,' Dinah put in slyly, 'Mr Farraday considers himself to *be* an intimate friend of Catrina's!'

Alice gave her a look of distaste and then ignored her. 'One can no more accept such an expensive gift, Catrina, from someone who is not even an acquaintance than one could invite him for Christmas.'

Catrina sighed. 'If you would keep an eye on Lucy, Alice, I shall go to the waterfront and thank Mr Farraday for his gift, but explain to him tactfully that we cannot accept it. Then we can ask Hobson to return the hamper to him afterwards.'

In the bedroom, Catrina retrieved Jake's note from the bodice of her gown and put it away in a drawer. Then she slipped on her cloak and left the house. A chilly mist hung over the Rock, but she had identified *Arabella* long before she had reached the waterfront. As she picked her way over coils of rope towards her anchorage, she saw Dominic's tall figure at the foot of her gangway.

She hurried to join him. 'What are you doing here?'

He turned his head to look at her. 'Since you were clearly not disposed to return Farraday's gift, I have come to pay for the contents of the hamper.'

She stared at him. 'How could you possibly have raised the money?'

'I pawned my signet-ring.'

The ring with its personal seal was as much part of him as his very identity. 'Your extreme behaviour, Dominic . . .' she began angrily.

At that moment Jake himself came walking down the gangway. He looked startled at the sight of them, but quickly recovered his composure. 'My crew-man told me that I had a visitor, but he did not say it was a family deputation!'

Before Catrina could speak, Dominic said, with such amiability that she was instantly alarmed, 'We have called in connection with the hamper which you sent.'

'It is a gift . . .' Jake began.

'Indeed it must be,' Dominic interposed smoothly. 'Only inspired intuition could have told you so precisely what goods we intended buying from you, and saved us the trouble of having to attend an auction to bid for them.' He reached into his pocket and brought out a handful of sovereigns. 'If it is not quite the correct amount, please let us know, so that we may make up the difference.'

Jake made no move to take the money. He hid his own anger. A great deal of calculation had gone into the sending of that hamper. He had been quite sure that it would be returned to him. By making his gift over-generous and controversial, he had felt confident of luring Catrina to him in person.

But he had intended that she should call on him at the Queen's Head, and by herself. To find the possessive brother-in-law with her, and turning the tables so neatly on himself, was not what he had bargained for at all.

Slowly, with an exaggerated gesture, Jake reached for his quizzing-glass, pausing to polish it with his silk handkerchief. Then he raised it in a theatrical gesture and allowed his languid gaze to rest upon the coins upon Dominic's outstretched palm, examining them as if they were oddities. It was a tactic which had often served him successfully in the past. In a moment or two the other man, flushed and discomfited, would turn on his heel and walk away.

Instead, Dominic said with a bland smile, 'I do beg your pardon. I should have realised that a man of your refinement does not stoop to handling money. I shall leave it to your crew to come and collect it.'

He tossed the coins into the air. One of them caught the quizzing-glass in Jake's hand and shattered the glass. It had happened so quickly that, for an instant, he appeared to be still staring disdainfully through the empty frame. From among the watching crew on board *Arabella* came a hurriedly-suppressed snort of laughter.

Catrina felt Dominic's hand on her arm. 'Now that Mr Farraday has been compensated in full,' he said smoothly, 'we may go home.'

Angrily she shook herself free. 'I should like you to know, Mr Farraday, that I, at least, appreciated the generosity with which you offered the gift . . .'

'Did you, Miss Beaumont?' In that moment of humiliation he hated her almost as much as he did Dominic Ross, simply for having been a witness to it. 'Perhaps your brother-in-law is right. They say that Greeks are not to be trusted when they come bearing gifts.'

'You are not a Greek,' she returned in a puzzled voice.

He did not comment, but merely swept her a bow. As Dominic began to draw her inexorably away, Jake called after her, 'I shall await your reply to my note, Miss Beaumont. Meet me at my lodgings, as usual.'

Dominic's fingers dug into the flesh of her arm. 'What did he mean? Have you been to his lodgings?'

'Yes, I have! And I shall go there again whenever I choose! Moreover, if I decide to marry him, I shall do so without consulting you . . .'

'*Marry him!* You fool, Catrina! Jake Farraday's kind do not marry anyone! They take—they use—and they discard women!'

'I know him rather better than you do!'

'You do not know him at all! Show me that note of his!'

'Certainly not! I have told you what it contains!'

His grip on her arm tightened, and she found herself in the humiliating position of having to run to keep up with him as he marched her towards the house.

He forced her to enter by the side door. She tried to move past him, but one arm seized her round the waist, while his free hand fumbled for the handle of the nearest door. She found herself propelled inside it, and discovered that it was one of the empty rooms whose furniture Alice had lent to needy friends.

Dominic's body pinned her against a wall. 'I want to see that note from Farraday!' he demanded.

'You have no right! And, besides . . .'

He thrust a hand down the front of her bodice, and encountered nothing but the smooth swell of her breasts. The intimate warmth of his hand against her flesh assaulted her senses, so that it was difficult to sustain her outrage. 'I—have put the note away,' she managed at last.

His own anger had left him. Slowly he removed his hand and looked at her with raw hopelessness in his eyes.

'There was nothing in the note, Dominic,' she said quietly. 'Nothing more than I had told you it contained. Jake pretended there was, in order to bait you. And even if there had been anything, I am of age, and responsible for myself.'

'You are a babe-in-arms when it comes to a man like Farraday, Catrina. He had an ulterior, self-seeking motive for sending that hamper, just as he'd had one for providing the food served at the King's birthday dinner. Keep away from him. He warned you himself, almost in so many words, that he is not to be trusted.'

'What do you mean?'

'A card-sharper is commonly referred to as a Greek.'

She made a sound of exasperation. 'But don't you see, that kind of self-denigrating remark is part of the façade he puts up for the world! I accept that he once cheated at cards. But is that the worst crime in the world, Dominic? And how do we know what the circumstances might have been?'

Dominic shook his head. 'Catrina, there are other things besides cheating at cards. Jake Farraday became involved with a sixteen-year-old girl. One of her brothers befriended him, and he repaid the friendship by encouraging the girl to run away from home and sail with him to Ireland.'

'I cannot imagine Jake, with his sophistication and sharp wit, being interested in a schoolgirl! It seems much more likely to me that she, hopelessly infatuated with him, stowed away on board *Arabella* without his knowledge!'

Dominic regarded her grimly. 'You are determined to defend him, aren't you? I cannot help wondering why!'

'It is because everything laid at his door since he cheated at cards seems to be based upon gossip and conjecture! And because what I *know* about him does not square with any of the stories being told about him. He helped me when I was desperate, and when I went to repay him he wanted to waive my entire debt to him. As it was, he would only accept interest at 5 per cent. Setting it at 50 per cent had been a sardonic joke. He had been behaving in the way the world expects Jake Farraday to behave.'

She moved to the door. 'Unless and until he does something to make me change my opinion of him, Dominic, I shall continue my friendship with Jake, whether you like it or not!'

Dominic said quietly, 'Would you like to hear, Catrina, what is rumoured to have happened to that young girl he took to Ireland?'

'Since you have just admitted that, once again, there are only rumours and no proved facts—no, I would not!' Her voice cracked. 'Dominic, I do not have much to cheer my life. Alice, for all her kindness, puts up a barrier between herself and me, and Dinah does not like me. I am an outsider; I do not belong to the same world as the service wives and daughters. And you . . .' She looked away. 'You may be my brother, as the law says you are. But all I get from that relationship are high-handed commands and angry lectures. No tenderness, no show of affection . . .'

He moved towards her, and touched her face. 'I dare not show you affection, Catrina, and you know it,' he said in a low voice. His fingertips trailed along the line of her cheek and rested briefly on her mouth. Then he dropped his hand.

She smiled drearily. 'So there you have it. Jake Farraday is the only one I can truly call a friend. Please try to put aside the prejudice you feel against him.'

Dominic shook his head. 'I can't, because it is not mere prejudice. Jealousy comes into it, I admit. But the rest is an instinctive knowledge of the kind of man he is. So—I am sorry, Catrina, but I shall continue to do my best to put whatever obstacles I can in the way of your friendship with him.'

'And I shall continue to defy you.'

But she did not see Jake again before he left the Bay, and with the passing days the bad weather closed in, imprisoning women and children inside their homes and adding to the misery of everyone. Catrina spent more time than ever in writing her diary:

> How dreary everything is! A little cheer was brought at Christmas, however, by the arrival of a large ship from Liverpool, which fought its way through the blockade. We have now entered the third calendar year of the siege. Just as my own obsessive longing for Dominic is doomed to make me a prisoner for life, will the enemy continue to incarcerate and menace all of us here on the Rock until the end of time?

But as if to answer her question, the first months of 1781 brought definite and encouraging signs of change.

'There has been a sudden alteration in the positioning of the Spanish fleet off Algeciras,' General Ridgeway announced one evening when he and Dominic arrived home. 'And repeated flag signals have been noted from the enemy towers. We think the new relief convoy we have been awaiting from Britain is on its way, and drawing near.'

Lucy interrupted the general exclamations of jubilation and hope by climbing on Dominic's lap, and saying plaintively, 'I do not feel well, Papa.'

'Don't you, my love? What is the matter?'

Catrina answered for her. 'I believe she is catching one of her chills again.' She moved towards them, and lifted Lucy from his lap, acutely aware of her hands pressing against his thighs as she did so. She hid her expression against Lucy's hair. 'I'll put you to bed, and bring your supper to you.'

Catrina retired to bed early too, but she was rudely awakened by the sound of church bells pealing, accompanied by excited voices and running footsteps. She struggled upright and lit a candle, peering at the clock. It was a few minutes to midnight. Every drama and crisis, she thought wearily, seemed to occur in the middle of the night.

Dinah was getting out of bed, and reaching for a gown. The entire household seemed to be astir, but Lucy had not awakened and Catrina was loath to disturb her unless the matter were vital.

A few minutes later Dinah rushed back to the bedroom and began to change into warm clothing. 'A British cutter, *Kite*, has slipped into harbour! Everyone is going down there to find out whether she is the vanguard of the approaching relief convoy!'

This time Lucy woke up, and sat rubbing her eyes. 'Well,' Dinah addressed Catrina, 'are you not coming also?'

'I think not. Lucy had best be kept warm and in bed.'

But the child began to whimper. 'I want to go with the others, Aunt Catrina. I want to see the ships coming in.'

'We'll hear all about it later, Lucy dear.'

Lucy pushed the bedcovers away. 'I'm better, Aunt Catrina! Please let us go and see the fun! *Please!*'

Catrina touched the child's forehead, and found that it was quite cool. 'We'll go,' she told Lucy. 'But you will have to be wrapped up warmly.'

Some minutes later they joined the others. The entire household, including the servants, had elected to watch the excitement. Dominic and General Ridgeway, Catrina discovered, had left for their posts some time before, in case the Spaniards decided to mount obstructive action. Hobson carried Lucy as they all streamed down to the waterfront, but once they had reached the edge of the waiting crowds, the child insisted on being handed over to Catrina.

It was cold, despite the denseness of the crowd, and the darkness was pierced only by the flickering torches that some of the people had brought with them. Apart from *Kite* lying in the harbour, there was not much to see. It seemed to Catrina a pointlessly long wait until morning, standing there with the heavy burden of the child in her arms.

Lucy, too, was obviously regretting her plea to be allowed to watch whatever was happening. 'My head aches, Aunt Catrina,' she whimpered.

Several of their party had become separated from them, but Alice was at Catrina's side. 'I'll help you to try and push a path through the crowd,' she offered.

But their efforts were in vain. The crush of people was too great, and they merely found themselves pinned in at a different spot. After a while the child fell asleep, and Catrina and Alice took it in turns to hold her, their arms becoming numb with the effort and with the cold. Hobson spotted them and thrust his way through to them, and relieved them of the burden of Lucy's weight.

Morning dawned, with a thick fog covering the sea. Catrina hoped that this would persuade the crowd to thin out so that they could return home with Lucy. But people were keyed up with excitement, and they refused to give up their long vigil until they had seen the relieving ships arrive in the Bay. The fog cleared, and a wild cheer went up. The British convoy could be clearly seen, moving towards the harbour in a compact body, with warships escorting them. Under the Barbary shore, the remainder of the naval squadron could be seen lying to.

As Catrina watched from among the crowd, she saw some fifteen Spanish gunboats forming a line. The cheering stopped. A short distance out from Algeciras the enemy gunboats opened fire on the nearest vessel of the British convoy.

The sound of the firing awakened Lucy. She stirred in Hobson's arms, and whined, 'I want Aunt Catrina to hold me. I want to go home.'

'Hush, Miss Lucy,' Catrina heard the butler tell the child sternly. 'We can't go home now, so you had best watch what is going on, because one day you will be able to tell your grandchildren about this morning.'

Lucy's attention had been successfully caught. 'What are the ships doing now, Aunt Catrina?' she wanted to know. 'Are we winning?'

'Yes, love, I think we are winning. The enemy is fleeing back to the shelter under the land!'

In their haste, Catrina noticed with satisfaction, several enemy ships ran aground and were swiftly abandoned by their crew, who were scrambling over the rocks to get ashore at Algeciras. In the meantime, the leading ships of the British convoy were advancing inexorably towards the harbour, scattering the enemy fleet. As they dropped anchor the crowds roared their jubilation.

Mighty as the sound was, it was drowned a moment later by savage mortar fire which rocked the town. The familiar, sickening pall of black smoke shot through with flashes of flame wrapped itself round the crowd as the long-prepared batteries of the Spaniards at last opened fire against the fortress.

With one arm round Alice's waist and her free hand holding on to Hobson's coat-tail, Catrina joined the chaos of scattering crowds as they rushed pell-mell through the battleground which the town had become, towards whatever safety they could find.

CHAPTER NINETEEN

EVERYTHING WAS CONFUSION and destruction. Fires had begun to rage unchecked in town as the Spanish guns thundered remorselessly from their batteries and forts. The crowd was gripped by the hysteria of terror, and seemed not to know in which direction to flee.

Hobson looked over his shoulder at Alice. 'Will we try for home, madam?'

'No. Too dangerous. The gulleys in the rocks would be best . . .'

'My place would be best,' Catrina interrupted. 'My cow-byre. But we must use care in making for it, or we shall be over-run by other refugees. I'll lead the way. We'll pretend to be making for the rocks.'

A building close by went up in flames as a shell hit it, and the crowd became united in their decision to reach the rocks and gulleys as swiftly as they could. Catrina felt herself being propelled along willy-nilly. She glanced over her shoulder and saw with relief that Alice and Hobson, with Lucy, were following her at an apparent tangent. It was only when they reached the cow-byre, and Lucy had been made as comfortable as possible on the palliasse, that anyone thought of Dinah and the female servants. Alice wanted to go and search for them in the gulleys, but Hobson advised,

'Leave them be, madam. We all know by now that the Dons will cease firing at one o'clock for their siesta. Mrs Forest and the servants are bound to go to the house then, and you can bring them back here with you afterwards. With your permission, madam,' he added, 'I wish to go to the waterfront, to offer my services in helping with the unloading of the stores brought in by the British convoy.'

He left, and Catrina and Alice sat in silence on the floor, listening to the sounds of destruction going on around them.

'I'm thirsty, Aunt Catrina, and the noise is making my

head ache,' Lucy complained.

Catrina remembered for the first time that she had left her cooking-pots in their old catchment area for the collection of water for her garden, and she went to bring one in. It had rained heavily two nights earlier, so that she knew the water would be fresh. She gave some to Lucy, and she and Alice drank deeply too, trying to still their hunger pangs.

At one o'clock precisely the enemy ceased their bombardment. Alice looked at Catrina. 'They'll start again in four hours' time. You'd better stay with Lucy while I go to salvage what I can.'

Catrina chewed at her lip. 'We need all the hands we can muster, and we cannot be sure that Dinah and the servants will return to the house. They may be too frightened.' She touched Lucy's forehead, which was still reassuringly cool in spite of the child's complaints and her lethargy. 'My love, would you promise to remain here and not wander outside? I want to help Aunt Alice to bring some blankets and food.'

Lucy yawned. 'I'll go to sleep. Tim will look after me while you are away, Aunt Catrina.'

As they left the cover of the palmettos and joined the stream of others rushing into town to take advantage of the enemy's siesta, Catrina addressed Alice in a worried voice. 'There is something wrong with Lucy, even though she has no fever. She did not once complain of being hungry, and she seems so strangely lacking in energy. Also, this—delusion—that Tim is still with her is something new.'

Alice touched her arm in a reassuring gesture. 'The child is tired and suffering from shock. And she has probably been consoling herself for a long time with the fantasy that Tim is still around. Half-asleep, she mentioned it aloud. That is all.'

'I hope you are right.'

They continued in silence. As they climbed over débris and rubble, some of which was still smouldering, Catrina knew that the same thought occupied both their minds. Would there be anything at all left to salvage? But the house was intact when they reached it, and Dinah was there, busy packing her gowns.

'You'll have to leave most of those,' Alice told her sharply. 'Blankets, food and candles are our first priority.'

One by one the female servants returned to the house and they helped to carry necessities in relays to the cow-byre. It was only when the operation had been completed, with ten minutes to spare before the Spanish ended their siesta, that Catrina realised some of the servants, in their urgency, had had slightly distorted views on what constituted necessities. Various pieces of small furniture cluttered the cow-byre, and a rare antique rug had been spread on its earthen floor.

Catrina chewed at her lip as she studied the assembled company. With the four servants, they totalled seven adults and one child.

'There is not enough room for us all,' she said apologetically. 'There is a crag in the rock close by, which opens into a cave. It is quite dry and spacious . . .'

'Me and the girls will take some bedding and make ourselves snug in there, miss,' Alice's personal maid, Jane, put in.

Lucy woke up and began to cry. 'My headache is worse, Aunt Catrina. I want the fighting to stop . . .'

'Have a little water, my love, and lie down again. I am going to light a fire, and make some pease-pudding. You'll like that, won't you?'

'No, I won't. Tim won't like it either.'

In the morning, Lucy was lapsing into bouts of delirium. 'Mama,' she muttered, 'I want to wear my Sunday pinafore . . . No, Tim, that's naughty! You must be a good dog, or Mama will say you make her sneeze . . .'

Alice came to kneel beside the palliasse. Lucy's eyes were fever-bright, her face flushed. 'There is no rash, or anything like that,' she said thoughtfully. 'It could be anything. An unusually severe feverish cold, possibly. I know there has been a recent outbreak of typhus in the town, so it could be that . . .' She allowed her voice to tail off.

'Oh, God!' Catrina tried to think. 'You and Dinah must take your bedding, and sufficient supplies, and get out of here. Go and shelter in the cave with the servants.'

'The child should be taken to the hospital, Catrina!'

'In all this?' She made a wild, sweeping gesture to comprise the hellish bombardment which had continued without ceasing throughout the night. 'Even if we were to reach the hospital unscathed, they would probably not admit her! The place will be full of casualties of the fighting.'

'That's true,' Alice admitted. 'But you cannot be left to cope with her alone.'

'Listen, Alice, you must do as I say! *I* have been in constant physical touch with Lucy, sharing my bed with her every night, so I have nothing more to lose if she *is* suffering from . . .' Catrina could not bring herself to use the word 'typhus' with all its dread associations, and so she qualified, 'something contagious or infectious. But you and Dinah must go, and keep away!'

Dominic thrust a weary hand through his hair. Apart from the blessed respite afforded by the siesta periods, there had been no breaks in the noise, the fury and the smoke of the assault by the Spanish. Thousands of pounds of shot and shell had been tearing into the town and its defences. He had almost lost all sense of time, and it needed a moment's concentration to realise that this was the third day of the bombardment.

A soldier came running up to him, his face blackened with soot, his uniform hanging in shreds. 'Captain, sir,' he panted. 'The town—most of it's on fire!'

'Wait until you've caught your breath,' Dominic ordered, 'and then tell me what has happened.'

The soldier coughed, and then drew deep draughts of air into his lungs. 'General Ridgeway sent me, Captain. The enemy—they're mixing all manner of stuff as will burn with the powder in their shells, and every building as is hit catches fire right away! General Ridgway says, Captain, sir, you must send men to fight the fires.'

Dominic forced himself to remain impassive. 'Have a rest before you return to General Ridgeway,' he told the soldier. He turned away, and hurried to pick a detachment of men from his regiment, ordering them to go and quench the fires in town.

As he and his depleted troops worked on, he tried to shut his mind to the blood-soaked casualties around them. He also tried to clear from his thoughts the question of what was happening to the women. To Alice and Dinah and Catrina and Lucy. But particularly to Catrina and Lucy.

At times Lucy seemed better. She would sit up and complain about the noise keeping her awake, and ask for water. At others the fever would take hold of her again, and she would shiver so convulsively that Catrina was forced to take her in her arms and attempt to warm the child with her own body-heat. The shivering would stop, only to be replaced by streaming perspiration that quickly soaked her clothes.

Alice brought water and food to the door of the byre, but Catrina ordered her sharply not to come closer.

'Has Lucy eaten anything?' Alice wanted to know.

'I've tried to feed her some gruel, but she refuses to swallow it.'

'I've just remembered!' Alice exclaimed. 'There is a little chocolate left at home. I had been hoarding it for a dire emergency. I'll send Dinah to the house as soon as the Spaniards stop for their siesta. Lucy likes chocolate, and it will provide her with the nourishment she needs.'

Long before she reached the Ridgeways' house, Dinah could see that it, together with neighbouring houses, was on fire. Outside one house which had been completely gutted she could make out clearly the charred corpse of someone who must have tried, in desperation, to salvage something from the dwelling.

She lost her self-control. Everything was too horrible to be endured. Where was Dominic? She began to run wildly towards the direction of the batteries. But something even more frightening than the Spanish bombardment, or the destruction of the houses and that grisly charred corpse, met her as she entered the area of the burning town she would have to cross before she reached the batteries.

It was here that the merchants had their shops, and the troops had discovered hidden supplies in them. The merchants had been pleading shortages, while all the time they had been hoarding liquor and livestock and other commodities! Soldiers were staggering about, clutching bottles from which they took copious draughts.

One of them saw Dinah, and lurched up to her. Before she could turn and run she was surrounded by soldiers in whom all sense of discipline had been blotted out by the effects of liquor. They began to pull at her clothes, cheering as they did so. She pleaded with them, terrified, but her very terror seemed to spur them into greater excitement.

One of them had pinned her against a wall, while several others were trying to strip off her gown, which was already hanging in shreds.

A shot suddenly rang out above their heads. 'The first man to lay another finger on the lady,' a voice said with menace, 'will receive a bullet to the brain.'

Soldiers hesitated, and then slunk away. Dinah clutched her tattered gown against her and looked at Jake Farraday. In spite of the destruction all round, he was as fastidiously dressed as he had been at the Governor's dinner.

He removed his embroidered coat, and held it out to her. 'Put this on, ma'am, and come with me.'

In Dinah's mind, the ugliness of the scene he had interrupted was instantly blurred. The whole episode became one of drama and romance. She, a beautiful lady in mortal danger, had been rescued by the notorious Jake Farraday. A man known for his self-interest would not have risked pitting himself against such an overwhelming mob of soldiers had he not been inspired by the sight of her standing there, so courageously holding them off with her defiant, scornful gaze . . .

His voice brought her back to reality. 'Your face is familiar, ma'am. Have we not met before?'

'Well—not precisely. I am Mrs Dinah Forest. You are acquainted with my sister-in-law-to-be, Miss Catrina Beaumont.'

'Ah, yes of course. You are betrothed to Captain Dominic Ross. Are they all safe?'

'Apart from Dominic, who is of course fighting at his post, and my cousin, General Ridgeway, the others are safely in hiding.' Dinah's voice invited him to enquire why she, alone, was wandering streets made lethal by enemy bombardment and fire and drunken soldiers. So,

'What brings you abroad?' he asked on cue.

'Lucy, my future stepdaughter, has a chill and refuses to eat the oatmeal we have been trying to feed her. So I decided to return home and see whether I could not find something left in the larder which would be more palatable and nourishing. But the house was on fire, so I thought I would see whether one of the merchants might be persuaded to sacrifice a small supply of something like chocolate, and instead I found myself surrounded by drunken, looting soldiers.' Even as she embroidered her story, Dinah was convincing herself of the truth of it.

'I am taking you to where *Arabella* is moored,' Jake Farraday said. 'My valet is extremely skilled with a needle, and will repair your gown. While you are waiting, a parcel will be made of victuals with which to tempt Lucy's appetite.'

A thrill passed through Dinah as she pictured the scene in her mind. She would be seated inside Jake Farraday's cabin on board *Arabella,* covered by a—yes, by a silken sheet. She was sure he slept between silk sheets. While his valet worked on her gown in his own quarters, she and Jake Farraday would sit together, making polite conversation. But all the while he would be aware of her body beneath the almost-transparent sheet. He would find it hard to contain his desire, but contain it he would, for he would be aware of a noble, untouchable quality about her . . .

'We had better run, now that we have reached the waterfront,' his voice broke through her dream. 'The enemy are concentrating a good deal of their fire on this area, and they may decide to cut short their siesta.'

He took her hand, but after she had stumbled a few times, he stopped and scooped her into his arms and ran with her towards *Arabella*'s anchorage. Dinah stored the memory in her mind, to be savoured fully later.

She was pleasantly surprised by the comfort and luxury of Jake's cabin. The next hour came as close to Dinah's dreams as it was possible for reality to resemble fantasy. Jake left her alone inside the cabin while she removed her torn gown, and she covered herself, not with a silken sheet but with an embroidered robe he had offered her. He returned after a discreet knock, and she tried to make herself look as small and vulnerable, and at the same time dignified, inside his voluminous robe as she possibly could.

The one irritating deviation from her dream was the way in which he continued to bring Catrina's name into the conversation. Where was she hiding? Now that a British convoy had once again arrived in the Bay, was she contemplating returning to England?

'I really couldn't tell you what Catrina's plans are,' Dinah said with a lilting laugh. 'At the moment she is concerned only with hiding from the enemy's fire.'

'Presumably she is caring for Lucy?'

'Yes, well, she is sitting with her while I am away,' Dinah conceded. She leant towards him. 'You know, Mr Farraday, I have a good deal of influence in society here in Gibraltar. When I have told people how you came to my aid, and how you behaved towards me with the utmost respect and decorum, I think you will find many a door, which was previously closed, thrown open to you!'

'Why, I cannot thank you enough, Mrs Forest,' he returned gravely. She was, he thought with amused contempt, as transparent as a silly schoolgirl. She obviously wished that he would behave towards her with a little less respect and decorum, even though she would, of course, put up a show of shocked outrage to begin with. But she would be the easiest conquest imaginable!

He toyed, fleetingly, with the thought of obliging her. The only pleasure he might possibly have gained from doing so would have been the thought that it was Dominic Ross's betrothed he was taking and using. But Ross did not love this silly, shallow creature, and he would probably be glad of a reason to be rid of her. More important, such a marginally enjoyable escapade would doubtless come to the ears of Catrina, and then he would have lost all hope of capturing that infinitely more desirable prize.

He would have liked to send a message to Catrina, but he did not trust Dinah to deliver it. Making up his mind, he said, 'I shall accompany you to where the others are hiding, and see if I can tempt Lucy's appetite with sweetmeats.'

'Oh no!' Dinah said with alarm. 'That will not be necessary.'

'I insist. Apart from anything else, I wish to make sure that you reach the others safely.'

Dinah shaded her eyes with her hand. 'I—I did not wish to speak of it,' she said brokenly, 'for what is the point in burdening others with one's fears and anxieties? The thing is—there is far more wrong with Lucy than a mere chill, and I cannot possibly allow you to expose yourself to infection.'

'What is wrong with the child?'

'She may be suffering from typhus.'

He stared incredulously at her. '*Typhus!* And you have

been sitting here, enacting . . . What makes you think she has typhus?'

Dinah had sensed the scornful criticism in his voice. 'Catrina thinks it is,' she said sullenly. 'It very probably is not. Catrina has isolated herself with Lucy and won't let anyone else come near them.' She gave a brittle little laugh. 'Of course, that means that Catrina may safely remain in hiding from the enemy's fire, so that *she* does not have to volunteer to face all the dangers and go and seek . . .'

'Tell me the child's symptoms,' Jake cut her short.

'See has a fever . . .'

'Naturally. What else? How long has Catrina been in close contact with the child?'

'They are almost always together, and they have been sharing the same bed for months. I think it is very unhealthy and undesirable . . .'

It did not sound like typhus to him. During his career at sea, members of his crew had, from time to time, contracted most of the serious contagious or infectious diseases, and what ailed Lucy did not match what he knew about any of them.

'Has Catrina complained recently of feeling ill?' he asked Dinah.

'Oh, no. Her constitution is extremely robust, her health rude. There is something rather unfeminine about such rugged, brawny health.'

He ignored the spiteful barb. If the child were suffering from a contagious ailment, Catrina would have displayed some symptom by now. At the very least, she would have felt too generally unwell to be able to go on nursing Lucy single-handedly. So whatever was wrong with the child could not be passed on to someone else.

He stood up. 'By now, my valet should have made such repairs to your gown as were possible to make. Get dressed, and then take me to where Catrina is nursing Lucy. I have medicine which I am confident will help the child, and may save her life.'

Dinah nodded. She had become reconciled to the fact that, for the moment, Lucy was to occupy the centre of the stage and already, in her mind, she was re-casting herself in a different drama.

Not only had she risked her life by entering the bombarded

town in search of nourishing food for Lucy; not only had she almost been ravished and murdered by drunken soldiers, but she had also gambled everything by accompanying the notorious, dangerous Jake Farraday to his cutter. And all in the hope that a poor little orphaned girl, her future stepdaughter, might be saved . . .

It had, once again, been impossible to spoon gruel into Lucy's mouth, for she shivered too convulsively. She did not recognise Catrina at all.

'No, Mama, please,' she kept repeating between chattering teeth.

Dear God, Catrina prayed inwardly, make her better. Save my poor Lucy.

She was trying to keep the blankets wrapped about the child when the light from the doorway was blotted out. She looked up in astonishment as Jake Farraday stood there, looking magnificent but incongruous in his embroidered coat and ruffled sleeves, and with an intricately-tied cravat at his throat.

'Stay away!' Catrina cried. 'We think it might be typhus.'

He remained in the doorway. 'Have any spots appeared on her body at all?'

'There are no marks of any kind.'

Reassured, he stepped inside the cow-byre, ignoring Catrina's cry that he should stay away. 'For how long has she been ill?'

'She began to complain of a headache just before the bombardment started, but I have remembered since that she looked pinched and pale for a few days before then.'

'If it had been typhus, I am certain the purple spots would have made their appearance by now. I've brought you something which will make her feel better, and also some bread and chocolate and fruit.'

'Oh, thank you!' Catrina said as he placed a wicker basket on the floor. 'Now, please go. Don't expose yourself to infection like this.'

He removed a flask of medicine from the basket. 'Give her three drops of this in water three times a day.'

Catrina looked at him with brimming eyes. 'Jake Farraday, I don't care what anyone says about you. I think you are quite magnificent!'

He veiled his eyes with his lashes so that she would not see their expression. He had achieved exactly what he had set out to achieve. He swept her a bow, and then left the cow-byre.

A short while later, Lucy had a lucid spell and Catrina was able to give her some of the medicine. Weak and exhausted, the child fell back on to the palliasse again, but she did not seem to be so feverish, and she even slept briefly.

She awoke when the Spaniards resumed their bombardment of the town. 'Aunt Catrina . . .' she whispered. 'Is it Sunday?'

'No, it isn't. Why?'

'Because I am wearing one of my Sunday pinafores.' She paused. 'Aunt Catrina?'

'Yes, Lucy?'

'I shouldn't sleep in my Sunday pinafore, you know.'

'I don't think it matters, just this once.'

'Don't tell Mrs Forest about it, will you? She would pinch me for wearing my Sunday pinafore in bed.'

'No, she won't. Could you try to drink a little chocolate now?'

Lucy nodded, and swallowed the chocolate which Catrina had made with hot water in which she had steeped some of the dates Jake had brought. Afterwards, she gave her more medicine, and Lucy fell asleep.

'How is she now?' Alice whispered from the doorway.

Catrina stood up and moved closer to her so that they could talk without disturbing the child. 'The medicine seems to be helping. She is no longer quite as feverish as she was, neither is she delirious. Her pulse has also become very much stronger.'

'One of the maids has tracked Hobson down,' Alice said. 'He is standing by, ready to go and fetch Dominic if you think it should be necessary.'

'Pray God it won't be necessary!'

Catrina returned to Lucy's side, and gently touched her forehead. The fever seemed to be much reduced, but her sleep was obviously not restful, for she was twitching and constantly moving her arms and legs.

Her eyes opened. 'Aunt Catrina,' she said. 'When Papa marries Mrs Forest, will I have to love her?'

Catrina was surprised, not only by the suddenness of the

question, but by the anxiety behind it. It was as if the child's illness had never been and she had been spending the past five days instead in pondering her future relationship with Dinah.

'If I peeled an orange, would you eat it, Lucy?'

'I'm not hungry. *Will* I have to love her?'

'No one can force themselves to love somebody, Lucy. You would have to try to be fair to her. Now go back to sleep.'

Catrina tucked the covers round her. There was something very restless about the child's wasted body but her brow had become almost cool to the touch. After a while she slipped into a doze, and Catrina went to the doorway to speak to Alice.

'Whatever the medicine was, it worked very quickly. She hardly has a fever at all now. The only thing that puzzles me is that she is restless, as if she is drawing energy from somewhere.'

'It sounds as if the medicine contains a stimulant,' Alice said. 'The main thing is that it has broken her fever. I don't think the restlessness matters, so long as she is not allowed to get up.'

Catrina returned to the palliasse, and found that Lucy was awake once again, and wriggling and fidgeting. 'Aunt Catrina . . .' she began.

'What is it this time, love?'

'Can I tell you a terrible, terrible secret?'

Catrina clasped the small hands in her own.

'What secret, love? I'm sure it couldn't really be all that terrible.'

'Oh, it is.' Lucy's over-bright eyes were very large in her pale little face. 'It's a black-sin secret. It's a cast-into-'ternal-darkness secret.'

'If it's about not loving Mrs Forest . . .'

'It's worse than that, Aunt Catrina! I think I'd better not say it out loud.' As Catrina placed her ear close to Lucy's mouth, the child whispered starkly, *'I don't like God.'*

The medicine, Catrina thought, was obviously stimulating into life all kinds of dormant fears, anxieties and feelings of guilt in the child's mind. She thought for a moment, and then she asked, 'Is it because he took your Mama and your grandparents and Tim?'

'Yes, but it isn't only that.' The child hesitated. 'It is because he is not a nice person. The new chaplain says so. The Lord-thy-God is a jealous God, he says. He smites people and he sends them plagues, and he gave Job sores, and he also teareth-ed him in his wrath.' She added in a small voice, 'I'm frightened of God, Aunt Catrina.'

Haltingly, trying to find the right words, Catrina said, 'Lucy, do you remember the pretty flowers that grow against the walls of the house in the summer? And the beautiful butterflies of different colours that flock to them? And do you remember how I explained to you that the flowers feed the butterflies, and the butterflies help to make flowers grow? Well, do you think it was a jealous, angry, frightening God who thought of making them so lovely, and arranged for them to help each other?'

'No . . .'

'And think of the Daddy-long-legs, Lucy. What an absurd, funny creature it is. Don't you think God must have been laughing to himself when he decided to create the Daddy-long-legs?'

The child gave an uneasy little giggle. 'You think God likes jokes, Aunt Catrina?'

'I'm sure he does, love.'

'I'd like an orange now, Aunt Catrina.'

After Lucy had eaten the orange, Catrina gave her some more of the medicine. The little girl yawned. 'I want to go to sleep now.'

After the child had been made comfortable and she was breathing evenly, Catrina went to the doorway and called Alice. 'She is very much better. It's growing dark and cold, and there is no need for you to remain on call any longer.'

Her heart filled with gratitude and relief, Catrina went to stretch out beside Lucy on the palliasse. She was so exhausted that she fell asleep almost immediately, until she was awakened by Lucy's voice, what seemed to be only minutes later. Alarmed, she felt the child's forehead, but the fever had not returned. She took the small hand in hers and found that the child's pulse was strong; miraculously strong for someone who had been so ill. All she needed now was long, unbroken sleep. If the bombardment would stop, perhaps she would get the rest she required.

Lucy heaved a long sigh. 'I'm not frightened of God any

more, Aunt Catrina.'

'I'm glad. Listen—the bombardment has stopped! Shall we both try to get some sleep before it starts it again?'

'Yes. Goodnight, Aunt Catrina.'

They settled themselves down again, and Catrina kept her arm about the child. But it was not long before Lucy's whispered voice broke the silence once more.

'Aunt Catrina?'

'Yes, my love?'

'Wouldn't it be nice to have a boiled egg for breakfast again?'

'You shall, just as soon as . . .'

The words froze on her lips. Convulsive spasms were tearing through Lucy's body. Catrina sprang up and groped for the candle and tinderbox. Its guttering light showed her that Lucy had her arms clasped over her head as if in unbearable pain. A sharp taste of terror and disbelief filled Catrina's mouth as she gathered Lucy to her.

The child's body arched in one last convulsive spasm, and grew still. Her head fell back limply across Catrina's arm. There would never be a boiled egg for Lucy's breakfast again.

CHAPTER TWENTY

THE EVENTS OF the next day were jumbled, and consisted of confused images in Catrina's mind. She remembered Alice appearing at the door of the cow-byre, and her own voice tonelessly reporting that Lucy was dead.

'Keep away,' she said over and over again as various people appeared and tried to remove Lucy's body.

Then Dominic was there, and *he* refused to keep away. He looked haggard with fatigue, and grief had carved harsh lines on his face. He knelt and lifted his dead daughter in his arms, his head bowed in sorrow.

'You should—have kept away,' Catrina said unevenly. 'If—what killed her—was contagious . . .'

He raised his head and looked at Catrina. '*You* have been with her.'

She swallowed. His meaning had been stark and clear. If she, too, was under sentence of death, he did not care whether he lived either.

He wrapped Lucy's body in a blanket and cradled it in his arms as he stood up. 'You can't take her!' Catrina cried wildly, spurred by some primitive sense of loss.

Alice spoke from the doorway, her voice gentle. 'Surgeon-Major Peters may be able to tell exactly what was the cause of her death.'

Catrina could never remember, afterwards, whether she slept then, or whether a fainting spell overcame her. The next thing she was aware of was that it had grown dark, and that the Spaniards had resumed their bombardment. Automatically she reached for Lucy, and then remembered.

Alice entered the cow-byre and lit a candle. She had brought bread wrapped in a napkin and a panikin of water.

'Poor Catrina,' she said softly. 'Poor child.'

'You—should not have come in here.'

'Surgeon-Major Peters examined Lucy's body, and I explained to him what her symptoms had been. He could find no evidence of contagious or infectious disease. He believes Lucy died of the ague.'

'Then it was all my fault!' Catrina cried in an agony of grief and guilt. 'If I had not taken her out into the cold night air to wait for the relief convoy . . .'

'Oh, my dear, you cannot blame yourself. Lucy fretted to go and watch the ships arrive in the Bay, and no one could have foreseen that we would become trapped among the crowd.'

'I should not have taken her outside in the first place! If I had not, she would still be alive.'

Alice put an arm round her shoulder. 'Catrina, consider the matter sensibly for a moment. You dressed Lucy warmly, and wrapped her in blankets. But if you had, indeed, forced her to stay in bed, think how it would have been when the enemy began to shell the town in the morning. You would have been alone in the house with Lucy; there would have been no time in which to do more than cover her with a blanket and flee the town. Even if you had not been caught in the enemy's fire, she would have been thoroughly chilled by the time you reached this place, and the result in the end would have been the same.'

Catrina began to weep helplessly. 'My poor little Lucy—I would have begged or stolen an egg for her breakfast if I had known . . .'

Alice held her and they wept together. 'I'll stay with you tonight,' she told Catrina when they were both calmer. 'I'll go and fetch my bedding.'

'What about Dinah?'

'She does not much care for the cave, but she is even more afraid of exposing herself to possible infection, no matter what Surgeon-Major Peters said. You must try not to mind if she treats you in the manner of a leper for some time to come.'

A toneless little laugh escaped Catrina. 'I can think of worse fates!'

Alice went to collect her bedding from the cave, and the two of them sat and listened to the sound of mortar fire for a while.

'Will—Will Dominic still marry Dinah, do you think?' Catrina broke the silence. 'He wanted a mother for Lucy . . .'

'Dinah will hold him to the marriage.' Alice's voice was cynical. 'She has already cast herself in her new role. She is to be Everything To Dominic. A man who has lost his wife and unborn child, and then his small daughter, will be an object of public sympathy. Oh yes, Dinah will revel in being seen to be Dominic's Whole New World.'

'I cannot understand why he ever proposed to her in the first instance!'

'She was available, and more than willing, and she pretended to be devoted to Lucy.' Alice added almost inaudibly, 'Since he could not have you, it did not much matter to him whom he chose.'

'Mrs Ridgeway—Alice—I want to leave Gibraltar! There is nothing, now, to keep me here. When the fleet sails . . .'

'It has already sailed, my dear.' There was sadness and regret in Alice's voice. 'Come, let us try and sleep. Tomorrow will be a harrowing day, for when the Spaniards break off for their siesta, Lucy is to be buried.'

Lucy's funeral turned out to be almost more than Catrina could bear. Supported by Alice, she left the cow-byre and walked through the town towards the place where the funeral service was to be held in the open.

'The King's Chapel inside the Convent is being used as an emergency store for supplies,' Alice explained.

Catrina merely nodded. The town, she was aware, was a pitiable sight. Scarcely a building remained unscathed, and most of Gibraltar lay in ruins. Heightening the grim effect were the bodies of soldiers who had been hanged in public for looting and other crimes committed while drunk.

Dinah was already among the crowd gathered at the spot where the service was to be held. Then Dominic appeared and went to stand beside her. Silence fell as the chaplain began to conduct the funeral service. Of necessity, it had to be brief, so that Lucy's small body could be interred beside her mother's grave before the Spanish bombardment desecrated the occasion. Dinah was weeping copiously, but Catrina's grief went too deep for public tears.

After a brief hymn had been sung, Dominic moved towards the small coffin. He gave the impression of having been carved of stone. General Ridgeway joined him, and together they lifted the coffin. Dominic's gait was stiff and mechanical as he led the way towards Lucy's burial-place.

Catrina had never thought of it before, but now she realised the importance of the conventional rituals of mourning; the gathering together of the bereaved to share funeral baked meats and sorrow. Lucy's hasty funeral left no time for this; the men had to return to their posts, and the women were forced to hurry away and seek refuge as far away from the town as they could before the enemy bombardment began again.

Catrina returned to her cow-byre. She knew that tents had been erected to the south of the Rock for officers' families, and that temporary huts were under construction. But although Alice pleaded with her to share their tent, she declined.

She felt closer to Lucy in the cow-byre. She wept as she remembered how the two of them had first discovered it, and then reflected on how the place had changed since then. Although much of the extraneous furniture had been removed, it still contained a tripod table and two chairs salvaged from the Ridgeways' house, and the incongruous, expensive Aubusson rug which softened the bareness of the earthen floor.

From time to time Hobson would appear, his manner as correct and punctilious as if these were normal times; he would bow and hand Catrina a parcel of food rations and say,

'With the compliments of Mrs Ridgeway and Captain Ross, ma'am.'

The enemy bombardment continued, and as if it were vying with the noise of the shelling, thunderstorms raged. Catrina knew that the officers, when they had time to sleep at all, would be sleeping in the barracks. But one afternoon during the siesta period, Dominic came to see her.

'I wish you would move in with Alice and Dinah,' he said.

'I prefer to remain here.'

'This place has too many unhappy associations,' he told her roughly.

'Wherever I went, I would be taking my unhappiness with me.'

Their eyes met. There were lines of strain around his mouth and she noticed a glint of silver in his dark hair.

'You should have gone back to England when you were

ordered to do so, Catrina!'

She sighed. 'There are many things I should, or should not, have done. I should never have come here in the first place. How long ago it seems now, that voyage in *Oriole* with Violet. Do you ever receive news of her, Dominic?'

He veiled his eyes with his lashes, and she knew that he was forced to lie when he said, 'No. As far as I am aware, she is still plying her trade in the *Linea*.'

So Violet was safe, and still carrying out her spying activities for the British. Not that they appeared to have any effect, judging by the never-ending enemy fire.

'Why don't we just give the Spaniards back their wretched Rock and be done with it!' Catrina burst out suddenly.

'Because it is not theirs.' He stood up, and pulled her to her feet. 'Go and share a tent with Dinah and Alice! This place is affecting your nerves!'

'To be brutally frank, Dominic, Dinah would affect my nerves far more than the solitude of the cow-byre does.'

He looked away. 'Yes, she is trying. I acted in foolish haste. She seemed to be devoted to Lucy, and the child was becoming too fond of you.' His voice cracked, and impulsively Catrina touched his cheek. His hand came up, covering her own, and they stood there gazing at one another, each conscious of the other's pain and desolation. He dropped his hand and moved away.

'There is something you had better know, Catrina. You would learn about it from others soon enough, in any case. Jake Farraday has slipped through the blockade again. He tricked the Spaniards by flying the Dutch flag, so they did not dare fire on his vessel, which he had renamed for the ruse. Then he hoisted the British colours while still within range of their guns. It was flamboyant, and an unnecessary risk to the lives of his crew and to other British ships anchored in the Bay, but I suppose you would think it a heroic act.'

'It is his nature to be flamboyant,' Catrina said. 'And I do think it was heroic.'

'You are not alone.' Dominic's voice was sour. 'He rescued Dinah from being molested by drunken soldiers in a manner which, if she is to be believed, would cast Saint George into the shade! The result is that there is now scarcely a woman in the garrison below the age of thirty who does not weave romantic dreams about him. But *you* are the one he wants . . .'

'Dominic, he did far more than save Dinah. I have not been able to tell you this before, but when we all thought Lucy was suffering from typhus, Jake Farraday risked infection by coming to the cow-byre with food and medicine for her. I realise, now, that she was far too ill for anything to save her, but the medicine did at least relieve her fever.'

Dominic's expression did not soften, although he said, 'I shall thank Farraday for what he did, but—I wish I could believe that I *am* wrong about him. In my career as an officer, Catrina, I have had to deal with men of all kinds and it has been necessary for me to become a judge of character. I sense that everything Farraday has done—for Dinah, for Lucy—was done to impress you. He is a predator, Catrina; the kind who does not care how long or how cunningly he needs to stalk his prey.'

'Oh, you are talking such nonsense! He and I are friends.'

'Friends! I have seen the way he looks at you! He is the kind of man who will not rest until he had possessed the woman he wants.'

'Very well,' she admitted. 'He does want me, but not in the way you believe. He asked me to marry him, and he refuses to accept that I will not do so.'

Dominic stared at her, long and hard. 'If he has asked you to marry him, then he knows about your fortune!'

She flushed. 'Thank you very much!'

He took hold of her shoulders. 'I did not mean that as an insult to you! But money—a great deal of it—is the only reason why Farraday would ask any woman to marry him! How large is your fortune, Catrina?'

'Mr Stanmore, my man of business, said that if I didn't touch the capital, I could count on an income of at least five thousand pounds a year.'

Dominic nodded grimly. 'A large fortune indeed! And if he married you, Jake Farraday would, as your husband, gain full legal control of it.'

'There is no possible way in which he could know the full extent of my legacy,' she protested. 'And in any case he has always been sceptical about its very existence!'

Dominic shook his head. 'Somehow he must have discovered exactly how much you inherited. It gives him a far stronger motive for pursuing you than I had imagined.'

Catrina gave a sigh of exasperation. 'What does it matter? I have no intention of marrying him.'

'Then leave this place, and go and stay with Alice and Dinah! He knows about the cow-byre, and there would be nothing to stop him from coming here.'

'Oh, very well,' she shrugged wearily. 'But not because I feel I have any need to fear Jake Farraday. I will do so, simply to put your mind at rest.'

He helped her to gather her belongings, and accompanied her to the tent which the two other women shared. Dinah muttered something about overcrowding, but Alice welcomed her warmly, and Catrina gained the distinct impression that the older woman could no longer endure to put up with Dinah as sole company.

But even though Catrina had bowed to Dominic's wishes and had left the cow-byre, she felt she owed it to Jake Farraday to thank him properly for the help he had tried to give in saving Lucy. She slipped away during the siesta the following afternoon, and walked through the ruined town. There could be no question that Jake was staying in lodgings; he must be living on his cutter.

She found Jake's vessel at its usual moorings. Members of his crew had painted out the Dutch name which had fooled the blockading Spanish and French vessels, and were re-painting ARABELLA in bold letters. One of them recognised her and left his work, wiping his hands on a rag.

'Why, miss, 'tis pleased I am to see you!'

Catrina blinked at him for a moment, and then remembered. 'You're Rawlings, aren't you? You carried my supplies for me—oh, such a long time ago it seems now!'

'It is that, miss. You made out then?'

Her mouth twisted as she thought of everything that had happened to her since that day. 'Oh, I made out. I wish to see your captain, Rawlings. He is on board?'

'Ay, miss. I'll take you to him.'

She climbed the gang-plank after him, and followed him across a deck and along a short companionway. His knock was answered by a man whom Catrina had never seen before.

'A lady to see the Cap'n, Bo'sun,' Rawlings announced.

'Miss Beaumont be her name.

From within, Catrina heard Jake give a soft laugh of pleasure. 'One moment please, Miss Beaumont!' he called. 'Bo'sun, over here, and close the door.'

As the door closed in their faces, Rawlings turned away. 'I'd best be back at my work, miss.'

Inside his cabin, Jake gave orders to the bo'sun in a low voice. 'I want all the crew to be set tasks which will keep them away from this companionway. I don't want to be disturbed *for any reason at all*! Tell the crew to ignore any sounds they may hear coming from in here. No one is to approach my cabin under any circumstances. Is that clear?'

'Ay, Captain.'

'Good. Tidy my desk, and then go and tell Miss Beaumont I am ready to receive her.'

Jake opened the door of a hanging cupboard and studied his reflection in the mirror set into the inside of it. This was the opportunity he had been waiting for.

There was only one way of forcing Catrina to marry him, he had decided. She fancied herself romantically and irrevocably in love with her brother-in-law, but that was because she remained, so far, properly unawakened. His expert knowledge of women told him that she possessed a strong sensual streak to which she had never given full expression. He planned to exploit it, to impose a strict restraint upon his own appetite and to concentrate instead on awakening in her such an overwhelming physical desire that she would be driven half crazy by the need for fulfilment. But he would deny her that to begin with. He would arouse her to fever-pitch and then call an abrupt halt, forcing her to take the next initiative.

He knew all the tricks it took to bring a woman to the point of abject, begging surrender, and he intended using them on Catrina. By the time he had finished with her, she would have developed such an insatiable appetite for more that she would not only be willing to marry him; she would be craving to do so! And then that large fortune in England would be his.

He turned away from the mirror, well satisfied both with his appearance and with the strategy he was planning.

* * *

The bo'sun opened the door of the cabin, and told Catrina respectfully, 'The Captain is ready to receive you now, Miss Beaumont.'

He stood aside for her to enter, and she heard the door closing behind her. Jake came forward, his hands outstretched. 'It is good to see you, Catrina.'

'Thank you,' she responded, and looked around her. In proportion to *Arabella*'s overall size, the cabin seemed unusually spacious. In spite of the outrageous risks he took in defying the blockade, he obviously liked his creature-comforts, for apart from a leather-lined desk and a comfortable-looking bunk, the cabin also contained several easy chairs.

He kissed Catrina's hands and then swept her a bow. He was as impeccably dressed as always, his cravat intricately tied, and wearing a rich coat of figured brocade. She took the easy chair that Jake offered her, and he sat down beside her.

'I came to thank you for trying to help Lucy,' Catrina said.

'Ah, yes. How did she fare?'

'She died,' Catrina told him quietly.

He leant across, and placed a hand on hers. 'I am so very sorry.'

'The medicine you brought for her really gave me hope for a while. It seemed to make her so much better, but then . . .' Catrina swallowed, and shook her head. After a moment she was able to go on. 'What was it—the medicine, I mean?'

He shrugged. 'Something I picked up on my travels. Many of the natives in primitive parts where we put in have remarkable remedies for all manner of conditions. Frequently they work, but they are not infallible.'

'Yes, well, you tried, and you risked possible infection to do so. And for that I thank you.' She rose. 'I had better leave now.'

She turned towards the door, but he slipped an arm about her waist from behind and forced her to face him. Before she could react, he caught her lower lip between his own, and then his tongue was probing her mouth, stirring an automatic pleasure inside her. But it was not sufficiently strong and overwhelming to blunt her judgment, and she pushed at his chest.

He raised his mouth from hers, but did not release her. 'Still obsessed by your forbidden love, Catrina?'

'It—It is no concern of yours!'

'No?' He slid his hands over her body. 'Why do you think I brave the blockade so often? There are other less hazardous runs I could make. I have been risking my skin, and I go on risking it, only in the hope of seeing you and perhaps being rewarded by one of your reluctant kisses. *That* is what you have reduced me to!'

She had always guessed that he was vulnerable behind the audacity, the mockery and the enigmatic shield he erected about himself. To have that vulnerability exposed so nakedly moved her deeply, and impulsively she offered him her lips.

With his mouth locked upon hers he steered her towards the bunk, but as his hands began to fumble at the fastenings of her bodice, she writhed away.

'No, Jake!'

'Hush, Catrina.' His hands became more urgent.

'Don't!' she cried out loudly.

His mouth descended on hers again, so that she could not have uttered another sound. Her mind seemed to be split into two. She knew that she herself was to blame for the present situation, for without stopping to consider the consequences she had encouraged him. And she also felt that, after he had revealed his feelings so nakedly to her, he would find her rejection doubly wounding. And yet she had to reject him, and soon—

She was spared the necessity of doing so, for at that moment a crashing sound came from outside the cabin, accompanied by male voices raised in anger. The door shook on its hinges and it was quite apparent that men were fighting outside.

Jake cursed, and raised himself from the bunk. Quickly Catrina straightened her clothing and stood up also. As Jake jerked the door open, the two combatants almost fell into the cabin, and Catrina was amazed to see that one of them was Rawlings.

Jake inserted himself between the two men, holding each by the collar, his face contorted with fury. 'What the devil do you think you are about?' he snarled.

'Cap'n, sir,' Rawlings said, passing a hand over his cut lip, 'it was *him* as started it . . .'

'No, it weren't!' the other man bellowed. 'Come at me like a madman, Cap'n, so he did! Just 'cause I points out some paint as he'd spilt on the deck! And then he said as how he was going to complain to you, Cap'n, and I tries to stop him, and he turns on me again . . .'

Catrina took the opportunity to squeeze past the men. 'I can see you have your hands full,' she told Jake. 'So I shall take my leave.' She shook her head at Rawlings. 'Surely you're too old for brawling!'

'A man ain't never too old to do as he thinks is right!'

Catrina left them, and skirted the area of wet black paint on the deck. She gave mental thanks to whoever had spilt it and saved her from a situation which had threatened to slip out of control.

She did not feel calm enough to face Alice and Dinah, and so she decided to pay a visit to Lucy's unmarked grave. It seemed so sad and anonymous: just a small mound of raw earth. Almost as if Lucy had never existed at all. A headstone would, at least, record the bare facts of her short life—

A sudden thought struck her. The fortune she had inherited was far too large for one young woman who had always lived simply and frugally. She would retain a reasonable amount on which to live comfortably, and with the rest she would establish a charitable fund for the needy children and the orphans of servicemen. It would be called the Lucinda Ross Fund, and would be Lucy's true memorial.

There were still almost two hours to go before the enemy would end their siesta and resume the attack, and Dominic decided, with deep reluctance, that he would have to go and thank Jake Farraday for trying to help Lucy.

When he reached *Arabella*'s moorings, there was no one about on the waterfront to announce him to her captain, and he decided to climb the gang-plank and announce himself. He wanted to get this task over and done with.

Farraday's crew were lined up, almost like spectators at a cock-fight, except that they showed none of the excitement of such a crowd, and they were watching their captain at work. A man was lashed to a mast, and Farraday was beating him with a cat-o'-nine-tails.

In the ordinary way, Dominic would not have interfered. It was none of his business, and as an officer in charge of men he knew there were occasions when, for the sake of discipline, punishment had to be dealt out. Personally, he abhorred the use of the fiendish cat-o'-nine-tails, but Farraday was master of his own ship, and no one could dictate to him as to how he should punish wrongdoers among his crew.

But this, Dominic quickly realised, was no ordinary punishment. For one thing, the man tied to the mast was well into middle age and must surely have been at sea for long enough to have learnt to avoid this kind of savage retribution. And Farraday did not give the impression of a man who was merely meting out justice. He was wielding the rope with its nine knotted lashes as if he were consumed by uncontrollable rage. The man being punished was covered in blood and was obviously unconscious, and there was no point in continuing to beat him, yet Farraday showed no sign of being ready to stop. The rest of the crew were shifting their feet uneasily, and it was clear that none of them had the courage to urge restraint on their captain.

'Farraday!' Dominic shouted. 'In God's name, man—enough!'

Jake paused only long enough to turn his head and snarl, 'Mind your own business, and get off my vessel!'

The cat-o'-nine-tails was whipping through the air again, and landing with a sickening thud on the unconscious man. 'You're killing him!' Dominic bellowed.

Jake seemed to put renewed force into the next stroke. Dominic lunged at him, grappling for the whip. He wrested it from Farraday's hands and threw it away, and it landed on the gang-plank. With a furious roar, Jake rushed to retrieve it, but Dominic stepped into his path.

Physical disgust rose inside Dominic, mingling with the contempt which he already felt for this man. Farraday was clearly bent on beating that poor brute tied to the mast until his own rage had been spent, and he did not care whether he killed the man or not.

Deliberately, Dominic took hold of his shoulder and spun him round, and used his superior strength to rush Farraday to the side and push him overboard. He hurried towards the bleeding, unconscious man at the mast.

'Cut him down,' he ordered the crew, 'and attend to his injuries. What was he being punished for?'

'Started a fight, sir. Don't know what got into old Rawlings.'

Dominic shook his head in distaste and perplexity. Fighting must be fairly common among crew members, and if it took place at sea, where total discipline was vital, it would be a serious matter. But *Arabella* was safely moored, so why had a brawl resulted in such a merciless beating? And why had Farraday chosen to carry out the punishment himself?

He moved away, and looked over the side of the vessel. Farraday was still floundering in the water, hampered by his boots and his heavy brocade coat in his efforts to reach dry land. The tails of the once-elegant coat billowed out around him, surrounded by all the flotsam and jetsam drifting on the water.

'Fetch a grappling-hook,' Dominic ordered the crew, 'and fish your captain out.'

When Farraday had been brought on board, dripping wet and filthy from the débris waiting to be carried away by the next tide, Dominic picked up the cat-o'-nine-tails and threw it as far into the Bay as he could, and then he turned to the Captain.

'I suggest that, in future, you deny yourself the pleasure of carrying out punishment in person,' he said.

Jake Farraday did not reply. Wait, he thought with cold, malevolent hatred. Just wait. You'll pay for this in full, Dominic Ross! And you'll pay in a way that will hurt you most—through the woman you want and can't have.

Catrina took care not to see Jake again before he sailed. Life inside the tent was cramped and without comfort, and she missed Lucy desperately. Her diary provided only limited solace, for with Dinah's constant, prying presence in the tent she dared not confide her longing for Dominic.

> The weather has become oppressive, with the sun beating down upon the tents and no wind blowing to give relief against the fierce heat. Everything, including the most dramatic events of the siege, contributes to

its monotonous pattern. Starvation is followed by supply ships getting through, only for the blockade to be resumed and hunger to set in once more.

Catrina laid her quill down as the light from the open tent-flap was blotted out. Dominic entered, looking strained and tired. She had hardly seen him at all since moving out of the cow-byre, and she was dismayed by the hopeless, aching longing which swept through her now.

If it was wrong in the eyes of God to love him, she thought rebelliously, then why did he in his omnipotence not do something to kill this feeling inside her and leave her at peace?

She made her voice neutral. 'A visit from you is a rare event, Dominic.'

'It is a flying visit only, to bring you this.' He held out a piece of soap. 'I knew you three ladies would appreciate it.'

Catrina seized it avidly. 'Where did you get it?'

'Confiscated it from a Spanish spy.' But he had veiled his eyes as he spoke, and she knew that he was lying; that he had recently met Violet, and that the soap was a gift from her.

'What is the altercation about outside?' he wanted to know. 'And where are Alice and Dinah?'

'Oh, it is the usual daily quarrelling between the women. Alice has gone to try and restore peace, and Dinah . . . Dinah has gone to derive what entertainment she can from the situation. But I can scarcely blame her for that. Almost any diversion is welcome in the monotony of our lives. What we need is some common purpose.'

'Then why not provide it?' Dominic challenged. 'Set them to make gardens.'

Her eyes widened, and a slow smile spread over her face. 'It would be wonderful if I could persuade them to do so! It would fill all those tense, boring hours!'

He said huskily, 'You look like an excited child . . .'

They moved at the same time, and stopped simultaneously just as they were about to touch. They stared at one another in hungry despair.

'Nothing changes,' Catrina whispered.

'No.' His mouth twisted in a bitter grimace. 'And I dare not touch you, dare not do so much as put an arm round you. For it would not stop there. And even if it did, no one walking in would be fooled. They would only need to look at us to realise that what they are watching is not a show of brotherly affection.'

Catrina made a defeated gesture. 'I'll go and see if I can get the women to listen to me.'

She pushed her way through the crowd towards Alice, and told her in a rapid whisper what she had in mind. 'An excellent scheme!' Alice applauded, and clapped her hands for silence.

'Miss Beaumont has a proposition to put to you,' she announced. 'Please give it serious consideration.'

Nervously, Catrina cleared her throat. 'Some of you may know that at one time I started an artificial garden where I grew vegetables. There are many similar rocky ledges to be found, and if we began gathering soil now we should have sufficient artificial gardens ready for sowing with autumn vegetables by the time the next foreign ship slips through the blockade. Most of them carry seeds as a matter of routine.'

She swallowed, and took a deep breath before she resumed. 'Apart from providing vegetables for our own tables, the work will give us something constructive to do, and also keep the children occupied. Everything I have learnt by experience I would happily pass on to you. Now—what do you say?'

There was a moment's silence. Then hands were raised in the air as the women signalled their willingness to take part in the scheme.

Catrina smiled. 'Good! Shall we make a start? You will need a utensil, such as a spoon or a ladle, to dig out soil from between rocks, and a dish or pail in which to carry it. But first, let us go and search for suitable sites for the gardens.'

The women hurried to arm themselves with the necessary tools, before spreading out among the rocks, and their enthusiasm grew visibly as more and more suitable ledges were discovered. They began to organise themselves voluntarily into groups and set to with a will, digging out soil and collecting it while others carried it to the ledges.

Catrina's days were full after that: helping, encouraging and advising the women. Only Dinah refused to be drawn into the scheme. 'I am not ruining *my* hands!' she declared.

The gardens were ready and waiting on the day a Portuguese vessel slipped through the blockade. As Catrina had predicted, she carried vegetable seeds among her cargo, and the women pooled their resources to buy a sufficient supply. Spontaneously they gave Catrina a cheering ovation before they hurried away to plant and sow their seeds. For the first time in months, a feeling of warmth and happiness stole over her.

During the following few days she had scarcely a moment to herself as she counselled the women, but at last all the gardens were ready, and as if to bless their efforts it began to rain gently but persistently. The next morning, none of the women could resist going to inspect the gardens, even though Catrina assured them, laughing, that germination would take considerably longer than one night.

They were still gathered in groups about their gardens when a body of troops approached, and as they drew nearer Catrina saw, with a leaping of her heart, that they were led by Dominic. During their brief meetings, she had kept him informed of the progress the women were making. Now that the Spaniards had again lapsed into their familiar spell of unnerving silence, Dominic and the troops had obviously come to see whether they might be of help to the women.

'The only assistance we need now,' she told him happily as she went to meet him, 'is from Nature!'

He ignored her and walked on, leaving her puzzled and disturbed by the total lack of expression on his face. She heard him raising his voice as he called the women together.

'Go home, ladies,' he commanded when he had the attention of all of them. 'And keep away. This whole area is out of bounds to you from now on.'

They stared at him in stunned silence. Catrina broke it by running to him and clutching his arm. 'Dominic, you can't issue such an order! We need to come here to tend our gardens . . .'

'The area is out of bounds,' he repeated.

'But our gardens!'

'They will have to be abandoned.'

She stared at him, hardly able to believe his treachery, when it had been at his suggestion that she had put the women to such hard work.

'Why?' she demanded.

'Because the gardens are to be blasted out of existence. And before you ask me again why.' he added savagely, 'the answer is—Mind your own damned business, Catrina!'

CHAPTER TWENTY-ONE

SICK AT HEART, Dominic watched the women return slowly to their tents and their shacks. Human nature being what it was, he knew that it would not be long before the women vented on Catrina their disappointment and their feelings of impotent anger at the futility of all their efforts.

He had fought as hard as he could to be allowed to tell them even a little of the reason for the destruction of their gardens, and yet he was still left with the feeling that he should have done more.

General Ridgeway had been adamant. 'It is the Governor's order that no one must know anything at this stage. We are all aware that this present cease-fire is no more than a lull before a far fiercer storm, and if the enemy should get wind of our plans, they'll bring forward their expected onslaught.'

He gave the order to his men to begin blasting. Galleries were to be formed in the solid rock, and 24-pounder guns mounted in the apertures, trained upon the enemy's works on the isthmus. At the same time underground caves were to be blasted in the rock, and batteries, galleries and magazines were to be built into the very heart of the great Rock of Gibraltar.

It was a bold, imaginative plan, and it might well be the deciding factor in ending this long siege. But all the same, Dominic could not help being haunted by the memory of Catrina's stricken face.

Catrina felt enclosed by the hostility of the women. They had seen all their hard work go for nothing and they had needed a scapegoat on whom to focus their bitterness. It could not be the army, for they were service wives and they accepted that whatever decision the army took, it must be for the ultimate best. So they had chosen her, because it had been she who had persuaded them to create the gardens.

Their resentment would probably have been short-lived had it not been for Dinah. As they all walked away from their doomed gardens, she had said airily, 'Of course, we few who are close to the men in high command always knew the army had plans of their own for the area.'

'That is nonsense!' Alice had exploded angrily. 'Neither Dominic nor John ever gave a hint that our work on the gardens would be for nothing!'

'If you say so, Alice,' Dinah had murmured. 'All the same, I know what my own reason was for not helping Catrina in her insatiable desire to be a heroine and to draw attention to herself.'

Angry mutterings had almost drowned her voice. Alice had appealed to the angry women. 'Let us put recriminations aside. For a short while we were united, and we showed that we could be again. Wasn't that a good thing in itself?'

The remark had been a mistake. It had implied that Alice, Dinah and Catrina had known about the army's plans, and that Alice had condoned the abortive making of the gardens in order to unite the women. Besides, she was the wife of a general, and could hardly have blurted out a secret which the army did not want to be known. Alice had been forgiven.

At least, Catrina thought with bitter irony, Alice had been granted her wish that the women should be united. They were now totally united in their enmity towards herself.

She had become an outcast to everyone but Alice, and she spent much of her time in solitary wandering along the waterfront, reflecting on Dominic's treachery. He must have been aware, she told herself, even while he was listening to her enthusiastic description of the women's work, how utterly doomed it was from the outset. And yet he had given no hint, no veiled warning, and had allowed them all to carry on right until the moment when he had so brutally ordered them to abandon their gardens.

One morning she was wandering near the waterfront when she saw that Jake's cutter had appeared in the Bay, and she strained to watch its progress. With his usual insolence, he steered clean across the bows of the Spanish admiral's ship of the line. In order to bring his guns to bear, the latter was forced to alter course and haul up-wind. While hanging uselessly with the westerly wind on her beam, the Spanish flagship fired two broadsides of round-and-grape-shot.

Catrina could see that Jake's cutter was hit, and that it was obviously taking in water. Even so, he mocked the Spaniards by impudently discharging his vessel's stern guns at the flagship as he put down his helm for the harbour. The flagship, caught by the wind and the current, was unable to give chase, and Jake's cutter limped into harbour.

A crowd had gathered round Catrina as they watched the scene, and cheers rent the air. Volunteers swarmed down to help *Arabella*'s crew to unload the cargo before the vessel could sink, and when the task had been completed, Jake himself was carried shoulder-high from the harbour. Catrina melted away so that he would not see her, but she remembered how he had said that he came to Gibraltar, running the gauntlet of the enemy ships, solely in the hope of seeing herself.

From that morning, everyone seemed to forgive Jake Farraday his past. He was now a national hero, and Catrina learnt that the Navy had gone so far as to accept his voluntary services as adviser on the strategy of slipping through the blockade. She met him by chance one day as she was on her way to tend Lucy's grave. He presented his usual handsome and flamboyant appearance, and studied her in her faded and patched gown.

'You look beaten,' he said, shaking his head. 'You have never looked beaten before. Defiant, yes. Determined, and full of fight. What has happened to you?'

'Too much. But circumstances change all of us, don't they? *You* have become respectable through circumstances . . .'

His lips flickered. 'Yes. I find it all vastly amusing.'

'But is it what you wanted?'

His eyes appraised her slowly. 'You know what it is I want.'

'I'm sorry, Jake. The answer is still no.' She began to walk on, and he fell into step beside her. He watched her as she pulled stray weeds from the mound of Lucy's still unmarked grave.

'There has obviously been no opportunity, yet, to erect a

headstone,' he remarked.

'No. It used to bother me that there is nothing to show she rests here. But since I thought of the idea of the Lucinda Ross Memorial Fund, I don't mind so much any more.'

'Tell me about it,' he invited without too much interest.

'I decided it was ridiculous that I should have such a vast fortune to spend on myself alone. It is far, far more than I could ever get through in a lifetime, so I am keeping just enough on which to live comfortably, and using the remainder to set up a charity for children in Lucy's name. I have written to my man of business in London, telling him what I wish him to do.'

Jake's thoughts were racing. As casually as he could, he said, 'You cannot have sent the letter yet, for no ships have sailed for Britain in a long while.' He hesitated. 'Keep this to yourself, Catrina, but I shall probably be sailing for England myself in the near future, and I could deliver the letter for you.'

'You are sailing for England? How? You have lost *Arabella*.'

'I have told you more than I ought to have done. But let me have the letter to your man of business, Catrina, and I shall see that it reaches its destination.'

'Thank you, Jake, but it went weeks ago, and will have arrived in England by now. A Dutch ship got through, and took with her all the mail bound for England.'

He turned his head away, pretending to study the other graves so that she would not see the rage in his eyes. He had spent months—no, *years*—in careful plotting and campaigning to get that money, and she had thrown it away on a charity! A damned memorial to a dead child!

Catrina had finished tidying Lucy's grave, and stood up. The child's grave never failed to stir her emotions, but today it was intensifying them. Life had become insupportable here in Gibraltar. Lucy was dead; Dominic avoided her on the few occasions when he came to the tent, no doubt because he felt guilty over his treachery; Dinah taunted her constantly, and the other women treated her like a leper.

'I want to go home,' she said wretchedly.

'Where *is* home now?' His response was mechanical.

'I am sharing a tent with Alice and Dinah. But that is not what I meant. I want to go home to England.'

He stared thoughtfully at her. 'I am going to trust you, Catrina. The Navy are placing at my disposal a vessel which I am to sail to England, taking home all the civilians who wish to leave Gibraltar. There will be a scramble for passages, and that is why the matter must remain secret until the last possible moment. There would be a risk, otherwise, of people cluttering up the quays with their bags and baggage for days in advance in order to make sure that they are taken aboard. But if you really wish to go home, I'll make sure that you have a berth.'

'And—there would be no conditions attached?'

'None whatever.'

'When are you sailing?'

'As soon as the wind and the weather conditions are right, and all the despatches and other documents which must also reach England are ready.'

'Would you allow me time to think about it?'

'Don't take too long,' he warned. 'When the right time comes for me to sail, I shall have to leave.'

After they had parted and she was walking back to the tent, Catrina wondered why she had not given him her answer there and then. After all, as the captain of a ship bulging at the seams with passengers, he would have neither the time nor the opportunity to continue pressing her to marry him. And it was not as if there was anything left to keep her on this besieged, hostile Rock.

As if to drive home this point, Dominic and General Ridgeway arrived at the tent that evening to spend a rare few hours of respite in what was the closest thing to domesticity now prevailing in Gibraltar.

Dinah took Dominic's arm, and said with a pointed look at Catrina, 'Shall we go for a walk, and allow John and Alice a little privacy?'

He nodded, and accompanied her outside. In spite of the protestations of the Ridgeways, Catrina took the hint offered by Dinah and wandered alone in the darkness, her thoughts bleak. There was no place for her here; she did not belong. The only solution was to take the one offered to her by Jake, and leave.

She told him so the following day. He took her face in his hands and said sympathetically, 'Poor Catrina. It is probably best that you leave, after all you have been through. However, I have a feeling that your brother-in-law would try to stop you from sailing on any ship captained by me.'

'He could not stop me even if he wished to! I am of age. However, he would probably make a fuss, so it would be best if no one knows that I intend leaving.'

'I shall send a messenger to you. Can you think of a message which would not sound suspicious to anyone else?'

Catrina considered for a moment. 'Yes. Let him tell me that Violet is in town, and wishes to see me.'

Jake made her a bow, and they parted. As she walked back through the desolate town towards the tents, Catrina told herself that she had made the only possible decision. Even if the British should finally triumph over the might of the enemy, there would be no triumph for herself. Peace would mean the marriage of Dominic and Dinah. Far better that she should leave now.

She did not even see Dominic again before the arranged message came from Jake. Guiltily, Catrina avoided Alice's eyes as she said, 'Violet must have fallen on hard times for her to have returned to town. I shall have to take such of my clothes as I can spare and offer them to her.'

Alice accepted the story without suspicion, and Catrina made a bundle of the minimum items of clothing she would need on the voyage. Then she followed the messenger to the harbour.

Jake was waiting for her. *Golden Sovereign* already had many passengers on board, squeezing into the berths, and as news reached people of the imminent sailing of a ship for Britain, they came streaming down to the harbour with their hastily-packed belongings. But while all others were forced to share crowded quarters, Catrina discovered that Jake had placed a private cabin at her disposal.

She was surprised to find that the Spaniards did not trouble to harass the vessel as she passed through the blockade, but when she went on deck one of the passengers told her, 'They don't care about ships taking people back to England. It's ships bringing in food, or supplies, or troop reinforcements they'll fire upon.'

As before, the vessel had scarcely entered the open sea when sea-sickness again struck Catrina down. But this time there was no kindly Violet to minister to her.

The door of her cabin opened, and Jake entered. He touched her clammy forehead as she lay racked with nausea on the bunk. 'My poor Catrina! I had quite forgotten that you are plagued by sea-sickness. I shall send a cabin-lad to you with some medicine.'

Soon after he had left, a boy who looked to be no older than fourteen knocked on the door and entered, handing her a flask of medicine. 'Cap'n says you're to take two drops in water, three times a day, miss.'

She swung her unsteady legs from the bunk and succeeded in measuring two drops into a mug, adding water from a flagon that fitted into a recessed space on the all-purpose ledge which had been fixed to one end of the cabin. After a while her nausea began to subside.

But as the days passed, she found that the medicine's benefits were overshadowed by its drawbacks. Although it did keep nausea at bay, it caused her heart to beat with disturbing palpitations and it also robbed her of sleep during the night. And being free of sea-sickness did not add to her enjoyment of the voyage.

Her fellow-passengers were mostly women, victims of the failed gardening scheme, and they were not at all disposed to be friendly. When they learnt, from a chance remark she made, that she had an entire cabin to herself while they were all forced to endure crowded conditions, they turned their backs on her entirely. There was not much fun in taking the air on a slippery deck, ostracised by everyone, and gazing at nothing but the surrounding ocean, while her heart beat uncomfortably fast all the time.

Catrina decided to take two drops of the medicine only at noon each day. The nausea returned, but not as violently as before. She was able to pick at the meals which Benny, the cabin-lad, brought to her, and to keep some of it down.

Whenever Jake snatched a few minutes from his duties on the bridge to look in on her, and found her lying on her bunk, she pretended that she was resting because of a sleepless night. She did not wish to hurt his feelings by admitting that she had stopped taking as much of the medicine as he had prescribed.

One advantage of being sea-sick, she sometimes reflected bleakly, was the fact that it blunted emotions. It pushed thoughts of Dominic to the background of her mind, and also the knowledge that she would probably never see him again. It helped, too, not to have to try and plan what she would do with the rest of her life.

One morning she awakened to the realisation that they had dropped anchor. When Benny brought her breakfast, he explained, 'We have docked at Lisbon, miss. We're to take on a cargo of fruit and wine, Cap'n says, and will be laying-to for some days.'

'What are all those bumping and shoving noises I can hear?'

Benny shrugged. 'Passengers dragging their trunks on deck, miss. Cap'n told them the ordinary Lisbon packet sails for England today, and many of them don't want to be kicking their heels here while we're laying-to. In a hurry, they are, to get home.'

'I suppose that's understandable,' Catrina said. There would be no question of herself transferring ships, and although she, too, would have preferred not to have the voyage delayed for any longer than necessary, she meant to take full advantage of the respite offered now that the ship was no longer lurching and heaving through the water.

She ate her breakfast, and rose with the intention of dressing and going on deck to see what Lisbon looked like. But she felt appallingly weak, and after the effort of washing, she decided to regain a little strength before venturing on deck. But she went back to sleep, in spite of the noise on board, and awoke only when the door of her cabin opened. She blinked at Jake, and tried to smile.

'I'm sorry I'm so disgracefully lazy . . .' she began.

'Not at all, my dear. It would have been an inconvenience if you had decided to join some shore-going party to look at the sights. Finding you abed in your shift suits me very well.'

She had struggled into a sitting position. 'I—I don't . . .'

'I have come for my reward, Catrina.'

Physical weakness blunted her reactions, and she did not fully understand until he ripped the covers away from her. She tried to fend him off as his hands went to the bodice of her shift. 'Jake, please!'

Violently he tore the shift so that her breasts were exposed. He crushed them in his hands and stopped her desperate cries by pressing his mouth to her lips. His kiss was hard and urgent, without tenderness.

When he raised his head she saw that his eyes were gleaming like those of a predator, and his mouth was curved in a cruel, triumphant smile. She tried to struggle from the bunk, but he dealt her a blow with his forearm which sent her crashing against the bulkhead.

He was dragging off his shirt and pulling off his breeches. For a moment she was too dizzy, too weak and too mesmerised with horror to move. Then she compelled herself to struggle from the bunk and lurch towards the door. But he overtook her before she had reached it, and he was laughing as he tore what remained of the shift from her body. 'By Christ, I have waited a long time for this!'

'Oh please . . .'

'I had planned it all quite differently, of course. But that was before you played me for a fool.' He lifted her in his arms and dropped her weakly struggling body on the bunk. And then, without warning, he was astride her, pinning her down with his full weight.

His mouth fastened on hers in another of those rapacious, urgent kisses, and she was totally unprepared for the shock of his knees forcing her thighs apart. She felt that frightening, angry symbol of his manhood, which she had tried not to look at as he pulled off his breeches, tearing into her, evoking a terrifying pain such as she had never imagined. She cried out, and tried impotently to fight him, but her efforts seemed to spur him on and he drove repeatedly into her, grunting and straining and biting into her shoulder as he did so.

When she thought that his animal assault would surely kill her, he gave a long shudder and crushed her body with his own weight for a moment while he lay panting for breath.

But the nightmare was not yet over. She tried to empty her mind, to divorce herself from the degradation of the acts which were perpetrated upon her already defiled body. It was hopeless to refuse or to resist, for he knew ways of inflicting pain which she had never dreamt existed.

At last he appeared to be sated, and he rolled from the bunk, pulling on his breeches. 'There are many, many more lessons in love, Catrina,' she heard him say, 'which I shall be teaching you. For the moment, duty calls. But I shall be back.'

The fainting spell which she had been praying for earlier overcame her then, and when she regained consciousness, he was gone. But she remembered his last words, and she knew that he would return to assault and degrade her again in the name of love.

CHAPTER TWENTY-TWO

AS SOON AS Dominic heard from Alice that Catrina had gone to meet Violet, he knew that something was terribly wrong.

'She can't have done so,' he said tensely.

'It seems that Violet is back in Gibraltar, and down on her luck. Catrina took a few things along for her.'

'She cannot have gone to meet Violet!' Dominic repeated, his voice sharp with anxiety. He himself had a secret rendezvous to keep with Violet on the isthmus that evening. Besides, the last time he had spoken to Violet, she had been anything but down on her luck.

'How long has Catrina been gone?' he demanded.

'About three hours.'

He made a fist and slammed it hard against the palm of his other hand. 'Good God in heaven, if she had gone to meet Violet, it would not have taken three hours!'

'I don't know why you are making such a fuss,' Dinah put in with sulky malice. 'Violet and Catrina are old friends; they have much in common and obviously have a great deal to talk about.'

He gave her a look of distaste and hurried out of the tent. If *Arabella* had not been sunk, he would have made straight for the waterfront. On this occasion, Jake Farraday could be ruled out. Since he was now attached, on a voluntary basis, to the Navy, his path did not cross Dominic's, but it was common knowledge that he shared a billet with two Naval officers. It was scarcely a place to which he would have been able to lure Catrina with any hope of privacy. And yet she had been lured somewhere, for Alice had seen the messenger who had arrived, and had heard him tell Catrina that Violet was in town and wanted to see her.

Without much hope, and only because he could think of nowhere else to search for her, Dominic went to the cow-byre. As he had feared, there was no sign of anyone having been there recently. He was preparing to leave it when he saw, from that high vantage-point, *Golden Sovereign* hauling up her anchor. Then she was drifting towards the open sea, taken by the wind and the tide, and allowed free passage by the blockading enemy ships.

It occurred to him, fleetingly, that Catrina might have decided to sail home to England. Then he dismissed the possibility. She did not have sufficient funds in Gibraltar with which to have paid her passage, and because the news that a ship was to sail for England had been sprung on the people of Gibraltar with so little notice, she could not have had time to borrow the money. Even so, Dominic made his way to the harbour. There was a bare chance that Catrina might be among the crowd which had watched *Golden Sovereign* departing. But even as he sped towards the waterfront Dominic knew that the real clue to Catrina's whereabouts lay in the message which had lured her from the tent.

By the time he reached the mole from which *Golden Sovereign* had sailed, most of the crowd had left. Dominic was about to turn back when he saw, approaching him, a young Naval officer whom he knew slightly. Apart from social occasions, members of the two services did not have a great deal of contact with one another.

Now, the young Naval officer grinned at Dominic and joked, 'Hoped to sail home on *Golden Sovereign*, did you, Ross? You wouldn't be alone in that!'

Dominic smiled perfunctorily. 'Why was her departure decided upon so suddenly?'

'It was no sudden thing. We kept it quiet because we didn't want civilians camping out on the moles and harbours for days on end with their baggage. It has been planned ever since Jake Farraday suggested himself as the captain in command . . .'

'Farraday!' Dominic stared at the other man in horrified disbelief. 'He is in command of *Golden Sovereign*?'

'Yes, indeed.'

Groaning an obscenity, Dominic strode blindly away and blundered along the mole to its furthest extremity, from which he could see *Golden Sovereign* making her way to the open sea.

This was the most terrible thing he could ever have imagined. She was on that ship with Farraday, and there was nothing at all he, himself could do about it. No physical effort, no flouting of military rules, no suicidal act of personal courage, would make the slightest difference. She might as well be on another planet for all the possibility there was of him reaching her and saving her from that depraved predator.

Catrina must have gone aboard the vessel of her own free will, and the false message from Violet was obviously a prearranged signal between herself and Farraday. How could she have done such a thing? She did not realise what Farraday was capable of; she had always shut her mind to warnings about him. But how could she have sailed for England without a word, without an explanation or a goodbye?

Then he dismissed that bitter thought as fear for Catrina overwhelmed him again. There were only a few crumbs of comfort he could cling to. *Golden Sovereign* was packed with as many passengers as she could carry, and that meant that she would have to share a berth with at least one other woman and possibly more. And Jake Farraday would have his hands too full with navigational duties on such a long voyage to be able to spare much attention for her.

No, the real danger would come when they arrived in England. But Jake Farraday wanted, above all, to marry Catrina. He would not jeopardise his chances of getting his hands on her money by doing anything to harm her in the meantime. It was a bleak grain of comfort for Dominic to cling to.

He could still think of little but Catrina when he went to the Land Port Gate at midnight for his rendezvous with Violet, who slipped through the darkness towards him. Dressed in black rags, she would have been taken for a gipsy woman, even if the enemy had spotted her.

'What news, Violet?' Dominic greeted her.

'Well, Captain, nothing as would cheer you, I fear. The *Linea* is crawling with Dons like flies round a rotten bit of meat. They has, I would say, more'n twenty thousand troops, and every man jack of them is working away at the defences. There's talk as how they're only waiting for a combined fleet before they storm Gibraltar from both land and sea.'

Ominous news, indeed. 'You're sure you have not mistaken what you heard, Violet?'

'Sure as can be, Captain. I've always had a quick ear for language, you know. Put me with gentry for a few months, and I can talk with a plum in me mouf if needs be. It didn't take me long to pick up the enemy's language, especially as my customers like to teach me, just so's they can fall over laughing at me accent.'

'You don't think they're beginning to suspect you?'

'Not they! They don't think I've got no brains. Their *own* women ain't got no brains, see, save for cooking and breeding and praying! No, the Dons just think me a common-or-garden whore. But tell me, Captain, how's things in town? How's Miss Beaumont?'

'She—has gone back to England,' Dominic answered with pain.

'Ah, poor love! It'd have been young Lucy dying what done for her.'

That, Dominic thought bleakly, and her sense of isolation caused by my own apparent treachery. I should have disobeyed orders and given her some hint that the gardens were to be blasted out of existence. It is small wonder that Catrina came to think of Jake Farraday as her only friend . . .

'Now, Captain, I'd best get back.' Violet's voice broke through his thoughts, and he took his leave of her.

He spent a sleepless night thinking of Catrina, worrying about her safety, and in the morning he reported his conversation with Violet to General Ridgeway. After the latter had been closeted with the Governor, he informed Dominic and other officers that the British would be moving on the the enemy camp that same night.

The Spanish, caught by surprise at the attack, became panic-stricken as columns of fire and black clouds rolled away from their burning fortifications, throwing a brilliant light over everything and so making the British task easier in destroying their batteries and stores.

Dominic wondered if Violet had had time and the quick wit to escape. A whore she might be, but she had the courage of an officer. She must have known, when she had told him last night of the Spaniards' preparations, that the British would be swift to react.

But for all the damage the British did that night, Dominic knew that there were overwhelming numbers of French and Spanish troops who would immediately begin the work of restoring their defences. Day and night, the British could hear the noise the combined enemy made as they employed thousands of workmen to toil away at the *Linea.* He took comfort from the fact that the British were no less busy. He threw himself into his own part of the preparations for the climax which everyone knew must come soon. But no matter how busy he was, no matter how preoccupied with military matters, the thought of Catrina was never far from his mind.

Catrina was bruised and bleeding and racked with pain, but she forced herself to get out of the bunk. She almost fainted again. Only the grim memory of that satyr's face, of Jake's animal lust and the many degradations which he had inflicted upon her, spurred her into superhuman effort.

She stumbled, retching, towards the slop-pail. Her flesh crawled with disgust at the knowledge of how her body had been used and abused, and what she wished for above everything else was to be able to sink into a tubful of hot water in an attempt to scrub herself clean.

But even if she had known how to lay her hands upon hot water and a tub, there would have been no time. She had to get away before Jake returned. Levering herself into an upright position, she steadied herself against the bulkhead and put on her cloak before she opened the cabin door.

She stumbled unsteadily towards the direction of the companionway. The sounds of footsteps descending caused her to freeze, and she shivered convulsively as she pulled her cloak tightly about herself. Her eyes sought wildly for some means of escape.

She almost fainted again, with relief this time, when the figure appeared at the foot of the companionway and she recognised Rawlings.

He stared at her in dismay. 'Miss! Oh, miss! I did hear tell as how the Cap'n had a fancy piece aboard—begging your pardon, miss. But it ain't never crossed my mind as how it was yourself . . .'

'I am not—not his fancy piece. I thought—he was my friend . . . I have to get off this ship, where he can't reach me.'

'You ain't in no state, miss, to go nowhere. Come with me, and we'll try and plan what to do.'

She submitted, and allowed him to support her. Her teeth were chattering as if she had the ague, and once in her cabin she submitted as Rawlings draped blankets over her shoulders.

'You didn't ought to have sailed with the Cap'n, miss! All them presents he sent you . . . Ain't you got the wit, miss, to know as he was softening you up?'

Don't trust a Greek when he comes bearing gifts . . . The thought slipped into her mind.

'I ain't no saint, miss,' Rawlings went on gruffly. 'And in the normal way I don't go poking my nose in the Cap'n's affairs. But—you was different, see? Making out all on your own, like you did. Got myself in bad trouble with the Cap'n, I did, stopping things that first time when I knew you was in his cabin and what was in his mind.'

'You mean,' she managed faintly, 'that time on *Arabella* ?'

'Ay. Twas all I could think to do, see—spilling paint on the deck, and spoiling for a fight so's I could break things up in the Cap'n's cabin. And then you goes and you sails with him, miss!'

She shook her head. 'He wanted to marry me, Rawlings. He asked me, over and over again.'

'Don't sound like the Cap'n at all, miss,' Rawlings said bluntly. He hesitated. 'Leastways . . . You got money, miss?'

'Yes. That is, I had a great deal of money until . . .' She stopped. Jake had not once repeated his proposal of marriage after she had told him about the Lucinda Ross Memorial Fund.

And what was it he had said to her, just before he violated her? *'I had planned it all quite differently. But that was before you played me for a fool.'*

'What am I to do, Rawlings?' she whispered. 'He—said he would be back . . .'

'Ay, he will that. Gone to see about the cargo as we're taking on. Only answer, miss, is for someone to share the cabin with you. Someone as'll stand up to the Cap'n.'

'On his own ship?' She laughed drearily.

Rawlings remained silently thoughtful for a moment. 'You leave it to me, miss.'

Catrina sat huddled on her bunk after he had gone. With hindsight she could see now what a fool she had been. An appalled sound escaped her as she realised something else. The medicine he had brought her to give to Lucy must have been the same stuff he had offered herself as a cure for sea-sickness. She remembered now how strong and rapid Lucy's heartbeats had been, and how she had been full of unnatural, restless energy towards the end, and unable to sleep. It was highly unlikely that the medicine had done anything to speed Lucy's death, for she was already mortally ill before Catrina made her drink the stuff.

But the truly dreadful thing was that Jake Farraday had offered the medicine to her, when he could not possibly have known what effect it might have upon so young a child. He simply had not cared. The medicine had been offered purely so that Catrina would see him in a sympathetic light. That was the measure of his ruthlessness in pursuit of what he wanted.

The cabin door opened again after a knock, and Rawlings entered with a tall, angular woman of about thirty. 'This here is Miss Nancy Bates,' he told Catrina.

The woman stared at her. 'You are Miss Beaumont.'

Catrina passed her tongue over her dry lips. 'I suffer most dreadfully from sea-sickness, and I cannot occupy my cabin alone . . .'

The woman gazed around her. 'You've plenty of space, I'll say that. I have been cooped up with my sister and brother-in-law and their three children, in spite of all the complaints I have sent to the Captain. Very well, I'll share your cabin. Rawlings, you'll fetch my trunks, if you please.'

'I'll do that, miss.' He gave Catrina a reassuring glance, and left.

Nancy sat down on the edge of the bunk. 'I'll sleep on the inside,' she said. 'I'll do what I can for you while the voyage lasts. All I ask in return is a bit of peace after the constant yammering of my sister's children.'

Catrina merely nodded. There was still a long way to go before they reached England, and Nancy seemed a formidable, iron-willed lady who would not easily budge once she had settled herself in.

Catrina became aware that her cloak had slipped, leaving one shoulder exposed, and that Nancy was staring at the marks on it. 'What happened to you?' she asked bluntly.

Catrina gathered her cloak about her. An obscure sense of guilt and shame prevented her from telling the truth. 'I—I fell,' she said at last, and changed the subject. 'How did Rawlings know about you?'

'I've made enough fuss about the overcrowded conditions since the beginning of the voyage for *all* the ship's crew to know about me! I would have takens the Lisbon packet, but I've heard that it's rat-infested and even more uncomfortable than this vessel.'

Catrina looked away. 'I—would be grateful if you did not mention Rawlings's name in connection with sharing my cabin.'

Nancy made no comment, but her gaze was thoughtful. Not long after her trunks had been brought to the cabin her mettle was tested, for Jake arrived and his face darkened when he found her installed with Catrina.

'This is a private berth,' he said tersely, 'and Miss Beaumont is travelling under my protection. I must ask you to return to your original quarters!'

Nancy gazed steadily at Jake, and then she glanced at Catrina, who had turned ashen and was shivering violently.

'Miss Beaumont needs taking care of,' she said smoothly. 'Anyone can see she has suffered greatly, and that she is not well. And, with due respect, Captain, you can't navigate the ship *and* look after a sick passenger, can you?'

Jake stared at her for a moment, and then he left, slamming the door behind him, and Catrina expelled her breath in a sound of incredulous relief.

No one, least of all that unattractive, raw-boned woman, would have been able to stop Jake from forcing himself on Catrina again if he had wanted to do so. The truth was that, having once possessed her, he did not really wish to do so again.

There was always the possibility that he might try to take her and fail, and that was a thought not to be borne. It was something which had been happening to him lately when a situation lacked stimulus. It might have been different if she had not fooled him by giving her money away. If he had married her, the need to go on pretending for a while longer might have supplied sufficient incitement to make him go on desiring her.

He could not remember the last time he had really desired any woman once he had taken her. The chase was always so much more exciting: the plotting and stalking and scheming to get his quarry into his power. The moment of victory was the climax, and memorable only if the quarry's violence were a match for his own. Everything after that was an anticlimax. He would conserve his appetite until another prospective quarry came within his sights, and in the meantime he would find his fulfilment and his ecstasy in what really satisfied him far more than any woman could—in playing mocking, lethal games of seamanship with the enemy.

His mouth twisted in a smile. Besides, the worst part of Catrina's punishment was yet to come, and Dominic Ross would be sharing in it.

Neither Catrina nor Nancy spoke for a while after Jake had withdrawn. That devil-may-care, sardonic wit which he had displayed in the past, Catrina was thinking, had been no more than one of his many poses.

'Protection!' Nancy snorted suddenly. 'I'd sooner be under the protection of a hyena! Raped you, did he?'

When Catrina gave her a shamed nod, Nancy said forcefully, *'Men!'*

In her own taciturn, emotionless way, Nancy proved to be as great a treasure as Violet had been. She seemed to sense that Catrina had a need to scrub her body in an attempt to rid herself of the memory of her defilement, and from somewhere Nancy found a tub and filled it with hot water.

When Catrina lay on the bunk afterwards, dressed in a clean shift, Nancy brought her some soup and a basket of fruit. She bullied Catrina into eating, and she appointed herself guardian against any further assault from Jake by never leaving her alone for more than a few seconds while they remained at Lisbon. And once they had set sail once more, and the familiar sea-sickness racked her, Nancy cared for her.

Catrina worried how she was to evade Jake once they had arrived in England. He would not, surely, allow himself to be outwitted without exacting punishment?

In an attempt to drive these thoughts from her mind she questioned Nancy about herself, and learnt that the woman had gone out to Gibraltar to join her sister, who had been widowed when her husband, an army corporal, had been killed in the bombardment by the Spanish.

'I was needed to help her bring the children back to England,' Nancy recounted. 'But before I knew where I was, and while we were still waiting for a passage home, my sister suddenly decided to marry again! He's a miner who'd gone out to Gibraltar to advise on the blasting of the galleries in the Rock. That's why I don't hold it against you too much about the gardens, you see. My sister and I knew all about the plans to mount guns inside the Rock; her husband had told us, but of course we were sworn to secrecy, and so we had to go on with the pretence of growing vegetables.'

But Dominic, Catrina thought with only the distant echo of pain, had not trusted herself sufficiently to warn her. If he had, she would have invented some plausible reason for abandoning the making of artificial gardens and saved the women all that hard work.

'So I wasn't needed in Gibraltar after all,' she heard Nancy go on. 'In truth, I became a nuisance. But that's life, I suppose. I'll tell you one thing—when we arrive back in England, I'm going to make it my policy to keep myself to myself from now on!'

When we get back to England, Catrina told herself, and I succeed in escaping from Jake Farraday, I shall crawl into a hole and never come out again . . .

She and Nancy awoke one night to the sound of gunfire. The vessel seemed to be weaving through the water, so that Nancy almost lost her balance when she climbed out of the bunk and lit a candle to go and investigate.

Catrina was leaning over the side of the bunk, her head bent over the slop-pail, when Nancy returned.

'We're back in Gibraltar,' she said flatly.

The shock of her statement was enough to stem even

Catrina's sea-sickness. 'We—We can't be!'

'We're ducking and diving through the Spanish blockade at this very minute,' Nancy assured her in a grim voice.

The vessel then steadied, and the sound of the firing grew more distant. If Catrina had needed added evidence that Nancy had told the truth, the calmness of the water in the Bay provided it.

Nancy helped her to wash and dress, and supported her on deck. The sun had not yet risen, and the Rock looked more brooding than ever in the grey light of early dawn. Catrina felt better in the open air, and Nancy went back to the cabin to collect their belongings.

A footstep sounded behind her, and Catrina turned. Jake was regarding her sardonically, his arms folded across his chest. Instinctively, she cringed from him. Nausea had risen in her throat, and it had nothing to do with the gently undulating waters of the Bay.

'When Dominic Ross learns what happened,' she heard him say, 'please remind him of a certain afternoon when he came on board *Arabella* uninvited, and interfered in something which was no concern of his. He will understand the message.'

She had won her battle against threatening nausea. 'Why have we not sailed on to England? What happened to make you turn back to Gibraltar?'

His smile was both mocking and malevolent. 'One of the things I have been looking forward to has been your reaction when you discover yourself to be back on the Rock. There was never any intention that *Golden Sovereign* should sail for England. It was a ruse, to fool the enemy. They had not expected to see the vessel back after so short a while, and in their surprise and speculation they failed to react swiftly enough to stop us from re-entering the Bay.'

Farraday stretched lazily. 'You see, my dear Catrina, there has been an outbreak of scurvy among the troops, and it was threatening to become an epidemic. Lemons and limes were needed to combat the disease, and I volunteered to sail to Lisbon to pick up a cargo of fruit. It had to be made to seem that *Golden Sovereign* was merely taking civilians back to England, for if the enemy had guessed at her real mission, they would have deployed all their might against her. That was why passengers had to be forced to rush to the harbour in droves, so that they could be clearly seen by the enemy as they competed with one another to embark. But as you may remember, they were advised to transfer to the regular packet when we arrived in Lisbon.'

She passed her tongue over her dry lips, the full scale of his treachery sinking in. He had lured and enticed her into embarking on what he had known would be a journey-to-nowhere, and his sole motive had been to violate and degrade her.

CHAPTER TWENTY-THREE

AS DAWN BROKE and the sun appeared on the horizon, Catrina realised that a crowd had gathered at the harbour, and then their cheers were ringing in the air as they gave Jake a hero's welcome.

He was the first to go ashore. The mob surged towards him, obviously to carry him shoulder-high, but a welcoming contingent of high-ranking Naval officers ordered them to fall back and let themselves through. Jake was borne away by the officers while the cheering mob followed.

Catrina went to look for Rawlings, and found him at work among the crew on deck. Pretending that she needed advice about getting her baggage ashore, she called him to one side and thanked him for what he had done for her. Afterwards, she returned to Nancy's side, and said,

'I cannot express what I owe you!'

'Then do not try. Do you have somewhere to go?'

'Yes. Oh yes.' Catrina hesitated, and looked away. 'Please—don't talk about what happened to me.'

'I won't, I promise. No one would believe it anyway, with *our hero* so firmly established in the public's esteem!'

Catrina kissed Nancy goodbye and watched her resignedly joining her sister and brother-in-law and three boisterous children. Then she streamed with the rest of the angry, outraged passengers down the gang-plank.

Like an animal going to ground, she made straight for the cow-byre. Because the rocks behind it did not point towards any of the enemy's lines of fortifications it had escaped blasting, and it was much as she had last left it.

In spite of what he had said, she knew that Jake could not be trusted at all. He would take it for granted that she had gone to Alice for safety and protection, and no doubt he relied on her feelings of shame and revulsion to ensure her silence. In any event, she thought bitterly, for a while he would be far too busy, being feted and honoured, to have time for seeking her out, and the cow-byre provided the solitude she needed.

Once again, she was gathering wild leeks and dandelions and stewing them into broth, and her thoughts made corrosive companions.

She remembered what Millicent had told her. *'Love!'* she had said. *'It is a trap which Nature sets for women.'*

And now Catrina knew that her sister had spoken the truth. Her own physical and emotional feelings for Dominic had been no more than another dream-fantasy, a more earthy version of Millicent's romantic pre-marital image of brushing her hair before the looking-glass while her husband watched her in adoration.

Men *were* animals, who wished only to do disgusting, loathsome things to one's body and force one into performing degrading acts. Millicent had said so; Violet had confirmed it; and it had been proved to Catrina in a way which she would never forget.

Men restrained themselves with skilfully seductive kisses and soft, intimate caresses until they had pinned their quarry down, whether in marriage or outside it, and then they became their true selves. And they called it love! Her bile rose as she recalled how Jake Farraday had promised to teach her more lessons in love. Had Millicent not said that Dominic had also wanted to teach *her* about love, when she had already discovered how abhorrent it was?

Well, now Catrina too knew love for what it was. It meant a brutal, bestial invasion by a man of a woman's body. It meant him biting and tearing at her flesh in an ugly display of lust. It meant being forced to do things which made her shrivel at the mere memory. She had experienced love once, and she wanted no part in it ever again.

Dear God, to think that she had wasted the best part of three years in longing for *that*! Now the very thought of Dominic or of any other man touching her in any way sickened her.

Although Jake was kept busy with his new duties as special adviser to the Navy, and so many now wished to befriend him that he scarcely had a moment to call his own, there was one particular task which still required his attention.

Catrina's punishment had to be completed in such a way that it would be calculated to hurt Dominic Ross in equal measure.

Jake guessed that Catrina had gone to the cow-byre. He had been keeping a secret eye on the tent she had previously shared with Alice Ridgeway and Dinah Forest, and there had been no sign of her.

Jake's opportunity came when Dinah emerged from the tent alone one morning. He approached her, and made her his most dashing bow. 'Mrs Forest, you are the very person I have been hoping to see!'

She flushed with pleasure. 'Have you, Mr Farraday? I would not even have thought you would have remembered me. May I say how very much I admire your spirit and courage?'

He gave a self-deprecating smile. 'I am no more than a simple sailor, ma'am. And as for not remembering you—I assure you, your lovely image has remained imprinted on my mind since the day I found you, helpless and vulnerable, at the mercy of a mob of drunken soldiers!'

She gave a little shiver of delight, and said archly, 'You must remember, Mr Farraday, that I am promised to someone else, and not free to accept such compliments.'

'The fact that you are promised to someone else is one of which I remind myself daily, with the greatest regret. Where are you bound for? May I accompany you?'

'I am not going anywhere in particular. Everything is so dreary, and I merely wished to get away from the settlement for a while.'

'Then may I suggest that we walk to the town? There is a plaza which escaped much of the bombardment and we could sit on a seat in the shade of trees while we talked.'

'I shall be delighted, Mr Farraday.' Dinah took the arm which he offered her.

When they reached the plaza and were sitting down, Jake began abruptly, 'Mrs Forest . . .'

'Oh, do please call me Dinah!'

'It would be an honour. Dinah, how is Miss Beaumont now?'

She stared at him. 'How should I know that? She is in England.'

'No, she isn't,' he interrupted quietly, and assumed a

troubled look. 'Am I to understand that Miss Beaumont has not been in touch with her family and friends since *Golden Sovereign* returned to Gibraltar?'

Dinah frowned in confusion. 'No. Are you suggesting . . . But we all assumed that she had transferred to the Lisbon packet and continued on to England.'

'I am afraid not.' He sprang up, and began to pace up and down. He whirled about suddenly, facing Dinah again. 'Dear Lord, I do hope she has merely gone into hiding, and that she has not done something quite desperate!'

'What do you mean? I am totally bewildered by everything you have been saying!'

He sat down again. 'Dinah, I know I can trust you, and I feel that for Miss Beaumont's sake I must tell you the whole truth, so that you may be able to help her.'

'Oh, yes, you may trust me!' Dinah breathed, and waited avidly.

'Well, as you know, I have always had a great regard for Miss Beaumont. She befriended me at a time when everyone else believed all the distorted rumours about me. So, I used to confide in her more fully than perhaps I should have done.'

'Do go on,' Dinah urged.

'I told Miss Beaumont about the Governor's plan that we should trick the Spaniards into believing *Golden Sovereign* was to sail for England with passengers. She begged to be allowed to make the voyage. She was tired of the austerity and grimness prevailing in Gibraltar and wished to go home. I agreed, and because she was a friend, I did the only thing any man of honour would have done. Conditions on the ship were vastly overcrowded, so I placed my cabin at Miss Beaumont's disposal and I shared a berth with the first officer.'

Jake paused for just long enough to give the impression that what he was about to say would give him no pleasure. 'I discovered, soon after we had put to sea, that Miss Beaumont suffered from sea-sickness. I gave her some medicine which I knew would cure it. Unfortunately the medicine—a distillation of herbs much used by the Moors along the Barbary coast—also has the effect of creating a great force of nervous, restless energy in those who take it, and I want you to remember that, Dinah, for I am sure it was to blame for much of Miss Beaumont's subsequent behaviour.'

'How *did* she behave?' Dinah asked eagerly.

'Well . . . She became—*demanding*. She would summon me to the cabin which she was occupying alone, on any pretext she could think of. I made her understand that I could not afford to be away from the bridge so often. At that stage, I thought she was merely bored, and wanted company. But then we arrived at Lisbon.'

'What happened at Lisbon? Dinah probed breathlessly.

'I advised the passengers to transfer to the packet which was sailing from there to England. Most of them agreed to do so. Then I went to the cabin to see Miss Beaumont. It had been arranged that I would lend her sufficient money to pay for a private berth on the Lisbon packet. The other passengers were to travel steerage at the British government's expense. When I arrived at the cabin, and she called to me to enter . . .'

Jake stopped, and looked away. 'I do not know how to put this with any delicacy, Dinah, so I shall have to be blunt. She received me, wearing nothing at all. I tried to withdraw, but she placed herself between me and the door. Then she embraced me, and . . .' He shook his head. 'I wish I were able to say that I pushed her away and told her to behave herself. But I am not a saint. I possess the weaknesses of any normal man, and I allowed myself to be tempted. I stayed with her and we . . . Well, you will have guessed what happened.'

Dinah allowed herself a little sound of shock, but inwardly she was trembling with glee. She had always known that Catrina was no better than she ought to be, making friends with a whore and forever drawing attention to herself!

'By the time I came to my senses,' Jake went on, 'Miss Beaumont had missed the Lisbon packet. I suggested that she put up at lodgings in the city and awaited the next sailing, and offered to lend her the money she would need. She wept, and said that she loved me, and that she wished only to be where I was. I was forced to be brutal, and to tell her that I did not love her in return. She refused to accept that, and she refused, also, to leave the ship.'

'You claimed,' Dinah put in shrewdly, 'that the medicine you gave her for sea-sickness was to blame for her behaviour.

But she could not have been sea-sick while you were in port, and therefore she could not have been taking the medicine at the time.'

'I had not considered that,' he agreed unhappily, and sighed. 'In any event, Dinah, I was forced to allow Miss Beaumont to remain on board *Golden Sovereign*, for she threatened that if I put her forcibly ashore in Lisbon she would tell everyone there that I was in reality returning to Gibraltar, so that the news would reach the enemy and they would be expecting me. She also threatened to cause all manner of scandals if I did not continue to share the cabin with her. She said, for example, that she would appear on the bridge unclothed, and offer herself to me in the presence of my men. I am afraid I showed my revulsion and disgust strongly, and I told her that I had no desire ever to touch her again. For my own protection against her threats, I placed her in the custody of a strong, no-nonsense woman among the passengers, who shared the cabin with her and acted as her gaoler.'

'My goodness . . .' Dinah breathed ecstatically. 'No wonder Catrina has gone into hiding! She must be terrified that those who witnessed her behaviour will be talking!'

'Yes,' Jake agreed gravely. 'And that is why I have told you the full story—so that when people do talk, you may leap to her defence. She is a very unhappy young woman.' He stood up. 'I think we had better leave now. I have duties awaiting me. Thank you for allowing me to confide in you, Dinah.'

He smiled as he took her arm. Dinah Forest, he knew, could be trusted to spread the story of Catrina's shame over the whole of Gibraltar in the shortest possible time. And what a satisfying twist it was that Dominic Ross's betrothed should be the one responsible for putting him through the torture of wondering whether, perhaps, the story did not contain some grains of truth!

A shadow fell across the doorway of the cow-byre, and Catrina stiffened, her muscles aching with tension. Dominic entered, his face expressionless. He looked as arresting as ever, with his silver-grey eyes bright in contrast with his tanned face and his dark hair falling over his brow. And she felt nothing but revulsion as she looked at him.

'Someone told me they had seen you among the passengers disembarking at the New Mole,' he said. 'Since you had not returned to Alice's tent, I guessed that you must have come here.'

She remained silent, watching him. He went on, 'It was as much a surprise to me as it must have been to you when *Golden Sovereign* returned to Gibraltar. The ruse was kept secret to all but the very highest level of command. I am sorry you had to make the journey for nothing.'

He broke off, and moved towards her. 'No, by God, I am not sorry! *Catrina* . . .'

'Keep—Keep away from me!' she said hoarsely, recognising the passion in his voice. She retreated so that her back was against the wall.

He frowned. 'Catrina, what is the matter?'

'Nothing! Just go away, and don't come here again!'

'You are still blaming me for the destruction of the gardens. Believe me, I wish I *had* disobeyed orders and told you about the blasting. But, at the time . . .'

'It has nothing to do with the gardens. Just leave me alone, Dominic. I don't want to see you.'

'Are you ill!' His voice held concern, and he was studying her with a frown. 'You are looking very pale and thin.' He advanced towards her, and as he touched her face blind panic seized her.

'Animal!' she screamed, kicking at his shins, drumming at his chest with her fists. 'You're—all animals! Depraved, corrupt beasts!'

Even in her frenzy, her mind registered the ferocious look which crossed his face. 'Go and sit down on the palliasse,' he ordered. 'I shall not come near you. Tell me what has happened to make you lash out at me in terror, when common sense must have told you that I merely wished to feel your forehead to find out whether you had a fever.'

She sidled towards the palliasse, her eyes never leaving his face. But he remained where he was. 'What happened, Catrina?' he demanded.

'*Love* happened,' she spat out bitterly, unable to cling to her resolve to keep the truth hidden away in her mind.

'Love?' Dominic's echo was a harsh whisper.

'What men call love! And I have no intention that it should ever happen to me again!'

A violent oath escaped him. 'Farraday forced himself on you!'

'*He* would not call it that! He called it teaching me lessons in love! Oh, he taught me well enough! I was unwell, and terrified, and completely helpless, but that did not stop him. He fell on me like a wild animal, and forced me to take part in unspeakable depravities, *and he talked about love*!'

Dominic said nothing more. His face set, he left her there and walked out of the cow-byre. For the first time, she was glad that the law would never allow him to do what Jake Farraday had done to her.

The story Jake had told Dinah, and which she had lost no time in repeating, spread through Gibraltar with the impetus of a bush fire. Like all such stories, it grew worse with each telling, and it was not long before most people had forgotten from whom they had first heard it.

Inevitably, the story reached Dominic too. He recognised its original author, and he was filled with such blind rage that if Jake Farraday had not remained within the protection of the Naval headquarters at all times, Dominic would have been quite capable of beating him to a pulp.

Perhaps, he told himself, it was as well that Farraday took care to remain inaccessible, for it was forcing himself to contain his rage and concentrate, instead, on finding some way of nailing the lie.

A false armistice was once again reigning over Gibraltar, leaving Dominic with time to spare. He traced some of the people who had been passengers on *Golden Sovereign* and who had refused to transfer to the Lisbon packet, and questioned them.

Their answers gave him no comfort at all. They were mostly women, and they remembered that Catrina had mentioned the fact that she was occupying a cabin by herself. 'Of course, we should have guessed it was the Captain's cabin, and that she was travelling as his doxy,' they said.

'I'm afraid, Captain Ross,' someone else told him, 'the story about your sister-in-law must be true. You see, there was a strong, forceful woman who used to collect food from the galley each day for someone else, and after we had left Lisbon, Miss Beaumont was not seen by anyone. We know,

now, that she was being kept locked up in the Captain's cabin with a women gaoler.'

Dominic tracked down Nancy Bates, and questioned her. 'I promised Miss Beaumont that I would not discuss the matter,' she said uncompromisingly.

'But, don't you see, it would help her if you were to break your promise, and state publicly what you know to be the truth!'

Nancy relented somewhat. 'I'll tell *you* what I know to be the truth, because you obviously care about her. But don't ask me to make a public statement, or to sign anything.'

'Why not?' he pleaded.

'Because bitter experience has taught me not to become involved in other people's lives and affairs. I'll do my best for Miss Beaumont by telling you all I know, but then I wish to be left in such peace as living with my sister's family allows me.'

With mounting angry despair, Dominic next obtained a list of the names of the crew who had sailed on *Golden Sovereign*. They could tell him no more than that it had been known the Captain had a 'fancy piece' aboard the vessel.

Then Dominic traced Rawlings, who had obtained temporary work as a labourer in a gang carrying out maintenance work at one of the moles.

'You're the man your Captain was close to beating to death when I intervened!' Dominic exclaimed.

'Ay, sir, and right grateful I am to you.'

Dominic began to question him. Rawlings was quite prepared to talk, but only in confidence, even though Dominic promised him protection against Farraday's anger. 'With respect, sir, the sea's all I know, and I ain't a young man no more. The Cap'n will get another ship, of that I'm sure, and I wants a place among his crew. I ain't saying as what he done to that young lady were right, for it weren't, but I has my living to think of.'

The matter, Dominic was forced to admit, was hopeless. There was no way of curbing the slanderous lies being told about Catrina, and no way of punishing Farraday. His frustrated rage became almost uncontainable when he learnt that the Governor was to give a reception at the Convent in Jake Farraday's honour, and that all senior officers of both services were expected to attend.

The Spaniards had launched no offensive for some days, but it had not escaped anyone's notice that great activity was going on at sea among their battery ships.

It had been observed, also, that when these large, awkward vessels attempted to return to their sheltered anchorage close to the isle of Algeciras, it required no less than ten gunboats to tow just one of them. For days now the British look-outs had reported that large quantities of powder and shot were being stowed on the floating batteries.

All the signs were ominous, and because the British could do little while they waited for events, the Governor had decided to honour Jake Farraday, the hero of the day, with an official reception.

Dominic arrived at the Convent just as the Governor was delivering his speech in tribute to Farraday's courage, his navigational skills, and the cool calculation with which he had carried out the ruse to bring in vital supplies from Lisbon to combat the outbreak of scurvy.

The Governor concluded what he had been saying in praise of Jake, and the audience cheered and clapped. The Governor held up his hand. 'Perhaps Mr Farraday would now like to say a few words.'

Jake rose to his feet. His first words were lost in the hum of startled speculation and excitement that followed Dominic's progress as he strode towards the rostrum. He positioned himself beside Farraday, and the audience waited, rapt with anticipation.

'I am sure Mr Farraday will be too modest to do so himself,' Dominic addressed the audience. 'So I want to tell you about one more dashing, courageous deed which is to be laid at his door. Most of the passengers who embarked on *Golden Sovereign* did so by their own free choice, and they were given the opportunity to transfer to the Lisbon packet. I have spent the past days tracking down passengers who chose not to transfer, and I have spoken to the crew, and I persuaded those who know the truth to recount it to me.'

'Really,' Farraday protested with a humorous smile at the audience which did not quite mask his alarm. 'I have received enough accolades as it is! One more will become a burden!'

'I cannot allow you to hide your light under a bushel!' Dominic interrupted, baring his clenched teeth in an answering smile. He looked at the avid, breathless audience again.

'My sister-in-law was one of those who embarked on *Golden Sovereign*. But, unlike the other passengers, she was deliberately persuaded to do so by Mr Farraday. He took advantage of the fact that her spirits were very low at the time, and he made her believe that the vessel was sailing for England. She felt it was pointless for her to remain in Gibraltar, and she accepted his offer of a free passage. She was not suspicious when a private cabin was placed at her disposal; after all, she regarded herself as a friend of Mr Farraday, and she did not expect a friend to be anything but chivalrous and kind.'

Dominic heard the other man muttering something, but he went on inexorably. 'Miss Beaumont had been suffering from sea-sickness and was in a weakened state and both defenceless and unwell when the ship docked in Lisbon. But our brave hero did what he had deliberately set out from the beginning to do.' Dominic's voice rose. 'He forced himself upon her, and brutally and violently raped her. She had no money and could not transfer to the Lisbon packet. All she could do was to appeal to another passenger, a determined woman of strong character, to share the cabin with her after that and prevent the courageous Captain from forcing himself upon her again.'

As he spoke the last words, Dominic turned and swung his fist with full force into Jake Farraday's face. The stunned silence of the audience erupted in a chaos of noise, but Dominic did not even look at the man as he fell unconscious to the ground.

Women were screaming, and a crowd had gathered round Farraday. Dominic felt his arm taken in a firm hold, and he looked at General Ridgeway, who was gesturing to him to move to one side. Dinah, weeping hysterically, followed him, and Alice brought up the rear.

'You are going to be disciplined for this,' General Ridgeway told Dominic heavily. 'You can thank God that Farraday is a civilian. Had he been in the services you would have faced a court-martial.'

Dominic shrugged. 'The truth *had* to be told. At least people will now be able to compare the two stories and decide for themselves which one is more likely to be the truth.'

'*No one* will believe that Catrina did not pursue Mr Farraday quite shamelessly!' Dinah cried in a shrill voice. 'Didn't she turn up in Gibraltar in the first place with a whore? You fool, Dominic! How could you believe that pathetic cock-and-bull story *she* obviously told you? Her true nature has always been . . .'

It was Alice who interrupted her. She stepped forward, and slapped Dinah's face hard. 'She was hysterical,' Alice explained calmly.

Dominic saw an aide pushing a way though the crowd towards them. 'The Governor wishes to speak to you in his office,' he was told.

Dominic nodded, and squared his shoulders. Governor Eliott was wearing his most austere look when Dominic entered his office.

'Sit down, Captain Ross. I will deal, later, with the public affront you offered our guest of honour, and which could not be excused for any reason.' The Governor leant forward. 'But in heaven's name, man, even if what you alleged were true, do you seriously believe you did your sister-in-law any service by shouting it to the world?'

Dominic stared at him in astonishment. 'Sir, have you not heard the gossip being spread about her?'

'Since I refuse to listen to gossip, people do not offer me any. But perhaps you had better tell me what is being said.'

With distaste, Dominic recounted the bare essentials of the story being spread about Catrina. 'It is my belief,' he added, 'that Farraday himself started the scurrilous whispering campaign, obviously to forestall anything Miss Beaumont might say about what had happened. By telling the truth in public, sir, at least I have ensured that some people will be prepared to give Miss Beaumont the benefit of the doubt, and begin to remember what Farraday's reputation was before he became a national hero. They may remember about a certain sixteen-year-old girl whom he seduced from her home and lured to Ireland on his cutter, and whose subsequent fate has never become known to the world. *Her* family would not speak out against Farraday, and what good did that achieve?'

The Governor sat in silence, his head bowed in thought. 'Farraday has been honoured, his past forgiven,' Eliott said at last, 'for one major reason. Grave trouble is brewing for Gibraltar, and we need the kinds of men who are willing to take risks. For that reason also, Captain Ross, I am going to punish you far more lightly than would reasonably have been expected. I accept your reasons for what you did, but you should not have done it in a place such as this, and on an occasion such as today's.'

A few minutes later Dominic left the Governor's office, having been privately reprimanded and given a token punishment. He stopped in town only long enough to collect some of his rations, and then made for the cow-byre. Somehow he would have to convince Catrina that what she had suffered at Farraday's hands had had nothing remotely to do with love.

She was young and beautiful, and it was right that she should marry one day. She was forever out of his own reach, and the thought of her belonging to some other man caused him immeasurable pain. But it was even more unbearable to imagine her wasting her youth in the barren existence of spinsterhood, afraid of ever being stirred to passion again.

She was sitting on a rock outside the cow-byre, staring into space. His heart contracted as he studied her. She had been washing her hair, and was drying it in the sun. She wore a simple gown without hoops, and he noticed that one of its sleeves was torn and that the hem had acquired a ragged edge. But she had never seemed more beautiful to him.

'Catrina . . .'

She started, and terror entered her eyes. He suspected that she would take flight at the slightest attempt to touch her, and so he kept his distance, finding another rock near by on which to sit down.

'I thought you might like to know that I have just publicly knocked Jake Farraday down.'

'What for?' she asked bitterly. 'Because he did what *you* would like to do?'

'It would not be remotely like that if *I* . . .' He stopped, and went on painfully, 'Some day you will meet a man who is able to offer you marriage. A decent, honourable man. It is important that you should not shut your mind to the thought of marriage and a family of your own because of what Farraday did to you.'

'I *have* shut my mind to it,' she said stonily.

'Then, for your own sake, I shall have to open it again.'

'You would be wasting your time.'

He was silent for some minutes, considering his next possible move. At last he spoke quietly.

'Catrina, do you remember that evening when Millicent caught us together, and you had removed your *peignoir*? She called us animals. Did you feel that we were behaving like animals at the time?'

Something stirred deep inside her. She tried to deny it, but it would not go away. Almost inaudibly, she said, 'That was Nature's trap.'

He moved slowly, so that she would not jump up in alarm, and came to sit beside her. 'What did you mean by that?'

'Millicent explained it to me. Nature traps women into a false illusion of love. Then, when it is too late, they discover the horrible reality.'

He thought for a moment. 'Now that you have discovered what you call the horrible reality, how do you imagine you would feel if we were to repeat what we did that evening?'

Her eyes flew to his face. He was looking at her very seriously. 'You know that you are safe with me, Catrina. I dare not do to you a fraction of what Farraday did, because in the eyes of the law I am your brother. I am trying to help you, love. I am trying to drive away the memory of what you had to go through. So—are you willing to take part in the experiment?'

She did not answer, and after a moment he stood up, holding his hands out to her. She did not take them, but she rose too, and followed him slowly into the byre.

They stood together, and facing one another, inside its walls. 'You showed yourself to me that evening without shame, Catrina,' he prompted.

She hesitated. It was true that she was safe with him. There had been so many times in the past when he could have taken advantage of what she had offered him in her tempestuous ignorance, and he had not done so.

And she was beginning to feel desperate, for the memory of what Farraday had done to her was slowly driving her mad, never leaving her mind, never giving her peace. Even when she slept she dreamt about the horror of it all. And, on the ship, there had been sea-sickness to take her mind partly away from it, but here there were no distractions. She had hoped that solitude would help, but it was only making it worse, and time was not proving to be a healer.

'Without shame, Catrina,' Dominic repeated gently.

Hesitantly she began to unfasten the bodice of her gown, and he remained quite still as she stepped out of it. He did not offer to help her to remove her stays, but sat down on the palliasse, watching her.

When she stood naked in front of him, he held out a hand, and she allowed him to pull her down on the palliasse.

He lay down beside her, and moved his hand gently from her throat to her breasts, exploring the smooth flatness of her stomach, and tracing the shape of her thighs. A long shudder shook her.

'Afraid?' he asked softly, with concern.

'N-No'

His hand continued its exploration, moving over the mound of soft down between her thighs, probing gently. 'Does this seem like animal behaviour, Catrina?' he whispered against her mouth.

The old, familiar response to him was pounding inside her, but she no longer trusted it. 'No, it does not,' she admitted. 'But this is just play-acting. Part of the trap. There is more—much more. And that *is* bestial and ugly and repellent, and I want no part of it! *Ever!*'

He sat up, and began to remove his coat and then his shirt. She shrank away. 'What are you doing?'

'Don't be alarmed. I intend only to take what you call the play-acting a little further.'

She began to tremble with remembered revulsion when he stood before her, naked as Farraday had been naked that day. But with a reassuring murmur he sank down beside her, and pulled her into his arms. He held her, touching her and kissing her, his mouth moving from her lips to her breasts and down to her thighs. He demanded nothing in return and he offered no threat. He seemed quite content with kissing and caressing her.

But a flame had begun to race through her, and *she* was no longer content with being touched and kissed. Her hands began an exploration of their own, and she moved herself against him, and as their mouths locked together she manoeuvred her body into position so that there could be only one inevitable outcome.

And it was not in the slightest as it had been with Farraday. Dominic moved within her slowly, lifting her body with his hands and encouraging her so that they achieved a matching rhythm. And all the while his mouth was kissing her lips and her breasts, his darting tongue heightening her arousal.

Their final mutual ecstasy was so intense that a cry escaped Catrina. Dominic held her to him. kissing the side of her mouth, and whispered,

'Have I convinced you, my love?'

'Yes. Oh, yes! Except—Dominic, what about those other perverted acts in which Jake Farraday forced me to take part?'

'He *forced* you, Catrina. That was the true perversion. Nothing willingly offered or received in love between two people can be called perverted.'

'I see . . .' Her voice rose in agitation. 'Dominic—*we have committed incest*!'

'We have not broken any *natural* law,' he said recklessly, pulling her against him once more. 'And they can't hang one twice for repeating the same crime, can they?'

CHAPTER TWENTY-FOUR

CATRINA HAD STEELED herself for the moment when he would have to leave her, but Dominic said with a laugh, 'As punishment for knocking down Jake Farraday, the Governor has stripped me of my command for twenty-four hours. I intend staying with you until the morning.'

They ate the rations he had brought, and they talked. They talked about everything except the fact that they had no future together, and that their love was a guilty secret which would have to be guarded with the utmost care.

'I know everything about you,' Catrina said, 'and yet I know almost nothing about your background. Millicent once told me that your family are wealthy landowners, and that you are the only son.'

'Yes. There was a coolness between my father and myself for a while, because he opposed my decision to make the army my career. But I enlisted as an ordinary soldier and worked my way up through the ranks, and he gradually accepted that the army was important to me. Now we are the best of friends.'

Catrina thought of her sister, who had been obsessed with the fear that her second child might also be a girl. 'It was important to you to have a son, wasn't it, so that he could take your place as your father's heir.'

'Yes. The family estate can be passed on only through the male line. I dare say when the time comes for me to inherit, I shall appoint an agent to look after the place, because I cannot imagine myself ever giving up the army.'

Catrina curled her fingers through his. 'Tell me about the rest of your family.'

He smiled. 'There is my mother, who is warm and wise and can do no wrong in my father's eyes. My two sisters, Ruth and Barbara, are both married with children of their own, and they live on neighbouring estates in Sussex, close to our parents. We all get on extremely well together, and my family had looked forward for so long to meeting Millicent and Lucy and welcoming them . . .' He broke off, and lapsed into silence.

Catrina could guess only too accurately why Millicent had never consented to visiting his family. It would have meant leaving the protection of their mother, and also the reassurance of that room of hers in which she had been able to lock herself away from Dominic's attentions.

Poor Millicent, Catrina thought. If only she had allowed herself to grow up. Aloud, she said, 'It must be wonderful to be part of a close family.'

He did not reply, but drew her roughly against him, and she sensed that he was trying to blot out the knowledge that it would be Dinah, and not herself, who would one day be a part of his family. And in the meantime, Catrina thought even as she responded to his kiss and his questing hands, she would have to content herself with what little she could get.

That night of love did not banish from her mind the memory of what Jake Farraday had done to her, but it put things into perspective. She knew, at last, what love truly meant.

She was awakened by Dominic in the morning. She stretched her arms out sleepily to him, but he said in an urgent voice, 'I have to go, Catrina. You must get dressed an join the other women.'

'What has happened?' she asked, alarmed.

'I have just come in from outside. New squadrons of Spanish and French vessels arrived during the night, and I have never seen so many warships in the Bay at one time before!'

He swore under his breath, and continued as if he were ticking off aloud the strength of the enemy. 'At least six Admirals' flags, besides God-knows how many frigates and zebecs. And I'd say some fifty ships of the line. But they are all as nothing compared with the floating batteries . . .'

'What are *they*?' Catrina asked as she dressed hurriedly.

'Specially constructed ships which the Spanish claim are incombustible and unsinkable, and our total fighting force numbers no more than seven thousand men! I know now how David must have felt, armed with his sling and waiting for Goliath to attack!'

She could not fully take in the enormity of what he had been saying. Uppermost in her mind was the feeling of having been cheated when she already had to content herself with so little. 'You told me you were suspended from duty for twenty-four hours . . .'

'Events have overtaken such a formality! I have to report for duty. The situation is serious, my love. Come, let us collect your things.'

They hurried away from the cow-byre together, and after a brief but intense kiss they parted company. Dominic ran towards the Convent where he had told her the Governor would be briefing his officers, and Catrina watched him for a while before she picked up her bundle of belongings and made her way to the tent of Alice and Dinah.

But Alice was there alone. She threw her arms about Catrina, and held her close. 'My poor dear girl! What you must have gone through at the hands of the vile man . . .'

'I was a fool. And—I am very sorry that I tricked you when I left with him.'

'I *was* hurt when I discovered that you had apparently sailed for England without saying goodbye, and more hurt when you returned and made no attempt to see me. I didn't believe the rumours, but all was made clear when Dominic explained what that vile man had done to you. I wanted to go to you last night, but John thought you would prefer to be alone.'

Catrina flushed guiltily. Had General Ridgeway really thought that, or had he suspected that Dominic was with her?

She changed the subject. 'When I saw the massed enemy fleet in the Bay, I decided that I had better join you.'

Alice nodded soberly. 'John says we must brace ourselves for the worst attack so far.'

Catrina looked about her. 'Where is Dinah?'

Alice seemed to have put the thought of their coming danger behind her, for a smile of malicious amusement played about her mouth. 'Dinah finally enacted the most dramatic role life could possibly have offered her. She ran away with the hero of the hour, Jake Farraday.'

'What?'

'Yes, indeed. She publicly apologised to Farraday on Dominic's behalf! I might tell you, I had to restrain myself from rushing after her and strangling her! In any event, she was not to be prised from Farraday's side for the remainder of the afternoon. He was obviously amused by the situation; Dominic had knocked him down, and there was Dominic's future wife hanging on his arm!'

'Yes, that would certainly have amused him,' Catrina confirmed.

'She did not return here with me. In the late afternoon a messenger arrived with a note from her addressed to Dominic. He has not yet seen it, and he doesn't know that she has gone.'

'She ran away with Jake Farraday . . .' Catrina frowned. 'But where could they have run *to*?'

'Like everyone else, Farraday sensed that a combined onslaught on the Rock was imminent, and he decided to depart while the going was good. He took—no, let us not mince words—he stole *Golden Sovereign* and rounded up all his crew. I don't know whether Dinah volunteered to go with him or whether he asked her to. But I am convinced he took her only because she is Dominic's fiancée.'

Catrina shook her head in pity for the rude awakening which was awaiting Dinah. There had never been any love lost between the two of them, but even Dinah did not deserve someone like Jake Farraday!

'Of course,' she heard Alice go on, 'Dinah had no way of knowing that her departure would be overshadowed by that frightening mass of ships in the Bay. She imagined that her name would be on everyone's lips today. She was to have been the talk of the garrison; the One Who Counted The World Well Lost For Love! The spirited, passionate young woman who abandoned respectability and dull duty for the romance and hazards of life at sea with her buccaneer.'

Catrina was silent. Poor, foolish Dinah with her habit of seeing life as sets upon a stage in which she was destined to play principal parts. It was too easy to guess what her future part would be. She would be abandoned by Farraday as soon as he tired of her, and it was possible to become tired of Dinah only too quickly.

'How did General Ridgeway take it? He was very fond of her.'

Alice shrugged. 'He is extremely angry and shocked by what she did. Poor John, unlike most other men, always hankered after a daughter rather than a son, and he never could see Dinah's faults. For my own part, I am glad to be rid of her and so, I believe, will Dominic be.'

But it would make no difference whatever to the situation between herself and Dominic, Catrina knew. And after last night, the fate which forced them to remain apart seemed crueller than ever.

The expected onslaught from the enemy came the following morning. Alice and Catrina joined the other women in scrambling for places of safety among the rocks, from where they watched the ten mighty battery ships draw out towards the Rock. Dozens of warships escorted them. Slowly they approached down wind, and the vessels dropped anchor no more than a thousand yards away from the town of Gibraltar.

'Why don't our side fire on them?' Catrina asked tensely.

'The British gunners will hold their fire until the floating batteries are securely in position,' Alice told her.

Suddenly, shockingly, the two sides engaged one another. Huge clouds of smoke wreathed the Rock and spread out across the sea, penetrated by trails of fire as the shells soared through the air. There was nothing but noise and smoke and guns flashing and hellish destruction.

Catrina could see that stretches of Gibraltar's line-walls were being blasted out of existence. The Spanish battery ships appeared to be living up to the reputation of invincibility that Dominic had described, for even the heaviest shells fired by the British rolled impotently down their sloping protective deck-covers or burst round them without achieving anything.

Catrina cowered with the other women in the shelter of the rocky gulleys, and thought fearfully of Dominic, who would be in the thick of the fighting.

Like those of his men, Dominic's face and hands were blackened by powder, and his eyes stung from the sulphur fumes as they toiled together at the British guns.

A similarly blackened figure appeared at his side, and he recognised one of his fellow-officers only when the latter spoke urgently. 'Your men are to leave what they're doing, and set to work firing kilns and furnaces instead.'

'Whatever for?'

'Governor Eliott has hit on the plan of heating cannon-balls before firing them at the enemy.'

'By God, if it could be made to work on those damned battery ships of the enemy! It has been like trying to break a window by lobbing breadcrumbs at it!'

Quickly, Dominic called his men together. Fires were kindled and stoked, and when the furnaces were at a high enough temperature, cannon-balls were dropped into their maws.

'Wait till the Dons get one of 'em hot potatoes hittin' their decks!' a soldier exulted.

Gingerly, using tongs, a relay of troops hurried with the red-hot cannon-balls from the furnaces so that the guns could fire them through the holes which had been blasted in the rock.

The Spaniards forsook their siesta period. A pity, Dominic thought grimly. They would have made such perfect sitting targets if they had broken off their firing! Early in the afternoon, the weary, smoke-blackened, sweating British broke into a cheer. One of the Spanish flagships was burning!

'By the Lord Harry!' Dominic heard someone shout, only minutes later. 'Look at that, will you! Invincible, they said! One of the buggers has caught fire!'

The flames spread rapidly, and the crew were forced to stop firing on the British lines as they rushed about in their efforts to put them out. But a brisk south-westerly wind had sprung up, Dominic noted with satisfaction, for this was not only hampering the efforts of the stricken ship's crew; it was also blowing the gunsmoke of the other battery ships well away from them, making them clearer targets for the Rock's gunners.

The persistent wind was the best ally the British could have hoped for, and Dominic sent up a silent prayer that it would not suddenly change direction. It was ensuring that whenever a fire started on board an enemy vessel, it spread rapidly and became out of control. The stricken battery ship presented a scene of chaos and confusion, and when it became clear to the enemy that she was doomed, the crew abandoned her.

Night was falling by now, and Dominic saw that the Navy were sending out small boats to rescue the Spanish crew. But while he himself, in common with other British officers, had given the order to cease fire while the rescue operation was being mounted, the Spanish-Franco forces showed no such restraint.

Even before the Spanish crew had been rescued, the enemy renewed their attack, and at the same time they bombarded the garrison without mercy from their lines on the isthmus, and the battle had to be resumed with no quarter given.

Catrina could not help thinking that this must be what Hell was like. The air was filling with the whistling of shells and the crashes of explosions, intermingled with the shouts, the groans and cries of pain from the human casualties. Her lips moved continually and silently in prayer for Dominic's safety. When dawn broke, she stared in numb silence at the scene of total devastation. The waters of the Bay were heaving with human corpses and wreckage of ships.

Three of the Spanish battery ships had disappeared, seemingly into oblivion. Others were smoking and burning, and every now and again there came a deafening roar from one of them as it, too, exploded.

'It happens when the gunpowder in their magazines becomes ignited by the fire,' Alice explained.

Whatever the reason for it might be, to Catrina it seemed like the final, convulsive death-rattle of a mortally wounded creature. But in spite of these sporadically exploding vessels, small boats manned by British crews, she noticed, continued to set out into the Bay to pick up enemy survivors.

By tacit agreement, the women began to return to their tents. The enemy had clearly been beaten, but no one felt any sense of triumph. The ugliness of the night's carnage had affected all of them.

In the afternoon General Ridgeway and Dominic arrived at the tent. They were blackened with smoke and gunpowder and were clearly exhausted. Catrina resisted the impulse to hurl herself at Dominic in fervent relief at his safety, and contented herself instead with saying, 'We have won, have we not?'

General Ridgeway sighed, and replied, 'It is by no means over. We have dealt the enemy a mortal wound, but they'll come back at us in their death-throes.'

Catrina drew Dominic to one side. 'Have you heard the news about Dinah?'

He nodded. 'Poor, silly girl. She did not even realise that all she was to Farraday was a joke. A final joke intended to be at my expense.'

Catrina gazed at him hopelessly. 'It changes nothing for *us*, does it?'

'No.' His mouth settled into grim lines. 'But let us take what we can, while we can. In future, when General Ridgeway comes to the tent, go to the cow-byre and wait for me.'

She nodded, and a short while later the men left again.

The General, Catrina soon realised, had been right when he had said the enemy would lash back in their death-throes. With sporadic breaks in between, the battle continued to rage.

When these welcome breaks did occur, Catrina and Dominic met in the byre for a few hours of stolen love. Each knew these moments were precious, for it would have to last them a life-time, and this knowledge added an extra dimension to their love-making.

They were locked on the palliasse, Catrina stirring against him, trembling in wordless ecstasy as his hands and lips caressed her. Her body was hungry to receive him, but each put off the moment, savouring the touch and the taste and the smell of one another until passion reached a frenzied urgency which demanded a climax.

Afterwards, Dominic lay with his arm about her, and she found him studying her with a sombre expression. 'When peace comes, as it soon must,' he said, 'it will not be long before my regiment is posted to some other part of the world.'

'I know,' Catrina whispered.

'You would have no legitimate excuse for joining me. You would have to return to England alone.'

Involuntary tears gathered in her eyes, and he drew her against him once more with a fierce and angry need.

Later the same day the thought came to her that they had probably spent their last few hours together, for news arrived that Lord Howe was approaching. He was heading a fleet sent to relieve Gibraltar and speed the death-throes of the enemy.

The Franco-Spanish alliance reserved their fire, and concentrated on preparing their ships to put out to sea and engage Lord Howe's approaching fleet. But the British remained at their posts, so that Catrina had only fleeting meetings with Dominic, and she awaited the end of the siege with very mixed feelings.

In the second week of October, a gale sprang up and increased until it was blowing at hurricane-force by nightfall, bringing with it driving rain, so that Catrina and Alice were awake all night, struggling to keep the water out and the tent in position.

Above the noise of the wind and the rain, the sound of gun-fire reached them. 'Surely,' Catrina demanded, 'the enemy are not choosing this of all nights to resume their bombardment?'

Alice shook her head. 'The pattern of the shots means that they are distress signals. I think the storm is causing havoc among the enemy ships in the Bay.'

It was not until morning, when the wind was blowing itself out and the ferocity of the rain was subsiding, that Catrina realised how right Alice had been.

The enemy ships in the Bay must have been ill prepared for the storm, for what remained of them were in a state of utter confusion and disarray. Many had obviously been driven from their moorings and been swept away.

Catrina could see a large Spanish two-decker only a few hundred yards away from the shore; she had lost her foremast and bowsprit and was in dire straits. She could not help wincing in sympathy as the British opened fire upon her, and she drove helplessly ashore, finally running aground near the line-wall. Catrina watched as a British flag was hoisted over the vessel's Spanish insignia as a token of surrender.

Other enemy shipping were in similar trouble. One French ship of the line and a frigate were fast ashore, along with many smaller craft; some had badly damaged masts and rigging, and it was clear that the heart had been torn from the enemy.

Later that day, news swept through the garrison that Lord Howe's fleet had been sighted. The battle-weary, hard-pressed troops set up a tremendous cheer, which was taken up by the women and children. Lord Howe's fleet entered the Bay with no more than token resistance from the enemy, swiftly quelled. The siege, which had lasted for more than three years, was all over, bar the formalities.

All around Catrina and Alice, people were hugging and kissing one another in euphoric joy. A senior officer's wife pushed her way through the crowd to join them, and said excitedly,

'The fleet has brought huge supplies of food and drink, among other things. A party is to be held at the Spanish Pavilion this evening. Will you come?'

Alice laughed. 'There'll be parties all over town tonight, I'd wager! Yes, we'd like to come, thank you.' She touched Catrina's arm. 'Shall we go and get ready?'

As they pushed their way through the jubilant crowd, Catrina asked doubtfully, 'Do you think I ought to attend the party at the Spanish Pavilion? Dominic told me about the stories spread about me, and while the fighting was going on no one would have had time to spare for such things, but now people might shun me, and I don't wish to embarrass you.'

'They will not shun you! Farraday has run off with Dinah in the meanwhile, which throws an entirely new light upon matters. You must certainly attend the party!'

As far as Catrina was concerned, getting ready for the party involved no more than washing, changing into the best of her few worn gowns and dressing her hair.

She was ready before Alice, and waiting for her outside the tent so that she could watch the sunset, when an officer approached. He bowed formally. 'Are you Miss Catrina Beaumont?'

'I am. Why?'

His eyes stared at an invisible spot above her head. 'My name is Major Connors, and I am acting on orders from the Governor. You are to accompany me to the Convent.'

'Why?'

'You are to be questioned by Lieutenant General Gregson in connection with a charge upon which Captain Dominic Ross has been arrested.'

'Arrested?' The blood in her veins seemed to have turned to ice. 'On—On what charge?'

Major Connors answered expressionlessly. 'That he did, on diverse occasions, participate with you in unlawful sexual commerce of near-kinship.'

CHAPTER TWENTY-FIVE

HER THOUGHTS FRAGMENTED, it had not even occurred to Catrina to offer some excuse to Alice. Blindly, she had accompanied Major Connors to the Convent. But instead of being questioned by anyone, she had been turned over to a sour-faced woman who had shown her to a room in one wing of the Convent.

'Lieutenant General Gregson will send for you in the morning,' the woman said, and went to the door. 'I shall bring you some food.' She locked the door after she had left.

Still numb with shock and disbelief, Catrina stared about her. The room was adequately but austerely furnished with a bed, a hanging closet, a wash-stand and a chair. With its small window set high into the wall, it could scarcely have altered since the days when it would have been occupied by a Franciscan friar.

Would Dominic be locked up somewhere inside the Convent in a similar room, she wondered. But no, the army would have premises built for the purpose.

Her hands clenched together in impotent anger. The authorities had waited until the siege was over, and Dominic's services no longer urgently required, before they had made a move. It was inconceivable that they had only just discovered today the situation between him and herself. *How* could they have discovered it? And what was to happen to both of them now?

She ignored the food which the woman who was clearly her wardress brought, and lay awake in silent despair for most of the night, listening to the far-off sounds of revelry as the town and the garrison celebrated the British victory. She slipped at last into a restless doze, and it seemed to her to be only minutes later that she was awakened by the sound of the key in the lock.

Her wardress entered, carrying breakfast on a tray. 'While

you are eating, I shall bring you hot water,' she announced. 'You are to wash and dress, and be ready for the moment when Lieutenant General Gregson sends for you.'

She was not sent for until mid-morning, and she did not know whether the delay was a hopeful sign or not. The only certainty was that it wore away at her nerves, and increased her feeling of trepidation.

At last her wardress was showing her into a book-lined room, and formally introducing her to Gregson. They had met before on several occasions, and somehow his equally formal acknowledgment of the unnecessary introduction added a new dimension of horror to the situation.

'Sit down, please, Miss Beaumont,' he said when the wardress had left.

She obeyed, keeping her eyes fixed upon his face. He was an elderly man whose normally friendly expression had been exchanged for one of neutral officialdom.

'You have been informed, I believe, of the charge upon which Captain Dominic Ross has been arrested. It is an unprecedented charge in military history, and will without doubt have to be changed to something else.' He made a vague gesture. 'Behaviour unbecoming an officer; bringing the regiment into disrepute—something of that nature. But you understand, I suppose, the meaning of the present charge?'

She moistened her dry lips with her tongue. 'I—I think it means incest . . .'

'It does. As your brother-in-law, Captain Ross had a duty to guide and protect you. He was responsible for your physical and moral welfare, more particularly since you have no other living male relatives. Far from carrying out those duties, he has abused the special position in which he stood as regards to you in a most flagrant and shameful and criminal manner.'

'How—how do you . . .' She stopped, and added recklessly, 'I utterly deny everything!'

'I am afraid there is no point in your denying it, Miss Beaumont. There were eye-witnesses, you see.'

She covered her face with her hands. This was the most dreadful, sordid end to something which had been beautiful.

She heard Gregson go on, 'One of the men under Captain Ross's command held a grudge against him. He considered that the Captain had punished him unfairly for some misdemeanour. This soldier began to notice that whenever the enemy gave some respite, Captain Ross would disappear into the same direction each time. He decided to follow him. There is no lock on the door of the cow-byre, and neither of you noticed it being opened a crack. To make sure that no doubt would be cast on his word, the soldier persuaded one of his friends to accompany him. So, I am afraid the case against Captain Ross is water-tight.'

'What—will happen to him?' she managed.

'That will be decided after his court-martial, of which I am to take charge. If found guilty, he will be dismissed from the army in disgrace, at the very least.'

She closed her eyes. The very least would be quite bad enough. The army was Dominic's life; he had risked quarrelling with the father he loved so that he might make it his career. And now he would have to leave it in disgrace, for there was no chance at all of him not being found guilty.

She looked up at Gregson, and then dropped her gaze. 'Why was I brought here? I was told you wished to question me. But you have simply told me what has happened and what will happen in future.'

'You were brought here in the hope that you might willingly confess to the actions with which Captain Ross is being charged, and so bring the date of the court-martial nearer. You were also brought here because you are to be confined within the Convent . . .'

'Am I to be charged also?'

'You did not allow me to finish. You are a civilian, and the army has no jurisdiction over you. However, your continual presence in Gibraltar is undesirable, and you are to be shipped back to England as soon as possible. In the meantime, you will remain here in the Convent, for your own sake as much as to ensure that you *do* sail for England.'

'For my own sake?' Catrina repeated.

Gregson's expression lost its neutrality, and he looked grim. 'Captain Ross has always been a popular officer. Public feeling will run high when it becomes known that he is to be punished while you will go scot-free. So, to protect you against possible physical assault, you will be given a room here in the Convent until your passage home can be arranged.'

He rang a hand-bell, and moments later the wardress appeared, and Catrina found herself dismissed.

Not long afterwards, General Ridgeway was brought to her room, and the door was locked after him. He hugged Catrina, and then took the chair while she sat down on the edge of the bed.

'Alice . . .' she began.

'She is extremely upset by what has happened, Catrina. But I am here in an official capacity, and she could not have accompanied me even if she had been sufficiently composed to do so. I am to conduct Dominic's defence.'

'How—How is he?'

'He does not confide his feelings to me, but I can guess what they must be. The army have not yet decided what the exact wording of the charge against him is to be. Catrina, it would be best if you were to refuse to make a statement, admitting anything. I might, then, be able to cast doubt on the word of the two soldiers who informed upon Dominic when I cross-examine them. It is a slim chance, but we have to grab at any straw.'

She nodded, and looked away. 'I—can guess what people are saying about me. Lieutenant General Gregson warned me that feelings against me would run high.'

General Ridgeway refused to be drawn on the subject, but after he had left the wardress was only too happy to enlighten Catrina about what was being said of her. Every story which had ever been told about her was being resurrected, beginning with the lies woven by Jake Farraday. Dominic's public defence of her was now being seen in an entirely different, meaningful, light. Catrina, it was being said, had not only pursued Jake Farraday in the most shameless manner, but when the truth leaked out, she had seduced Dominic and made him believe a completely false version of the events. After all, did she not begin her brazen adventures in Gibraltar by arriving in company with a whore?

It was even being rumoured now that Millicent's death had been no accident. Had it not been the case that the poor, pregnant woman had been alone in the house with her sister and the whore? And if Catrina had set fire to her sister's room, the whore would have turned a blind eye.

Catrina listened to the calumnies which were being heaped

upon her head, but she scarcely cared. Her thoughts were with Dominic, whose career and reputation and entire future had been ruined because of her. She turned away, cursing the impulse which had brought her to Gibraltar in the first place.

General Ridgeway came to see her again later that day, and brought a brief message scrawled by Dominic. *'Whatever may happen,'* he had written, *'I regret nothing.'*

Catrina turned her head away so that the General would not see her tears, and tucked the note inside her bodice. But as if he had known what it contained, General Ridgeway said heavily, 'Others might think you will get off scot-free, but you won't. The scandal will follow you back to England and dog you for the rest of your life.'

She hardly cared; her only concern was for Dominic. And it was not until after the General had left her that Catrina began to perceive how she might help Dominic. Since public opinion was casting herself in the role of chief villain, she argued, there was a chance that he might escape being found guilty. Plans began to race through her mind.

If General Ridgeway could somehow arrange for her to give evidence at Dominic's court-martial, she might turn the tide in his favour. She would swear that she had instigated the acts of which he stood accused, and that he would have to be a saint to have resisted her determined advances.

Through her wardress, Catrina requested that General Ridgeway should be brought to see her again, and the next day she waited in almost unbearable tension for him to arrive. But it was not until well into the afternoon, when her nerves were stretched almost to breaking-point, that Catrina heard the wardress's key in the lock.

'You're to follow me,' she said.

Catrina was surprised. On both previous occasions, General Ridgeway had visited her in her room.

She was even more surprised, and bewildered, to be shown inside Gregson's office, and to find him there in the company of the Governor, and of Alice and John Ridgeway. Since the General had once again called in an official capacity, why had he brought his wife with him?

The wardress withdrew, and Catrina took the chair offered to her by Gregson. For a brief moment her eyes met Alice's, and Catrina experienced a stab of guilt. The General had been understating the case when he had said his wife was upset by what had happened. Alice had clearly been devastated, judging by her swollen eyelids and her ravaged face, and the muscle which twitched spasmodically at the corner of her mouth.

Catrina turned away from Alice. Later, she would try to explain and ask forgiveness for having caused so much distress. At the moment she had to concentrate on something far more important. Breathlessly, she addressed General Ridgeway. 'Something has occurred to me; something which could prove vital to the defence at Dominic's court-martial . . .'

'We have not called to discuss the court-martial,' he cut her short, his voice heavy. 'Alice has something to tell the Governor, and it is necessary for you to hear it also.'

'Oh,' Catrina said blankly, her glance going to Alice. What could possibly be more important than the court-martial facing Dominic?

Alice kept her head bowed, her gaze fixed upon her hands which she twisted together on her lap. Her voice was barely audible as she began to speak. 'You and Millicent were not sisters, Catrina, and therefore you are not, and have never been, Dominic's sister-in-law. The Beaumonts were not your parents.'

Catrina stared at her in total disbelief. For a moment there was silence in the room. Then the Governor said in his austere, clipped voice, 'You are telling us, Mrs Ridgeway, that Miss Beaumont was an adopted child?'

'In—In a manner of speaking, yes.'

Fragments of memories were flashing through Catrina's mind like images. There was Millicent, arriving with the Beaumonts for one of their periodic duty-visits, and taunting, 'Papa and Mama love me, but not you!' It had been so patently true that her own protests and denials had lacked conviction.

Catrina shook her head. 'I don't understand. Why did the Beaumonts adopt me, when they never wanted me at all? And why was I never given a hint? Why was it kept secret—from me, from the world . . .' She stopped as understanding dawned. 'I see. The truth was too scandalous. I am a bastard, of course!!'

The ugly little word brought a sharp intake of breath

from one of the men, but the lines of distress around Alice's mouth told Catrina that she had been right. She nodded slowly. 'I was not simply an adopted child who had been born on the wrong side of the blanket—was I? I was the skeleton somewhere in the Beaumont family cupboard, and sending me to live with Lady Prudence was as close as it was possible to get to bricking me up in a cupboard.' Her glance went from Alice to John Ridgeway. 'And the two of you knew it.'

'Catrina . . .' General Ridgeway began.

She made a sound which started as a bitter laugh and ended almost on a sob. 'The—The circumstances must have been so sordid that you judged it preferable to keep me in ignorance. Who was my mother? Some half-witted scullery-maid?'

The Governor decided to take control of the conversation. 'The army's only concern is to establish whether there was, or was not, a close kinship between Miss Beaumont and Captain Ross which rendered punishable the acts they committed together. We shall require something more than just a statement that she was adopted by the Beaumonts.'

'I know,' Alice said quietly. 'And that is why I have come in person to tell you that *I* am Catrina's true mother.'

The room had begun to spin round Catrina. This was the very last thing she had expected! She had been certain that she would be told some squalid story about the Beaumont family, something sensational enough to have justified the Ridgeways' silence.

She heard Gregson say with deep concern, 'I am sorry, Alice, but you will have to be rather more specific than that. I take it that John was not the father of your child?'

She shook her head, but seemed unable to voice the necessary explanation. General Ridgeway rose, and moved to her side, placing a comforting hand on her shoulder. He began without inflection,

'Briefly, the situation is that Alice and I were betrothed and I was serving with the regiment abroad when she . . . Well, it was a very difficult, vulnerable period in her life, and she became infatuated with another man. He was not someone she could possibly have married. Her friend, Mary Beaumont, was already married at the time, and between them they concocted a plan which would ensure that the world would regard the coming baby as the child of the Beaumonts.'

Alice had begun to weep. General Ridgeway drew her to her feet and held her, stroking her hair. He glanced up, and went on, 'When Dominic was arrested, and Catrina locked up inside the Convent, Alice knew that her secret would have to come out. She confessed everything to me and then asked me to bring her here. You will appreciate that it was not an easy thing for her to do. And now, with your permission, Governor, we will withdraw so that I may comfort my wife.'

The Governor gave him a look of sympathy. 'By all means, General.'

My mother, Catrina was thinking, staring at Alice. But they were no more than words; a dispassionate statement of fact. In the past, she had always felt instinctively drawn towards Alice. So why was there nothing but this cold hostility inside her now?

As if Alice could somehow read her thoughts, she freed herself from her husband's embrace and raised her ravaged face to Catrina's. 'Forgive me,' she pleaded brokenly.

I will not forgive you, Catrina thought with stony enmity. Alice had only told the truth when she had been forced into it to stop Dominic's court-martial. If it had not been for that, she would never have claimed the relationship between them, and it was a form of rejection which Catrina found unforgivable.

The Ridgeways had reached the door when something occurred to Catrina. 'Who was my father?' she demanded. 'Did I ever know him?'

'No.' Alice's reply was almost inaudible. 'He worked for my family—as a groom.'

Catrina fought a wild desire to laugh. It was, after all, a very commonplace little tale. Nothing dramatic or sensational to lift it above the ordinary. A good-looking groom and a bored young mistress whose betrothed was serving a long period abroad with his regiment.

'Please,' she heard Alice say, 'come to my tent after—when you leave here. Let me explain . . .'

Catrina did not reply. As the door closed behind them, something else darted into her mind. Since Millicent had not been her sister, there was nothing whatever to stand between herself and Dominic! That one simple, joyous fact swamped everything else which had been revealed today.

She became aware that the Governor was addressing Gregson. 'I believe my presence is no longer required. You will deal with the procedure for having Captain Ross released. Miss Beaumont's detention, of course, has never been official.' He made Catrina a bow and left the room.

She rose too, and faced Gregson. 'Will you tell me, please, where Dominic is being held? I wish to go there and await his release.'

'Miss Beaumont,' the officer said quietly, 'please sit down again. There is something I want you to consider very carefully.'

She gave him a sharp look. 'Well?'

'Dominic was faced with a ruined career. Alice Ridgeway's confession has offered him a second chance. Are you going to snatch that chance away from him, and allow his career to be ruined after all? For believe me, it *would* be ruined if he married you.'

This time she did sit down, groping numbly for a chair. She fixed her gaze on the officer's face. 'Because—Because I am illegitimate?'

'Not only that. But the sensational disclosure that you are Alice Ridgeway's love-child will certainly add fuel to the fire. A regiment is far more than a military unit, you see. It is a community, and its harmony depends upon everyone fitting in. And you, I'm afraid, have attracted too much attention of the wrong kind to fit in.'

She gave a harsh, bitter laugh. 'Too much mud has been thrown at me, and we all know that some of it will stick for ever. And because of it, none of the other officers and their wives will accept me. Is that what you have been trying to say?'

'Something like that,' Gregson admitted. 'Dominic's position would be untenable, just as General Ridgeway's has become untenable. Like the General, he would have to leave the army. But unlike the General, Dominic is young, the best of his career still before him, many of his ambitions not yet realised. He made many sacrifices to join the army. He risked a breach with his family, who did not wish him to become a soldier, and he worked his way up through the ranks. Could you really allow him to make the sacrifice he would have to make if he married you?'

Catrina sprang up and began to pace the floor. 'Since Dominic has to choose between me and the army, I'm sure he would choose me . . .'

'Of course he would. And that is why I have not yet put into motion the official procedure for ordering his release. There is a ship in the harbour, Miss Beaumont, ready to sail for England with the tide. You could leave with her and be beyond reach by the time Dominic is set free. You could allow him to take the second chance which he has been offered.'

'You are asking too much!' Catrina cried desperately.

'It is *you* who would be asking too much if you stayed, and Dominic married you. It is not only his career which is at stake. He is the only son of a proud and prominent landowning family. How do you think they would feel about him marrying someone whose name has been linked with so much scandal?'

'We would have one another . . .' she began.

'And that is all you *would* have,' Gregson put in swiftly. 'Dominic would lose contact with all his friends, for those who are not in the regiment are long-standing friends of his family. You would have to be everything to one another. If you married, Miss Beaumont, all the sacrifices would have to be made by Dominic. Even if he did not come to resent you in time, do you think you could live for the rest of your life with the knowledge that Dominic had given up everything for you?'

She closed her eyes. Right from the start the fates had been conspiring to keep her and Dominic from one another, and at last she had to concede that they had won.

She turned to face Gregson. 'You are right,' she said dully. 'Can you arrange for me to sail on that ship leaving for England?'

He nodded, and tugged at the bell-pull beside his desk. 'A passage will be secured for you. Go and fetch your belongings.'

CHAPTER TWENTY-SIX

WITHIN MOMENTS OF Catrina boarding the ship the anchor was hoisted, and the breeze was bearing her away from Gibraltar and from Dominic. She discovered that she was to share a cabin with five other women.

They were army wives returning home in advance of their husbands. They knew who she was, and as she placed her possessions underneath her bunk, the women's comments washed over her.

'I thought cockroaches and rats was all we'd have to put up with . . .'

'There ought to be a special berth set aside for her sort . . .'

'Don't know about any of the rest of you, but I'm beginning to feel sick already, and it's nothing to do with the sea . . .'

Oh God, Catrina thought, clenching her hands together, she would not be able to expect help from any of these hostile women when the miserable, familiar sea-sickness struck her.

She escaped as soon as she could, and went on deck, watching through a blur of tears as the menacing shape of the Rock receded. How would Dominic take the lying message she had written for him, and left with Lieutenant General Gregson?

'The shock of your arrest,' she had scrawled, 'and of my confinement in the Convent, followed by Alice's confession that I am her daughter, have all helped to change me. Forgive me, but all I wish now is to leave Gibraltar, and never again be reminded of this past, wretched chapter in my life. I hope you will soon forget me also.'

Catrina brushed the tears from her eyes and turned her bitter thoughts to Alice. Alice, who was at that very moment waiting in her tent to 'explain'. As if any explanation would possibly justify the fact that Catrina had been abandoned to the harsh custody of Lady Prudence.

For the first time, it struck her that Lady Prudence had been her grandmother. It must have been Alice's affair with the groom that had caused the bitter rift between mother and daughter. It seemed strange that the old woman should have agreed to give a home to the child of that affair when the Beaumonts decided that they did not wish to keep her after all. And strangest of all was the fact that Lady Prudence had left her entire estate to Alice's lowly-born daughter.

Catrina shrugged. That had probably been done solely to spite Alice. What did any of it matter? She herself had never mattered to anyone, that was clear. She had not mattered to her father, the humble groom who had never even seen her. She had not mattered to Lady Prudence, and she had certainly not mattered to Alice, for all her tears.

The shell of hostility hardened round Catrina. What difference did it make which 'mother' had rejected her? Let Alice go on waiting vainly for the chance to 'explain' and beg forgiveness . . .

'Well,' a familiar voice broke into Catrina's thoughts, 'that's me last sight of Gibraltar for a good while.'

Catrina whirled about. *'Violet!'*

'Like old times, ain't it, love?' Violet grinned.

It was not remotely like old times, Catrina thought, studying Violet. How prosperous and well turned out she looked in her gown of ruby-coloured velvet, while Catrina herself was shivering in her thin, almost threadbare stuff gown.

'Oh Violet, I am so happy to see you,' Catrina said, and burst into tears.

A comforting arm encircled her waist, and she felt herself being guided towards the companionway, and propelled inside a cabin. Gradually she succeeded in forcing some control over her grief, and she took in, with bemusement, the comparative luxury of the cabin which Violet obviously occupied alone. How well and truly their situations had been reversed!

'So what is it, love?' she heard Violet ask with concern. 'Something to do, has it, with the man as you always wanted—Captain Ross?'

'You knew?'

'From the first minute you clapped eyes on him! But he ain't for you, ducks, is he, and you've had to face it.'

'It's—far more complicated than that. But you're right. I *have* faced the fact that the best thing I could possibly do for Dominic is to disappear from his life.' Catrina changed the subject. 'What are you doing aboard, Violet, and so obviously prosperous?'

'The Dons paid me well, and I put a bit aside. And then, you see, dear, the army paid me real handsome for the information I carried back to them.' Violet chuckled. 'There's even talk of a public honour for me! Hard to credit, ain't it?'

'Not at all! I am sure you deserved it. What will you do when you reach London?'

'Open me own gown-shop,' Violet replied promptly. 'Got a bit of capital now, see, and one of me customers was a Frenchman. What he didn't know about fashion! Helped me to design this here gown, he did, besides sketching for me what the ladies of Paris are wearing. Two of me sisters work in slop-shops; I'll hire 'em meself instead. Oh yes, I'll be right and tight from now on.'

'I'm glad,' Catrina said sincerely, and rose. 'I suppose I'd better return to my own berth. I don't quite know what one is supposed to do about mealtimes. Perhaps you'd tell me?'

Violet gave her a shrewd look. 'How many you sharing with, love?'

'Five.'

'And giving you the cold shoulder, ain't they?'

'Well—yes.'

'Right! You come with me, and we'll fetch your things. Then you'll move into my cabin, ducks.'

'Oh, Violet . . .' Catrina felt a constriction in her throat.

'No more'n you woulda done for me,' the other girl said gruffly, and held out her hand. 'Come, let's get it over with.'

Violet, too, was recognised by the five women with whom Catrina had been doomed to share, and their comments became more pointed when the two of them arrived together. But Violet riposted with some even more pointed comments of her own, and soon afterwards they were on the way to her cabin with Catrina's belongings.

'Old hags!' Violet grunted. 'Now for supper, dearie. We're s'posed to collect our rations from the galley, but I've squared a galley-hand to bring mine to me cabin. I'll nip along, and tell him to make it two.' She glanced at Catrina, and shook her head. 'Though I dare say it won't be long before you starts feeding yours to the fishes!'

But in that, to the surprise of both of them, she had been wrong, for the familiar sea-sickness did not assail Catrina when *Seagull* entered the open waters.

'Got your sea-legs at last,' Violet commented.

Catrina told herself that she would have to learn to be grateful for minor blessings, such as freedom from sea-sickness, and the presence of Violet on this voyage. Not that Violet came within the category of a minor blessing, she amended. The voyage would have been utter purgatory if it had not been for her friendship, and for the sanctuary which her private cabin offered.

It was some time before Catrina could bring herself to tell Violet the whole truth about herself. She felt obscurely ashamed of the fact that both Mary Beaumont and Alice Ridgeway had rejected her; as if she were having to admit that there was something wholly unlovable about herself. But one day when Violet was talking about the Ridgeways, and remarking on how good they had always been to Catrina, the latter could restrain herself no longer.

'Let me tell you how good they really were to me, Violet! Not the General,' Catrina amended fairly. 'He was kept in the dark as much as I was. And indeed, I feel sorry for him. It can't be very pleasant to learn, after so many years, that your wife had betrayed you with a common groom.'

Violet stared at her. 'What you talking about, love?'

'Alice Ridgeway is my mother,' Catrina said baldly.

Violet sank down heavily on her bunk. 'Well, if that don't beat everything!'

'Oh, there is a good deal more to beat it,' Catrina corrected with a bitter smile. 'Alice knew how I felt about Dominic. She alone knew that he was not my brother-in-law, and that we could have married after Millicent died. But she said nothing. She allowed him to propose to Dinah instead. She would have allowed that marriage to go ahead, still saying nothing.'

Catrina's voice took on a corrosive edge. 'Every single thing that happened—every scandal in which I became involved—was the direct result of my believing I was

Dominic's sister-in-law. Alice stood by and watched it all happening, and still she said nothing. That was true motherly behaviour, wasn't it, Violet?'

'Oh, you poor dears,' Violet sighed. 'Both you and your Ma.'

'I'm afraid I don't feel any pity for her at all.'

Violet shook her head. 'Can't you think of how it must have been for Mrs Ridgeway? Scared out of her wits, she was, poor thing. Remember as how I always said she was scared?'

'If she was, it was entirely on her own account! She was afraid that I might somehow stumble upon her guilty secret.'

'No, dearie, it wouldn't have been that. It were fear that *she* might give the show away by making it plain how she felt about you. I see it all now. Kept you at a distance, didn't she?'

Catrina made no answer. Violet had been quite right about Alice keeping her at a distance, but she did not want anything to undermine the shell of bitter hostility she had erected around her feelings. She changed the subject. 'I heard one of the deck-hands say that if the wind continues in our favour we'll be docking tomorrow. We'd better pack our things.'

The wind did remain in their favour, and in the morning the two of them stood together on deck and watched England's shoreline drawing closer.

'What will you do when you get to London, ducks?' Violet wanted to know.

Catrina shrugged. 'Go back to the house in Belgravia, I suppose.'

'The one as your godmother—no, your grandmother—left you,' Violet nodded.

'You'll come and visit me, won't you?'

' 'Course I will, dear, just as soon's I've got me gown-shop on its feet.'

After they had disembarked the two of them took the mail-coach to London, and at the final staging-post they hired a carriage to convey first Catrina to Belgravia, and then to drop Violet at her parents' home near Billingsgate.

Catrina's spirits were as bleak and dreary as the English winter when she climbed the familiar steps to the front door of the house where she had spent her early years, and which she had left to travel to Gibraltar what seemed like a lifetime ago.

She banged the knocker, and waited, but nothing happened. Then she realised what must have occurred. After Mr Stanmore, her lawyer, died so suddenly and no one else had official authority to act for Catrina, the servants she had left to look after the house would not have been paid. During the months—years—which had elapsed before her written authority reached Mr Stanmore's son, the servants had obviously left and found other employment.

She sighed, and hailed a sedan-chair, and asked to be taken to the address where Mr Stanmore had had his business premises. She was welcomed by his son, a plump, unctuous young man whom she disliked on sight. But he confirmed that the servants had left when it had been impossible to pay them, and by the time he was legally able to pay them what was owing, they were already installed in new positions and unwilling to return.

'I did not press the matter, Miss Beaumont,' he added, 'since I did not know for how long you would wish to remain in Gibraltar. When you sent me your instructions regarding the Lucinda Ross Memorial Fund, I thought you might—er—have formed an attachment to an army gentleman, and that your long-term plans might not include returning to your house in Belgravia.'

She looked away. 'Perhaps you would kindly let me have the key to the house, Mr Stanmore, and sufficient funds for my immediate needs.'

He jumped up and unlocked a safe. 'Certainly, Miss Beaumont.'

She slipped the keys and the money he had handed her inside her reticule and stood up. Mr Stanmore hovered, over-anxious to please. 'If you would like me to attend to the matter of hiring new servants, Miss Beaumont . . .'

'Later, perhaps. I shall be in touch with you.'

When she had returned to the house and had unlocked the front door, Catrina tried to see it through fresh eyes. She tried to imagine Alice as a child, running down the curved staircase, her laughter ringing in the air. Or had laughter ever echoed in this house?

Catrina sighed, and wandered from room to room, looking at the shapes of the furniture which the departing servants had left draped in dust-covers. Grossly neglected as they had been during Lady Prudence's life-time Catrina had taken the pieces of furniture for granted. It was only after the old woman's death, when Mr Stanmore senior had called in the valuers, that she had discovered their worth. She had had them restored to their former glory. Now, she scarcely cared whether or not they ever emerged from their dust-covers again.

Before returning to the house, Catrina had stopped at a nearby victualler's shop to buy bread and butter and cheese. She had emerged from the shop with its crowded, bounteous shelves and had gazed about her. How peaceful and civilised London is after Gibraltar, she had thought, and how utterly lonely . . .

She had that same feeling now as she walked from room to room, remembering her pleasure in refurbishing everything after Lady Prudence's death had brought it into her possession. She would joyfully have exchanged it all for the cow-byre and Dominic . . .

She forced herself to cut the thought off in her mind. If she was to survive, she could do so only by concentrating on keeping all thoughts of Dominic ruthlessly suppressed.

She carried logs in from outside and lit a fire in the small sitting-room that Lady Prudence had always used for general purposes, because it was cheaper to heat one modest room.

Catrina sat on the hearth-rug by the fire and ate her bread and cheese. Afterwards she fetched blankets and a pillow and made up a bed for herself on the sofa. Later, tomorrow perhaps, she would bestir herself and ask Mr Stanmore to engage a few servants so that the house could be properly heated and aired. She ought, really, to sell the property and buy a smaller, more manageable house.

But somehow she could not find the will or the incentive to do anything about any of it. She continued to camp there in one room, and she called daily to buy supplies from the butcher, the fishmonger and the grocer just as she had done so many times in the past, and cooked her own meals and ate them alone.

She bought every newspaper, broadsheet and pamphlet on sale in London and scanned them all in the hope of finding news of some kind about Dominic, anything at all to explain the fact that he had not written to her.

At first, she had not wanted to admit to herself that she was hoping he would ignore her own message to him and bombard her with angry letters. But as the days passed and the newspapers listed the names of the vessels that had recently set sail from Gibraltar, and no letter came for her, she admitted her secret hope to herself, and wept as it slowly withered.

One afternoon Violet called upon her, carrying a parcel. Catrina welcomed her warmly, and invited her inside the small sitting-room. Violet shook her head as she took in the fact that Catrina virtually lived in that one room.

'I know,' Catrina said with a wry smile. 'I am becoming as peculiar as Lady Prudence was. I shall probably end up like her, pinching pennies and blaming my own poverty for everything that is lacking in my life.'

Violet looked troubled, but all she said was, 'I brung you this, love. It's a present, see.'

Catrina unwrapped the parcel, and stared at the gown of pale-green wool trimmed with velvet in a deeper shade. 'But it's beautiful! Did you make it?'

Violet nodded. 'Been doing quite well with me gown-shop. Why don't you come and pay me a visit, love, and order a new wardrobe? Do both of us a lot of good, that would. Profit for me, see, and something better for you to wear than them rags you're clinging to! With proper clothes, you could begin to make friends . . .'

'Where, Violet? Where do I start? I know no one. Unless you count my lawyer, and he makes my flesh creep.'

Violet hesitated. 'Captain Ross—he has family in England, don't he? Why don't you visit them, dear, and introduce yourself? That'd start you off making friends.'

Catrina interrupted her with laughter which was not quite under control. 'What shall I say to them, Violet? "My name is Catrina Beaumont. You have probably heard of me. Apart from sundry other scandals in which I was involved, I am the one who caused Dominic to be arrested and face a court-martial. Would you mind overlooking those facts and help me to find friends?" Should I ask them that, Violet?'

'No dear,' Violet said quietly. 'It were a stupid idea. Look, why don't you try on the gown and see if it fits?'

Catrina nodded, forcing control over herself. 'Thank you

for the thought. And you're right—I *do* need clothes, and who better to order them from than yourself? Give me a hand, Violet, would you?'

Catrina was helped into the new gown, and afterwards she and Violet stood before the cheval mirror in the room and studied her reflection.

'It fits like a glove, dear, and suits you a treat,' Violet said. 'Now let me just pin your hair up for you.'

The front-door knocker banged at that moment. 'Expecting someone?' Violet wanted to know.

Catrina frowned. 'No. I can only imagine it must be the curate, come to lecture me for not having attended church. Oh, dear . . .'

'Want me to see him off, love?'

'Oh, would you? I don't think I could face a sermon.'

Violet was gone for so long that Catrina guessed, guiltily, that the curate was reading *her* a lecture on the subject of regular church attendance. Then footsteps sounded outside, and the door was flung open.

'I'll leave you now, love,' Violet said. 'I think you'd best be left alone with your visitors.'

She picked up her cloak, and as she stood away from the door, Alice and John Ridgeway entered the sitting-room. Catrina stared at them, her mind registering the sound of the front door closing behind Violet. Alice, she noticed, had lost weight and a good deal more grey showed in her hair than when she had last seen her. Catrina looked at her, and felt nothing but hostility.

General Ridgeway spoke. 'Philip Gregson told me what had passed between you, Catrina. It was both wise and courageous of you to leave as and when you did.'

She glanced away from them. 'How did—Dominic take it?'

'He kept his thoughts to himself. And, of course, Alice and I were rather preoccupied with our own affairs. We left Gibraltar only a few days after you did.'

Catrina moved, and made a show of attending to the fire. 'I hope you are warm enough,' she said with unnatural politeness. 'Oh, please do sit down.'

They seated themselves on the sofa, and Alice leant forward. 'My dear . . .'

'When did you arrive in England?' Catrina asked quickly.

'About three weeks ago,' General Ridgeway answered. 'Hobson and the servants came to London ahead of us, and he searched for a furnished house to rent on our behalf while Alice and I stayed with friends in the country. Even though the house which Hobson found for us in Mayfair is adequate, we are looking for a suitable house to buy.'

Catrina laid the poker down in the grate and turned away from the fire. 'So you have left the army.'

'Yes.'

Alice spoke suddenly, in a rush. 'I have to explain matters to you, Catrina. I must make you understand. If you knew what my life was like in this house . . . I lied when I said my father was devoted to my mother. She dominated him and kept him dancing to her tune, and when he died she expected me to take his place.'

'I'll go and make some tea,' Catrina interrupted. She did not want to listen to Alice's excuses.

'A capital idea,' General Ridgeway approved, and added, 'Alice, would you not go and give the child a hand?'

So Catrina found herself being accompanied into the kitchen by Alice, but the latter merely said, looking round her, 'Do you know, this is the very first time I have ever seen inside this room? Until I left, there was a cook and an army of servants, and we all kept very strictly to our own domain . . .'

'*My* domain,' Catrina interrupted sardonically, 'was to prepare the meals when the cook was too drunk to do so, and to do the cleaning which the half-witted maid had neglected, and generally to wait upon Lady Prudence. But now that I know myself to have been the bastard daughter of a groom. I understand why that should have been allowed to be so.'

'You are very bitter,' Alice said in a voice which sounded close to tears.

'I have cause to be.'

Alice looked as if she meant to say something. Then she obviously thought better of it, and suggested diffidently instead, 'While we are waiting for the water to boil, would you mind if I showed you the bedroom which used to be mine?'

'If you like,' Catrina answered stiffly, and thought,

Anything, provided you do not go on seeking to justify your actions.

As they climbed the stairs, Alice shuddered. 'What a sad, dismal house this always was, and still is!'

Catrina was about to retort that she had had the house completely refurbished after Lady Prudence's death, and that it had looked most elegant and not in the least dismal. But it came to her that Alice was right. No matter what one might do to the house, an atmosphere of bleakness seemed ingrained in its very walls.

'If what I am hoping to find in my old bedroom is still there,' she heard Alice go on quietly, 'it will explain to you certain things in a way which I could not possibly make you understand by recounting them to you. This is the room, Catrina.'

Ever since she could remember, that particular room had been used to store broken furniture and other jumble. *The rubbish-room,* Lady Prudence had called it., How implacable and malevolent her bitterness must have been towards her daughter!

In the depths of her own hostile anger and bitterness, Catrina wanted to hurt Alice by telling her about the use to which the room had been put. But she restrained the impulse and opened the door. She had had the room cleared of lumber and left empty, with the vague intention of furnishing it as a spare bedroom some time in the future.

Alice looked about her for a moment, her expression sad and abstracted. Then she moved towards the window-seat. A cupboard had been constructed beneath it, and Alice knelt to open its doors. It was empty, as Catrina knew. But while she watched, Alice pulled at a floorboard in the back of the cupboard, and after a moment she had prised it up.

Alice groped inside the recess beneath the boards, and a sound escaped her as she brought out a leather-bound journal. She wiped dust and cobwebs from it with her handkerchief.

'Like yourself, I also kept a diary,' she told Catrina. 'I have often wondered why I left this particular journal here. Was it because I sensed that the time might come when it would be needed? I don't know. But read it after John and I have left. Now, shall we go down and make the tea?'

Catrina nodded, glancing at the journal. She could guess

at its contents; the love-sick jottings of an infatuated girl; an account of her secret meetings with the handsome young groom. Reading it would alter nothing. The fact remained that Alice, her mother, had allowed her to grow up, wretched and rejected, with a cold and bitter old woman who had never had the slightest regard for her at all. Her own mother, and Catrina had never even known of her existence until she went to Gibraltar! And now she was supposed to read Alice's diary, and forgive her?

Catrina carried the tea-tray into the living-room, while Alice followed with the journal. She placed it on the table, and as if she sensed that Catrina did not want explanations or excuses from her, she addressed her husband.

'This journal, John dear, was begun during that first period after our betrothal when you were sent abroad with the regiment. I cannot describe to you how wretched things were in this house at the time. My father had just died, and Mother was beside herself. She had long ago alienated all our friends and relatives and suddenly she perceived that she was doomed to end her life on her own—unless I could be persuaded or forced to break off my engagement.'

'I think,' General Ridgeway put in, 'she had a terror of being left on her own because in her heart she did not like herself.'

'Perhaps,' Alice conceded. 'She certainly needed someone to dominate. I thought I would be driven mad by her, for there were no diversions whatever. You were abroad; my only friend, Mary Beaumont, had recently married and was totally absorbed in her new husband. I was desperate for company—any company other than Mother's . . .'

'I am perfectly aware,' Catrina interrupted in a hard voice, 'of what you are both trying to do. You are trying to excuse the inexcusable. But I have lived all these years with the knowledge that I had been rejected. It does not really matter to me whether I had been rejected by you, Alice, or by the Beaumonts.'

General Ridgeway put his tea-cup down and rose, helping his wife to her feet. 'I had hoped, Catrina, that you might be ready to accept Alice's explanation. But you are obviously still very bitter. We are staying at Number 15, Cadogan Square. Please call on us when you feel ready to do so.'

Alice turned to her. 'Please—try to forgive me. I did not

give you away lightly, and I never stopped thinking of you.'

Catrina made no reply. Being thought of constantly had done nothing at all to make her dreary life with Lady Prudence easier to bear.

'Read my journal, Catrina,' Alice begged. 'And then call on us. I shall be waiting for you every day.'

When they had gone and she was alone again, Catrina stared unseeingly into the fire, her spirits utterly quenched and her thoughts bleak. Dominic must have been fully aware that the Ridgeways were leaving Gibraltar for England and that they would call on her, and yet he had not troubled to send her so much as a message. He had obviously decided to take her at her word, and forget her.

She picked the journal up and placed it high on a shelf. Let it gather dust there, and let Alice go on waiting vainly for forgiveness! What she had done was totally unforgivable.

CHAPTER TWENTY-SEVEN

VIOLET ARRIVED AT the house one morning a week later, in a hired chair and with her arms full of fashion sketches.

'Well, love,' she scolded Catrina, 'I reckoned since you didn't come to me shop, I'd best call on you so's we can decide on the clothes you'll be needing.' She gave Catrina a searching look. 'Had things out with your Ma, did you?'

Catrina gave a harsh laugh. 'If she had told the truth when Millicent died, Dominic and I could have married. Because she kept silent I have lost him, and I shall never forgive her.' She changed the subject. 'Let me see your sketches, Violet.'

For a while they discussed modes and fabrics and the use of trimming materials. Then Violet said suddenly, her voice gentle, 'Ducks, put yourself in your poor Ma's place. We was in Gibraltar, outnumbered hundreds to one by Frenchies and Dons, with more and more men—like my Eddie, the rat—deserting to the enemy. And Mrs Ridgeway, she weren't no ordinary army wife. Her husband were a General, someone in command, a gentleman as needed to keep all his wits about him for the work as had to be done. Think how it would've been if his wife suddenly ups and says to the world, "Miss Beaumont is my daughter from the wrong side of the blanket. I let one of me Pa's grooms crack me pitcher afore I married." Well . . . What would've happened to discipline, dear? The poor General would've been in a daze, and the other officers all abroad, and the troops agreeing among theirselves like pickpockets in a fair! We wouldn't've stood a chance against the enemy, love, not with things all skimble-skamble like that!'

Catrina was silent for a moment, and then she said stonily, 'I think I would like the cloak made up of fine wool, Violet, and lined with silk. In contrasting shades of green, perhaps. Could you call again tomorrow, and bring some swatches of fabric with you?'

Violet sighed, and did not refer to the matter again, but confined herself to taking Catrina's measurements and marking sketches of various garments.

But the following morning when she called, she asked abruptly, 'How-and-about did your Ma come to give you away to Mrs Beaumont in the first place? I mean, why did Mrs Beaumont take you, and give you her name, and then let the old harpy have you instead?'

'I don't know,' Catrina shrugged the matter aside.

'But didn't your Ma explain?'

Catrina's glance went to the shelf. 'She gave me her journal to read. She said it would explain many of the things that happened.'

'Read that there journal, ducks,' Violet advised gravely. 'Otherwise, you're going to get that bitter and hard inside, you'll end up just like the old woman, your grandma!'

The thought of becoming in any way like Lady Prudence moved Catrina to reach reluctantly for the journal that evening after Violet had gone. She sat down by the fire, and opened it. The first entry read:

> I left this wretched, unhappy house this morning, determined to visit Mary and Rodney Beaumont even if I were to be less than welcome. Instead, I never went further than the stables, for I became drawn into a most surprising conversation with a most surprising young man. He is a new groom Papa had hired just before his death; he is from Ireland, and his name is Patrick Fogarty.
>
> I wish my humble pen could convey the sheer poetry of his lilting voice and his manner of speech! He makes every sentence sound like a line from a sonnet, and he has strong, refreshing views on everything. He also has the most striking hair I have ever seen; the colour of polished copper, and the most tender green eyes imaginable. After listening to Mama's angry, demanding tirades, talking to him was both soothing and uplifting. Although he received no formal schooling he has taught himself to read, and is familiar with Carey's *Poems on Several Occasions*. I have promised to lend him my volumes of Savage's *The Wanderer*.

Catrina laid the journal thoughtfully aside and rose, moving to the cheval mirror and staring at her reflection. So it was from her father that she had received her dark-copper hair and her green eyes. He was beginning to assume the properties of a real person, and not the standard character of handsome, earthy, and rather coarsely sensual servant she had been imagining.

She sat down again and picked up the journal. The following entries were so revealing that, although Catrina became absorbed in what she was reading, she could not help feeling that she was eavesdropping on something intensely private. It was quite clear that Alice was falling head over heels in love with Patrick. She wrote of his sensitivity and his talent and his humour; of the drama in blank verse which he was writing during his spare time, and of the way his hair curled when the weather was damp. No one else appeared to have existed for her during that long period; she made no mention of her mother or of John Ridgeway or her friend Mary Beaumont. Her whole world had been bounded by Patrick.

It was growing late, so Catrina put the journal aside and prepared for bed. But she lay awake for a long time, thinking about what she had read.

When Violet arrived the next day she saw the journal on the table, and nodded approvingly. 'You made a start.'

'Yes.' Catrina hesitated. 'She seems to have felt as deeply for her Patrick—my father—as I feel for Dominic. That part I *do* understand.'

'Talking about Captain Ross, ducks—it's a real surprise to me that he took your leaving Gibraltar without no fuss.'

Catrina shrugged, and said bleakly, 'I suppose it was spelt out to him, as it was to me, that the army would never sanction a marriage between us. And he would hardly have been granted home leave so that he could go after me.' *But he might have written,* she added dolefully to herself, *or sent a message through the Ridgeways.*

That evening Catrina reached for Alice's journal with something akin to eagerness. A sound escaped her as she turned a page and read the next raw entry.

> Oh, dear God, I wish I were dead! The unthinkable has happened. Somehow, Mama found out about

> Patrick. I dare say the servants must have gossiped. I went to the stables this morning, and discovered that she had summoned him late last night and dismissed him on the spot, and he is even now on his way to Ireland. He had to accept her terms. She would not furnish him with a reference, and if he attempted to seek another position in England, she threatened to blacken his character. She has given him sufficient money with which to return home, but if he uses it for any other purpose, or sets foot in England again, she will charge him with having stolen it. Oh, how am I to go on . . .

The ink recording the rest of the sentence had been blurred, as if by falling tears. There was a lump in Catrina's throat as she read the more legible entry which followed.

> Mama sent for me after breakfast, and called me such terrible names that I felt physically ill. My greatest sin, apparently, is that I consorted with a common groom. Oh, if only I knew where to find him I would leave this wretched house and go after my beloved Patrick, and share his life, no matter how humble it might be.

There were no entries for several weeks, and her silence was explained once Alice had taken up her pen again.

> My entire world has crashed about my head. I had thought I had plumbed the depths of despair when Patrick left, but I was wrong. I have been unwell for some weeks, and this morning Mama explained it to me. I am to have my darling Patrick's child. My every instinct is to treasure this small part of him, but it is not to be. Mama has made that clear.
>
> In spite of her rage and disgust, she is not altogether displeased at the turn of events, for it has delivered me into her hands. She is demanding that I write and tell John our betrothal is at an end, and that I wish to devote myself to my widowed mother. Then she plans to take me away so that I may have the infant

> in a town where I am not known. Afterwards the child I long so much to keep will be sent away to foster parents 'belonging to the lower orders like its father' as Mama puts it. And I am to remain with her for the rest of her life. Dear God, how she will kepp me in bondage now that she has such a hold over me!

Overcome with emotion, Catrina put the journal aside. She blew out the candles and wept for the poor distraught girl who had committed her plight and her wretchedness to the pages of her diary.

Violet noticed the dark shadows beneath her eyes the next morning, for she glanced at the journal and said, 'Bad, was it?'

Catrina nodded. 'I think Lady Prudence must have been the most evil woman who ever lived. I thought *I* had suffered by being made to live with her, but I can see now that because she had no feelings for me other than contempt, I escaped lightly. In her own warped way she loved Alice, and would have done anything to keep her daughter exclusively to herself.' She hesitated for a moment. 'Violet, would you mind carrying on with the making of the garments we have already decided upon? We can discuss, later, the details of the rest of the wardrobe. I should like to read the remainder of the journal and—and decide what to do.'

'I understand, ducks. Me and me sisters'll get on with the morning gown and the travelling dress and the cloak, and I'll call again, day after tomorrow. That do you?'

'Very well indeed. Thank you, Violet.'

When she was alone again, Catrina picked up the journal. Later entries were brief at times, and often erratic.

> Spoke to Mary today, and told her the truth. Rodney will soon be joining the regiment abroad. Mama keeps pressing me to write to John and end our engagement.

Catrina turned the page.

> John is now my only hope, my only means of escape from Mama. I know it is wrong of me to wish to make use of him, but I am quite desperate. Could I

> confide in him, and beg his forgiveness? Mary and Rodney assure me that no man could possibly forgive, and even if he were still willing to marry me, John would never allow me to keep my baby.
>
> Tuesday, 11th June. I am at my wits' end. Mama never gives me a moment's peace. She talks about my poor unborn baby as if it were some kind of freak, merely because its father is a humble groom. Oh, I want my baby, and I want Patrick! And at the same time I cannot bear to abandon the life-line which John represents, my only chance to escape from the life which Mama has mapped out for me. No baby, no Patrick, no John, no hope.

Catrina wiped away tears as she went through the pages of the journal.

> Today I threw myself upon Mary's mercy, and I persuaded her, in the name of friendship, to help me. She and Rodney and I have made a plan, and I could never repay what they have agreed to do for me. The regiment will not be returning to England until after my baby has been born, and John will probably not be given home leave in the meantime. Mama is beside herself, and says she will cut me out of her life. She says I have sinned, and that I should live with my punishment for the rest of my life.
>
> But tomorrow Mary, Rodney and I will move into lodgings in Islington where we are not known, and the day after Rodney leaves to join the regiment. What a mercy that Mary is poor in close relatives, and that all of Rodney's family live in Scotland. There is a reasonable chance that we may succeed with the deception, for I do not believe even Mama would wish to create a scandal which could be lampooned against by the broadsheets. I am to call myself Mrs Beaumont until after the birth of my baby, and Mary will be Alice Welles. As soon as the infant has been registered as being the child of Mary and Rodney Beaumont, we shall change lodgings again and await the return of John and Rodney. May God forgive me for the deception, and may John never find out that

> he has been tricked into being second-best.
>
> This is the last entry I shall be making in my journal. Tomorrow I become Mary Beaumont who is awaiting the birth of her child. My great comfort is the knowledge that, with Mary and I being such friends and our husbands serving in the same regiment, I shall always be close to my dear baby and watch it growing up.

Catrina put the journal away and wept for the young, desperate and unhappy Alice who had, after all, been parted from her child. How had that come about?

All the questions against which Catrina had so resolutely set her mind to begin with were demanding to be answered. She heated water and poured it into a tub, and after she had bathed and dressed in the gown which Violet had presented to her, she left the house and hailed a chair.

Hobson greeted her at the door of the rented house in Mayfair as if none of the drama, crisis or scandal in Gibraltar had ever been, and as if hardly a day had gone by since he had last seen her.

'The General and Madam are in the drawing-room, miss,' he said. 'I have been told that you were to be taken straight to them when you called. If you would follow me, please.'

The General stepped forward to kiss her hand and Catrina dropped him an automatic curtsy, wondering how much of the true story so painfully told in that journal was known to him.

Then her glance went to Alice. They stared at one another for a moment and moved simultaneously, flinging their arms about one another.

Alice's eyes were wet with tears when they broke apart, but she was in control of herself. 'Have you found it in your heart to forgive me?' she whispered.

'There is nothing to forgive.'

'Ah, but there is. I should have made a clean breast of things long before Dominic's arrest forced me to do so.'

'It must have taken a great deal of courage to tell the truth at all,' Catrina said with new understanding. 'I no longer blame you for delaying. You had, after all, to destroy your own reputation and good name.'

'*My* reputation and good name were never my main

concern. But John had given so much of his life to the regiment and I knew that, if the truth ever became known, he would have to resign. As, of course, he has been forced to do,' she added sadly.

Her husband slipped his arm through hers, and said, 'Stop blaming yourself, my dear. Indeed, I am glad that I shall have more time to spend with you from now on.' But there was a look of loss in his eyes which did not escape Catrina's notice.

Alice slipped a grateful hand over the General's, and looked pleadingly at Catrina. 'I don't want you to think that it was only my husband's career which stopped me from acknowledging you. I learnt to love John after we married, and I realised that my feelings for Patrick, your father, had been a young girl's infatuation. I was so afraid of losing John's love, and that forced me to make a choice between you and him. I feared he would have nothing but bitterness and contempt for me if my secret became known.'

'But it was not a complete secret, was it?' Catrina pointed out. 'The Beaumonts knew, and so did Lady Prudence.'

General Ridgeway poured a glass of canary wine for each of them, and they sat down. 'As you say,' Alice agreed, 'the Beaumonts knew. They, after all, pretended to the world that they were your parents.'

'But they rejected me,' Catrina said with a frown. 'Since they were willing to make such a sacrifice before I was born, why did they change their minds afterwards?'

'They had no choice in the matter,' Alice explained. 'At first, we thought my mother was allowing the deception to be entered into because if she had spoken out it would have caused a scandal. What we did not know was that she had a far more devilish revenge up her sleeve. After you were born, Catrina, she issued her ultimatum. The Beaumonts could keep you during your infancy, she said, but as soon as you were three years old she demanded custody of you.'

'What?' Catrina exclaimed, staring at her.

'Yes, indeed.' Alice smiled sadly. 'By taking my child she would not only punish me, but she would also provide herself with the life-time companion which I had refused to be. She declared that there was only one person who could bring you up as you deserved to be brought up, and that was herself. If we did not agree, she would tell the truth to the world.'

'She had no affection for me at all,' Catrina said.

'She did not regard you as her grand-daughter. To her, you were no more than the base-born child of a common Irish groom. But we were forced to give in to her demands, and because the Beaumonts knew they would have to hand you over to her when you were three years old, they kept you at an emotional distance and did not allow themselves to love you. So it was not unnatural, perhaps, that they poured out all their love on Millicent after she was born.'

Catrina thought of Alice, watching her baby growing in the care of Mary Beaumont, knowing that the infant was deliberately being deprived of love, living with the knowledge that at the age of three she would have to be handed over to a vindictive, spiteful woman, and she shook her head in pity.

'I made one last attempt to reason with Mother,' she heard Alice go on. 'When you were three, I took you to her myself, and I pleaded with her. She was implacable. She made it clear to me that she never wanted to see me again, but she agreed to allow the Beaumonts to visit you. They kept the truth of your wretched existence from me, but after I had heard from you what conditions were like, I understood why she had allowed the Beaumonts to see you. She obviously hoped they would add to my punishment by describing how wretchedly miserable you were with her.'

Hobson entered at that moment to announce that dinner was ready, and Catrina accepted an invitation to join them for the meal. She could not help noticing that, in spite of the fact that this was a rented house with furniture chosen by strangers, Alice had already placed her own individual stamp upon it. There was a warmth and a homeliness about the place which made the house in Belgravia seem all the bleaker by contrast.

A thought occurred to Catrina, and she turned to Alice. 'Why did Lady Prudence leave her entire estate to me, when she regarded me with such contempt?'

'I insisted on it as *my* condition for leaving you with her. I guessed, rightly, that nothing would give her greater pleasure than to send for her lawyer and tell him, in my hearing, that she no longer regarded me as her daughter and was cutting me out of her will. I could only pray, as the years passed, that she would not change her will. But as you have told us, she came to believe herself to be penniless, so I dare say it did not occur to her.'

Catrina lapsed into silence, and merely nodded as General Ridgeway extolled the excellence of the sirloin he had been carving. After a moment, Alice said diffidently, 'John and I are planning to leave for Bath tomorrow, Catrina, to take the waters. Why don't you go with us, and make your home with us afterwards?'

'Yes, indeed!' General Ridgeway urged. 'And if you could come to look upon me as a father, I should be honoured.'

Catrina was greatly touched. 'Thank you. But . . .' *Dominic might still write,* she added mentally. *And if I left Belgravia, he would not know where to reach me . . .*

'I wish you would go with us to Bath,' Alice pleaded a while later when she and Catrina were alone in the drawing-room, and the General had been left to finish his port. 'I am anxious to find as many diversions for John as I can. I am very conscious of the fact that he misses the regiment, and that it is all because of me. He has been trying to hide it from me, but I know that he is feeling pulled down at present. The regiment has left Gibraltar and is bound for India.'

'Oh!' Catrina moved to the window and pretended to stare outside. There was a kind of finality about the news that Dominic had gone to India. It signalled the death of any lingering hope that he might, after all, refuse to accept that they had no future together.

She turned away from the window, and spoke as steadily as she was able to. 'I shall accept the invitation, and go with you to Bath. But I cannot do so if you are leaving tomorrow. This gown is the only one I possess. Violet is at present making a new wardrobe for me, and it will not be ready for at least another week.'

General Ridgeway entered the drawing-room then, and it was arranged that their departure for Bath was to be postponed until Catrina was ready.

A while later, as she waited for the carriage to be brought to the front of the house, she said her goodbyes to the Ridgeways. The General gave her a tentative, almost shy smile. 'Alice is your mother, and I—I hope you might come to regard yourself as being the daughter I always longed for and never had.'

Catrina moved, spreading her arms wide so that she could fold both of them in a close embrace. She had lost Dominic, but she had gained parents. She would have to take comfort from the fact, and learn not to yearn for more.

Trails of fog drifted on the cold night air as the carriage drove her home. Thanking the driver, she climbed the steps, fumbling in her reticule for the key. Then she gave a faint cry as she looked up and saw a large figure in a caped coat draped against the door.

'I was,' Dominic's voice reached her, 'beginning to contemplate forcing an entry.'

'Dominic!' she said with incredulity, her heart drumming a tattoo in her breast.

'Unlock the door, and let us go inside, for pity's sake!'

Mechanically, she obeyed. Inside the hall he fumbled for a tinderbox and lit the nearest branch of candles. He stood framed against its guttering flames, his face cast into inscrutable planes of shadow and light.

'You never wrote,' she blurted out.

He laughed shortly. 'There is a very simple explanation for that. I knew, only, that Lady Prudence's house was somewhere in Belgravia. Finding you has been the devil's own task, Catrina!'

'Why are you not on the way to India with . . .' she began.

'For heaven's sake,' he interrupted, 'is there nowhere in this gloomy house where we may talk in comfort?'

She lit another branch of candles and led the way into the room which she used as her living quarters. She had left a fire laid in the grate, and she watched as Dominic bent down to light it.

He straightened, and moved towards her, pulling her into his arms. 'It has been a long time, Catrina, and it's fortunate for you that my first anger has cooled. How dared you make decisions for both of us, without waiting to hear what my views on the matter were?'

She moved her head so that his lips brushed her temple instead of finding her mouth. 'Dominic, Gregson explained to me why you could not marry me.'

'He had no right to interfere!' Dominic said roughly.

'Come and sit down.'

Reluctantly she allowed him to lead her to the sofa, but she took care that they should not touch. 'I have been half out of my mind, Catrina, trying to track you down! All papers kept by Millicent's family had been destroyed by the fire, and it was not until after the Ridgeways had left Gibraltar that I realised I did not know your address. By that time it was impossible for me to contact them, for I had no address for them either. I was contemplating knocking on the door of every house in Belgravia when I suddenly remembered the Lucinda Ross Memorial Fund.'

'Oh . . .'

He reached for her hand. 'I first learnt about it in Gibraltar. I was staying with my family in Sussex, wondering what more I could do to trace you, when I suddenly remembered about the Memorial Fund. I travelled hot-foot to London, to the army headquarters, where I obtained the address of the Fund's administrator, your man of business Mr Stanmore. Through him I was able to find you.'

'But what are you doing here, Dominic, in England—when your regiment is on its way to India?'

'I have left the army.'

She sprang up. 'Oh, I admit that, against all common sense, I harboured secret, foolish hopes . . . But you cannot, you *must not,* leave the army on my account, Dominic!'

He rose, catching her hands in a firm grasp. 'Did you really imagine for one moment that I would abandon you after all there has been between us? Did you doubt that I would plan for us to be together?'

'I will not allow you to make such a sacrifice!'

'It has already been done.' He forced her to sit down once more. 'I have bought myself out of the army.'

'Then you must tell them you have changed your mind!' Catrina cried in agitation. 'Dominic, believe me, you will live to regret it if you don't, and you will grow to hate me for being the cause of it all. I have only to take General Ridgeway as an example to know that I am right. No matter how deeply and sincerely he loves Alice, he is lost without the army. But at least he is an old man and could not have been expecting to continue his career for much longer in any case. But *you*—you have so many years ahead of you which would be wasted, and become filled with resentment . . .'

Dominic stopped the flow of words by kissing her, hard. He held her away from him afterwards, and said seriously, 'Catrina, there *is* life outside the army! Apart from taking an interest in the management of the family estate I shall one day inherit, I intend involving myself in local affairs, and perhaps even enter Parliament one day.'

Unconvinced, she shook her head. 'You cannot deny that your heart has always been with the army. You told me so yourself.'

He made a cynical sound. 'Perhaps. But like many another disillusioned lover, I came to perceive its imperfections. How do you imagine I felt when I realised that my superiors had waited until the siege had ended, and my immediate usefulness was over, before they arrested me? And when I learnt that Gregson had persuaded you to disappear from my life—well, my disenchantment was complete.'

She went to kneel by the fire, coaxing it with the bellows. When the flames were roaring up the chimney she pretended to busy herself with sweeping ashes from the hearth.

'Gregson said many things,' she began, 'and some of the points he made were only too valid.' She formed the words with difficulty. 'Yours is a close family, and I will not be the cause of coolness between you. No matter how you may try to gloss things over, my reputation gained in Gibraltar is bound to follow me, and become known to your family.'

'They already know it, and I have glossed nothing over.' He was kneeling beside her on the hearthrug, and she saw that he had removed his coat. 'I have told my family everything. I knew it was important, not only for myself but also for you, that they should accept you without reservations. You had told me once how you longed to be part of a close family. And that is why I wished to make quite sure that my family would welcome you.'

'They—They cannot possibly welcome me if you have told them everything.'

'I started by telling them about my marriage to Millicent. I told them about Lucy . . .' His voice caught for a moment before he went on, 'and how you cared for her. I told them how you undertook all the work in the house after the servants deserted.'

'There were—other things,' Catrina muttered, 'which you

must have suppressed, or they would not want to know me.'

His lips twitched. 'Oh, they cannot wait to meet you! My father wants to know precisely how you fashioned the artificial garden, and how you coaxed your vegetables to grow in such unfavourable conditions. And my mother has nothing but admiration for someone who would steal a bullock shot by the enemy, and cut it up herself. She also wishes to know your recipe for stewed dandelion-leaves; she means to serve it as a side-dish at a dinner party in your honour, to demonstrate your ingenuity to Sussex society! As for my sisters—they consider the whole story too romantic for words, and wish to hear every detail of it from your own lips.'

'Even the details of how I was violated by Jake Farraday?' Her voice was raw.

'As to that,' Dominic said quietly, 'my father holds me to blame for not having broken every rule of the army and challenged him to a duel.'

Catrina shook her head in bemusement. Dominic had made the winning over of his family sound so easy, but she could imagine how carefully and with what subtlety he must have proceeded.

'You obviously have a dangerously honeyed tongue,' Catrina said at last, 'to have persuaded your family to see me in such a heroic light. But even you, Dominic, could not have given a romantic gloss to the fact that I am the illegitimate daughter of an Irish groom . . .'

'That reminds me,' Dominic interrupted. 'Before leaving the Rock, and after I had heard the full story from Alice, I made it my business to seek out some Irish officers. You have no need to be ashamed of your father, Catrina. He is quite well known in Dublin as a poet and dramatist.'

'Oh . . .' She had been wondering about her father, and whether it would be possible to trace him.

As if Dominic had guessed her thoughts, he went on, 'Patrick Fogarty is married, with four children. From what Alice has said, he does not know of your existence. It would be better for him and his family, and also for Alice and John Ridgeway, if you were to leave well alone.'

'I expect you are right.' She sighed. 'But even though my father may have gained modest fame in his homeland, it does not alter the fact that I am illegitimate.'

Dominic grinned. '*That* is the last point on which my family would have made an issue! How could they have, when they have always boasted of the fact the my father's grandmother was the product of an affair between a Royal duke and a gipsy dancer from a travelling fair?'

Suddenly she was in his arms, and he was kissing her with all the hunger of their long separation. He held her away from him. 'You cannot refuse to marry me when my entire family is waiting with eager enthusiasm to welcome you!'

'Well,' she laughed shakily, 'it is a difficult decision. The alternative, after all, is so inviting. I *could* decide to continue living here, growing more peculiar by the day . . .'

Her voice was cut off by his kiss. He began to unbutton the bodice of her gown, cupping her breasts in his hands. 'Shall we,' he teased, 'see if some of the magic has gone, now that we no longer believe it to be a crime?'

The magic was heightened, if anything, by the knowledge that there was now no need to be furtive or secretive or afraid of discovery. Each helped the other to undress by the leaping light of the fire, and she moved her fingers over his naked chest, to the hollow of his stomach and against his hard-muscled thighs. The physical sensation of his warm flesh beneath her fingers filled her heart and her mind, and a soft moan escaped her as he began to kiss her with lingering intimacy.

Like floodgates opening, she found herself taking the initiative, making demands, uttering sounds of urgency as they moved together to a glorious height of fulfilment.

Dominic laughed deep in his throat. 'There is one thing which I kept secret from my family. I judged it best not to tell them what an utterly, satisfyingly, shameless creature you are!'

She made a purring sound of contentment and happiness, and coiled her naked legs about his. 'Violet will be so pleased . . .' Catrina broke off. 'I will not turn my back on her, Dominic! She is trying to establish herself in business with a gown-shop, and I will not withdraw my patronage.'

He kissed her mouth. 'I confidently predict that my mother and sisters will offer her their custom also. I have told them about Violet, and they admire her almost as much as they admire you.'

Catrina moved her forefinger along the curve of his lips. 'And, Dominic—Alice is my mother, and I will not have her slighted.'

'Nor will she be. My family accept that she will wish to arrange our wedding.'

'You seem to have left nothing to chance.' As she sat up, she chanced to catch a glimpse of her reflection in the cheval mirror. 'So that was it!' she exclaimed. 'Why did I never realise? It was so obvious.'

'I wish it was to me, whatever it may be.' His hand moved over her thigh, re-awakening an instant arousal to match his own.

'Violet always said that Alice was afraid. I did not believe it at first, and then I realised it also, but I thought it was because she guessed how you and I felt about one another. Later, Violet said Alice had been afraid of showing her feelings for me. But there was something else as well.'

'I don't have the faintest idea what you are talking about,' he murmured against her mouth.

She tangled her hands in his hair, restraining him from kissing her for the moment. 'Don't you see? Apart from my colouring, I resemble Alice! When I first met her, I wondered of whom she reminded me. And then she took to wearing pince-nez when she obviously had no need of them. She was desperately afraid that John would look at me one day, and suddenly see me as *she* had looked when she was young!'

Dominic sat up, and she found his gaze travelling from her hair down to her full breasts and slim thighs, and his silver-grey eyes were soft with love and desire.

'I have always considered Alice to be beautiful,' he said, 'but I had never realised, until now, how utterly irresistible she must have been in her prime.'

Catrina stretched out her arms to receive him as he covered her body tenderly but ardently once more with his own.

HISTORICAL NOTE

THE Deceased Wife's Act was passed in 1907 enabling people for the first time to marry the sister/brother of their deceased spouse. It was not until 1960 that it became possible to marry one's sister/brother-in-law if the ex-spouse was still alive.